Thomas Edward Bridgett

Life of Blessed John Fisher

Bishop of Rochester, cardinal of the Holy Roman church, and martyr under Henry

VIII

Thomas Edward Bridgett

Life of Blessed John Fisher
Bishop of Rochester, cardinal of the Holy Roman church, and martyr under Henry VIII

ISBN/EAN: 9783337038236

Printed in Europe, USA, Canada, Australia, Japan

Cover: Foto ©Raphael Reischuk / pixelio.de

More available books at **www.hansebooks.com**

LIFE OF
BLESSED JOHN FISHER,

BISHOP OF ROCHESTER,

CARDINAL OF THE HOLY ROMAN CHURCH,

AND

MARTYR UNDER HENRY VIII.

BY THE

REV. T. E. BRIDGETT,

OF THE CONGREGATION OF THE MOST HOLY REDEEMER.

FIFTH EDITION.

LONDON
BURNS, OATES & WASHBOURNE LTD.
PUBLISHERS TO THE HOLY SEE

TABLE OF CONTENTS.

		PAGE
PREFACE,	... ...	vii

CHAPTER

I.	Early Years, ...	1
II.	Cambridge, ...	17
III.	The Bishop in his Diocese, ...	53
IV.	Extra-Diocesan Labours, ...	71
V.	Fisher and Erasmus, ...	91
VI.	Preacher and Writer, ...	105
VII.	The Divorce, ...	141
VIII.	Parliamentary Struggles, 1529, ...	178
IX.	Supreme Head, ...	191
X.	The Beginnings of Sorrows, ...	212
XI.	The Holy Maid of Kent, ...	234
XII.	The Oath of Succession, ...	264
XIII.	In the Tower, ...	287
XIV.	The New Supremacy, ...	305
XV.	Royal Snares, ...	332
XVI.	Papal Honours, ...	354
XVII.	The Trial, ...	361
XVIII.	The Martyrdom, ...	388
XIX.	Contemporary Judgments, ...	412
XX.	Lessons of the Martyrdom.	429
CHRONOLOGICAL TABLE,	... ...	449

PREFACE TO SECOND EDITION.

THE name of JOHN FISHER, the learned theologian, the saintly prelate, the heroic martyr, is familiar to everyone who has acquired the mere outlines of history ; yet many deep students of the period in which he lived will be ready to confess that their knowledge is restricted to a few facts of his life, and perhaps the details of his death. The days in which his lot was cast were evil, and a man of his noble character could occupy no very conspicuous place in them, except by contrast, protestation, and martyr-dom. He could not fill the foreground like Luther, Calvin, and Cranmer, or even like Cardinal Wolsey or Bishop Stephen Gardiner. And though the same remark applies to his friend and fellow-martyr Sir Thomas More, yet there were many circumstances that made the character of the latter more generally attractive to the biographer and to the reader. It was a new thing at that period for a layman to rival the best ecclesiastics in learning, eloquence, and theology, as well as in law and in statesmanship. The chancellor's charming family life, where virtue and letters, religion and wit, united with patriarchal simplicity, was, if not a new development of the social system, yet a return, after ages of ignorance and barbarism, to the best Christian traditions of the days of St. Basil and St. Paulinus. In his own family, too, the Blessed Thomas More found those who were capable of recording, as well as appreciating, his virtues, and of telling the incidents of his life and death throughout Europe. Thus multitudes are acquainted with the words and acts, the public and private life of More, whose knowledge of Fisher is merely that he was a learned and virtuous bishop, tyranically put to death by Henry VIII. The memories of the two martyrs are typified in the fate of their pictures. The picture of Sir Thomas and his household, by Holbein, still fresh, and often reproduced by the engraver, has made us all familiar with his gracious and noble aspect ; while more than one old canvas or panel, without a history, and showing only a pale, ascetic face on a faded background, left the beholder uncertain whether he had been gazing on a Warham, à Tunstal, or a Fisher.

But it is not yet too late. After lying long forgotten, an authentic portrait of the martyr bishop was found by Queen Caroline in a secret drawer in the royal palace, and we now know how he looked in 1527 ; for the sketch is by Holbein's faithful pencil.* And so, too, by the opening of the national and of foreign archives, and the diligence of their guardians, documents unknown for centuries have once more been brought to light, and enable the student to fill in many details of Fisher's life and character.

* See *infra.* p. 15.

To the present writer no books are of such living interest as these great volumes of *State Papers.* But I am quite aware how few share this taste, and that for the great majority of readers the facts embodied in ancient records cannot be said to have been " brought to light " until someone has gathered them out, and grouped them together, and clothed them in modern form.

Using an author's privilege to say somewhat of himself, or at least of his motives and labours, in a Preface, I will now state how I have been led to write this life, and how far I am indebted to previous biographers. Although the recent decree of the Sovereign Pontiff permitting the public *cultus* of the Blessed John Fisher* has been the occasion and impulse of my work, I formed the resolution only because I had previously made many of the necessary studies and gathered most of the materials. When, just forty years since, I first entered the refectory or hall of St. John's College, Cambridge, my attention was at once arrested by the portraits of the foundress, Lady Margaret, mother of Henry VII., and of her confessor, John Fisher, Bishop of Rochester ; and the quaint rebus of a fish and an ear (of corn) in the coat-of-arms of the latter, in the chapel window, somewhat distracted my mind amid psalms and prayer. I wished at once to know something of those worthies ; and as the senior tutor of my college, Dr. Hymers, had reprinted Fisher's funeral sermon of Lady Margaret, with notes, I was soon able not so much to

* See at the end of this Preface.

satisfy as to excite still more my curiosity. It was certainly not the intention of the editor, a clergyman of the Protestant Church of England, that the perusal of his reprint should lead any student of St. John's College a step back to the Catholicity of Bishop Fisher. Yet such was the case. I soon purchased a copy of the first edition of Fisher's first treatise against Luther, printed in 1523, and, without entering very deeply into controversy, I received a deep impression of the violence and malice of the Reformers, and a gentle drawing towards the defenders of the old faith, which all subsequent studies increased. Though I read no more of Fisher's writings at that time, his spotless character and heroic death gave weight to other arguments, which made me refuse the oath of royal supremacy then required for a degree, and thus obliged me to leave Cambridge in 1850 and seek reconciliation with the Catholic Church.

I never forgot those first impressions, and at intervals have made myself familiar with the whole of Fisher's writings, both in Latin and in English. I had also read the *Life of Fisher* by Dr. Baily, printed in 1655, and the much larger *Life* by the Protestant Lewis. Some years ago I entertained a thought of editing the original MS. *Life of Fisher* by Dr. Hall, of which a transcript had been placed at my disposal, and for that purpose I had searched the *Epistles of Erasmus* and a good deal of the literature of the early days of Henry. It was, however, reported that the Early English Text Society was engaged upon this MS., and

I left the work to hands which I hope will prove as competent as they have been dilatory.

Among Protestant writers, the first to do complete justice to the character of Bishop Fisher, and to investigate correctly his judicial murder, was Mr. Bruce. " It is a shame to our biographers," wrote that gentleman in a paper read to the Society of Antiquaries in 1831, " that there does not at this time exist a life of Bishop Fisher of any value or authority. Dr. Fiddes, Lewis, the biographer of Caxton, and Mr. Alban Butler were all engaged upon the subject, but without any profitable result. Of Fiddes' collections I know nothing. Mr. Lewis' work was some time since in the hands of the Rev. Theodore Williams, and Mr. Alban Butler's collections were in the possession of Mr. Charles Butler, but have been destroyed. In the meantime Dr. Baily's, or rather Dr. Hall's, *Life of Fisher*, printed in 1655, and now seldom met with, is the only book upon the subject.

" I have abstained," he adds, " as much as possible from having recourse to Hall's work, because I was desirous of ascertaining how much might be gathered from other sources, either to corroborate or contradict his statements. The result is, in most instances, favourable to his correctness, although many things in his volume are clearly fabulous.* His account of the trial and execution of Fisher, which is copied into our State Trials, appears to me to be written in a

---

* It must be noticed that he is speaking of Baily's Hall. I do not think he would have said this of the genuine Hall, of whom I will speak immediately.

style so plain and simple, and with such an air of truth, that if considered merely as a composition it ought to render the book of considerable value."*

Since Mr. Bruce wrote his Essay, the *Life of Fisher*, left in MS. by the Rev. John Lewis, has been published with an Introduction by Mr. Hudson Turner. It contains a large Appendix of valuable documents, but Mr. Lewis' own narrative is written throughout in an antagonistic spirit. Mr. Bruce, without having seen it, refuted its principal misrepresentations. I have made much use of Lewis' collections, but have generally abstained from historical controversy. The best answer is the simple record of historic facts.

Dr. Baily's *Life of Fisher* I have altogether put aside, having access to the original *Life* by Dr. Hall, to which Baily added nothing but verbiage and blunders.† Of Hall's *Life*, however, I must say something, since for some incidents he is the only authority. His MS. has not yet been published, except in Baily's adaptation, and I do not find that anyone has examined its real value. Baily made several additions, some of which are palpably false and have brought discredit on Hall, from whom they were supposed to be taken. I have pointed these out

---

* *Archæologia*, vol. xxv., p. 88.

† Dr. Thomas Baily, son of a Protestant bishop, had been sub-dean of Wells. He became a Catholic during the Commonwealth. Sir Wingfield Bodenham had lent him a MS. of Hall's *Life of Fisher*. He made a copy introducing what he doubtless considered improvements. Wood says: "He sold his copy to a bookseller for a small sum of money, who caused it to be printed at London under the name of Thomas Bayly, D.D.". Of this there have been several editions—London, 1655, 1739, 1740 ; Dublin, 1740 ; and London, 1835.

in their proper places. The value of this English
life, its sources, and its authorship I shall discuss in
full in the Appendix. Though it has supplied me
with many interesting details, yet I have tried to
work independently of it as much as possible. It
will be seen that by far the greater part of this *Life* is
drawn from papers the authenticity of which is beyond questions.

As regards official or state records, it may be mentioned, for those unfamiliar with such matters, that a
collection of the principal documents of the reign of
Henry VIII. was published by the Government from
1830 to 1852 in eleven volumes. These are commonly quoted as *State Papers of Henry VIII.* They
must not be confounded with *Letters and Papers of
Henry VIII.*, still in course of publication. These
latter are Calendars of documents rather than tran-
scripts; but they are on a much larger scale, and
cover a wider field than the former. Nor are they
altogether like other Calendars printed for the Master
of the Rolls. Owing to the exceptional importance
of that period of history, a great latitude was given to
Mr. Brewer, the first editor, and since his death to
Mr. Gairdner, to indicate, abridge, or print in full, not
only papers in the Record Office, but whatever documents, MS. or already printed, would illustrate the
public transactions in England in that reign. This
great work has fortunately been brought down beyond
the death of Bishop Fisher.

Among these new sources for the history of our
holy Martyr none are more important or interesting

than the despatches of Eustache Chapuys, the ambassador of the Emperor Charles V. at the Court of
Henry VIII., from the end of 1529 until after the
death of Fisher. Mr. Paul Friedmann has defended
his accuracy against the animadversions of Mr.
Froude: "Partial his accounts may be; he may
blame that which to many people appears right; he
may call his adversaries bad names; and he may take
pleasure in repeating the malevolent gossip of the
town. But his statements as to facts are always
made—as he takes care to show—on what seems to
him good authority, and I have found no 'untrue
accounts in his letters'." *   The letters of Chapuys
are printed—at least for the period on which I am
engaged—in an English translation by Don Pascual
de Gayangos in the *Spanish Calendars*, published for
the Master of the Rolls, and again, though slightly
abridged, in the *Letters and Papers*, edited by Mr.
Gairdner. I have preferred, as a rule, the translation
of Mr. Gairdner; but as M. De Gayangos is more full,
I have occasionally given his version, especially when
by his quoting the original French I felt assured of
his accuracy.

I must now leave my work to the reader. I have
spared no pains in getting together the materials, and
have sought accuracy above all things. If I have in

---

* Preface to *Anne Boleyn: a Chapter in English History*, by Paul
Friedmann (1884), p. 12. Mr. Froude, who had seen a few of the
letters of Chapuys, says: "In some instances his accounts can be
proved untrue". But of this he gives no proof, and his own reputation for accuracy is not so great as to give weight to his mere statement, especially against one whom he calls a "bitter Catholic".

the latter part of the work somewhat overloaded my pages with dates, it was because there is nothing in which historians of this period are more deficient, while the importance of an event or the very meaning of a term—such as, for example, Supreme Head—may depend on the year or month in which the event occurred or the term was used. For the beginnings of the schism in England are a real Evolution, as will be shown in the proper place.

I have not forgotten that I am writing the life of a saint ; but for that reason I have above all things eschewed imaginary details and general panegyrics. The facts must be carefully ascertained and fully stated before the lesson can be drawn. A saint is not an author's puppet, like the hero of a novel, that he should make him speak and act according to his will. I am very conscious of want of skill in grouping authentic details into a consistent whole, and in giving interest to the dry labours of an antiquary. Yet I hope that I have moulded in clay a faithful, if somewhat rude, likeness, which a more skilful hand may reproduce in marble, perhaps in smaller size, and without my blemishes.

DECREE

[OF THE CONGREGATION OF SACRED RITES]

CONFIRMING THE HONOUR GIVEN TO THE
BLESSED MARTYRS,

JOHN CARDINAL FISHER, THOMAS MORE,

AND OTHERS,

PUT TO DEATH IN ENGLAND FOR THE FAITH

FROM THE YEAR 1535 TO 1583.

ENGLAND, once called the Island of Saints and the Dowry of the Virgin Mother of God, as even from the first ages of the Church it had been renowned for the sufferings of many Martyrs, so also, when it was torn by the fearful schism of the sixteenth century from the obedience and communion of the Roman See, was not without the testimony of those who, *for the dignity of this See, and for the truth of the orthodox Faith, did not hesitate to lay down their lives by the shedding of their blood.* *

In this most noble band of Martyrs nothing whatever is wanting to its completeness or its honour : neither the grandeur of the Roman purple, nor the venerable dignity of Bishops, nor the fortitude of the Clergy both secular and regular, nor the invincible firmness of the weaker sex. Eminent amongst them is JOHN FISHER, Bishop of Rochester and Cardinal of the Holy Roman Church, whom Paul III. speaks of in his Letters as *conspicuous for sanctity, celebrated for learning, venerable by age, an honour and an ornament to the*

---

* Gregory XIII. Constitution, *Quoniam divinae bonitati*, May 1st, 1579.

b

kingdom, and to the Clergy of the whole world. With him must be named the layman THOMAS MORE, Chancellor of England, whom the same Pontiff deservedly extols, as *excelling in sacred learning, and courageous in the defence of truth.* The most authoritative ecclesiastical historians, therefore, are unanimously of opinion that they all shed their blood for the defence, restoration, and preservation of the Catholic Faith. Gregory XIII. even granted in their honour several privileges appertaining to public and ecclesiastical worship ; and chiefly that of using their relics in the consecration of altars, when relics of ancient Holy Martyrs could not be had. Moreover, after he had caused the sufferings of the Christian Martyrs to be painted in fresco by Nicholas Circiniani in the Church of St. Stephen on the Coelian Hill, he permitted also the Martyrs of the Church in England, both of ancient and of more recent times, to be represented in like manner by the same artist in the English Church of the Most Holy Trinity in Rome, including those who, from the the year 1535 to 1583, had died under King Henry VIII. and Queen Elizabeth, for the Catholic Faith and for the Primacy of the Roman Pontiff. The representations of these martyrdoms painted in the said Church remained, with the knowledge and approbation of the Roman Pontiffs who succeeded Gregory XIII., for two centuries, until, about the end of the last century, they were destroyed by wicked men. But copies of them still remained ; for in the year 1584, by privilege of the said Gregory XIII., they had been engraved at Rome on copper-plate with the title : *Sufferings of the Holy Martyrs who, in ancient and more recent times of persecution, have been put to death in England for Christ, and for professing the truth of the Catholic Faith.* From this record, either by inscriptions placed beneath them, or by other sure indications, many of these Martyrs are known by name ; that is to say, fifty-four. They are,—

Those who suffered death under King Henry VIII. : *John Fisher,* Bishop of Rochester, Cardinal of the Holy Roman Church ; *Thomas More,* Chancellor of England ; *Margaret Pole,* Countess of Salisbury, mother of Cardinal Pole ; *Richard Reynolds,* of the Order of St. Bridget ; *John Haile,* Priest ; eighteen Carthusians, — namely, *John Houghton, Augustine Webster, Robert Laurence, William Exmew, Humphrey Middlemore, Sebastian Newdigate, John Rochester, James Walworth, William Greenwood, John Davy, Robert Salt,*

Walter Pierson, Thomas Green, Thomas Scryven, Thomas Redyng
Thomas Johnson, Richard Bere, and *William Horne ; John Forest,*
Priest of the Order of St. Francis ; *John Stone,* of the Order of St.
Augustine ; four Secular Priests,—*Thomas Abel, Edward Powel,*
Richard Fetherston, John Larke ; and *German Gardiner,* a layman.

Those who suffered under Elizabeth : Priests,—*Cuthbert Mayne,*
John Nelson, Everard Hanse, Rodolph Sherwin, John Payne,
Thomas Ford, John Shert, Robert Johnson, William Fylby, Luke
Kirby, Laurence Richardson, William Lacy, Richard Kirkman,
James Hudson or *Tompson, William Hart, Richard Thirkeld,*
Thomas Woodhouse, and ——— *Plumtree.* Also three Priests of the
Society of Jesus,—*Edmund Campion, Alexander Briant,* and *Thomas*
Cottam. Lastly, *John Storey,* Doctor of Laws ; *John Felton,* and
Thomas Sherwood, laymen.

Until lately, the Cause of these Martyrs had never been officially
treated. Some time ago, in the year 1860, Cardinal Nicholas Wise-
man, of illustrious memory, Archbishop of Westminster, and the
other Bishops of England, petitioned the Sovereign Pontiff Pius IX.,
of sacred memory, to institute for the whole of England a Festival in
honour of all Holy Martyrs, that is to say, even of those *who, though*
not yet declared to be such, have in latter times, for their defence of
the Catholic Religion, and especially for asserting the authority of the
Apostolic See, fallen by the hands of wicked men and resisted unto
blood. But as, according to the prevailing practice of the Congregation of Sacred Rites, a Festival can be instituted in regard only to
those Servants of God to whom ecclesiastical honour (*cultus*) has
been already given and rightly sanctioned by the Apostolic See, the
said petition was not granted. Wherefore, in these last years, a new
petition was presented to Our Holy Father the Sovereign Pontiff Leo
XIII., by His Eminence Cardinal Henry Edward Manning, the
present Archbishop of Westminster, and the other Bishops of England,
together with the Ordinary Process which had been there completed,
and other authentic documents, in which were contained the proofs
of Martyrdom as to those who suffered from the year 1535 to 1583,
and also the aforesaid concessions of the Roman Pontiffs in regard to
those above-mentioned.

Our Holy Father was pleased to commit the examination of the
whole matter to a Special Congregation, consisting of several

Cardinals of the Holy Roman Church and of Officials of the Congregation of Sacred Rites,—the examination to be preceded by a Disquisition, to be drawn up by the Right Reverend Augustine Caprara, Promoter of the Holy Faith. In this Special Congregation, assembled at the Vatican on the 4th day of December of the present year, the undersigned Cardinal Dominic Bartolini, Prefect of the said Sacred Congregation, who had charge of the Cause, proposed the following question : " *Whether, by reason of the special concessions of the Roman Pontiffs, in regard to the earlier Martyrs of England—who, from the year 1535 to 1583, suffered death for the Catholic Faith, and for the Primacy of the Roman Pontiff in the Church, and whose Martyrdoms were formerly painted, by authority of the Sovereign Pontiff Gregory XIII., in the English Church of the Most Holy Trinity in Rome, and in the year 1584 were engraved at Rome on copper-plate by privilege of the same Pontiff—there is evidence of the concession of public ecclesiastical honour, or of this being a case excepted by the Decrees of Pope Urban VIII., of Sacred Memory, in the matter and to the effect under consideration* ". The Most Eminent and Most Reverend Fathers, and the Official Prelates, after hearing the written and oral report of the aforesaid Promoter of the Holy Faith, and after the matter in regard to the 54 Martyrs above-named had been fully discussed, were of opinion that the answer to be given was : " *Affirmatively, or That it is proved to be a case excepted* ".

The undersigned Secretary having made a faithful report of all that precedes to Our Holy Father POPE LEO XIII., His Holiness vouchsafed to approve the decision of the Sacred Special Congregation, on the 9th day of December, 1886.

The present Decree was issued on this 29th day of December, sacred to the Martyr Thomas Archbishop of Canterbury, whose faith and constancy these Blessed Martyrs so strenuously imitated.

     D. CARDINAL BARTOLINI,
        PREFECT OF THE CONGREGATION OF SACRED RITES.
            LAURENCE SALVATI,
                Secretary.

L. ✠ S.

LIFE OF
BLESSED JOHN FISHER.

——✳——

CHAPTER I.

EARLY YEARS.

THIS work is not a history of the times of the martyred Bishop of Rochester, but an arrangement of such authentic details concerning his life, labour, and sufferings as can now be gathered together. Before, however, considering the details of that life, it will be useful to locate it, so to say, as a whole, among our historical associations; and for this purpose it is important to observe that, although his martyrdom connects him with the well-known epoch of the Reformation, he belongs to an earlier, less familiar, and very different period.

There is a passage in his writings which will enable us to look at that period from his own point of view, and in which he has unconsciously sketched his own position in it as by the words of a seer. In the first decade of the sixteenth century, preaching on the Seven Penitential Psalms, he came to these words: *Tu exurgens misereberis Sion, quia tempus miserendi ejus, quia venit tempus* *—"Thou shalt arise and have mercy upon Sion; for it is time to have

* *Ps.* ci. 14.

i

mercy upon it, for the time is come". These words led
him to review and to bewail the state of Christendom, and
to pray for its re-establishment:

"The religion of Christian Faith is greatly diminished;
we be very few; and whereas sometime we were spread
almost through the world, now we be thrust down into a
very straight angle or corner. Our enemies hold away
from us Asia and Africa, two of the greatest parts of the
world. Also they hold from us a great portion of this
part, called Europe, which we now inhabit, so that scant
the sixth part of that we had in possession before is left
unto us. Besides this, our enemies daily lay await to have
this little portion. Therefore, good Lord, without Thou
help, the name of Christian men shall utterly be destroyed
and fordone. . . . Therefore, merciful Lord, exercise Thy
mercy, show it indeed upon thy Church, *quia tempus est
miserendi ejus.* If there be many righteous people in Thy
Church militant, hear us, wretched sinners, for the love of
them; be merciful unto Sion, that is to say, to all Thy Church.
If in Thy Church be but a few righteous persons, so much
the more is our wretchedness, and the more need we have
of Thy mercy."

He then reminds our Lord of His promise that the
Gospel should be preached throughout the whole world, as
a testimony to all nations, and prays Him to raise up men
fit for such a work. He recalls how the Apostles were but
soft and yielding clay till they were baked hard by the fire
of the Holy Ghost. He then proceeds as follows:

"So, good Lord, do now in like manner again with Thy
Church militant. Change and make the soft and slippery
earth into hard stones. Set in Thy Church strong and
mighty pillars, that may suffer and endure great labours—
watching, poverty, thirst, hunger, cold, and heat—which also
shall not fear the threatenings of princes, persecution,
neither death, but always persuade and think with them-

selves to suffer, with a good will, slanders, shame, and all
kinds of torments, for the glory and laud of Thy Holy
Name. By this manner, good Lord, the truth of Thy
Gospel shall be preached throughout all the world. . . .

"Oh! if it would please our Lord God to show this great
goodness and mercy in our days, the memorial of His so
doing ought, of very right, to be left in perpetual writing,
never to be forgotten of all our posterity, that every generation
might love and worship Him time without end." *

These last words refer to the verse of the Psalm on
which he was commenting: "Let those things be written
unto another generation, and the people that shall be
created shall praise the Lord". The preacher did not
foresee, when uttering them, that they would be the justification for writing his own life. His words, coming from
the depths of his heart, described himself, his aspirations
and resolutions; and the Providence of God over him
makes them now read like a prophecy. But they are here
quoted rather as showing the period, in the Church's and
in England's history, in which that Providence had placed
his whole life.

The sad tone in which he speaks of the narrowing of
Christendom reminds us that his birth, early in the second
half of the fifteenth century, almost coincides with the
taking of Constantinople by the Turks. The boy must
have heard from his parents and teachers, with awe, of that
great calamity of recent occurrence, which seemed to
threaten the very existence of Christianity. The fear of
his youth was to endure and increase throughout his life. He
beheld with a bleeding heart the continual encroachments
of the infidels, the continual division and quarrels of

* *English Works* of John Fisher (Early English Text Society),
pp. 171, 178, 191. In this and future quotations I modernise the
spelling, but change the words as little as possible. These sermons
were first printed by Pynson in 1505.

Christian princes. A few years after the discourse above quoted, he had to grieve over the taking of Belgrade and of Rhodes, but he was not to live to triumph at the heroic defence of Malta and the victory of Lepanto.

If he watched with anxiety the attacks of "our enemies," as he calls the Mahommedans, from without, he had no reason as yet to fear defection from within. Whatever he might deplore in the state of England, and whatever chastisements he might anticipate and seek to avert, he did not and could not contemplate at that period the schism and heresy that were so soon after his death to separate his country for centuries from Catholic Christendom. Since his childhood he had heard of—perhaps had been an eye-witness of—the ravages of civil war ; and, though the red and white roses had been intertwined, and peace restored to the land twenty years before he preached those sermons, that hateful strife had caused a confusion so universal, and had so lowered the morality of both the clergy and laity, and the discipline of monastic life, that the preacher might well be allowed to make the supposition that there were "but few righteous people in the Church militant" in England. Nor would anything he might hear of the state of religion in France or Spain, Germany or Italy, make such a supposition very extreme, even when extended, as it was by him, to the Church in general.

The inspired and prophetic prayer that he makes, that God would now at last come to the succour of His suffering Church, and send great and apostolic men to rebuild her walls and extend her territories, was fully granted, but the fruits were not to be seen by him in this life. He had heard, of course, of the discovery of new lands in the western ocean by Columbus in 1492, and he may not improbably have himself conversed with Sebastian Cabot, the discoverer of Newfoundland, when that brave sailor was in England in 1497. In the privy purse expenses of

Henry VII. for 10th August, 1497, is an entry o. £10 "to him that found the new Isle," and again, in 8th April, 1504, of £2, as gift "to a priest that goeth to the new Island"; and, considering the relations of Fisher at that time with the King's mother, the Lady Margaret, which brought him often to Court, it is not unlikely that he bade God-speed to that very priest, and may have had a dim vision of a new sphere and of better days for the Church, than in that "strait angle or corner" of Europe in which it was then cooped up. At the time he uttered that prayer for apostolic men, St. Ignatius, a youth of fourteen, was a page in the Court of Ferdinand the Catholic. He was still "the soft and slippery earth," but the fire of the Holy Ghost would before many years bake and harden him into one of the strong pillars of the Church. And two years after his prayer, the great Apostle of the Indies, St. Francis Xavier, was born. Their names were never heard on earth by Fisher; but those who believe in the power of prayer, and who remember the words, "Beg the Lord of the harvest that He send labourers into His harvest," will not doubt that He who destined the gift to His Church inspired the prayer, which in God's ordinary Providence is the condition of all great graces.*

The life of Fisher began amidst the horrors of civil war, and ended amid the horrors, far greater to a soul like his, of religious rebellion and impiety. The darkness of night seemed to him to be gathering more deeply over the world and the Church. He was not permitted to see the streaks of dawn which had already begun to appear. But he was himself, both in life and death, "a burning and a shining light," all the brighter by contrast with the shades around.

---

* On the words of the 2nd Psalm : *Postula a me et dabo tibi gentes in possessionem tuam*—" Ask of Me and I will give thee the gentiles for Thine inheritance," Suarez remarks that prayer was a condition even of the promises made to the Incarnate Son of God.

These reflections may appear more fitted for a retrospect of a life already narrated, than for an introduction to one not yet known to the reader; yet there is an advantage in reading the details of a life lived long ago, with that general knowledge of its surroundings with which we approach the study of the life of one of our own times.

Dr. Hall places the birth of John Fisher in the year 1459. If this is correct, he would have been about seventy-six at the time of his death, on 22nd June, 1535. But the Bishop of Faenza, who was Papal Nuncio in Paris, and who had known the Bishop of Rochester in England, writes on the very day of his death: "The English call him a valetudinarian of ninety, reckoning him twenty-five years older than he is".* If he was really only sixty-five at the time of his death, he must have been born in 1470 or 1469; and this calculation corresponds with his own saying, that he was very young when made bishop: *Qui paucos annos habuerim;* for if he was born in 1459, he would have been about forty-five years old, when raised to the episcopate, which he could scarcely have called an early age,† especially in those days, when youths were often made bishops, and when men were called old at fifty, and were marvels of longevity at sixty. ‡ Another reason, which seems to show

---

* *Letters and Papers of Henry VIII.*, vol. viii., No. 909. He repeats the same thing in another letter, No. 910.

† Fisher thus spoke in a solemn academical address to Henry VII. in 1506. Henry was then only forty-nine, yet he was considered old; and Fisher, being then engaged in eulogising his great wisdom and experience, would not have spoken of himself as having been too young to be made a bishop at the age of forty-five. I am here supposing that this speech was made by Fisher in 1506, and not by John Blyth, Bishop of Salisbury, in 1495, as it was conjectured by Mr. Gairdner, in *Letters and Papers of Richard and Henry VII.* See the proofs in Professor Mayor's notes to Cooper's *Memoir of Lady Margaret*, p. 249, and in this vol., ch. ii.

‡ "Old John of Gaunt, time-honoured Lancaster," was only fifty-

that Hall has dated the birth of John Fisher too soon, is that he is known to have taken his bachelor's degree in 1487. Had he been born in 1459, he would then have been twenty-eight, whereas eighteen was a much more usual age for graduating in those days. We may conclude, then, from these two facts, that the Bishop of Faenza's statement is correct, and, as it was made contrary to appearances and general opinion, we must suppose he would not have made it without good grounds. I venture, then, to place the birth of the future martyr in the year 1468 or 1469.

The place of his birth was Beverly, in the East Riding of Yorkshire, at present a decayed town, but then, owing to its magnificent collegiate church and ecclesiastical establishment, of considerable importance.* His parents were Robert and Agnes Fisher. They had four children, as we learn from the father's will, made shortly before his death in 1470. If the date above assigned for his birth is correct, John was the youngest.† He had a brother Robert, who remained a layman and died a few months before the bishop. We shall find him an inmate of the bishop's palace at Rochester, acting as his steward, and afterwards supporting the bishop at his own great cost when in prison. In a list of debts‡ due to the bishop at his attainder, there is mention of a Ralph Fisher as well as

nine when he died. St. Teresa says St. Peter of Alcantara was *a very old man* when she first knew him, yet he was not sixty.

* Leland, in 1539, writes: " The town of Beverly is large and well builded of wood. It is not walled."

† Lewis, in his *Life of Fisher*, says he was the eldest, but gives no authority. He says the father died in 1477, whereas the will (given by him in App.) says 1470. As Robert received his father's name, it is probable that he was the eldest son.

‡ See *Letters and Papers of Henry VIII.*, vol. viii. 888. In the same document we find Robert, John, and Edward White as indebted to the bishop.

Robert, and this may have been the name of another
brother.* Edward White is spoken of as the bishop's
brother-in-law, and since by his mother's second marriage he
had only one sister (who became a nun), one of the children
of Robert Fisher must have been a daughter.† His father's
sister Ellen had married Thomas Wickliffe, as we find from
the will to be given immediately. The Wickliffes, in spite
of the heresiarch, remained very staunch Catholics; and a
great part of the inhabitants of the village of Wycliffe, in
the North Riding of Yorkshire, are Catholics to this day.
Robert Fisher appears to have resided in St. Mary's Parish
in Beverly, and was by trade a mercer. He died when
"his children were of a very tender age," writes Dr. Hall.
John, in fact, according to the computation we have adopted,
was only a year old; according to Hall's he would be eleven.

The will of Robert Fisher was drawn up in Latin, and
runs as follows: "In the name of God, Amen. The 30th
day of June in the year of our Lord 1470, I, Robert Fisher
of Beverly, mercer, being in good mind, make my last will in
this way. First, I bequeath my soul to Almighty God and to
the Blessed Mary, His Mother, and to all the saints of the
heavenly court, and my body to be buried in the Church of
the Blessed Virgin Mary at Beverly before the crucifix.
Then I give and bequeath to each alms-house in Beverly
20 pence.‡ I give and bequeath for tithes forgotten 20

---

* Mr. Lewis (*Life of Fisher*, i. 4), mentions some letters of frater-
nity obtained for John and Ralph Fisher, brothers, from the hospital
of the Holy Trinity. He doubts whether it is the same John Fisher.

† Robert Fisher and Edward White generosi literati infra Ebora-
censem oriundi et infra Roffensem dioceses commemorantes, are witnesses to a deed in October 1519, together with the bishop (Memoir
of Lady Margaret, p. 161). After his brother-in-law's death Edward
White went abroad (*Letters and Papers*, xi. 524). He is said to be
of Lynne-Bishop. (Also *Ib.* 1247, *iv.*)

‡ We may multiply all these sums by twelve at least to find their
equivalents in modern money.

pence. I bequeath to the fabric of the collegiate church of S. John of Beverly 20 pence. I bequeath to the fabric of the cathedral church of St. Peter's, York, 8 pence. I give and bequeath to each of the two houses of the Franciscans at Beverly 3s. 4d. I give to the chaplain of Holy Trinity to pray for my soul 13s. 4d. I will that a fit chaplain cele-brate for my soul during one year. I bequeath to Sir Robert Cook,* vicar of the Church of the Blessed Virgin Mary, 6s. 8d. I bequeath to John Plumber, chaplain, 6s. 8d. I bequeath to Thomas Wickliffe, my brother, 6s. 8d. I bequeath to my sister Ellen, his wife, 6s. 8d. I bequeath to my brother William 40s. which he owes me by bond, and besides his bond I leave him 14s. I bequeath to the abbot and convent† of Hagnaby in Lincolnshire 10s. for one trental of masses‡ to be celebrated there for my soul. *Item*, I bequeath to Clementia Charington 2s. *Item*, to the fabric of the church of Holtoft in Lincolnshire 3s. 4d. *Item*, I bequeath to each of my children of my own property (*de mea propria parte*) £2 13s. 4d., and should one of them chance to die while under age, then the portion of the deceased to be divided equally between the three survivors. The residue of all my goods not hitherto disposed of or be-queathed, after the payment of my funeral expenses and debts, I give and bequeath to Agnes my wife, which Agnes and John Siglestorn I appoint executors of this my last will and testament, and William Fisher, my brother, and Thomas Wickliffe, trustees (*supervisores*), the witnesses (of my will)

* Priests without a university degree are always called Sir with the Christian name (in Latin *Dominus*), but graduates Master or Master Doctor. The word Reverend was not in use, except in the formal address of a bishop : the Reverend Father in God.

† Convent in that period means community. It was never applied to a building either for men or women.

‡ That is, one each day for a month. A groat, or 4d., was the usual honorary of the priest, equivalent to four or five shillings in present value.

being Robert Cook, vicar of the Church of the Blessed Virgin Mary, John Wollar, John Copy, and others.

"The present will was proved on the 26th day of June in the above year (1470), and the administration granted to the executors therein named, having taken the oath required by law." *

Agnes Fisher does not seem to have acted unwisely nor unkindly to her children in marrying again. Her second husband's name was White, and by him she had three sons, John,† Thomas, and Richard, and a daughter named Elizabeth. This Elizabeth White became a nun in the Dominican monastery of Dartford, in her brother's diocese of Rochester. For her he wrote two treatises when in prison.

This is all I have been able to discover about the family, and the glimpse, slight as it is, shows them united in affection to the end.‡

Education was easily obtained in a town like Beverly, and John most probably received his first training for the priesthood in the grammar school attached to the collegiate church of St. John. His early writing, some of which may be still seen in the proctor's books at Cambridge, is noted as very

* The Latin is given by Lewis (ii. 253). There is an error in one of the dates, for the will is made on 30th of June and proved on 26th. Perhaps the first date should be 20th. The mention of two churches in Lincolnshire perhaps points to the birthplace of Robert Fisher. The patronymic Fisher would indicate a seaside origin, and Hagnaby was not far from the German Ocean. The name of Fisher was not among the burgesses of Beverly in the middle of the 15th century, so that Robert Fisher may have been born elsewhere.

† The name John may perhaps have been given to the Blessed John Fisher in honour of St. John of Beverly, Archbishop of York. Fisher's mother called her eldest son by her second husband by the same name.

‡ John Fisher occurs as Protestant curate of the Minster at Beverly in 1579, probably a relative of the martyr, since the name was not common in that town.

good, and his elegant Latinity may be taken as a proof of his diligence in early years ; for though it was not learnt altogether at school, it is seldom that much progress is made in higher studies when the foundation has been carelessly laid.

Were I writing the life of a mere scholar like Erasmus, or of a learned and zealous priest like Colet, it might be fitting to speak with some detail here of the grammar school education in England, before printed books had come into general use, and to dwell on whatever other influences, secular or religious, would have helped to form the mind and character of a clever, studious, and pious boy, in a town such as Beverly ; and following him to Cambridge, there might be something picturesque to tell as to the horses, the roads, the inns, the company, when a youth left his home for the first time for what was then so long and venturesome a journey. But I am engaged on the life of a martyr, and there will be so much to say of his public career and later life, that I feel bound to confine myself, in his earlier years, to such special facts as have been recorded of Fisher personally, leaving it to my readers to fill up the details of the picture.

The range of study in those days was narrow and the grammar school had soon taught whatever it was capable of teaching. It was usual for boys to enter the universities at the age of fourteen or fifteen.* John Fisher was sent to Cambridge in the year 1483. Were the usual date assigned to his birth correct, he would then have been twenty-three or twenty-four years old, which is utterly improbable, since nothing has been recorded or can be reasonably con-

* *History of the University of Cambridge*, by Professor J. Bass Mullinger, vol. i. 346. To this book I may refer in general for an account of the life of mediæval students. as well as for a complete investigation of Fisher's influence on Cambridge, in the first quarter of the sixteenth century.

jectured to account for so unusual a delay. We are
therefore confirmed in the opinion that he was born about
1469. There is a somewhat uncertain tradition* that at his
first entrance into the university he was a member of a new
foundation called "God's House," which was subsequently
by his influence refounded as Christ's College. If this was
the case the connection did not last long, for he was certainly
in his first years at Cambridge under the care of William de
Melton, fellow of Michael House. This college stood on a
part of the ground now occupied by Trinity; it was indeed
at a period after Fisher's death absorbed into that foundation of Henry VIII.

William de Melton was a native of Yorkshire, and perhaps
a friend of Fisher's parents. He was eminent in his day as
a philosopher, a theologian, and a preacher. He was elected
Master of his college in 1495, and shortly afterwards Chancellor of York. Fisher always speaks of him with affection
and reverence.† The following passage of one of his controversial works carries us back to his undergraduate days:
"My master, William Melton, Chancellor of York, a man
eminent both for holiness and for every kind of erudition, used
often to admonish me when I was a boy and attended his
lectures on Euclid, that if I looked on the least letter of any
geometrical figure as superfluous, I had not seized the true
and full meaning of Euclid. But if the disciple of Euclid
must be so careful in points of geometry, certainly the disciple of Christ must weigh well each word of his Divine
Master, and be thoroughly convinced that there is not a
word without its purpose." ‡ Another allusion to his youth

* Cooper's *Memoir of Lady Margaret*, p. 100.

† In 1527, Fisher, in preface to Book I. of his treatise against
Œcolampadius, says: "Meltonus . . . theologus eximius de quibus
dam capitibus heresum Lutheri scripsit, sed liber ejus hauddum prælo
commissus est". Melton died in 1528.

‡ *Proœmium* in 5 librorum contra Œcolampadium (1527).

is found in a treatise against Luther: "Now I begin to see by experience the truth of what I heard as a boy, that heretics must be avoided at least for this reason, that other heretics arise from their ashes. I see that John Huss lives again in you. But God in His Providence has mercifully provided this remedy, that you can never agree together. . . . Blessed be God who reduces you to confusion, by that very spirit of division that you strive to introduce into the Church." *

Fisher became Bachelor of Arts in 1487, and three years after took his degree of Master (1491), and was soon chosen Fellow of his college,† a proof both of his learning and of the esteem in which he was held.

He must have been ordained priest on the title of his fellowship. Never perhaps lived a man in England who more thoroughly illustrated the heavenly character of the Christian priesthood, as his own pen has described it. He wrote as follows in his defence of the priesthood against Luther: "God's Providence has arranged that the inferior or earthly bodies, prone to change and to corruption, should be refreshed, vivified, and perpetuated by the influence of the higher or heavenly bodies, to which he has given not only greater durability, but also the virtue of shining, illuminating, warming, moistening, enlivening, thundering, and lightening. So it is in the Church; and therefore the Holy Ghost in the Psalms compares the Apostles and other ministers of God to the heavens, the people to the earth. 'The heavens show forth the glory of God.' Like heavenly bodies, the ministers of God illuminate by the splendour of their lives, warm by the ardour of their charity, moisten by their counsels, vivify by their promises, thunder by their threats, flash by their miracles. This was so not only in the days of the Apostles; the Church is ever one and the same,

* *Confutatio Assertionis Lutheranæ*, Art. 30 (1523).
† Lewis i., 4.

and now stands in need of these ministries no less than
then."* No words could better describe his own beneficent
influence, first on the University of Cambridge, then on his
diocese, and finally on the whole of England and on the
Church throughout the world. We will confine ourselves
in the next chapter to his influence on his university.

But now that he has arrived at full age, let us try to get a
glimpse of him. I know not why biographers generally
describe their heroes after relating their deaths. It is
surely a help to have, in one's imagination, while reading a
life, some genuine picture of its subject. I take the following description from Dr. Hall: "In stature of body he was
tall and comely, exceeding the common and middle sort of
men, for he was to the quantity of six feet in height, and
being therewith very slender and lean, was nevertheless
upright and well-formed, straight-backed, big-jointed, and
strongly sinewed. His hair by nature black, though in his
later time, through age and imprisonment, turned to
hoariness, or rather to whiteness. His eyes long and
round, neither full black nor full grey, but of a mixed colour
between both. His forehead smooth and large; his nose
of a good and even proportion; somewhat wide-mouthed
and big-jawed, as one ordained to utter speech much,
wherein was, notwithstanding, a certain comeliness; his skin
somewhat tawny, mixed with many blue veins. His face,
hands, and all his body so bare of flesh, as is almost
incredible, which came the rather (as may be thought) by
the great abstinence and penance he used upon himself
many years together, even from his youth. In his countenance he bore such a reverend gravity, and therewith in
his doings exercised such discreet severity, that not only of
his equals, but even of his superiors, he was both honoured
and feared.

"In speech he was very mild, temperate, and modest,

* *De Sacerdotio*, Congressus ii., Tertium Axioma.

saving in matters of God and his charge, [and in the affairs] which then began to trouble the world, and therein he would be earnest above his accustomed order. But vainly or without cause he would never speak; neither was his ordinary talk of common worldly matters, but rather of the Divinity and high power of God, of the joys of heaven and the pains of hell, of the glorious death of martyrs and strait life of confessors, with such-like virtuous and profitable talk, which he always uttered with such a heavenly grace that his words were always a great edifying in his hearers."

Hoping that the reader may, from the facts to be related, be able to paint in his own mind a correct image of the soul and character of Fisher, I will add a few words regarding the various portraits that profess to give a likeness of his body.

There is one now (1888) in the Hall of St. John's, Cambridge, which represents "a very mortified and meagre personage with a crucifix before him".* This was presented to Baker, the well-known antiquary, by the Marquis of Bath. It is either not Fisher at all or a mere fancy portrait. A bearded portrait, belonging to Major Brooks, in 1866 was shown in the Portrait Exhibition as an original portrait of the Bishop of Rochester, by Holbein. According to Dr. Woltmann, it is neither by Holbein, nor does it represent Fisher. Holbein is not known to have *painted* any portrait of Fisher, but there still exist two beautiful sketches in red chalk made by his hand. One of these is in her Majesty's collection at Windsor, the other in the British Museum. These were made in the year 1527, when the bishop was about fifty-eight years old (according to the computation we have adopted). Dr. Woltmann says: "The worn countenance, with its honest, modest, but anxiously conscientious expression, shows completely the man, whose

* Cole, quoted by Turner, in his Introduction to Lewis, i., xxvi.

wonderful purity of life, combined with profound and unostentatious learning, as well as incredible kindliness of demeanour towards high and low, is extolled by Erasmus ".*

The frontispiece of this volume is from the drawing in the Windsor collection. A former keeper has written the following words on it : *Il Epyscopo de Resester fo tagilato*† *il capo l'an°.* 1535—(The Bishop of Rochester was beheaded in the year 1535 ‡).

---

* *Holbein and his Time* (Eng. Tr., p. 313).

† *Sic*, for *fu tagliato*.

‡ These words, in the lower part of the drawing, do not appear in the frontispiece, which is shorter. They are hard to decipher, but the words "Bishop of Rochester" are quite clear. I am indebted to the courtesy of the Secretary of the Science and Art Department, at South Kensington, for leave to reproduce this portrait by the auto type process.

CHAPTER II.

CAMBRIDGE.

IN a Latin oration addressed to Henry VII.. in 1506, Fisher, speaking as chancellor of the university, extolled its antiquity and past grandeurs, but deplored the state to which it had been reduced before the king came to its succour. He described what he had seen and experienced in the following words : " Either from continual lawsuits and wrongs inflicted by the town, or from long-continued pestilence, by which we lost many of our more cultured men, and no less than ten grave and very learned doctors, or from the want of any patrons and benefactors of arts and letters, studies had begun generally to languish, so that many were deliberating how they might best get away. We should indeed have fallen into utter desolation, had not your majesty, like the orient from on high, looked down upon us." * No doubt King Henry VII. was a real bene- factor to the University of Cambridge, both by his personal interest and visits, and by his munificence † in carrying on the splendid foundation of St. Mary and St. Nicolas (more commonly called King's College), begun by Henry VI. But while it is probable that much of this interest and generosity was due directly or indirectly to Fisher's influence, it is certain that Fisher himself, by the advice he gave to the king's mother, the Lady Margaret, and his own co-

---

* Lewis, ii. 269.

† This, however, was principally by money left at his death.

2

operation in her royal bounties, proved himself one of the greatest benefactors Cambridge has ever known. This noble lady had so great a place in the life of Fisher, as well as he in hers, that it is necessary to say a few words of her history and character.

Margaret Beaufort, the mother of Henry VII., was the only child of John Beaufort, the first Duke of Somerset, who was grandson of John of Gaunt, Duke of Lancaster, and great-grandson of Edward the Third. She had been married in childhood (as was the custom) to the son of the Duke of Suffolk, but did not ratify the marriage when of age to consent, and was given to Edmund ap Tudor, Earl of Richmond, brother of Henry VI. Her husband dying in 1456, not many months after his marriage, left her a widow at the age of thirteen. Their child, subsequently King Henry VII., was born after his father's death, on 28th January, 1457.* In 1459 she married Lord Henry Stafford, her second and third cousin, being like herself descended from Henry III. He died in 1482. She took for her third husband (or her fourth, if we include the matrimonial contract of her childhood), Thomas, Lord Stanley, afterwards Earl of Derby, also her third cousin. Thus she became Countess of Derby as well as Richmond. It was through her intervention that the wars of the Roses came to an end, by the alliance of her son Henry, Earl of Richmond (and by the victory of Bosworth in 1485, King Henry VII.), with Elizabeth of York, daughter of Edward IV. A contemporary poet called the Lady Margaret "mother, author, plotter, counsellor of union ".†

---

* The bishop declared in her own presence and that of her son that he was born before she had completed her fourteenth year. —Lewis, ii. 265.

† Mr. Cooper, the well-known author of the *Annals of Cambridge* and of *Athenæ Cantabrigienses*, left in MS. a *Memoir of the Lady Margaret.* It is rather a chronological series of every document he

The first mention of Fisher in connection with the Countess of Richmond is in 1495. So great was his reputation in the university, that in 1494 he had been chosen senior proctor. Business of the university took him to the Court, which was then at Greenwich. The Proctor's Book contains the note of the expenses of this journey in his own handwriting (in Latin) : " For the hire of two horses for 11 days, 7 shillings ; for breakfast before passing to Greenwich, 3 pence ; boat-hire, 4 pence. I dined with the lady, mother of the king. I supped with the chancellor," &c.*

The acquaintance then, or perhaps previously, begun between the young priest and this noble lady must have continued and ripened into mutual esteem, though we have no record of it for the next seven years. In the meantime Fisher continued to reside at ·Cambridge, and in 1497 was chosen Master of Michael House, in place of Dr. Melton.† On the 5th July, in the year 1501, he commenced Doctor of Divinity, and on the 15th was chosen vice-chancellor of the university.‡ In 1502 the Countess of Richmond made him her chaplain and her confessor in the place of Dr. Richard Fitzjames, promoted to be Bishop of Rochester.§

could discover touching on her in any way than a life. It is, however, a valuable compilation, and has been edited with appendices and notes with the greatest care by Professor Mayor, and published at the expense of Christ's and St. John's Colleges.

Another Life was published in 1839, by Miss Halsted. It is written in a sympathetic spirit, and does justice, as far as was in the power of a Protestant writer, both to the Countess and to her confessor, the Bishop of Rochester.

* Lewis, i. 5.

† Lewis throws doubts on this, but Mr. Bass Mullinger gives it as quite certain. Cooper and others make Fisher Vicar of Northallerton in Yorkshire. Probably some other John Fisher has been mistaken for the future Bishop of Rochester. He declared more than once that he was unbeneficed when made bishop.

‡ Proctor's Book *apud* Lewis.

§ He was afterwards Bishop of Chicester, and lastly of London.

This holy lady was much older than her spiritual father, and
while she loved, esteemed, and cherished him with the affection of a mother, she yet obeyed him with the docility of a
child, not only after her husband's death making a public
vow of chastity in his hands,* but also a vow of obedience:
"To the intent all her works might be more acceptable and
of greater merit in the sight of God," says Fisher in her
funeral sermon, "such godly things she would take by
obedience, which obedience she promised to the fore-named
father, my lord of London [Dr. Fitzjames], for the time of
his being with her, and afterwards in like wise unto me".
On the other hand, her confessor declared publicly, in the
statutes for the fellows of St. John's of his foundation, that
"he was indebted to her as to his own mother," and willed
therefore that she should be prayed for at mass like himself.†

The first fruits, as regards the university, of Fisher's
guidance of the Countess of Richmond, who had long
since devoted both herself and her great riches to every
kind of good works, was the endowment of a readership in
divinity in both Cambridge and Oxford. The foundation
charters bear date the 8th September, 1503, the feast of
the Nativity of the Blessed Virgin Mary, to which Lady
Margaret seems to have had a special devotion.‡   Dr. John

---

* Widows frequently made such public vows. . . . They received
mantle, scapular, veil, and ring. (See form of blessing in Bishop
Lacy's Pontifical.) There is an example of this vow in Bishop Fisher's
register, April 21, 1510. (See Lewis's *Life of Fisher*, vol. i. 42.)
Lady Margaret "obtained her husband's licence a long time before
he died" to take the same vow in the hands of Dr. Fitzjames; after
his death she renewed it to Dr. Fisher. (See her *Funeral Sermon* (E.
E. Text Soc. Ed.), p. 294.)

† *Memoir of Lady Margaret*, p. 248.

‡ See the digression on Our Blessed Lady on the feast of her
Nativity in the sermons on the Penitential Psalms, preached by
Bishop Fisher in presence of the Countess, p. 44.

Fisher was the first reader appointed at Cambridge. His duties were sufficiently onerous. He was bound to read such works of divinity as the chancellor or vice-chancellor, with the college of doctors, should judge necessary, for an hour daily throughout term, and up to the 8th September in the long vacation, but to cease in Lent if the chancellor thought fit, in order to be occupied in preaching. He was to receive no fee besides his salary, which was £13 6s. 8d., paid half-yearly,* a fair endowment in days when the average income of a chantry priest was not more than £5. Owing to his duties as vice-chancellor, Fisher soon resigned this lectureship.

Another foundation of the countess followed in 1504. This was of a preacher "to the praise and honour of the Holy Name of Jesus and the Annunciation of the Blessed Virgin Mary". He was to preach six sermons annually— viz., once in the course of two years on some Sunday at St. Paul's Cross, if the preacher can obtain permission, otherwise, at St. Margaret's, Westminster; but if not able to preach there, then in one of the more notable churches of the city of London, and once during the same term of two years on some feast day in each of the churches of Ware and Cheshunt in Hertfordshire; Bassingbourne, Orwell, and Babraham in Cambridgeshire; Maxey, St. James Deeping, St. John Deeping, Bourn, Boston, and Swineshead in Lincolnshire. The stipend was £10 per annum, and the preacher was to be unbeneficed, but a perpetual fellow of some college in Cambridge.†

A matter of even greater importance than these was the foundation of Christ's College at Cambridge. William Bing ham, parson of St. John Zachary in London, had begun a college called God's House, and had resigned the honour of founder to Henry VI. But the king, being occupied in the greater foundation of his own magnificent College of St.

* *Memoir of Lady Margaret*, p. 89.　† *Ibid.*, p. 93.

Mary and St. Nicolas (King's), left that of God's House incomplete. Its revenues were only sufficient for the maintenance of a proctor and four fellows. Previous to placing herself under Dr. Fisher's direction, the Countess of Richmond had planned a magnificent chantry foundation for herself and the king at Westminster, and had received from the king the necessary licences in mortmain. Fisher judged that it would be more for the glory of God to devote her bounty to the promotion of learning.* The countess agreed, but as it was necessary to obtain the king's approval, she committed the negotiation to Dr. Fisher, with the result that appears in the following letter of the king to his mother:

"MADAM, my most entirely well-beloved lady and mother, I recommend me unto you in the most humble and lowly wise that I can, beseeching you of your daily and continual blessings. By your confessor, the bearer, I have received your good and most loving writing, and by the same have heard at good leisure such evidence as he would show unto me on your behalf, and thereupon have sped him in every behalf without delay, according to your noble petition and desire, which resteth in two principal points: the one for a general pardon for all manners and causes; the other is for to alter and change part of a licence, which I have given unto you before, for to be put into mortmain at Westminster, and now to be converted into the University of Cambridge, for your soul's health, &c. All which things, according to your desire and pleasure, I have with all my heart and goodwill given and granted unto you. And, Madam, not only in this, but in all other things that I may

---

* In the Register at St. John's, it is expressly said: "By the persuasions and counsel of the said reverend father the said princess altered her mind from the said foundation in the said monastery to the foundation of Christ's College in this university".—*Memoir of Lady Margaret*, p. 158.

know should be to your honour and pleasure and weal of your soul, I shall be as glad to please you as your heart can desire it. And I know well I am as much bounden so to do as any creature living, for the great and singular motherly love and affection that it hath pleased you at all times to bear towards me. Wherefore, mine own most loving mother, in my most hearty manner I thank you, beseeching you of your good continuance in the same. . . . Written at Greenwich, the 17th day of July (1504?), with the hand of your most humble and loving son,

" H. R."*

Under the authority of a licence obtained from the king, 1st May, 1505, the countess refounded God's House by the title of Christ's College, for a master, twelve fellows, and forty-seven scholars. The countess reserved to herself certain chambers over those of the master, of which during her absence Bishop Fisher (for he was now bishop, as will be explained directly) was to have the use for his life, and on his death they were to belong to the master. Bishop Fisher was appointed visitor during his life. †

The king had been greatly impressed by what he had seen of Dr. Fisher. He had been for some time uneasy in conscience as to the men he had promoted to bishoprics. It was one of the greatest abuses of those days, and the main source of all the evils that abounded, that the selection to the episcopal office having fallen into the hands of the Sovereign, men were chosen whose qualifications were merely those of courtiers or statesmen. The episcopal revenues were looked on as means of supporting or rewarding foreign ambassadors or functionaries of the State, and

* *Memoir of Lady Margaret*, from copy in St. John's Register.

† For the statutes and other particulars, see *Memoir of Lady Margaret*, pp. 100-104, and Mullinger's *University of Cambridge*, i. 446 462.

there were bishops who either never saw their dioceses or were absent from them for years, drawing their revenues and governing them by officials, with mere auxiliary or, as they were called, suffragan bishops, to perform epis-copal functions. The following letter, however, does as much honour to King Henry VII. as it does to Dr. Fisher :

" MADAM,—An' I thought I should not offend you, which I will never do wilfully, I am well minded to promote Master Fisher, your confessor, to a bishopric ; and I assure you, Madam, for none other cause, but for the great and singular virtue, that I know and see in him, as well in cunning [*i.e.*, talent] and natural wisdom, and specially for his good and virtuous living and conversation. And by the promotion of such a man I know well it should encourage many others to live virtuously and to take such ways as he doth, which should be a good example to many others hereafter. How-beit, without your pleasure known I will not move him nor tempt him therein. And therefore I beseech you that I may know your mind and your pleasure in that behalf, which shall be followed as much as God will give me grace. I have in my days promoted many a man unadvisedly, and I would now make some recompense to promote some good and virtuous men, which I doubt not should best please God, who ever preserve you in good health and long life."*

The countess was no doubt pleased by the honour con-ferred on her confessor, and by her persuasion, as well as that of Richard Fox, Bishop of Winchester, Dr. Fisher was

* The king promised his confessor, in the last Lent of his life, and made known his promise to many persons, "that the promotions of the Church that were of his disposition should from henceforth be disposed to able men, such as were virtuous and well learned". —Fisher's *Funeral Sermon of Henry VII.*, p. 271 (Ed. of E. E. Text Society).

induced to accept, not the honour, but the "good work" of a bishop. This may be an appropriate place to quote his own words on the subject, though they were not written until 1527. He dedicated his work, *On the Truth of Christ's Body and Blood in the Eucharist* (against Œcolampadius), to Fox, Bishop of Winchester—first, Because he was the founder of Corpus Christi College, Oxford, and if there was no truth in the Real Presence he would have given an empty title to his college; and, secondly, for the reason that follows: " Ever since our first acquaintance, your lordship had taken so affectionate an interest in me, that I felt myself impelled most ardently both to learning and to virtue. You also recommended me to King Henry VII., who then, with the greatest prudence, held the reins of this kingdom, so that by the esteem he had for me from your frequent commendations, and of his own mere motion, without any obsequious ness on my part, without the intercession of any (as he more than once declared to myself), he gave me the bishopric of Rochester, of which I am now the unworthy occupant. There are, perhaps, many who believe that his mother, the Countess of Richmond and Derby, that noble and incomparable lady, dear to me by so many titles, obtained the bishopric for me by her prayers to her son. But the facts are entirely different, as your lordship knows well, who was the king's most intimate counsellor, as you were also of the illustrious King Henry VIII., who now by most just right of succession fills his father's throne, as long as your health allowed you to frequent the Court. I do not say this to diminish my debt of gratitude to that excellent lady. My debts were indeed great. Were there no other besides the great and sincere love which she bore to me above others (as I know for a certainty), yet what favour could equal such a love on the part of such a princess? But besides her love, she was most munificent towards me. For though she conferred on me no ecclesiastical benefice, she had the

desire, if it could be done, to enrich me, which she proved
not by words only, but by deeds; among other instances,
when she was about to leave the world.   However, as I have
spoken her praises in a funeral oration, I will not pursue the
subject here, though she could never be praised too much.
This only I will add, that though she chose me as her director, to hear her confessions and to guide her life, yet I gladly
confess that I learnt more from her great virtue than ever I
could teach to her.   But to return to your lordship, to
whom after the deceased king I owe whatever benefits have
accrued to me or mine from this bishopric, though others
may have greater revenues, yet I have the care of fewer
souls, so that as I must before long give an account of both,
I would not wish them one whit increased," &c.*

Reserving for a time the consideration of Dr. Fisher as a
bishop, it will be as well to conclude here what has to be
said regarding his benefits to the university.   His appointment to Rochester did not sever his connection with Cambridge, but gave him greater scope and influence.   In the
year 1504 he was chosen to be chancellor, and was re-
elected for ten years successively, when he was chosen for
life, as will be related presently.   This office did not require
residence in Cambridge, and was often conferred on those
who but rarely, if ever, visited the university.   The authority,
however, was great and the duties many.

On the resignation of Dr. Wilkinson, president of Queens
College, Cambridge, in April, 1505, the fellows at once
elected in his place the Bishop of Rochester.†   (He had

---

* The bishop repeats almost the same thing in his statutes of St.
John's.   There also he uses the word " citra *obsequium* aliquod," one of
the coincidences that prove the speech mentioned at the beginning of
this chapter to be his and not Dr. Blyth's.   He there says: "Qui nunquam in curia obsequium prœstiterim".   (See Professor Mayor's note
to *Memoir of Lady Margaret*, p. 248.)

† Lewis, ii. 260.

resigned the mastership of Michaelhouse on being appointed chaplain to the countess.*) This college had been founded in 1448, by Margaret of Anjou, Queen of Henry VI., and having absorbed the hostel of St. Bernard, was dedicated to St. Margaret and St. Bernard. It was then, as now, more commonly spoken of as Queen's College. The bishop retained this office only three years, for, according to Dr. Hall, it had been offered to, and accepted by, him, principally that he might have a residence at Cambridge when he went there to superintend the building of Christ's College. The foundation profited by his presidentship; for it · was his influence, no doubt, that led the Duke of Buckingham, in June, 1505, to increase the endowment. The duke did this, as he declares, at the instance of the Countess of Richmond, who was connected with him by marriage. In 1505, the countess paid a visit to Cambridge, and was lodged in the president's house at Queens'. †

On 22nd April, 1505, King Henry VII., being on a pilgrimage to Our Lady of Walsingham, with his young son, Henry, Prince of Wales, afterwards Henry VIII., arrived at Cambridge on his way thither, and was met by the chancellor within a quarter of a mile of the town, and conducted by him to his lodgings in Queen's, from which, after an hour's rest, vested in the robes of the Garter, as it was the eve of St. George, he proceeded to King's College. Though the magnificent chapel was still unfinished, the chancel was fitted up and adorned with the escutcheons of the knights of St. George, and the chancellor-bishop officiated at solemn vespers,‡ as well as at high mass and vespers on the following day.

---

* Hall's *Life of Fisher* (MS.). The date, however, is not certain. His successor was not chosen until 1505 (Mullinger, i. 446).

† *Memoir of Lady Margaret*, p. 250.

‡ Ackermann, in his *Cambridge*, i. 254, only mentions the first vespers, but the statutes required that all members of the order should

The king prolonged his visit, and was present at the discussions throughout the various schools.* The next day he provided a great banquet for the whole university.

In the following year he returned, with his mother, the countess, and with his son, and the chancellor addressed to him, in the Franciscan Church,† the Latin oration from which we have already quoted.

Another great academical work, the foundation of St. John's, was not merely due to the bishop's initiation, but owed its completion entirely to his indefatigable labour. This was, however, neither an entirely new work, nor, like that of Christ's, the enlargement of a work of a similar kind. It was the conversion of a religious house into a college of secular priests and scholars. Some persons have maintained that such transformations as this, of which we have another example in Jesus College, Cambridge, by Bishop Alcock of Ely, and a greater and more famous in Cardinal Wolsey's foundations of Ipswich and Oxford, prepared the way for

---

keep the feast of St. George, either at Windsor, or wherever the Sovereign might be, as he should appoint. They were bound to be present at first vespers on the vigil ; at matins, procession, high mass, and second vespers on the feast ; and at the solemn requiem on the following day. Even though the feast of St. George could not be celebrated on the 23rd April because of Holy Week or Easter Week, the king and the knights still assisted on the 22nd and 23rd at the solemnities of the Church, wearing the blue mantle and collar. (See the statutes in the *Register of the Most Noble Order of the Garter*, vol. i. 42, 43, and 299.) It adds to the mournful interest of the noble chapel of King's, that the Blessed Fisher once at least pontificated within its walls.

* " Anno superiori ad nos venisti, dignatus es disceptationibus interesse, atque id per omnes omnium facultatum scholas ; neque id fecisti cursim et perfunctorie, sed longo temporum tractu."—*Oratio Cancellarii, anno* 1506, *habita.* The speech is printed in Lewis, ii. 263.

† See *Memoir of Lady Margaret*, pp. 108, 249. The large and beautiful church of the Grey Friars was pulled down forty years later, to make room for and provide materials for Trinity College.

the general suppression of the monasteries. And it is no doubt true that Thomas Cromwell may have conceived the general project, as well as become familiar with the methods of suppression, while he was Wolsey's agent. Yet, in fact, there is no similarity between the two things, or, at least, no greater similarity than there is between lawful execution in the name of the State and private and indiscriminate murder. Should a headsman take to the trade of an assassin, the Government would surely not deserve blame for giving him the taste of blood. During the French wars, Henry V. transferred the property of some alien priories from French to English monasteries, or at most from the regular to the secular clergy. What resemblance has he to Henry VIII., who plundered the monasteries and squandered the proceeds in pageants and gambling, bribes to his courtiers, and rewards to his tools? The transference from one ecclesiastical purpose to another was carried out, not simply by the State, but with the full sanction of the Sovereign Pontiff. That there was no abuse in any of Wolsey's suppressions I would not maintain, but certainly no such fault can be found in those in which Fisher cooperated. He brought about the suppression of the " Hospital " of St. John, in Cambridge, because it was involved in most serious pecuniary difficulties, and its few remaining members were living in total disregard of their rule and character. The hospital, or Maison Dieu, at Ospringe, in Kent, was also dissolved and given to the foundation of the college. But it had been utterly abandoned and left desolate in the time of Edward IV., and had by royal patent been granted in charge to seculars. The vested interests of these were, however, entirely respected ; and, in the transformation of both houses all spiritual obligations of the former possessors were transferred to the members of the new college.

At a somewhat later period, by the bishop's influence, two

nunneries were suppressed and their property handed over to St. John's. In these cases foundations once flourishing had dwindled down to disorderly houses of two or three inmates. Every effort at reform had been tried in vain by their diocesans, one of whom was the bishop himself, and at last, with the licence of the king and the approbation of the Holy See, the nuns were pensioned upon other houses, and the scandal together with the priories came to an end. Nothing can better prove the reforming zeal of the bishop, his justice and careful observance of every canonical rule, than the documents still preserved regarding the suppression of the Priory of Higham near Gravesend, in the diocese of Rochester.   Processes of law were not less tedious then than now, and sixteen years of the bishop's life were consumed before all the business connected with these transformations could be thoroughly effected. He has himself written an account † of his difficulties and labours in the foundation of St. John's, but the details belong rather to a history of the university or of the college than to his life.

The bishop was a great lover of the monastic state, as appears by many places in his writings, and by many acts of his life; and if, out of reverence for it, he would cut off incurable scandals, he would in no way lend himself to any general measure of suppression. He did not live till 1536, or he would certainly have made a strenuous opposition to the parliamentary measures on this suject. Dr. Hall indeed tells us that the question was first broached in 1529, and gives us the bishop's speech in Convocation which caused it to be laid aside for a time. " My lords," he said, " I pray you take good heed what you do in hasty granting to the king's demand in this great matter. It is here required that we should grant unto him the small abbeys for the ease of his charges; whereunto if we condescend, it is like the great will be demanded ere it be long

* Lewis, ii. 307.   † *Ibid.*, ii. 277.

after. And, therefore, considering the manner of this dealing, it putteth me in remembrance of a fable, how the axe
that lacked a handle came on a time to the wood, and
making his moan to the great trees, how that for lack of a
handle to work withal he was fain to sit idle, he therefore
desired them to grant him some young sapling in the wood
to make him one. They, mistrusting no guile, forthwith
granted him a young small tree, whereof he shaped himself
a handle, and being at last a perfect axe in all parts he fell
to work, and so laboured in the wood, that in process of
time he left neither great tree nor small tree standing."

This speech is not, I think, mentioned elsewhere ; but as
we have not the debates of Convocation, a question like the
above may have been mooted and then laid aside, without
leaving other record than in the memories of those from
whom Dr. Hall gathered his information.

But to return to the foundation of St John's. While the
first steps were being taken in England and in Rome for the
transformation of St. John's Hospital into St. John's College,
the Lady Margaret died, 29th June, 1509. Her son, Henry
VII., had preceded her on 21st April; and on each
occasion the Bishop of Rochester was selected to preach
the funeral sermon. Fisher was one of the executors named
in her will, in a codicil to which she stated her intention to
found a college, consisting of a master and fifty scholars, with
divers servants, and to provide buildings and endowments.
Baker says very truly that "had she not lodged this trust
in faithful hands, this great and good dowry must have died
with her ". The same zealous and careful historian adds :
" Though all was transacted and carried on in the name of
the executors, yet it ought never to be forgot that the Bishop
of Rochester was the sole or principal agent. The men of
quality amongst the executors, as they had little concern for
foundations of learning, so I scarce meet with any footsteps
of their agency herein. Bishop Fox, who had a great in-

terest in the last reign, began to decline in this; and besides
he began now to have designs of his own, and to turn his
thoughts towards Oxford and his foundation there. The
two other executors of the clergy, Dr. Hornby and Mr. Hugh
Ashton, as they had a true zeal for the design, so they wanted
power, and though they were very useful instruments, yet
what they did was chiefly in subordination to Bishop Fisher.
Almost the whole weight of this affair leaned upon this good
bishop, whose interest was yet good, deservedly esteemed at
Rome, valued by the king, and reverenced by all good men."*

Leaving the details of the endowment and building of the
college to be sought for in the pages of Baker, I will merely
mention here that the chapel was consecrated by the Bishop
of Rochester, with the licence of the diocesan, the Bishop
of Ely, at the end of July, 1516.† It was also to the Bishop
of Rochester that the executors of the foundress committed
the difficult work of drawing up the statutes.‡

The benefactions of the bishop were not confined to influence and labour. He founded at Christ's College a solemn
annual commemoration and mass for his own soul and those
of his parents and his heirs, with a distribution to be made
to the fellows and scholars ;§ and at St. John's College he
founded four fellowships and two scholarships. On this
subject he must speak for himself. I translate some parts of
the statutes of his own foundation. In the preamble he
writes: "The noble princess, Lady Margaret, Countess of

* Baker's *History of St. John's* (ed. by Prof. Mayor), i. 66.

† The chapel was pulled down a few years since, and replaced by a
much larger one. The gate-tower belongs to the original college.
The arms of Lady Margaret, and the statue of St. John the Evan-
gelist, are seen over the gate.

‡ *Early Statutes of St. John's* (ed. by Prof. Mayor), 1857. The first
statutes of 1516 were very like those of Christ's College ; the second
statutes of 1524 more like those of Corpus Christi, Oxford, made by
his friend Bishop Fox.

§ Lewis, ii. 272.

Richmond, the foundress of this college, in her great conde-
scension had a great desire to procure me a richer bishopric.
But when she saw that her approaching death would frustrate
this desire, she left me a no small sum of money to use
according to my own will and for my own purposes,* which
I mention lest anyone should think that I have made this
large endowment with other people's money. Now, as I
receive from the annual revenue of the bishopric of Rochester
quite enough for the decent maintenance of a prelate, and
since the college has sustained certain losses, I have considered that it was better that both that legacy of hers, and
also a considerable addition of my own, should be spent for
the good of my own soul, in the education of theologians,
than squandered on my relatives, or wickedly and uselessly
consumed for other vain purposes, according to the custom
of the world. And this I do, not only for my own soul, but
by my example to excite others to lend a helping hand to
the college." He then mentions that besides £500 already
made over to the master and fellows for this purpose, and
besides the gift of valuable ornaments (for the chapel), he
makes over a sufficient sum to purchase land to the annual
value of £60.† Three of the fellows were to be of the
county of York, and one of the diocese of Rochester, two of
them at least to be already priests. He also appointed four
examiners in humanities, dialectics, mathematics, and philo-
sophy; and two lecturers—one in Greek for younger students, and one in Hebrew for the more advanced. He
wishes twenty-four trentals of masses to be distributed
annually to the most virtuous and indigent priests in the
college, to be offered for his soul, leaving for each trental
10s.‡ For his Obit he appointed solemn office on the vigil,

* "Quâ in privatum meum commodum uterer."
† I have already mentioned that we may multiply by ten (roughly)
to get modern value.
‡ That is, the usual stipend of a groat (4d.) = 4s.

3

with mass on the day itself, at both of which the master and
all fellows and scholars should assist, with lights burning on
the high altar and on his tomb ; the master to receive
on the occasion 6s. 8d., each fellow 3s. 4d., each scholar
1 s.*

The chalices and other plate given by the bishop to the
college weighed 163 ounces, and, besides other things, a magnificent suit of vestments of red cloth of gold—the vestment
valued at £26, the cope at £34.† From the mention of
the portcullis embroidered on these vestments, it is probable
that they had been a gift to himself from the Lady Margaret.
There is a passage in the bishop's explanation of the Penitential Psalms, regarding the comparative insignificance of
rich vessels and robes in church, which might be misunder-
stood without this practical commentary. In the Apostles'
days, he says, " were no chalices of gold, but many golden
priests. Now be many chalices of gold, but almost no
golden priests."‡ The ambition and labour of the bishop
in all these foundations was to multiply golden priests.

His labours were not unappreciated. The university, as
has been already said, selected him as chancellor for many
years. In 1514, he thought it would be for its greater advantage to choose Wolsey instead. The senate reluctantly
acquiesced, and addressed to the retiring chancellor a most
honourable and affectionate letter. In his reply he deplores
the little he had been able to do, and promises them much
greater things from the zeal and power and influence of
Wolsey. He tells them that though he sets little or rather

* Lewis, ii. 287.

† A set of vestments costing £600 would be extraordinary at the
present day. At Eton a chasuble, two tunicles, two copes of white
satin embroidered with gold, cost £83 6s. 8d. in 1445, or more than
£800 modern. (See Mr. Maxwell Lyte's *History of Eton College*,
p. 29.)

‡ I have given the passage at length in my *History of the Holy
Eucharist*, vol. ii., ch. ix., " On Riches in Churches ".

no value on the mere honour of being chancellor, he greatly esteems the honour of being chosen to it by such a body. He promises his help on every occasion, and prays that, as the university has lately grown in collegiate buildings (St. Mary's Church, King's College Chapel, Christ's and St. John's Colleges), it may advance in learning and in virtue in Christ.

Wolsey, who was then Bishop of Lincoln, declined the honour on the score of his cares of State, but promised that he would regard the university with the same affection and interest as if he were chancellor. Thereupon, by unanimous vote, the dignity of chancellor was conferred on the Bishop of Rochester for life. Notwithstanding his attainder and imprisonment, the university did not consider that his office was vacated; and it was not till after his death that another chancellor was chosen. Then, alas! in self-defence, the university replaced him by Cromwell, the man who, either as instigator or tool of the king's malice, had hunted him to death.*

It would be both unnatural and foolish to have recalled all these things, and not to ask ourselves what have been the results of all the labours and sacrifices of Bishop Fisher and Lady Margaret; or whether those results are altogether such as they would have approved, could they have been anticipated.

God's providence brought these two holy souls into this close relationship, not only for their mutual edification, but for the good of the university, which still profits by their zeal and generosity, though in many things it has cast aside what they held dearer than life. It is impossible to speak too highly of the eagerness shown by the two colleges of the Lady Margaret's foundation, especially by St. John's, to keep alive the memory of their noble foundress, and of her

* Mullinger's *History of the University of Cambridge,* ii. 1.

confessor and co-operator, Cardinal Fisher.[*] But though the pictures of Lady Margaret in the attitude of prayer adorn the wall and window of Christ's College chapel, and her statue, with that of Fisher, occupies the porch of St. John's, what boots it to recall the memory of their devotion, when the great objects of their devotion are banished and proscribed? The Blessed Eucharist that hung day and night in the Pyx before the altars has been absent for three centuries; the altar stones on which Fisher, with streaming eyes, offered the Divine Sacrifice, have been broken in pieces; the Divine Sacrifice itself repudiated as idolatry and an outrage to Jesus Christ; devotion to Our Lady and to God's saints has been cast away as folly and superstition. The virtues of Cardinal Fisher and of the Countess of Richmond are not denied, but on the contrary are generously extolled, with the exception that, when their attachment to doctrines and practices like the above cannot be passed over without some allusion, a vague phrase like "attachment to the tenets in which they had been brought up," or "the superstitions of their times," is used as an excuse for them and a plea for rejecting their example.[†] But this is disingenuous and cowardly. If any one thing is historically certain, it is

---

[*] Her portrait at the present day (1888) hangs in the chapel of Christ College and in the hall of St. John's. Quite recently a stained glass window, representing Henry VII. and Lady Margaret in prayer before St. Edward, which had been long ago removed from the window of Christ's College chapel and cast aside, has been replaced. The *Memoir of Lady Margaret*, by Mr. Cooper, edited with immense pains by Professor Mayor of St. John's, has been printed at the joint expense of the two colleges. Professor Mayor's edition of Baker's *History of St. John's*, and his *Early Statutes of St. John's*, and Professor Babington's *History of the Infirmary and Chapel of the Hospital and College of St. John's*, are all worthy monuments of esteem and affection towards the illustrious founders.

[†] "He was a learned and devout man, much addicted to the superstitions in which he had been bred up."—Burnet's *Reform.*, book iii., vol. i., p. 708.

that neither Lady Margaret nor Bishop Fisher would have
spent their money and their labours on those scholastic
foundations, on preacherships and professorships, except for
the propagation of the Catholic Faith as they held it, and as
it is held by the Church at this day in communion with
Rome. Lady Margaret with her own hand transiated and
had printed the fourth book of the *Imitation of Christ* to
teach devotion to the Real Presence. In her funeral sermon
Fisher thus spoke: " That this noble princess had full faith
in Jesus Christ it may appear if any will demand this
question of her that our Saviour demanded of Martha. He
said to her, ' *Credis hoc?*'—' Believest thou this?' What
is it that this gentlewoman would not believe, she' that
ordained two continual readers in both the universities to
teach the holy divinity [*i.e.*, doctrine] of Jesus, she that
ordained preachers perpetual to publish the doctrine and
faith of Christ Jesu, she that builded a college royal to the
honour of the name of Christ Jesu, and left till [to] her
executors another to be builded to maintain His faith and
doctrine; besides all this, founded in the monastery of
Westminster, where her body lieth, three priests, to pray for
her perpetually? She whom I have many times heard say,
that if the Christian princes would have warred upon the
enemies of His faith, she would be glad yet to go follow the
host and help to wash their clothes for the love of Jesus?
She that did openly witness this same thing at the hour of
her death (which saying divers here present can record).
How heartily she answered, when the Holy Sacrament
containing the Blessed Jesu in It was holden before her, and
the question made until her, Whether she believed that there
was verily the Son of God that suffered His Blessed Passion
for her, and for all mankind upon the Cross?—many here
can bear record how with all her heart and soul she raised
her body to make answer thereunto, and confessed assuredly
that in the Sacrament was contained Christ Jesu the Son of

God, that died for wretched sinners upon the Cross, in whom
wholly she put her trust and confidence. . . . And so, soon
after that she was aneled, she departed and yielded up her
spirit into the hands of our Lord. Who may not now take
evident likelihood and conjecture upon this, that the soul of
this noble woman, which so studiously in her life was occupied in good works, and with a fast faith of Christ and the
Sacraments of His Church, was defended in that hour of
departing out from the body, was borne up into the country
above with the blessed angels deputed and ordained to that
holy mystery? For if the hearty prayer of many persons, if
her own continual prayer in her lifetime, if the Sacraments
of the Church orderly taken, if indulgences and pardons
granted by divers popes, if true repentance and tears, if faith
and devotion in Christ Jesu, if charity to her neighbours, if
pity unto the poor, if forgiveness of injuries, or if good works
be available, as doubtless they be—great likelihood, and
almost certain conjecture, we may take by them and all these
that so it is indeed."

In the funeral sermon of Lady Margaret's son, Henry
VII., Fisher said: "The cause of this hope was true belief
that he had in God, in His Church, and in the Sacraments
thereof, which he received all with marvellous devotion;
namely, in the Sacrament of Penance, the Sacrament of the
Altar, and the Sacrament of Aneling. The Sacrament of
Penance, with a marvellous compassion and flow of tears,
that at some time he wept and sobbed by the space of three-
quarters of an hour. The Sacrament of the Altar he received at Mid-Lent and again upon Easter-day, with so
great reverence that all that were present were astonyed
thereat; for at his first enter into the closet where the Sacrament was, he took off his bonnet, and kneeled down upon
his knees, and so crept forth devoutly till he came unto the
place self where he received the Sacrament. Two days next
before his departing, he was of that feebleness that he might

not receive It again; nevertheless he desired to see the monstrant wherein It was contained. The good father, his confessor, in goodly manner as was convenient, brought It unto him; he with such a reverence, with so many knockings and beatings of his breast, with so quick and lively a countenance, with so desirous a heart, made his humble obeisance thereunto; with so great humbleness and devotion kissed, not the self place where the Blessed Body of Our Lord was contained, but the lowest part, the foot of the monstrant, that all that stood about him scarcely might contain them from tears and weeping. The Sacrament of Aneling, when he well perceived that he began utterly to fail, he desirously asked therefor, and heartily prayed that it might be administered unto him; wherein he made ready and offered every part of his body by order, and as he might for weakness turned himself at every time, and answered in the suffrages thereof. That same day of his departing, he heard mass of the glorious Virgin, the Mother of Christ, to whom always in his life he had singular and special devotion. The image of the crucifix many a time that day full devoutly he did behold with great reverence, lifting up his head as he might, holding up his hands before it, and often embracing it in his arms, and with great devotion kissing it, and beating oft his breast. Who may think that in this man there was not perfect faith? Who may suppose that by this manner of dealing he faithfully believed not that the ear of Almighty God was open unto him, and ready to hear him cry for mercy, and assistant unto these same Sacraments which he so devoutly received?"

Such is Fisher's testimony to his own faith, and that of King Henry VII., and of Lady Margaret. He has declared frequently his own absolute conviction that the things which his colleges now repudiate, and Margaret Professors now denounce, are no accidental or indifferent matters, that can be put aside, leaving the substance of Christian faith

intact. "HE WHO GOES ABOUT TO TAKE THE HOLY SACRI-
FICE OF MASS FROM THE CHURCH PLOTS NO LESS A CALA-
MITY THAN IF HE TRIED TO SNATCH THE SUN FROM THE
UNIVERSE." * A few years passed, and men brought up in
his university, many of them fed by his bounty, blotted out
that sun. Pilkington, a fellow of St. John's, and afterwards
Bishop of Durham, knows no bounds in his scurrility when
he speaks of the holy Mass; Grindal breaks altar-stones,
destroys vestments and missals, in the hope that the very
name and remembrance of the Holy Sacrifice may be obliterated; Parker classes together as equally unavailable for
his Protestant communion "profane cups, dishes, bowls,
and *old massing chalices";* and Latimer, preaching before
Edward VI., says: "All these that be mass-mongers be
deniers of Christ, which believe and trust in the Sacrifice of
the Mass and seek remission of their sins therein; for this
opinion hath brought innumerable souls to the pit of
hell".†

Time went on, and some, at least, grew ashamed of this
violence. At the beginning of the 18th century, Thomas
Baker, a fellow of St. John's, after a long study of all
the documents in his college archives, thus wrote of the
Bishop of Rochester: "The college was first undertaken
by his advice, was endowed by his bounty or interest, preserved from ruin by his prudence and care, grew up and
flourished under his countenance and protection, and was at
last perfected by his conduct. In one word, he was the
best friend since the foundress, and greatest patron the
college ever had to this day. His full character I do not

---

* "Quo fit ut quisquis hoc sacrificium ab ecclesia tollere moliatur,
nihilo minorem ei jacturam intentat, quam si mundo solem eripere
studuerit."—*Assertionum Regis Angliœ Defensio,* vi. 9.

† Pilkington, *Works* (Parker Soc.), *passim;* Grindal, Injunctions
of 1571, in *Remains* (Parker Soc.), pp. 123-144; Parker, *Visitation
Article,* No. 5; Wilkins, iv. 258; Latimer, *Sermon on False Doctrine*
(Parker Soc. Ed.), p. 522.

meddle with. I must be no advocate for his private opinions, and his private virtues do not want one." *

This is certainly the language of sincere gratitude and admiration. Yet, is it consistent? Can the opinions and the virtues be thus separated? What Baker calls opinions were with Fisher articles of faith. They were, moreover, the principles of conduct that moved him to those virtues and those works that Baker justly praises. Other men have founded colleges with equal generosity and from different motives; but Fisher's zeal and bounty had one end in view—to provide a body of learned and virtuous Catholic priests. It is more than doubtful whether he would have given either his time or his money for merely secular science; and it is most certain that he would have shuddered at the thought of endowing that form of religion which Baker professed, and he did, in fact, die rather than co-operate in its first beginnings.

When recording the suppression of St. John's Hospital, Baker rightly said that its fate was "a lasting monument to all future ages, and to all charitable and religious foundations, not to neglect the rules or abuse the institutions of their founders". Yet, what fidelity to founders' wishes can be found in the College of St. John, of Baker's day or of our own? I do not speak of immoral life, but of change of worship and of faith. Is it no neglect of a founder's institutions to continue to teach logic and mathematics, Latin, Greek, and Hebrew, but to teach another theology, and not only to omit the prayers and masses that he made a condition of his benefits, but to reject, repudiate, and spurn them?

Baker drew much nearer to the faith of Fisher than most of the members of his foundation, yet he addressed the following lines to his founder :

* *History of St. John's,* p. 102.

" To thee I dare appeal, if thou dost know
Or now concern'st thyself with things below ;
Oft had I sent my fervent vows to heaven
Were this the time, or aught were now forgiven.
Oft had I pray'd for thee, as thou desires,
Could I believe thee hurt by purging fires.
Thy past desires they were, nor are they so,
'Twas thy mistaken wish when here below."

Baker was a fellow on the foundation of Hugh Ashton, archdeacon of York, one of Lady Margaret's executors, and a zealous co-operator with Fisher. It is probably to him the above lines are addressed; for, in describing the Ashton chantry in St. John's Chapel, he says : " Might I choose my place of sepulture, I would lay my body there, that as I owe the few comforts I enjoy to Mr. Ashton's bounty, so I might not be separated from him in death. May I wish him that happiness, which I dare not to pray for, but which my hopes are he now enjoys ! I daily bless God for him, and thankfully commemorate him ; and could I think he now desired of me what his foundation requires, I would follow him with my prayers and pursue him on my knees."

This was written sincerely, and sounds, perhaps, plausible and liberal. Yet, if it is thus allowed to interpret founders' wills on one's private judgment, and presume on their change of mind in an unseen world, not only may an Anglican reject the holy Mass, but a deist may put aside revelation, and an atheist the existence of God, on the same plea. Strange that, during three centuries and a half, this convenient ἐπιἐίκεια by which Protestants claimed the right to enjoy the bounty of a Catholic founder, never led them to extend that bounty to those for whom it was expressly intended, who held the founder's faith, and would have complied with his conditions.

The most recent historian of the University of Cambridge, who is also a member of St. John's—Mr. J. Bass Mullinger—

though he has dealt out praise to Bishop Fisher with no stinting hand, yet, in discussing the statutes drawn up by him, has allowed himself the following reflection : "His life presents us with more than one significant proof, how little mere moral rectitude of purpose avails to preserve men from pitiable superstition and fatal mistakes". Pitiable superstition is a strong but, at the same time, a very vague word. To one man the belief in modern miracles is very pitiable, while another pities the state of mind that can despise the evidence for modern miracles and accept that for the miracles of the Gospel. One thinks prayer to the Blessed Virgin pitiable superstition, and another prayer to Jesus Christ. A Unitarian sees no more superstition in belief in Transubstantiation than in the Incarnation. To Pilate, Our Lord's declaration that He came into the world to give testimony to the Truth seemed pitiable superstition. What was the special superstition of Bishop Fisher, that provokes the pity and contempt even of his panegyrist, Mr. Mullinger does not state. I am sure that he does not share Pilate's absolute scepticism as to the attainability of any truth whatever in matters supra-sensual, and that he does not pity his founder merely because he held dogmatic truth. His expression, then, can only mean that he differs from him in certain details of belief. But would it not be more modest to abstain from accusations of superstition and indulgence in pity, until assured that his own standard of judgment in these matters is something more solid and lasting than the prevalent liberalism of English men of culture in the 19th century? The Rev. T. Mozley, in his *Reminiscences of Oxford*, made a very apposite reflection. When on a visit to Normandy, he was startled by certain popular forms of devotion to the Blessed Virgin. He checked his first movement to brand it all as pitiable superstition by this thought: "For more than a thousand years saints, theologians, martyrs, the salt of the earth, the

men that had held fast the faith and preserved it for us, and
that had continually rescued the civilised world from re-
lapsing into prehistoric savagery, had done what these
simple folk were doing. They had undoubtedly worshipped
and invoked the Virgin, and bound themselves in special
devotion to her service. But for the place long held by the
Blessed Virgin in the heart and mind of man, *I should not
have been a fellow of Oriel, for Oriel would never have been,*
and I should not have gone to Normandy ; nay, I am very
sure I should never have been at all." *

A similar train of thought ought to have occurred to the
fellows of St. John's, when they broke down the altars and
removed Our Lady's image, and renounced the pope's
supremacy. The pope, they said, has no more authority
outside his own see than any other bishop. Had it been
so, St. John's would never have been founded ; for the
Bishop of Ely had retracted the consent he had given to
the Lady Margaret to the suppression of the religious house
of St. John's, and it was only by the bull obtained from Julius
II. by the Bishop of Rochester, overriding the consent of
both king and diocesan, that the pious foundress's intention
could be carried out.†

Professor Mullinger also contrasts Dean Colet's "prophetic liberality" in leaving the trustees of his school power
to modify his statutes with Fisher's "unreasoning dread of
change and pusillanimous anxiety to guard against all future
innovations whatever". But he seems to have misunder-
stood both Colet and Fisher. Most certainly Colet did not
anticipate changes of faith, nor give any licence to make
them, since the liberty he grants to trustees is founded on

* *Reminiscences*, ii., ch. cxxi., p. 351. Fisher writes as follows :
" Væ miseris illis qui virginis hujus gloriosæ præcellentiam vel pilo
minuere student, quod tamen a Lutheranis audio factitatum. Prop-
ter quod haud dubie manet eos ultio divina nisi maturius resipiscant"
(*De Sacerd.*, col. 1294). This was written in 1526,

† Baker's *St. John's*, p. 66.

his trust "in their fidelity and love that they have to God and man, and also as believing verily that they shall always dread the great wrath of God ". He foresaw the likelihood of changes in scholastic methods and external circumstances, and his permission to modify his statutes went no further. And if Bishop Fisher made no such explicit provision, he knew that there resides in the Holy See the requisite power to make wholesome modifications according to the times. He had invoked that power himself to change worn-out religious foundations into a college of students; and he knew it would be equally open to future chancellors or masters to apply to the Holy See for power to suppress or add to, to modify or widen, the statutes drawn up by himself. But he certainly did not foresee, nor would he have consented, that his purpose of educating Catholic priests in the Catholic Faith should be set aside, and that his magnificent work should become the exclusive possession of one among a number of Protestant sects. When a great and munificent foundation has been so absolutely wrested from its original purpose, that all those who have shared the faith of its founders, and were willing to carry out their founders' intentions, have been persistently shut out from it for more than three centuries, more appropriate reflections might have occurred to the historian of the university than to bewail the illiberality and want of prophetical foresight of one of its greatest benefactors.*

After this digression, if it is such, I return to the bishop's conduct as chancellor. One of his duties was to guard the

* As one who had to leave my college and my university without a degree, in 1850, because I had returned to the faith of Blessed John Fisher, I plead a right to make the above protest. I am told that the exclusion is now at an end. Fénélon and Wesley figure side by side among the decorative paintings of the new chapel of St. John's, though it is reserved for Anglican liturgy! Why not make Fisher walk hand in hand with Luther, and Lady Margaret with Catharine Bora ?

faith of the students and the orthodoxy of the teachers.
Dr. Hall has related at great length an incident which has
been travestied by his copyist Baily, and through him by
subsequent writers. The substance of Dr. Hall's narrative
is this. A Norman *priest*, named Peter of Valence, having
imbibed some of the errors of Luther, fled to England, and
sought to hide himself and propagate his heresy in Cambridge. When Fisher, as chancellor, published a grant of
indulgences by Leo X., especially to such as should with-
stand the Lutheran heresies,* this Peter wrote in the night
over the grant : " Beatus vir cujus est nomen Domini spes
ejus et non respexit vanitates et insanias falsas (*istas*) " ; *i.e.*,
" Blessed is the man whose hope is in the name of the
Lord, and who has not regarded vanity or mad follies " (*such
as these*). The chancellor, having failed to detect the author
of this outrage, published an excommunication, but with a
promise of pardon on condition, not " of an open acknowledgment of his fault," as Lewis says, but of a secret confession, the fact of which, but not the person, the confessor
should have leave to make known to the bishop.† As no
such acknowledgment was made, after the three usual admonitions, the chancellor tried to read the excommunication,
but could not proceed for emotion, and again deferred the
matter. When, amidst a great concourse, he at last solemnly
published the censure, he did it " not without weeping and
lamentation, which struck such a fear into the hearts of
his hearers, when they heard his fearful and terrible
words, that most of them being present, especially of
the younger sort, looked when the ground should have
opened and swallowed [the culprit] up presently before

* Probably in 1521, not in 1515, as Lewis conjectures.
† " He moved the author to repentance," says Hall, " and by confession of his fault to ask forgiveness at God's hands, which if he
would do by a certain day, so as himself might also have knowledge
thereof, he promised on God's behalf remission."

them, *as a right reverend and worthy prelate one• told me, which then was a young man and present at all the business,* such was the bitterness of his words and gravity of his sentence. But although for that present time the mind of the miserable man was so hardened with obstinate stubbornness that it could by none of these means be induced to repentance and confession of this so detestable act, but still continued in that wilful blindness with deep and close dissimulation for a space after, yet did not this holy man's zealous words and pitiful tears spent in compassion of the wretched soul altogether perish ; for not long after they wrought so in him that they never went out of his mind, but engendered such remorse of conscience in his heart, that although mere necessity forced him hereafter to forsake the university and become a servant* to Dr. Goodrich, then Superintendent of Ely, a vehement heretic and ill-disposed person, yet could he never be brought to think otherwise but that he had sore offended Almighty God in contemning Him in one of His so worthy vicars. Insomuch as when any of his fellow-servants or others in that house would jest at him, and put him in remembrance of his former act, as many times they would, he would ever blame them for so doing, rehearsing to them this verse of the Psalmist : ' Delicta juventutis meæ et ignorantias ne memineris Domine'.'' (The sins of my youth and my ignorances remember not, O Lord.) †

* The word "servant" was not confined to menials, but included all officials in a large household, as a secretary, tutor, or chaplain.

† Dr. Hall's reputation as a historian, as I shall have frequently to show, has much suffered by means of the changes in his narrative made by Baily. His long account of this incident is no doubt accurate, since he had the circumstances from an eye-witness. The clause making this known is omitted by Baily. Baily's style is extravagant ; while Hall simply relates that the bishop's emotion prevented him from speaking. Baily says : " When the words began to sit heavy upon his tongue, according to the weight of the sentence, the fire of love, as

The respect paid to the bishop's learning, as well as the need for it, is apparent from the following letter of Archbishop Warham to Cardinal Wolsey. He writes that on 8th March, 1521, he has received letters from Oxford stating that the university is infected with Lutheranism, and many books forbidden by Wolsey had obtained circulation there. He regrets that this should have happened in a place where he was brought up, and of which he is now chancellor. The university desires him to be a mean to Wolsey, that such order may be taken for the examination of the suspected as that it incur no infamy. He thinks it a pity that a small number of incircumspect fools should endanger the whole university with the charge of Lutheranism : a thing pleasant to the Lutherans beyond sea, and a great encouragement to them, if the two universities—one of which, Oxford, has been void of all heresies, and the other, Cambridge, boasts that it has never been defiled—should embrace these heretical tenets. It would create great slander if all now suspected were brought to London ; he desires, therefore, that some commission may sit at Oxford, to examine not the heads but the novices. The university will be glad if he

within some limbeck or beneath a balneo Mariæ, kindling within his breast, sent such a stream up into his mind, as suddenly distilled into his eyes, which like an overflowing viol reverberates the stream back again to the heart, till the heart surcharged sends these purer spirits of compassion out of his mouth, which could only say that he could read no further ". Baily has also changed facts. He says that after the excommunication Valence was taken notice of for his altered countenance, left Cambridge, and fled as it were for sanctuary to Dr. Goodrich, till, pursued by remorse, he returned to Cambridge, and wrote up the words indicating his sorrow on the same place where he had formerly written the scoff, that he was then absolved and ordained. Mr. Lewis shows the impossibility of all this, since Goodrich was not bishop till about a year before Fisher's death. But Hall says none of these things. Valence wrote up no retractation ; he was not absolved ; he was priest before he came to Cambridge ; yet nothing is more likely than that after Fisher's martyrdom he should have felt and expressed remorse even in Dr. Goodrich's household.

will request the Bishop of Rochester or London (Tunstal) to draw up a table of Lutheran writers who are to be avoided, and send it down to Oxford.*

As yet only a few of Luther's books had appeared. He had published his theses on Indulgences in 1518, but on 3rd March, 1519, he had written a submissive letter to the pope, and on 15th January, 1520, had written to the emperor, Charles V. (just elected) that he would die an obedient child of the Church. But on 20th June he had published his address to the Germans on the Christian state, and in October his *Captivity of Babylon*, in which he utterly and for ever broke away from all Catholic obedience and doctrine; and on 11th December he publicly burnt the pope's bull and the canon law at Wittenberg. But other heretics were springing up, and wise men, even at these first beginnings of the Reformation, augured what would be its ultimate results in general infidelity.†

It was therefore resolved that a public demonstration or

---

* The original is in the British Museum (Calig., book vi. 171), and is printed by Ellis (3rd Series, i. 239); and by Brewer, *Letters and Papers*, iii. 1193.

† Cuthbert Tunstal, on 7th July, 1523, wrote to Erasmus: "Luther has put forth a book on the abolition of the mass, which he never understood. What can he do more unless he intends to write on abolishing Christ? The man's malice leads in that direction, since already the Blessed Virgin is abolished by his followers, as I hear" (Inter *Ep. Erasmi*, 656). In his answer Erasmus says: "I hope your prognostications regarding the end of this affair may turn out false. But the Anabaptists (as they are called) are muttering anarchy, and other monstrous doctrines are growing up, which if they spread will make Luther seem almost orthodox. They say that baptism is necessary neither for adults nor children. And if they persuade the people, as some are trying to do, that there is nothing in the Eucharist but bread and wine, I do not see what is left of the Sacraments. No sect has yet risen which preaches impiously about Christ, but this tumult of opinions has given courage to many to dare to speak blasphemously of Christ's Divine Nature, and to doubt about the authority of the whole of Scripture."—*Ep.* 793.

4

protest against the German heresies should be made. A
number of books of Luther, Carlstadt, and others were
seized and brought to London, and the 12th May (1521),
being the Sunday within the octave of the Ascension, was
appointed for their burning. The place chosen was St.
Paul's Cross. Cardinal Wolsey presided in great state.
The pope's ambassador and the Archbishop of Canterbury
were on his right, the imperial ambassador and the Bishop
of Durham on his left, and the rest of the bishops were
seated around.* The Bishop of Rochester had been selected
to preach, both on account of his learning and his fame as
an orator. I cannot consider his effort in this instance a
happy one. The great length of the sermon would not
have been found fault with in those days;† but it consists
of four parts with little unity of arrangement, and is rather a
theological treatise than a discourse to the people. Without
the coarseness of Luther or the buffoonery of Latimer, Fisher
might, by a simple and more popular sermon, have produced
greater effect. The sermon, however, was so well liked by
the king that his Latin secretary, Richard Pace, translated it
into Latin.‡

Notwithstanding all precautions, heresy found its way into
both universities. This led to another sermon at St. Paul's,
preached by the Bishop of Rochester also, before Cardinal
Wolsey and a great number of bishops and abbots, on the

---

* *Letters and Papers*, iii. 1274.

† When the sermons were preached at mass they were short
enough; but the grand discourses pronounced on public occasions
such as this, and apart from all other religious service, were often of
enormous length. But their infrequency made this tolerable or even
agreeable.

‡ After the king's quarrel with the pope, this sermon, which defends the pope's supremacy, became extremely displeasing to the
king, and in more than one proclamation he ordered all copies to be
sent to Cromwell for destruction.—*Letters and Papers*, viii. 55 and
ix. 963.

retractation of Dr. Barnes in 1527. This man was prior of the Augustinians at Cambridge, and got mixed up with a party of Lutherans there, though he always denied that he held Lutheran doctrine. On Christmas Eve, 1525, he preached a sermon on a text taken from the Epistle of the day: " Let your moderation be known unto all men ". His text, says Mr. Mullinger, " was one which might well have made him to reflect before he indulged in acrimony and satire. But controversial feeling was then running high in the university, and among his audience the prior recognised some who were not only hostile to the cause with which he had identified his name, but also bitter personal enemies. As he proceeded in his discourse his temper rose ; he launched into a series of bitter invectives against the whole of the priestly order ; he attacked the bishops with peculiar severity ; nor did he bring his sermon to a conclusion before he had indulged in sarcastic and singularly impolitic allusions to the pillars and poleaxes of Wolsey himself."* He was cited before the vice-chancellor, and at last sent for to London, where he was examined by six bishops. " So far as may be inferred," writes the same author, " Fisher inclined to a favourable view of the matter ; and when the first article, charging Barnes with contempt for the observance of holy days, was read over, he declared that he for one ' would not condemn it as heresy for a hundred pounds. But,' he added, turning to the prior, ' it was a foolish thing to preach this before all the butchers of Cambridge.' " Severer views, however, prevailed on that or other articles, and he was adjudged a heretic, but on his promise to recant was condemned to bear a faggot. On Quinquagesima Sunday, 1527, Barnes, with other penitents, came in procession to the north door of St. Paul's, each bearing a faggot, and after a sermon by the Bishop of Rochester before eighteen bishops, with as many abbots and priors, they

* *History of University*, i. 576.

made their confession of heresy, threw their faggots into the fire, on which were heaped a great number of heretical books and copies of Tyndall's New Testament, and at last the bishop absolved them from their censures.* The sermon preached on this occasion does not exist.

* Froude, ꜱ. 43, ꜱ̵ꜱꜱ ꜱ̵ꜱ̵ꜱ ꜱꜱꜱ ꜱ̵ꜱ̵ꜱ.

CHAPTER III

WE have seen that Fisher's conception of the functions of a priest was that of the influence of the heavenly bodies on the earth: enlightening, warming, fertilising. No one can call in question his beneficent action on the University of Cambridge and the general education of the clergy. But the doubt may have occurred to some whether the presidency of a college, the chancellorship of a university, and the superintendence of new foundations were not works incompatible with the duties of a bishop. We must now, therefore, consider him as the chief pastor of his diocese. His episcopate was unusually long, more than thirty years, and (a thing very rare in those days) it was exercised over one flock only. It is to be regretted that more details have not come down to us on the subject of his pastoral and diocesan labours; but we know enough to be sure that no energy, spent elsewhere, was at the expense of his primary duty to his own people. He was known, not only throughout England, but to all Europe, as the model of a perfect bishop. Writing to Wolsey, in 1518, Erasmus calls Fisher "a Divine Prelate," and to Reuchlin, in 1520, "There is not in that nation a more learned man or a holier bishop".*

* "Cum tantum absim ab illius divini præsulis eruditione" (Ep. 317; ed. Le Cleve, 1703). "Episcopus ille Anglus, quo non alius in ea gente vel eruditior vir vel præsul sanctior" (Ep. 541).

We shall meet with abundance of such testimonies as we proceed. That of Cardinal Pole expresses not only his own opinion, but the universal esteem of all good men. In his *Apology*, addressed to Charles V., he writes as follows: " Nothing could be so reasonable a prejudice against the new supremacy as the integrity of the leaders who opposed it. If anyone had asked the king, before the violence of his passions had hurried him out of the reach of reason and reflection, whom of all the episcopal order he chiefly considered? on whose affection and fidelity he most relied? he would, without any hesitation, have answered, The Bishop of Rochester. When the question was not put to him, he was accustomed, of his own accord, to glory that no other prince or kingdom had so distinguished a prelate. Of this I was witness, when, turning to me, on my return from my travels, he said that he did not imagine I had met with anyone, in foreign parts, who could be compared to him, either for virtue or learning.

"This advantageous judgment of his prince was repaid by an equal zeal and fidelity in the bishop. He constantly professed, that besides the obligation common to all subjects, he had that of the king being born in his diocese [at Greenwich], and residing more frequently in it than elsewhere; and that his majesty's grandmother, whose ghostly father he had been, and who survived the late king and queen, had recommended her grandson to his peculiar care. She was a person of great prudence, who was aware of the dangers of royalty, when it falls to the lot of youth; and, being about to leave the world, she, with many tears, entreated the bishop, though several excellent men were also present, to assist the king by his instructions and advice, and desired her grandson to have a deference for him preferably to all others, as what would most contribute to his felicity both here and hereafter. He had, moreover, this inducement to be vigilant in the king's welfare, as he was the only surviving counsellor of his late majesty."*

The fact here mentioned by Cardinal Pole, that Fisher had a special regard for Henry, as for one of his own flock, born in his diocese, and frequently residing there, shows the view he cherished of his duties as a pastor. Let us now go back to the time when he received this charge.

We have seen the letter in which Henry VII. expressed to his mother his desire to raise her confessor to a bishopric, as some atonement for other promotions made from worldly motives. Fisher's Protestant biographer Lewis expresses his surprise or displeasure, because, " notwithstanding the bishop's so frequently, and with so much gratitude, ascribing this his promotion to the king, and acknowledging him for his patron, in the bishop's register it is entered as entirely owing to the pope". Yet one would have thought a boy could distinguish between the right to present to a benefice and the right to confer it. Is the patron of a living among Anglicans the source of clerical jurisdiction? Would Fisher have been grateful to the king for choosing him for presentation to the pope, if he had considered such presentation as an invasion of papal prerogative? The fact that the king's nominee was regularly elected by those to whom the *congé-d'élire* was sent, may be·urged against the freedom of election on the part of chapters or convents, but it has nothing to do with the question of the confirmation by the Sovereign Pontiff. The bishop's registrar followed the usual formula and expressed the simple truth, when he set down the bishop's appointment to his See as emanating from the pope. The entry ran as follows: " The Register of the Reverend Father in Christ, my Lord John Fisher, doctor in theology, and by the grace of God Bishop of Rochester. Our Most holy Father

* *Apol. ad Carolum V. Cæs.*, § 20 (Philips' Trans.).

in Christ, and Lord Julius, by Divine Providence second (of that name), when the cathedral-church of Rochester was vacant by the translation of the Reverend Father in Christ, Richard, to the cathedral-church of Chichester, appointed the aforesaid venerable Father to be its bishop and pastor, as appears by the bulls given in Rome at St. Peter's in the year of Our Lord's Incarnation, 1504, the seventh indiction, and the first year of his pontificate. He was consecrated by the Reverend Father in Christ, Lord William, by Divine permission, Archbishop of Canterbury, primate of all England and legate of the Apostolic See, in his chapel within his manor of Lambeth, in the diocese of Winchester, on Sunday before the feast of St. Catharine, virgin, viz., on the 24th day of November, in the aforesaid year, in the presence of Master Hugh Ashton and Richard Collet, doctor of laws."

The assistant bishops were William Smith of Lincoln and Richard Nykke of Norwich. At the same time William Barons, Bishop of London, was consecrated. He did not survive a year.

The Bishop of Rochester chose Dr. Thomas Head to be his Vicar-General, and in his person as his proxy was installed and enthroned in his cathedral-church on the 24th April, 1505. The bishop seems to have been happy in the choice of his officials. Nicolas Metcalf was his archdeacon for at least twenty-four years, and rendered the greatest service in the foundation of St. John's College, and as its third master, from 1518 to 1537. Though he yielded when the oath of supremacy was exacted, he was considered "a papist," and, retiring from his office two years before his death, we can have little doubt that by the prayers of the holy martyr in heaven he repented of his weakness and was reconciled with God and with the Church. Roger Ascham, though a Protestant, speaks of him in the highest terms. "He was a father to everyone in the college; there was none so poor, if he had either will to goodness, or wit to learning, that could lack being there, or should depart from thence for any need.   I am certain myself that money many times was brought into young men's rooms by strangers that they knew not.   In which doing this worthy Nicolas followed the steps of good old St. Nicolas, that learned bishop.   He was a Papist, indeed; but would to God, among all us Protestants, I might once see but one that would win like praise, in doing like good, for the advance-ment of learning and virtue."*

Another of Bishop Fisher's intimate friends, who, like Metcalf, imbibed his own spirit, was Dr. John Adison, his chaplain.   He was condemned with the bishop, as we shall see, to perpetual imprisonment, in the affair of the Maid of Kent, but must have been released ; for three years after his master's death he wrote a book in defence of the supremacy of the pope.†

Before entering on any particulars regarding Fisher's episcopate, it may be well to say a few words with regard to the oath which he, in common with all English bishops of that day, took to the king.   At his consecration he made, of course, the usual oath of allegiance to the pope, as it is still in the Roman Pontifical.   But with it he took the following oath of allegiance to the king : " I, John, Bishop of Roches-ter, utterly renounce and clearly forsake all such clauses, words, sentences, and grants which I have or shall have hereafter of the pope's holiness, of and for the bishopric of Rochester, that in any ways have been, are, or hereafter may be hurtful or prejudicial to your highness, your heirs, successors, dignity, privilege, or royal estate.   And also I do swear that I will be faithful and true, and faith and truth will bear to you, my sovereign lord, and to your heirs, kings of the said realm, of life and limb, and earthly worship,

* Ascham's *Works*, p. 315.

† See Cooper, *Athenæ Cantab*. It was to this book that Tunstal of Durham and Stokesley of London made a reply.

above all creatures, for to live and die with you and yours,
against all people. And diligently I shall be attendant on
all your affairs and business, according to my skill and
power; and your counsel I shall keep, acknowledging myself
to hold my bishopric of you only,* beseeching you for the
temporalities of the same, promising as before that I shall
be a faithful, true, and obedient subject to your highness,
your heirs, and successors during life; and the services due
to your highness for the restitution of the temporalities of
the said bishopric I shall truly and obediently perform. So
help me God and the holy evangelists."

It has been asserted by Dr. Hook, the late historian of
the Archbishops of Canterbury, that this oath is exactly
parallel to the protest made by Cranmer at his consecration,
before taking the oath of obedience to the pope. Hence
either Fisher and the other bishops must share in the charge
of perjury cast by Catholics on Cranmer, or both they and
he must be freed from any such stain. But the two cases
differ entirely. When the bishops took the two customary
oaths, the pope was fully aware of that taken to the king,
and neither forbade it nor issued any protest against it.
Hence, even if the oath to the king had really limited anything contained in that to the pope, the limitation being
known to the imposer or recipient of the oath, and tacitly
accepted by him, there would have been no shadow of perjury. In reality, however, there was no contradiction. The
caution or protest contained in the king's oath is not against
any promise contained in the papal oath, but against other
possible acts or words coming from Rome; and though it
was certainly in no way honourable to the Sovereign Pontiff,
it was such as he could and did tolerate. But Cranmer's
protest was a real limitation of the very essence of the oath
about to be taken; it was a private limitation, and, though

* Not, of course, the jurisdiction, but the temporalities, of which
there is mention in the next phrase.

made before witnesses, was utterly secret and unknown as regarded the pope himself, by whom the oath was imposed. Had he known it he would not have consented to Cranmer's consecration. Burnet has said "that if Cranmer did not wholly save his integrity, yet he intended to act fairly and above board ". If any meaning can be attached to these words, it is that, if he committed perjury, he took care to have witnesses of his intention to commit perjury. As to Fisher, we shall find him faithful to both king and pope, obedient to each in his sphere, but paying court and flattery to neither for any earthly gain. Let us now consider the sphere of his episcopal action.

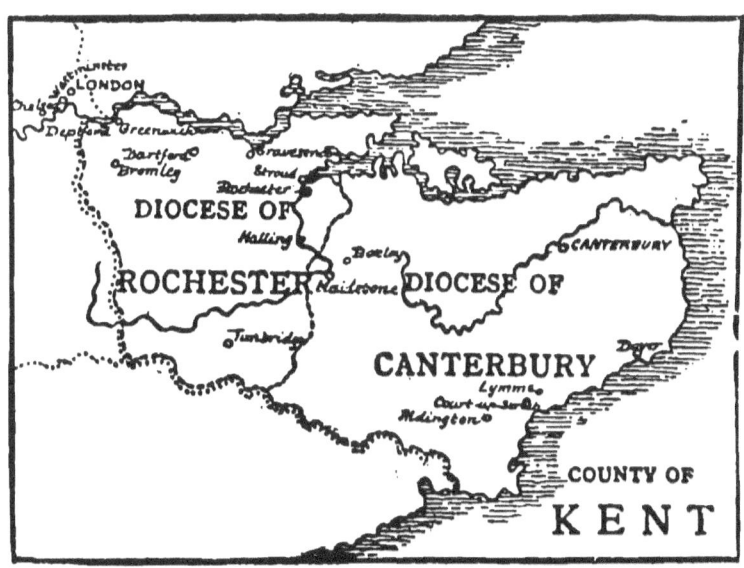

The diocese of Rochester, formed by St. Augustine himself, was the smallest in England. It consisted of ninety-nine parishes, almost all in the western part of the county of Kent. There were three deaneries—Rochester, Malling, and Dartford, divided by the deanery of Shoreham, belong

ing to Canterbury.* Rochester, the episcopal city, was
insignificant in size. Leland, writing soon after Fisher's
death, said : "The cathedral-church and the palace, with
other buildings there, occupieth half the space of the compass within the walls of Rochester".† In the time of
Queen Elizabeth there were but one hundred and forty-four
houses within the walls. But it was an ancient British and
Roman station or fortress, on the river Medway, where the
high road between Canterbury and London crosses it. It is
thirty-three miles from London and twenty-nine from Canterbury. It was called by the Romans Durobrivæ or Duro-
brivis, contracted into Roibis, to which the Saxons added
ceaster (from *castrum*), and thus it became Hroveceaster, or
Rochester.‡ The ecclesiastical name is Roffa, whence
Bishop Fisher is commonly known among theologians as
Roffensis. Whatever importance it acquired after the Conquest, either as a city or a see, was due to the zeal and energy
of Bishop Gundulf, formerly a monk of Bec, and a friend of
Lanfranc and St. Anselm. He built, at least in part, the
castle whose massive ruins still overtop the cathedral. The
nave and other parts of the present cathedral are also his
work. The dedication of the church is to St. Andrew. At
his appointment to the see Gundulf found only three secular
canons, almost without endowment. By the advice and
assistance of Archbishop Lanfranc he replaced these by a
large body of Benedictine monks. The monks were
governed by a prior, the bishop, though not necessarily or
even usually a monk, standing to them, as it were, in the
place of an abbot. Though Gundulf obtained very con-

* The deanery of Shoreham on the map in the *Valor Ecclesiasticus*
comprises the parishes given in 1810 as "Peculiars," belonging to
Canterbury, though they are attributed to the deaneries of Rochester,
Malling, and Dartford.

† *Itinerary*, vi. 9.

‡ Halsted's *Kent*, vol. iv.

siderable revenues, in the division which he made he gave the far larger share to the monastery, so that the Bishop of Rochester was the least wealthy in England, his revenues not amounting to £300 a year.* Fisher's six immediate predecessors had been translated to richer sees. Far from seeking to imitate them, Fisher used to say that it was safer to have fewer souls and less money to account for, and that he would not desert his poor old wife for the richest widow in England.

In days when shops were still few, and society was less subdivided than now, each man of position was obliged to have a large body of retainers, and drew from his own estates the maintenance of his family. A dwelling-house, sometimes very humble, but sufficiently large to accommodate a fair number of domestics, according to the rude mode of life then common, would be erected on more than one of the manors. The word palace, applied to a bishop's house, should present to us no vision of princely magnificence. The Bishop of Rochester had houses at Halling, Bromly, and Trottescliffe, at Rochester, adjoining the cathedral, and at Lambeth, used when his duties in Parliament or Convocation called him to London. This house stood near the river, not far from the present Westminster Bridge, and was called La Place.†

The palace at Rochester had been rebuilt about 1450, but owing to the neglect of Fisher's predecessors, and from its situation too near the river, it was far from salubrious, and Fisher was the last bishop who dwelt in it. The site is

* So valued at collection of subsidy, but in the *Valor Ecclesiasticus*, made in 1535, the revenues are given as £411. Those of the monastery of Rochester are £486, of the nunnery of Malling £219, of the nunnery of Dartford £380.

† It came into Henry VIII.'s hands not long after Fisher's death, and was granted to the Bishops of Carlisle, and thence called Carlisle House. In 1647, it was sold by the Parliament and destroyed. (See Brayley's *Surrey*, p. 86.)

now occupied by private houses, but the remains of one hall of the old palace are still shown." *

Erasmus, who had resided there as Fisher's guest, gives some description of it in the following letter, written to the bishop on 4th September, 1524: "It was with the utmost concern I read that part of your letter wherein you express your fear of ever living to see my book arrive. My concern was still heightened by the account your servant gave of the ill state of your health. . . . I shrewdly suspect that the state of your health principally depends upon your situation. The near approach of the tide, as well as the mud which is left exposed at every reflux of the water, renders the climate unwholesome. Your library, too, is surrounded with glass windows, which let the keen air through the crevices. I know how much time you spend in the library, which is to you a very paradise. As to me, I could not live in such a place three hours without being sick." †

The Protestant bishops who succeeded Fisher abandoned both this house and that of Halling, also on the river, for a better palace which they built at Bromley.

On the 27th April, 1534, immediately after the imprisonment of the bishop for refusing the Succession Oath, all his goods being thereby confiscated to the Crown, commissioners were sent to take an inventory of his palace furniture. This document enables us to some extent to visit the bishop at home, and gives a striking picture of episcopal poverty. It deserves, therefore, to be given in all its detail.

"*In his own bedchamber.* A bedstead with a mattrass, a counterpoint of red cloth lined with canvas. A celer and tester of old red velvet nothing worth. A leather chair with a cushion. An altar with a hanging of white and green satin of Brydges (*Bruges*), with Our Lord embroidered on it. Two blue sarcenet curtains. A cupboard with a cloth. A little chair covered with leather and a cushion. A close

---

* *The Reliquary* (New Series), vol. i., n. i.   † *Ep.* xviii. 47.

stool and an old cushion upon it. An andiron, a fire pan, and a fire shovel.

"*In the great study within the same chamber.* A long spruce table and other tables. Three leather chairs. Fire irons. Eight round desks and shelves for books.*

"*In the north study.* Divers glasses with waters and syrups, and boxes of marmalade, which were delivered to his servants. A table, four round desks and bookshelves.

"*In the south gallery.* Fifty glasses of divers sorts, with a curtain of green and red say.

"*In the chapel in the end of the south gallery.* A cushion in the seat of the chapel, the altar cloths, two pieces of old velvet and a superaltare (altar-stone). Four gilt images with a crucifix.

"*In the broad gallery.* Old hangings of green say. Old carpets of tapestry set under the said books. An altar cloth painted with green velvet and yellow damask. A St. John's Head standing at the end of the altar. A pontifical book. A painted cloth of the image of Jesus taken down from the Cross. Two old sarcenets.

"*In the old gallery.* Certain old books pertaining to divers monasteries.

"*In the wardrobe.* A kirtle of stamnel, a Spanish blanket, a pair of coarse blankets, a limbeck to distil *aqua vitæ*, with divers old trash. A trussing bedstead, a pair of sheets, six boards, two pair of trestles.

"*In the little study beside the wardrobe.* Divers glasses and boxes with syrups, sugar, stilled waters, and other certain trash sent to my lord.

"*In the great chapel.* The altar hung with white sarcenet, with red sarcenet crosses, and under it two hangings of yellow satin, of Brydges, and blue damask ; eight gilt images upon the altar ; two laten candlesticks. A diaper cloth upon the altar, and hanging over it. A pix, with a

* This is no doubt the library described by Erasmus.

cloth hanging over it garnished with gold, with tassels or red silk and gold.* At the ends of the altar, two curtains of red sarcenet upon the desk where he sits. Two pieces of tapestry, and two cushions covered with dornexe. A mass book. An old carpet on the ground before the altar. Hangings of painted red say. An altar beneath, in the same chapel, hung with old dornexe, and a painted cloth of the three kings of Coleyn. Five images of timber. A table of Doomsday. A crucifix with the images of the Father and Holy Ghost.

"*In the little chamber next the great chapel.* Hangings of old painted cloths, a great looking glass broken. An old folding bed.

"*In the old dining chamber.* Two leather chairs. A black velvet chair. A table and trestles. Two cupboards. Two carpets in the windows. Two joined forms."

There is no need to enumerate the chairs, and trestles, and boards in the other rooms. We have seen all the finery of the house.

The inventory of the bishop's manor house at Halling is more scanty and still more wretched.†

Let the reader note especially one item: The figure of the head of St. John the Baptist standing on the altar. We shall see more of the meaning of this when we come to the bishop's action regarding the king's divorce.

Such, then, was the sphere allotted for the bishop's labours, and such the provision for his residence within that sphere. All accounts agree that he never left it willingly. He was very little at Court, and the only absence from his diocese that we can trace during those many years was

---

* The hanging pix for the Blessed Sacrament, with its silk covering, was almost universal in England before the 16th century.

† *Letters and Papers*, vii. 557. The books were seized, and are not in this inventory, nor the plate. The inventory fills ten pages. The above are the principal items.

connected with university matters, or with his duties in
Parliament and Convocation. The bishop began by the
visitation of his diocese, correcting abuses, preaching, confirming, and relieving the needy. He was well persuaded,
as he had written just about this time, in his sermons on the
Penitential Psalms, that "all fear of God, also the contempt
of God, cometh and is grounded of the clergy".* His first
care, therefore, was with them. He had complained in the
same sermons, when commenting on the words, *Qui juxta
me erant de longe steterunt*—" My neighbours stood afar off,"
that pastors, who ought to be the nearest neighbours of all,
stand aloof either by bodily absence or by silence.
" Bishops be absent from their dioceses and parsons from
their churches. . . . We use bye-paths and circumlocutions
in rebuking. We go nothing nigh to the matter, and so in
the mean season the people perish with their sins."† As
we shall see the bishop devoid of all human fear, when he
has to resist the king in all the fury of his passions, we may
believe Dr. Hall, when he tells us that he was dauntless in
reproving scandalous pastors : " Sequestering all such as he
found unworthy to occupy that high function, he placed
others fitter in their room ; and all such as were accused
of any crime he put to their purgation, not sparing the
punishment of simony and heresy, with other crimes and
abuses ".

Dr. Hall, who has told us the names of the eye-witnesses
from whom he learnt what he relates, gives a beautiful
picture of the bishop's ordinary life : " He never omitted so
much as one collect of his daily service, and that he used
to say commonly to himself alone, without the help of any
chaplain, not in such speed or hasty manner to be at an end,
as many will do, but in most reverent and devout manner, so
distinctly and treatably pronouncing every word that he

* *Penit. Psalms* (E. E. T. Society). p. 179.   † *Ibid.*, p. 77.

5

seemed a very devourer of heavenly food, never satiate nor filled therewith. Insomuch as, talking on a time with a Carthusian monk, who much commended his zeal and diligent pains in compiling his book against Luther, he answered again, saying that he wished that time of writing had been spent in prayer, thinking that prayer would have done more good and was of more merit.

"And to help this his devotion he caused a great hole to be digged through the wall of his church of Rochester, whereby he might the more commodiously have prospect into the church at mass and evensong times. When he himself used to say mass, as many times he used to do, if he were not letted by some urgent and great cause, ye might then perceive in him such earnest devotion that many times the tears would fall from his cheeks.

"And lest that the memory of death might hap to slip from his mind, he always accustomed to set upon one end of the altar a dead man's scull, which was also set before him at his table as he dined or supped. And in all his prayers and other talk he used continually a special reverence to the Name of Jesus.

"Now to those his prayers he adjoined two wings which were alms and fasting, by the help whereof they might mount speedier to heaven. To poor sick persons he was a physician, to the lame he was a staff, to poor widows an advocate, to orphans a tutor, and to poor travellers a host. Wheresoever he lay, either at Rochester or elsewhere, his order was to inquire where any poor sick folks lay near him, which after he once knew he would diligently visit them, and where he saw any of them likely to die, he would preach to them, teaching them the way to die with such godly persuasions that for the most part he never departed till the sick persons were well satisfied and contented with death.

"Many times it was his chance to come to such poor

houses as for want of chimnies were very smoky, and thereby so noisome that scant any man could abide in them.* Nevertheless himself would then sit by the sick patient many times the space of three or four hours together in the smoke, when none of his servants were able to abide in the house, but were fain to tarry without till his coming abroad. And in some other poor houses where stairs were wanting, he would never disdain to climb up by a ladder for such a good purpose. And when he had given them such ghostly comfort as he thought expedient for their souls, he would at his departure leave behind him his charitable alms, giving charge to his steward and other officers daily to prepare meat [*i.e.*, food] convenient for them (if they were poor) and send it unto them. Besides this he gave at his gate to divers poor people (which were commonly no small number) a daily alms of money, to some two pence, to some three pence, to some four pence, to some six pence, and some more, after the rate of their necessity.† That being done, every of them was rewarded likewise with meat, which was daily brought to the gate. And lest any fraud, partiality, or other disorder might rise in distribution of the same, he provided himself a place, whereunto immediately after dinner he would resort, and there stand to see the division with his own eyes. If any strangers came to him he would entertain them at his table, according to their vocations [*i.e.*, position], with such mirth as stood with the gravity of his person, whose talk was always rather of learning or con-

---

* The fuel would be turf or wood at best.

† Skilled labourers engaged in building the church at Eton in 1441 received only 6d. a day, and other labourers 4d. (*History of Eton College*, by H. Maxwell Lyte, p. 14). In the year 1515, we find from the cellarer's accounts of the monastery of Holy Trinity, London, that labourers' wages were 5d., a pair of shoes 8d., hose (*i.e.*, trousers) 17d., two shirts 2s. 4d., a gallon of Rhenish wine 1s., of Malmsey 8d., a quart of ink 4d., a preacher's honorary on the first Sunday of Lent 3s. 4d. (*Letters and Papers of Henry VIII.*, vol. ii. 115.

templation than of worldly matters. And when he had no
strangers, his order was now and then to sit with his chaplains, which were commonly grave and learned men, among
whom he would put some great question of learning, not
only to provoke them to better consideration and deep
search of the hid mysteries of our religion, but also to spend
the time of repast in such talk that might be (as it was
indeed) pleasant, profitable, and comfortable to the waiters
and standers by.

"And yet was he so dainty and spare of time that he
would never bestow fully one hour at any meal. His diet at
table was, for all such as thither resorted, plentiful and good,
but for himself very mean. For upon such eating days as
were not fasted, although he would for his health use a
larger diet than at other times, yet was it with such temper-
ance that commonly he was wont to eat and drink by weight
and measure. And the most of his sustenance was thin
pottage, sodden with flesh, eating of the flesh itself very
sparingly. The ordinary fasts appointed by the Church he
kept very roundly,* and to them he joined many other
particular fasts of his own devotion, as appeared well by his
own thin and weak body, whereupon though much flesh was
not left, yet would he punish the very skin and bones upon
his back. He wore most commonly a shirt of hair, and
many times he would whip himself in most secret wise.

"When night was come, which commonly brings rest to
all creatures, then would he many times despatch away his
servants and fall to his prayers a long space. And after he
had ended the same, he laid him down upon a poor hard
couch of straw and mats, for other bed he used none,
provided at Rochester in his closet near the cathedral-
church, where he might look into the choir, and hear
Divine service. And being laid, he never rested above

* Every Friday was then a fast-day in England, besides very many
vigils.

four hours at one time, but straightway rose and ended the
rest of his devout prayers.

" Thus lived he till towards his latter days, when, being
more grown into age, which is, as Cicero saith, a sickness
of itself, he was forced somewhat to relent of those hard
and severe fasts; and the rather for that his body was much
weakened with a consumption, wherefore, by counsel of his
physician and licence of his ghostly father, he used upon
some fasting days to comfort himself with a little thin gruel
made for the purpose.

"The care that he had of his family was not small; for
although his chief burden consisted in discharge of his
spiritual function, yet did he not neglect his temporal affairs.
Wherefore he took such order in his revenues, that one part
was bestowed upon reparation and maintenance of the
church, the second upon the relief of poverty and maintenance of scholars, and the third upon his household
expenses and buying of books, whereof he had great plenty.
And, lest the trouble of worldly business might be some
hindrance to his spiritual exercise, he used the help of his
brother Robert, a layman, whom he made steward as long
as his said brother lived; giving him in charge so to order
his expenses that by no means he brought him in debt.
His servants used not to wear their apparel after any court-
like or wanton manner, but went in garments of a sad [*i.e.*,
sober] and seemly colour, some in gowns and some in coats,
as the fashion then was; whom he always exhorted to
frugality and thrift, and in any wise to beware of prodi-
gality. And where he marked any of them more given to
good husbandry than others, he would many times lend
them money, and never ask it again, and commonly when
it was offered him he did forgive it. If any of his household had committed a fault, as sometimes it happened, he
would first examine the matter himself, and, finding him
faulty, would, for the first time, but punish him with words

only, but it should be done with such a severity of speech
that whosoever came once before him was very unwilling to
come before him again for any such offence. So that, by
this means, his household continued in great quietness and
peace, every man knowing what belonged to his duty.

"Some among the rest, as they could get opportunity, would
apply their minds to study and learning, and those above
others he specially liked, and would many times support
them with his labour and sometimes with his money. But
where he saw any of them given to idleness and sloth, he
could by no means endure them in his house, because out
of that fountain many evils are commonly wont to spring.
In conclusion, his family was governed with such tem-
perance, devotion, and learning that his palace, for conti-
nency, seemed a very monastery, and for learning a university " *

* Dr. Hall's *MS.*

CHAPTER IV

EXTRA-DIOCESAN LABOURS.

ON the 18th July, 1511, Pope Julius II. published a Bull of Indiction for a general council, to meet in the Lateran Church, on 19th April, 1512. The bull is signed by the cardinals then present in Rome, amongst whom was Christopher Bainbridge, Archbishop of York, and Cardinal of St. Praxedis.* He was then resident ambassador of the King of England.

The objects of this council, which is known as the 5th Lateran, were the suppression of the schism of Louis XII., peace between Christian princes, reformation of morals, and defence of Christendom against the Turks. In November, 1511, Henry VIII. made a "holy league" with Ferdinand, King of Arragon, and Joanna, Queen of Castile, against France, the objects of which were the defence of the Church and the acknowledgment of the Lateran Council.† Though he had already his representative in Rome, in Cardinal Bainbridge, he determined to send a special embassy, or orators, as its members were called, and a commission was issued, on 4th February, 1512, to Silvester de Giglis (an Italian), Bishop of Worcester; John Fisher, Bishop of Rochester ; Thomas Docwra, Prior of the Knights of St. John ; and Richard Kidderminster, Abbot of Wynch-

---

* In Colet's *Councils*, another Christopher, Cardinal of St. Peter and Marcellinus, is entered as Eboracensis, p. 690.

† *Letters and Papers of Henry VIII.*, vol. i. 1980.

combe, to proceed to Rome for the opening of the council.*
For some reason not known to us the commission was
revoked, and another issued, on 1st April, to the Bishop of
Worcester and Sir Robert Wingfield.† Even these, however, did not go, and England had no representative at the
opening except Cardinal Bainbridge. At some of the later
sessions we find the Bishop of Worcester present. ‡

By the absence of a bishop so wise, so learned, so holy,
and so fearless, there is no doubt the Church at large
suffered a loss. The incident is interesting as showing the
great esteem in which the bishop was held by the king.
Silvester de Giglis would have been no fit associate for such
a bishop, and was probably chosen as being an Italian, and

---

* *Letters and Papers*, i. 2085-3108.   † *Ibid.*, i. 3109.

‡ There is much mystery about this embassy, and it may save
trouble to future explorers to unravel it as far as possible. Burnet,
in his *History of Reform.*, i. 19, and Wharton, in *Anglia Sacra*, i.
382, Collier, in his *History*, iv. 5, Lord Herbert, and others, all
suppose that Fisher went to Rome. Baker, in his *History of St.
John's*, i. 78, proves that he did not go; so does Lewis, in his *Life
of Fisher*, i. 43. Mr. Brewer, however, in his Preface to vol. i. of
Letters and Papers, p. 95, writes: ' When the Bishop of Rochester,
the Prior of St. John, and the Abbot of Wynchcombe were sent as
ambassadors to the pope, 5th February, 1512, the first and second
received £800, the third 800 marks, for their expenses during one
hundred and sixty days," and he refers to the warrants directed to the
Treasurer of the Chamber. This would seem good evidence. Yet it
is certain that they did not go. Fisher himself, in his account of his
labour and difficulties in the foundation of St. John's, says: " *Sixth*,
After this I was moved by the king to prepare myself to go unto the
general council, for the realm, with my Lord of St. John and others.
. . . *Seventh*, When I was disappointed of that journey," &c. (Lewis,
ii. 279, 280). Again, there is no record of his presence in the acts of
the council. There is also evidence in the State Papers that Docwra
was in England in May, 1512 (i. 3173). Wingfield, instead of going
to Rome, was ambassador to the emperor. The "diets" of the
ambassadors were paid beforehand, as appears from the king's book
of payments, February, 1512 (*Letters and Papers*, ii. 1454). Of
course, when the commission was revoked, the money was refunded.

versed in diplomacy. Fisher would have been a poor diplomatist, and was selected to do honour to the English Church, and to render service to the Church universal. He would have found in the Abbot of Winchcombe, Richard Kidderminster, a man of congenial mind. A letter written to him by Colet in 1497, represents him as learned and a patron of learning, "ardent in the love of all sacred wisdom," and of a sweet and hospitable character.* In 1521, like Fisher, he wrote a treatise against Luther.

Thomas Docwra or Dokray, prior of the hospital of St. John of Jerusalem in London, more commonly known as Lord of St. John's, held as a knight the very highest place, and had a seat in the House of Lords. He had been the king's ambassador in France in 1510. He took part with the Earl of Shrewsbury in the French wars in May, 1513.

The Council of Lateran was opened on 3rd May, 1512, and continued its sessions at intervals. Pope Julius died on 21st February, 1513, but the council was continued under Leo X. It was probably by the pope's desire that a second project was entertained of sending special ambassadors, and again the choice fell on Fisher and Docwra. Wolsey alludes to their projected journey in a letter to De Giglis, which Mr. Brewer has placed at the end of October, 1514.† On 3rd March, 1515, Polydore Vergil writes from London to Adrian de Corneto, Cardinal of St. Chrysogonus, and Bishop of Bath : "The king's ambassadors leave on the 10th with letters for the cardinal. Perhaps it will not be allowed without the permission of *le. mi*" (this was a cipher designating Wolsey), "who are hateful to heaven and earth. The Bishop of Rochester will be glad to visit him. Will send by his hands the king's gift." ‡

* See Seebohm's *Oxford Reformers*, p. 45 (2nd ed.), and Knight's *Life of Colet*, p. 311.

† *Letters, &c.*, i. 5542.

‡ I cannot reconcile the date assigned to this letter, with others (ii.

The University of Cambridge wrote to him a most com-
plimentary letter, begging him to use his influence when at
Rome in its favour and in the confirmation of its privileges.*

On 10th March, 1515, the bishop appointed William
Fresel, the prior of his cathedral, and Richard Chetham,
prior of Ledes in Kent, as his proctors during his absence
to confer benefices, to reconcile churches, license quæstors,
&c.† But these procuratorial letters, as well as letters of
introduction which he had obtained for presentation in
Rome, are now in the archives of St. John's College, Cambridge, which proves that his journey was again prevented.‡
Wolsey was then intent on the cardinalate, and perhaps
Fisher was not judged a fitting agent in such a matter.
Whether for this or other reasons, his commission was a
second time revoked, and the Church lost his services.

Dr. Hall mentions a third projected visit to Rome. He
does not give the year, but from various circumstances
mentioned it must have been in 1518. "He was taken,"
writes Dr. Hall, "with a great desire to travel to Rome,
there to salute the pope's holiness, and to visit the tombs
of the holy Apostles St. Peter and St. Paul, with the rest of
the holy places and relics there. But you shall understand
that this was by him determined from the time that he first
received his bishopric, which by certain occasions was twice

238, 312), but the matter is of no importance. The letter of Polydore
was filled with scurrility against Wolsey. It was intercepted in Rome
and sent to Wolsey, who threw Polydore into prison. In prison he
wrote to Wolsey : "Lying in the shadow of death, he has heard of
Wolsey's elevation to the cardinal's throne. When it is allowed him
he will gaze and bow in adoration before him, and then my spirit will
rejoice in Thee, my God and Saviour." When he was set free and
arrived safe in Italy, he took his revenge on the cardinal and made up
by abuse for his adulation. (See *Letters, &c.,* ii. 970.)

* Prid. Id., Feb., 1514 (*i.e.,* 1515); Lewis, ii. 286.

† Lewis, ii. 286.

‡ Baker's *History of St. John's,* i. 75.

before disappointed.* Whereupon, having now gotten (as he thought) a good opportunity, he providently disposed his household and all his other matters, and after leave obtained of the king and his metropolitan, he began to prepare for his journey to Rome. To this voyage he had chosen learned company. But behold, when everything was ready and the journey about to begin, all was suddenly disappointed, and revoked for other business to be treated of at home, which of necessity required his presence.

"The cause of his revocation was by means of a synod of bishops then called by Cardinal Wolsey, who (having lately before received his power legatine from the pope) at that time ruled all things under the king also at his own will and pleasure. To this synod the clergy of England assembled themselves in great number, when it was expected that great matters for the benefit of the Church of England should have been proposed. Howbeit, all fell out otherwise. For, as it appeared after, this council was called by my lord cardinal rather to notify to the world his great authority, and to be seen sitting in his Pontifical Seat, than for any great good that he meant to do, which this learned man perceived quickly.†

"Wherefore, having now good occasion to speak against such enormities as he saw daily arising among the spiri-

---

* Dr. Hall has made no mention of the Council of Lateran, or the intention to send the bishop there as king's orator, yet this statement about the double "disappointment" is correct, and confirms the accuracy of his information. This I mention because what follows about the bishop's speech to the English bishops rests on his authority only, as far as I can discover. Baily has misplaced the matter in 1522, after the publication of the king's book.

† The priests who, like Dr. Hall, remained faithful to the Catholic cause after the overthrow of the Catholic religion in England were very prone to throw the blame of what had happened on the pride and ambition of Cardinal Wolsey, giving a sinister intention even to his good works, perhaps unjustly.

tuality, and much the rather for that his words were among the clergy alone, without any commixture of the laity, which at that time began to hearken to any speaking against the clergy, he there reproved very discreetly the ambition and incontinency of the clergy, utterly condemning their vanity in wearing of costly apparel, whereby he declared the goods of the Church to be sinfully wasted, and scandal to be raised among the people, seeing the tithes and other oblations, given by the devotion of them and their ancestors to a good purpose, so inordinately spent in indecent and superfluous raiment, delicate fare, and other worldly vanity, which matter he debated so largely, and framed his words after such sort, that the cardinal perceived himself to be touched to the very quick. For he affirmed this kind of disorder to proceed through the example of the head, and thereupon reproved his pomp, putting him in mind that it stood better with the modesty of such a high pastor as he was to eschew all worldly vanity, specially in this perilous time, and by humility to make himself conformable and like the image of God.

"'For in this trade of life,' said he, ' neither can there be any likelihood of perpetuity with safety of conscience, neither yet any security of the clergy to continue, but such plain and imminent dangers are like to ensue as never were tasted or heard of before our days. For what should we (said he) exhort our flocks to eschew and shun worldly ambition, when we ourselves, that are bishops, do wholly set our minds to the same things we forbid in them? What example of Christ our Saviour do we imitate, who first executed doing, and after fell to teaching? If we teach according to our doing, how absurd may our doctrine be accounted! If we teach one thing and do another, our labour in teaching shall never benefit our flocks half so much as our examples in doing shall hurt them. Who can willingly suffer and bear with us, in whom (preaching humi-

lity, sobriety, and contempt of the world) they may evidently
perceive haughtiness in mind, pride in gesture, sump-
tuousness in apparel, and damnable excess in all worldly
delicacies?

" ' Truly, most reverend Fathers, what this vanity in temporal things worketh in you, I know not. But sure I am
that in myself I perceive a great impediment to devotion,
and so have felt for a long time. For sundry times, when
I have settled and fully bent myself to the care of my flock
committed unto me, to visit my diocese, to govern my
church, and to answer the enemies of Christ, straightways
hath come a messenger for one cause or other, sent from
higher authority, by whom I have been called to other
business, and so left off my former purpose. And thus, by
tossing and going this way and that way, time hath passed,
and in the meanwhile nothing done but attending after
triumphs, receiving of ambassadors, haunting of princes'
courts, and such like, whereby great expenses rise, that
might better be spent many other ways.'

"He added, further, that whereas himself for sundry
causes secretly known to himself was thrice determined to
make his journey to Rome, and at every time had taken
full and perfect order for his cure, his household, and for
all other business till his return, still by occasion of these
worldly matters he was disappointed of his purpose. After
he had uttered these with many more such words in this
synod, they seemed all by their silence to be much astonied,
and to think well of his speeches; but indeed by the sequel
of the matter it fell out that few were persuaded by his
counsel; for no man upon this amended one whit of his
accustomed licentious life, no man became one hair the
more circumspect or watchful over his cure, and many were
of the mind that they thought it nothing necessary for them
to abate anything of their fair apparel for the reprehension
of a few, whom they thought too scrupulous, so that (excuses

never wanting to cover sin) this holy father's words, spoken
with so good a zeal, were all lost and came to nothing for
that time." *

From this account of Dr. Hall it appears that according
to His usual providence God was pleased to send a warning
before His anger fell on the Church in England. Reformation was indeed needed, but not such reformation as has
falsely usurped the name. That has been in many respects
but a development and legal establishment of the evils
against which such men as Fisher raised their voices; and
when it came it was welcomed by those of loose and unworthy life, and resisted by those whose life was holiest and
whose voice had been raised most boldly against abuses.

It would, however, be doing an injustice to the many
learned and excellent prelates who were Fisher's contemporaries if I let it be supposed that no serious effort was
made to remove scandals from the Church. The venerable
Bishop of Winchester, Richard Fox, had retired from Court,
and was labouring in the sanctification of his diocese, when
he heard that Wolsey, in 1527, was really resolved to take
stringent measures in a national council; thereupon he wrote
him a warm letter of thanks and encouragement.† The
miserable affair of the king's divorce came to thwart this
effort or project; but on Wolsey's disgrace the Archbishop
of Canterbury, having recovered the plenitude of his supre-

---

* This national and legatine synod was convoked on 1st Monday of Lent, 1518, and was to have concluded on 9th September.
It was, however, interrupted by the plague, and was prorogued to 1st
Monday in Lent, 1519. Constitutions were made and published, but
they have not come down to us. From the register of a diocesan
synod of Hereford, held in 1519, for the promulgation of the decrees
of the national synod, we find that, amongst other matters, they
regarded the dress of the clergy, and the life of candidates for ordina-
tion, &c. For greater facility they were published in English (Wilkins,
iii. 682).

† Wilkins, iii. 708.

macy, took measures at once for the desired reforms. New laws were not needed, but the enforcement of the old and the abolition or curtailment of the innumerable exceptions and dispensations. A Convocation or Provincial Council of Canterbury, begun in November, 1529, and continued in 1531, drew up a code of decrees and instructions for prelates and pastors, for religious orders and for preachers and schoolmasters, as excellent and full as Fisher himself could have desired.* But alas! the king had other matters in hand than the moral reform of clergy or laity. The decrees were scarcely committed to paper before, by arts and threats, he first deprived the clergy of their liberty, and then cast them headlong into schism and heresy, as will be related in a future chapter.

To go back to the synod of 1518. That the complaints uttered by the Bishop of Rochester were not querulous and censorious reproaches of other men, but the cry of agony of a soul zealous for God's glory and men's salvation, may be seen almost at a glance, when we recall the vain pomps and pageantries of which the chronicles of those days are full, and contrast the labour and expenses with which they were carried out with the apathy and indolence with which every attempt at reformation was received.

As Rochester was on the high road between Dover and London, Fisher had perhaps more than his share of State pageantry. He might not object to show honour to the pope and king when a messenger passed bearing some token from the former to the latter. Thus, in the first year of Fisher's episcopate, Julius II. sent a sword and cap of maintenance to Henry VII., which were received with "many and great ceremonies," says Stow. In 1510, he sent the golden rose to Henry VIII. In 1514, Leo X. sent him the sword and cap, and Clement VII. a magnificent gold

* Wilkins, iii. 717-724.

rose-tree in 1524.* What these things involved may be seen from the following order of the council (12th May, 1514):

"To MY LORD OF ROCHESTER,—My Lord, we commend us unto you in our hearty manner. So it is the king's grace hath knowledge that an ambassador, sent from the pope's holiness to his grace, with a sword and cap of maintenance, is come to Calais, and intendeth immediately to take shipping to arrive at Dover. Whereupon it is appointed that the prior of Christ's Church of Canterbury shall meet with the said ambassador beyond Canterbury, and so to entertain him in his house, and afterwards upon monition to be given to him, shall conduct him to some place convenient between Sittingbourne and Rochester, where the king hath appointed that your lordship, the Master of the Rolls, and Sir Thomas Boleyn shall meet with him and so conduct him to London. . . . And in case ye be not now at Rochester, ye will upon knowledge thereof repair thither, where the Master of the Rolls and Sir Thomas Boleyn shall be with you accordingly. And Jesu preserve your lordship. At Baynard Castle the 12th day of May.

"P. NORFOLK, P. DORSET, RI. WINTON, P. DURHAM." †

Such duties as the above belonged to the bishop's position, and so, again, he might accept willingly enough the expensive and onerous duties which devolved upon him when the Cardinal's Hat was sent to Wolsey in November, 1515. When Warham, the Archbishop of Canterbury, sung mass at Westminster, at the ceremony of investiture, there were present the Archbishops of Armagh and Dublin, the Bishops of Lincoln, Exeter, Winchester, Durham, Norwich, Ely, and Llandaff, with the Abbots of Westminster, St. Alban's, Bury, Glastonbury, Reading, Gloucester, Winchcombe, Tewkes-

---

* See on all these Cooper's *Lady Margaret*, p. 43.

† Lewis, ii. 297. For an accouut of the grand ceremonial at the king's investiture, see *Letters and Papers*, i. 4835 and 5111.

bury, and the Prior of Coventry. The Bishop of Rochester acted as "crosier" to the archbishop. Dr. Colet, Dean of St. Paul's, preached the sermon, of which the heralds, who have treasured up all the ceremonial of that day of magnificence, have only preserved this brief notice, that "a cardinal represented the order of seraphim, which continually burneth in the love of the glorious Trinity, and for their consideration a cardinal is only apparelled with red, which colour only betokeneth nobleness". He exhorted Wolsey to execute righteousness to rich and poor, and desired all people to pray for him.* Such functions as these were ecclesiastical, but the bishop complained that he had to go to great expense, or to submit to long interruption of his work, for mere State pageantry. Thus, when the Emperor Charles V. visited England, in May, 1522, he was met by the king at Dover, and the two monarchs proceeded by easy stages to London. At Canterbury the clergy and religious lined the streets to the cathedral, where the Archbishop, Warham, assisted by the Bishops of Rochester, Bangor, and many others, met them. The emperor was lodged at the archbishop's palace, the king at St. Augustine's. The next stage was Sittingbourne, then Rochester, and at Rochester they spent the Sunday, and were entertained by the bishop. As the emperor's attendants alone amounted to two thousand, and half the English nobility and prelacy, with their followers, were also present, it is a marvellous thing how all found beds in the little city of Rochester and its neighbourhood.†

But this was little in comparison with the meeting between Henry and Francis I. at the famous Field of the Cloth of Gold, in 1520. I shall not transcribe the gorgeous descriptions that have come down to us of that ceremonial. It

---

* *Letters and Papers*, ii. 1153-1248.

† The full account is given in Hall's *Chronicle.* Also In *Letters and Papers*, iii. 2288.

is enough, as regards the Bishop of Rochester, to say, that though the meeting did not take place until the 7th June, the feast of Corpus Christi, arrangements were made long before. On 26th March, it was notified to the bishop that he was appointed to ride with the King of England, at the embracing of the kings, together with the Bishops of Durham, Ely, Chester, Exeter, and Hereford, the Archbishop of Armagh, the Archbishop of Canterbury, and the Archbishop of York and Legate (Wolsey). The list was afterwards modified, but he retained his place, as being member of the Privy Council. He was to have with him four chaplains and twenty persons, eight of whom should be gentlemen. He was to provide twelve horses to be transported beyond the sea. It seems that a further change was made, and he waited on the queen instead of the king.[*]

It is curious that, though he often proposed to visit Rome and Germany, the only occasion on which he ever crossed the sea was with this crowd of courtiers. The magnificence of the ecclesiastical functions on Corpus Christi, and especially on the Sunday within the octave, when the Bishop of Rochester was one of the assistants at the mass celebrated by the cardinal, in the presence of the kings and queens, and the nobility of the two countries, was equal to that of the Court ceremonial; but whether it caused much joy to the heart of Fisher may well be questioned. His words, preached in 1505, may have recurred to his memory: " Our joy is the testimony of a clean conscience—*Gloria nostra hæc est, testimonium conscientiæ nostræ.* Which joy without fail shone more bright in the poor Apostles than doth now our clothes of silk and golden cups. . . . Truly, neither gold, precious stones, nor glorious bodily garments be not the cause wherefor kings and princes of the world should dread God and His Church, for doubtless they have

* Rymer, xiii. 711 ; *Letters and Papers*, iii. 702, 703, 734.

far more worldly riches than we have. But holy doctrine, good life, and example of honest conversation be the occasions whereby good and holy men, also wicked and cruel people, are moved to love and fear Almighty God." *

We may now bring together such notices as have been preserved of the bishop's action in Convocation, previous to the year 1530, which will require special attention. As Convocation is an institution peculiar to England, and may not be familiar to some of my readers, I will say a few words as to its nature and functions.

Convocation was the name given to the assemblies of the clergy in England, especially as called together by royal authority and for State purposes ; when summoned by merely ecclesiastical authority and for merely ecclesiastical legisla- tion, such assemblies were called synods or councils, and they were either diocesan, provincial, or national.† But a Convocation could pass into a synod, and a purely ecclesias- tical synod might, if it pleased, vote a subsidy for the king.

Each province (Canterbury and York) had its own Con- vocation ; and each Convocation, like Parliament, consisted of an upper and a lower house. When Edward I. first sought to organise the clergy into a third estate, especially for the purpose of granting subsidies, the clergy were indisposed to admit any right in the civil power to summon them together; and at last it was settled that while the king issued his writ (called *præmunientes*) to the archbishops, they should issue their writs, as of their own authority, to the bishops, deans, archdeacons, abbots, priors, chapters, and clergy (represented by their proctors), calling them to Convocation. But the archbishop claimed and exercised the right to summon synods without waiting for royal writ,

---

* *English Works* (E. E. Text Society), p. 180.

† A national synod could only be convoked by one having authority as papal legate over both provinces, and was hence called legatine.

and when royal business was over could dissolve the Convocation or continue it as a synod. *   Unfortunately no detailed record exists of the meetings of Convocation. Colet, Dean of St. Paul's, preached a well-written and very earnest sermon to the clergy at the opening of Convocation on 4th February, 1512, and this was shortly afterwards printed both in Latin and in English. †   It is an urgent cry for reform, and traces the prevalent evils principally to the want of care in the selection of the clergy. This sermon has been greatly lauded as if it contained the seeds of Protestantism. Nothing can be further from the truth. It is not only orthodox, but imbued with true Catholic feeling. It is just the kind of fearless address to the clergy that saintly men have made in every age. Fisher would have listened to it with joy. In some respects it resembles the discourse made by himself a few years later. What Colet recommended to the clergy in general, Fisher was practising in his own diocese.

In 1515, Leo X. had exhorted Warham, the Archbishop of Canterbury, to induce the clergy to grant a subsidy to the king, that he might take part in the defence of Christendom against the Turks. Warham brought the matter before Convocation. Dr. Taylor the orator of the bishops, advised them utterly to refuse. He said that "more tenths had been paid by the clergy in one sitting than to any other kings in the whole of their lives. They should not open a window to so perilous an example as the pope required, lest,

---

* By the Act of Submission of 1532, to be mentioned later on, all such independence was surrendered : "Since that period the Convocation cannot assemble, even for Church purposes, without the royal permission, nor, when assembled, proceed to business without a special licence from the Sovereign ".—Lathbury, *History of Convocation*, p. 111 (2nd ed.).

† The sermon is printed in full (in English) in Mr. Lupton's recent *Life of Colet.* He thinks the translation probably Colet's own.

when they wished it, they might not be able to close the door." (Here the orator got his metaphors mixed.) "They had paid already six tenths to defend the patrimony of St. Peter." The orator's eloquence prevailed. The Lower House of Convocation also refused. They called to the pope's mind the efforts they had made in the time of Julius II. They said that the victories of Henry over the French had removed all dangers from the Holy See. Such was the selfish policy of the English Church. Yet Christendom at that time was in the greatest danger, and the popes alone were taking measures to avert it; and Leo X. would have succeeded at that moment in uniting the Christian kings against the Turks but for England. The clergy refused a tenth to the pope, and before many years they had to pay an enormous sum to the king, who had cast off the pope's yoke.*

We can judge from his own writings what were the Bishop of Rochester's views and action in this matter. In his answer to the *Assertions of Luther*, which he published some years later, he defends the general system of the Crusades, and shows that they were on the whole successful, and in some instances brilliantly successful. He shows that when they failed it was from one or other of three causes : first, the general neglect and indifference of Christendom, as when Constantinople fell; secondly, the wicked lives of the Crusaders, which forfeited God's blessing; thirdly, self-glorification after victories, to which he attributes the failures of John Hunniades after the glorious victory of Belgrade. To Luther's almost inconceivable enmity against the popes,

---

* *Letters and Papers of Henry VIII.*, vol. ii. 1312, with Mr. Brewer's remarks in the introduction to that volume. Dr. Stubbs also remarks that after 1534 the tenths formerly granted to the pope continued to be paid to the king (*Lectures on Mediæval and Modern History*, p. 250). Christendom lost, but the clergy gained nothing, by the schism.

the bishop replies : " If you spoke thus of only one or the
other of the popes, whose life had been publicly detestable,
one could scarcely tolerate your conduct.   But when you
thus without discrimination bark cynically against all, and
even against the See itself, in which so many holy pontiffs
have succeeded one to the other, who can bear it patiently ?
Certainly no man who wishes to be considered a Christian
and loyal to Christ.   You call on the emperors to bring the
popes to order, but if you compare the conduct of the
popes with that of the emperors in these wars, certainly you
will not consider that the resistance to the Turks and the
collecting of the necessary money should be entrusted to
the latter rather than the former.   The emperors have put
more obstacles in the way of this great work than any, and
have committed greater frauds with regard to the funds collected."   He instances Frederick II. and others, and concludes : " If, then, the necessity of undertaking this war
shall occur, certainly the collection of the funds should be
entrusted to no one rather than to the pope ".

He highly praises the popes who sought to move the
Christian nations to prayer and penance as well as to active
resistance to the infidel ; and in doing so almost prophesies
of St. Pius V. and the victory of Lepanto : " Give me popes
like these," he says, alluding to Innocent III. and Callixtus,
" who will take measures to obtain assiduous prayers.   Give
me soldiers such as St. Augustine wished Count Boniface to
be, who while their hands grasp the sword, by their prayers
assail the ear of the Giver of victory ; give me a leader such
as Godfrey, who refused to wear a golden crown in the city
where Christ had been crowned with thorns.   With such
leaders, such soldiers, such pontiffs, let no one doubt of full
success against the Turks." *

Another important affair came before this Convocation of

---

* *Assert. Luth. Confutatio,* in Art. 34.

1515. The Abbot of Winchcombe, Richard Kidderminster, had preached at St. Paul's and spoken strongly against the judges who violated ecclesiastical exemption. The king called an assembly of divines on the matter, and the guardian of the Franciscans, Henry Standish, opposed the doctrine of Winchcombe and the rest, maintaining the right of the civil power to punish criminal clerics, and rejecting ecclesiastical exemption. Standish was prosecuted for his opinions by the bishops, and appealed to the king. He was supported by the temporal lords, and a second assembly was held by the king at Blackfiiars. The bishops denied that they had prosecuted Standish for any advice given by him as king's counsellor, but for speeches of his on other occasions. The secular lords and the judges determined that the whole Convocation which had taken part against Standish was subject to a *præmunire*. Wolsey, in the name of the clergy, disavowed any intention of diminishing the king's prerogative, but asked that the matter might be referred to Rome. The king said : " We are, by the sufferance of God, King of England, and the kings of England in times past never had any superior but God. Know, therefore, that we will maintain the rights of the Crown in this matter like our progenitors ; and as to your decrees, we are satisfied that even you of the spirituality act expressly against the words of several of them, as has been well shown you by some of our spiritual council. You interpret your decrees at your pleasure ; but as for me, I will never consent to your desire any more than my progenitors have done." * Thus at least the king is reported to have spoken by a lawyer named Kellwey, writing in the time of Queen Elizabeth ; but it is probable enough that, though Kellwey had original documents before him regarding the quarrel, he may have himself composed this speech, or given a colouring to it. It seems to represent the Henry of 1530

* *Letters and Papers*, ii. 1314.

better than the Henry of 1515. However, it is not unlikely that even in his youth, without being inclined to quarrel with the pope, the king would have been glad of an opportunity to give a humiliation to his bishops at home, and to enhance his own prerogative.

Standish was made Bishop of St. Asaph's in 1518. The unfixed spelling of those days acting on the pronunciation, and the slovenly pronunciation reacting on the spelling, St. Asaph's was commonly written and pronounced St. Ass's, whence Standish, who was a great opponent of Erasmus, got called by him St. Asinus or Episcopus de St. Asino.* In spite of some singularity in his opinions, he was an advocate of Queen Catharine and an opponent of the Reformation, though not, like Fisher, "usque ad sanguinem".

Though the Bishop of Rochester's name does not occur in the Standish controversy, there can be no doubt as to which side he favoured. Among the MS. seized by the king at his attainder, and now preserved in the Record Office, is an English treatise, partly in Fisher's handwriting, on the rights and dignity of the clergy, and a paper on the same subject in Latin.† These may have been drawn up on this occasion.

Parliament was disolved on 22nd December, 1515, and was not reassembled till after an interval of eight years. It met at Blackfriars on 15th April, 1523, and Sir Thomas More was Speaker. The southern Convocation had assembled at St. Paul's on 20th April, and the Mass of the Holy Ghost had been sung; but, on the first day of meeting, Cardinal

---

* Dr. Taylor, who was both Prolocutor of Convocation and Clerk of Parliament, has made a note in the *Lords' Journals*: "In hoc parliamento et convocatione periculosissimæ seditiones exortæ sunt inter clerum et sæcularem potestatem, super libertatibus ecclesiasticis, quodam Fratre Minore nomine Standish, omnium malorum ministro ac stimulatore".

† *Letters and Papers*, viii. 887.

Wolsey, wishing to assert his superiority as legate over the primate, summoned the members to adjourn to Westminster The poet Skelton thereupon made the epigram :

> " Gentle Paul, lay down thy sweard,
> For Peter of Westminster hath shaven thy beard ".

The legality of this meeting was objected to, and a fresh summons had to be issued that the two Convocations should appear before the Cardinal at Westminster on 7th May. " I pray the Holy Ghost be among them and us both," writes a member of Parliament, on hearing that the Mass of the Holy Ghost, owing to these confusions and jealousies had been three times sung.* The country was then engaged in war with France, and the practical question before Parliament and Convocation was a grant of a large subsidy. It was with difficulty obtained from the Commons, though More, the Speaker, did his best to enforce the wishes of the king and his minister.† His friend Fisher had other views, or perhaps we may say had no official responsibility to cause him to maintain reserve as to his views. Polydore Vergil says that when it was proposed to grant the king a moiety of one year's revenue of all benefices in England, to be levied in five years, the grant was energetically opposed by Fox, Bishop of Winchester, and Fisher, Bishop of Rochester. It was, however, carried.

This matter is in itself one of minor interest. Yet the resistance of the bishop to the wishes of the king is a matter of great importance in estimating his character. He was one of the very few who dared to exercise their judgment and maintain what they judged to be right in days of almost unexampled subserviency and want of principle. Fisher did

---

* *Letters and Papers*, iii. 3024. After all, the legatine synod was soon dismissed, and the Convocation in the two provinces assembled as before.—Lathbury's *History of Convocation*, p. 101 (2nd ed.).

† In Tudor Parliaments the Speaker represented the king rather than the Commons, and promoted the king's plans.

not approve of the king's policy of meddling with continental politics and quarrels. He was therefore conscientiously opposed to levying loans and taxes to carry out this policy. Though it was the ambition of the king and of Cardinal Wolsey to make England important as an arbiter or at least a weight in Europe, Fisher could not see how this promoted the glory of God, or the protection of Christendom against the infidels, or the prosperity of England; and he had the courage to express his conviction, at the risk of displeasing the great cardinal and making an enemy of the imperious king. In a very few years he was called upon to oppose the king in a matter that lay nearer to his heart—that of his divorce; and later on, as the king's will grew more and more perverse, to resist his impious usurpations against the Church and the Holy See. But before entering on the history of these contests, we must consider him as a preacher and a writer during the years of peace and prosperity, when he walked, as it were, hand in hand with the Defender of the Faith.

CHAPTER V.

A MAN may be a great patron and promoter of learning without being a great scholar himself or an assi- duous student. But Fisher was all these. His rhole life was spent among books, and his love of study ncreased rather than relaxed with years. He strove against reat disadvantages in his youth, and profited by every pportunity as he advanced in age. The interruption of the ld intercourse with continental universities, caused by the 'rench wars, retarded the revival of Latin literature in Ingland, and our universities were scarcely recovering from he awful devastations of the great plague of the 14th cen- ury, when they were again thinned and discouraged by the ivil wars of the 15th. Ten years before Fisher entered Cam- ridge, the university library consisted of no more than three undred and thirty volumes, and among these were no Greek uthors, and but few of the heathen classics.* It was ot until 1511 that lectures in Greek were given in Cam- ridge. This language was, therefore, either altogether or lmost unknown to Fisher, while resident at the university.)f his zeal to acquire it and to promote its study, at a later eriod, I will speak presently. The cultivation of a purer atinity than that of the Middle Ages had begun much earlier, nd the style of Fisher is easy and elegant. His writings very eldom lead him to mention the heathen authors, nor do I

* See Mullinger's *University of Cambridge*, i. 324, 327.

know of anything that would suggest that he took any deep
interest in them.   This, however, will not deprive him of a
place among the Humanists, unless it is also refused to his
friend Colet, Dean of St. Paul's, and founder of St. Paul's
school, who, while ordering that the best and purest Latin
should be taught, wishes that Christian authors should be
especially used, mentioning, in particular, Lactantius, Pru-
dentius, Proba, Sedulius, Juvencus, and Baptista Man-
tuanus.*

Fisher's reading must have been incessant, and have
occupied almost every moment he could spare from works
of duty, piety, and necessity.   He is said to have got together
the best private library in England, perhaps in Europe.
Very many of the works he quotes must have been in MS.,
but he evidently procured every new work as it came from
the press.   When replying to Le Fèvre, who made light of
the scholastics, he can quote later authors, as Simon of
Cassia, Ubertin de Casali, Nicolas of Cusa, Mark Vigerius
(Senegallensis), Pico della Mirandula, Baptist of Mantua
(Spagnuoli), and Petrarch.†   In his controversies with Luther

---

* Lupton's *Life of Colet*, p. 279.   Colet writes very strongly
against "the barbary and corruption and Latin adulterate which
ignorant blind fools brought into the world, and with the same hath
distained and poisoned the old Latin speech and the very Roman
tongue, which in the time of Tully and Sallust, and Virgil and Terence,
was used, and which also St. Jerome, and St. Ambrose, and St. Austin,
and many holy doctors learned in their time.   I say that filthiness
in all such abusion, which the late blind world brought in, which
more rather may be called blotterature than literature, I utterly
abanish and exclude out of this school."   This intemperate language
is in great contrast with the moderation with which Fisher speaks of
the later scholastic Latin.   Latin was to some extent a living
lauguage in the Middle Ages, and therefore words had to be coined
to express new ideas.   It was the very same process which made
Colet coin the word "blotterature," which is quite as barbarous as
anything in Scotus.

† *De Unica Magdelena*, lib. iii.

and Œcolampadius, there is scarcely a Greek or Latin Christian writer, now contained in the great collection of Migne, from the 1st to the 13th century, from whom he does not make apt citations, which he could not have borrowed from other writers, since they regarded new controversies, and are introduced by remarks which show conclusively that they were the fruit of his own reading.*

Whether he read any of the Greek fathers in their own tongue does not appear. Sometimes he mentions the translator of the particular book of St. Chrysostom from which he quotes.† But that he had acquired, by his own labour, a fair knowledge of Greek is certain. It was not until after the Greek text of the New Testament, by Erasmus, had appeared, in 1516, with his translation, annotations, and criticisms, that Fisher turned his attention seriously to the study of this language. The book contained a letter of approval of Leo X. to Erasmus, and was published with the express approbation of the Bishop of Basel, in whose diocese it was printed. It had been prepared by Erasmus in great part at Cambridge, where he resided from 1511 to 1513. No wonder, therefore, that the chancellor should be deeply interested in such a work. Erasmus had sent him an early copy.‡ When he was at Cambridge, he had promised to

* See especially, in his work against Œcolampadius, the preface to the fourth book. A very curious investigation might be made from Fisher's works as to the activity of the press up to the end of the first quarter of the 16th century. After quoting from Angelomus, "quia rarior est hujus commentarius," he excuses himself from making citations from Remigius, Druthmarus, Strabus, Rabanus, Haymo, Alcuin, Theodore, Bede (he is dealing with the 7th, 8th, and 9th centuries), "quandoquidem eorum libri communiter habentur".—Ed. Werceburg, 991.

† E.g. (col. 726), "Chrysost., Homil. lxix., Bernardo Brixiano interprete"; (col. 1440), "Hoc scripsit Chrys., Hom. lxxxi. sup Mat., ex traductione Trabezuntii".

‡ Fisher thanks him. Inter Ep. Erasmi, in Append., 103 (Ed. Leyden).

dedicate his book to the Bishop of Rochester, and had only
omitted to do so because he had obtained the privilege of
dedicating it to Pope Leo X.* Archbishop Warham, on
receiving his copy, had greatly praised it to several bishops,
amongst whom was certainly Fisher.† With such stimu-
lants, Fisher would at once devour the Introduction (or
Paraclesis) and the Notes. In June, Erasmus himself came
to England, and, at the express invitation of the bishop,
spent a great part of the month of August with him at
Rochester. Soon after his departure, the bishop writes to
him: " In the New Testament translated by you for the
common good, no one of any judgment can take offence.
. . . I am exercising myself in the reading of St. Paul (in
Greek) according to your directions. I owe it to you that
I can now discover where the Latin differs from the Greek.
Would that I could have you for my master for some
months." ‡ In answer to another letter, Erasmus congratu-
lates him on his progress : " I am very glad that you do
not regret the labour you have spent on Greek ". This is
written on 8th September, 1517.§ The bishop, however,
was not satisfied with the progress he could make without a
master, and begged Erasmus to introduce him to someone
well acquainted with the language, from whom he might
receive a thorough course of instruction. He was then
about forty-eight years old, according to the computation I
have adopted—an age by no means unfit for acquiring
perfectly a new language for one of the bishop's studious
habits, yet which would deter most men from the attempt.
Both Erasmus and Sir Thomas More tried to persuade
William Latimer ‖ to undertake the task. He had learned
Greek in Italy, and was considered an excellent scholar.
He excused himself, however, alleging the time it had taken

* *Erasm. Ep.*, vii. 9.   † *Ibid.*, in App., 65.   ‡ *Ep.* 428, in App.
    § *Ep.* 178, in App.   ‖ Not Hugh Latimer, the heretic.

him to acquire what he knew, his imperfect knowledge, and his disuse of study. He was urged again, but it is not known whether or not he yielded.*

Neither age nor occupation daunted the bishop in his pursuit of sacred science, and in addition to the study of Greek, he took lessons in Hebrew from Robert Wakefield, a Cambridge scholar who had gone abroad in quest of learning, and was supposed to possess not only Greek and Hebrew, but Arabic, Chaldee, and Syriac. It is not likely that his knowledge of these latter languages was very deep, but he was a good teacher of Hebrew, and had already been professor at Tubingen, Paris, and Louvain, and in 1524 lectured in Cambridge. Four years earlier he had given private lessons

---

* Mr. Mullinger has thrown a doubt on Mr. Lewis's assertion that Bishop Fisher did acquire *some* knowledge of Greek (*University of Cambridge*, i. 519, 520). He must have overlooked the assertion of Fisher and the congratulation of Erasmus quoted above; to which I may add the following references in his writings. P. 994, he refers to the mass of St. Basil : " Quam Græco sermone reverendus pater episcopus Londoniensis nobis communicavit ". This was Tunstal, himself a good Greek scholar, and who would have seemed to taunt the Bishop of Rochester with his inferiority, had he given him a book he knew he could not read. Fisher refers also critically to the force of the Greek pronoun (col. 158), to the gender of Greek words (col. 1442), not as to points learnt from another—"omnes qui græce latineque quicquam sciunt " (col. 167), to the meaning of a Greek word (col. 252) ; he corrects the Latin by the Greek (col. 286, 671), and especially (col. 570) whree he has a dissertation on the words ποίμενε and βόσκε (in *John* xxi. 15-17), with a reference to the use of the former word in the Septuagint. Such examples—which might be added to—prove indeed nothing like scholarship, and might, in one less humble and sincere than the bishop, be mere affectation of knowledge not possessed, but transferred from the pages of another. But certainly there is no ground for such a suspicion in a man of so great ability and indomitable energy. The apparatus for learning Greek was scanty enough in those days, but there were several grammars, and with one of these, and the help of the Latin versions of Erasmus and the Vulgate, it was no very difficult thing to become familiar with the Greek Testament.

to the Bishop of Rochester.* Fisher's zeal for Hebrew had been excited by a book of the famous German scholar Reuchlin (or Capnion, as he sometimes called himself), which had been sent to him by Erasmus at the end of 1516.†
His studies, without going very far in that difficult language, caused him at least to pay great attention to the observations of St. Jerome, of Lyra, and of Reuchlin on the Hebrew text.‡

It is more surprising to find the bishop writing with enthusiasm about a new treatise on logic and rhetoric. In his university career the text-book had been the *Parva Logicalia* of Petrus Hispanus.§ Erasmus had recommended to the bishop a treatise, *De Inventione Dialectica*, by Rudolphus Agricola. He writes to Erasmus in 1516, that "he never

* Wakefield says, in his *Syntagma* that it was eighteen years since he taught Hebrew to Fisher and to Thomas Hurskey, the general of the Gilbertines. The date of this book is not known; but as Wakefield died in 1537, even if it appeared only in his last year, the date of teaching Fisher could not be later than 1519. Nor could it be earlier, for it was at the end of that year Wakefield returned from the Continent. (See Mr. Pocock's notes to Harpsfield's *Treatise on the Divorce*, pp. 307, 319.) He became a great opponent of Fisher on the subject of the divorce, with regard to which he played no honourable part. (See his letter to the king, *ibid.*, p. 317.) Harpsfield refutes his book, which seems to have been a conceited and empty production.

† The bishop's interest in Reuchlin was so great that he more than once thought of paying him a special visit.—*Ep. Eras.*, 541, of 8th November, 1520.

‡ He knew enough to consider it no affectation to use such phrases as "ut cuique vel mediocriter in Hebraicis erudito dilucidum est" (col. 675). He reproaches Luther with taking the Hebrew, the Greek, or the Latin in interpreting the Old Testament as it best suited his purpose (col. 676). He relates Hebrew etymologies, and contests the accuracy of Luther's translation (col. 675). He adopts and quotes at length Reuchlin's derivation of "Missa" from the Hebrew. "Non abs re fuerit huc citare quid amicus noster Joannes Capnion, vir in omni literatura celebratissimus, hac de re scripserit" (col. 204).

§ Mullinger, i. 350, and letter of Erasmus to Boville.

read anything .nore learned and delightful on the subject.
Would that he had known it when younger. He would
prefer that to being an archbishop." *

From what has been said the friendly relations subsisting
between Fisher and Erasmus are apparent, but the subject
demands a greater development. How can we explain an
intimate friendship and mutual esteem between men so very
different in character? The reality of their friendship
admits of no doubt. Erasmus is not always straight-for-
ward; and now that his letters are gathered together, we can
see that he wrote many pleasant things concerning his
patrons, in letters likely to come to their knowledge, while
he has far different appreciations in other times and places.
But his letters will be searched in vain for anything unfavourable to the Bishop of Rochester. Everywhere he
speaks of him in the very highest terms. The only approach
to criticism or depreciation is in a letter addressed to Henry
VIII.'s Italian secretary Ammonius. With him Erasmus
was very intimate, and on easy and (so to say) convivial
terms. Erasmus writes to him from the bishop's palace at
Rochester on 17th August, 1516 : " Rochester has prevailed
on me to spend ten days with him. I have regretted it
more than ten times." But his regret arose either from the
place, of the insalubrity of which he speaks strongly elsewhere, or from his anxiety to get to the Continent. So at
least Ammonius interprets him, for in his reply he says that
he dares not ask Erasmus to stay with him ten days, since
he is in such a hurry to get away. He will venture, however, to invite him, though all are not like the Bishop of
Rochester.† In fact, Erasmus protracted his visit beyond
ten days. It was on this occasion he put the bishop on the
road of his Greek studies.

* *Ep.* 429, in App. This treatise had only recently been published, long after its author's death.
† *Ep.*, viii. 26, 27 (Lond. Ed.).

7

Erasmus was born in 1465, and was therefore a few years older than the bishop. His first visit to England was made in 1497, at the invitation of William Blount, Lord Mountjoy, who had been his pupil in Paris. On this occasion he made the acquaintance of Colet and More, and other of Fisher's friends, and not improbably of the bishop also. In the spring of 1506 he was again in England, and was admitted Bachelor and Doctor of Divinity at Cambridge, as well as at Oxford.* At that time Fisher was president of Queen's, and must certainly have met him, but Erasmus left almost immediately for Italy, and did not return to England until the end of 1509. He was at first the guest of Sir Thomas More, in whose house he wrote his *Moriæ Encomium*. In a letter written in 1510 he thus speaks of the Bishop of Rochester : " Either I am greatly mistaken, or Fisher is a man with whom no one in our time can be compared, either for holiness of life or greatness of soul. I except only the Archbishop of Canterbury." † It was, no doubt, by the influence of Fisher that Erasmus, having resolved to make a stay in England, settled at Cambridge rather than at Oxford. The zeal for Greek, however, in the university did not answer the expectations of the chancellor or of the lecturer. Erasmus' lectures were scantily attended. His own health was bad, and the plague drove away many of the students. By Fisher's influence he was appointed Lady Margaret Professor of Divinity. Of the subject or success of his lectures nothing has been recorded ; but as there is no record of collision or contradiction, we must conclude that his efforts in behalf of Patristic studies aroused no alarm, even if they excited little enthusiasm. ‡

* For Cambridge, Mullinger, i. 453 ; for Oxford, Seebohm's *Oxford Reformers.*

† *Ep.* 109 (Ed. Leyden).

‡ The eagerness of some modern writers to see in every advance in liberal studies a dawning of the " Reformation," and their perplexity at finding so little opposition, is amusing. Speaking of Colet's

Erasmus had certainly no reason to complain of his treatment in England. Archbishop Warham had presented him to the rectory of Aldington in Kent ; and though non-resident, he drew from it an income of £20. The Bishop of Rochester gave him an annual pension of a hundred

lectures on S. Paul at Oxford in 1496, Mr. Seebohm writes: "The announcement of Colet's lectures was likely to cause them (*i.e.*, the Oxford doctors) some uneasiness. They may well have asked, whether, if the exposition of the Scriptures were to be really revived at Oxford, so dangerous a duty should not be restricted to those duly authorised to discharge it" (*Oxford Reformers*, p. 4). This is a fair specimen of Mr. Seebohm's book. It is theory, not history—what was "likely," what "may have well been". He has no vestige of any "uneasiness" or opposition to record. Erasmus tells Colet: "There is not a doctor who will not lend him (Colet) a hand or give him attentive audience, though he is so much younger" (*Ib.*, p. 131). Erasmus, describing the success of Colet's lectures, says: "Nullus erat ibi doctor vel theologiæ vel juris, nullus abbas, aut alioqui dignitate præditus, quin illum audiret etiam allatis codicibus "—which is all to their praise. Mr. Seebohm's Protestant imagination thus interprets Erasmus: "The very boldness of the lecturer and the novelty of the subject were enough to draw an audience at once. Doctors and abbots flocked with the students into the lecture hall, led by curiosity *doubtless* at first, or *it may be*, like the Pharisees of old, bent upon finding somewhat whereof they might accuse the man whom they wished to silence (!). But since they came again and again, as the term went by, bringing their note-books with them, it soon became clear that they continued to come with some better purpose " (p. 32). "Allatis codicibus " I should take to mean their copies of St. Paul, not their note-books, but that is unimportant. Mr. Seebohm has written much about Pseudo-Dionysius, but he has surpassed the author of the Divine Hierarchies in the imagination with which he has drawn a Pseudo-Colet. Mr. Mullinger has been too much under the influence of Mr. Seebohm's style of writing when he regards it as "certainly a remarkable circumstance" that Erasmus "succeeded in avoiding anything approaching to a collision " (*History*, i. 495); but he does not, like Mr. Seebohm, draw a fancy picture of men who came to scoff and stopped to pray. Mr. Lupton's *Life of Colet* is not disfigured, like Mr. Seebohm's, with groundless theories and modern speculations. A Catholic may read it with pleasure as well as instruction.

florins. He held the Margaret Professorship, which was well endowed, and other emoluments, so that it has been calculated that "his total income could scarcely be less than £700 in English money of the present day".[*] If then he complained to some of his friends, it must be set down to a certain avarice from which he was not quite free, or to his bad health. On looking back a few years later to the results of his labours, he took a more cheerful view. "England," he wrote, "has two universities, Cambridge and Oxford. Greek literature is taught in both, but in Cambridge peacefully, because the chancellor of that university is John Fisher, Bishop of Rochester, whose life is no less theological than his learning."[†] In 1521, he wrote to Louis Vives, complaining that Louvain still opposed the revival of learning, and contrasting it with Cambridge: "Three years ago," he says, "the Bishop of Rochester, a true bishop and true theologian, told me that in place of (the old) sophistical argumentations, now sober and wholesome disputations are carried on between theologians, at the end of which they are not only more learned, but also better men".[‡]

If Erasmus eulogises Fisher, Fisher also has great esteem for Erasmus. In writing his answer to Œcolampadius in 1527, he thus speaks of that heresiarch's contempt of Peter Lombard, St. Thomas, and the scholastics. "Do you think that all were asses and men without judgment who approved the books of the Master of the Sentences? You are greatly mistaken if you think so. The scholastics may have been deficient in eloquence—that I will not contest—but they were not deficient in knowledge of the Scriptures. Does St. Thomas appear to you to have been ignorant of the Scriptures, whose commentaries have been admired by those

---

[*] Mullinger, i. 505.
[†] The contrast implied is to the faction of Greeks and Trojans at Oxford in 1519.
[‡] *Ep.* 611.

who are the acknowledged leaders in eloquence? Erasmus, a man of admirable judgment, as is clear from his annotations (to the New Testament), thus extols St. Thomas: 'In my opinion there is no modern theologian who has equalled him in diligence, or has a sounder judgment or more solid erudition'. And John Pico Mirandula says that St. Thomas is justly called the flower of theology."* It would be easy to quote similar passages where Erasmus is named with honour, but facts are stronger than words. In addition to the bishop's recommendation of Erasmus for the Divinity professorship at Cambridge, he selected him to be his companion in travel and theologian in the Council of Lateran. † We have seen that this project fell through. It was Fisher who urged Erasmus to write his paraphrase of St. John's Gospel, ‡ and who first suggested, and then urged over and over again, his work on preaching. §

As no one will call in question the orthodoxy of Fisher or his zeal for the Catholic faith, it is clear from all this that the bishop was thoroughly convinced of the sincerity of the attachment of Erasmus to the Church. He has nowhere expressed a general approbation of all that Erasmus wrote, but he refused to join in the outcry against him, on account of certain opinions, which he had put forward rashly but not obstinately maintained, or certain expressions which he might himself regret. Erasmus was not a mere humanist; he regretted and protested against the *paganism* of many of the Italian humanists. His indefatigable toil was given to the translation of the Greek fathers, the editing of the Latin fathers, and to the exegetical study of Scripture. These labours gained him the support and approbation not only of Fisher, but of Wolsey, Warham, Fox, and Tunstal in England, of many of the holiest and most lear..ed bishops of the

---

* *Contra Œcol.*, i., cap. 2.   † *Ep. Erasm.*, 167.
‡ *Ep.*, 29th Nov., 1522.   § *Ep.* 661, 698, 746.

Continent, and still more of the Sovereign Pontiffs Leo X., Adrian VI., Clement VII., and Paul III.

There are letters of Erasmus to Fisher in which he speaks very strongly against the abuses in the Church, and ' he clearly feels that in this he may speak openly, and has with him the bishop's sympathy. But he never indulges with him in the sarcasms and levities that show the less favourable side of his character.

It is very probably owing to Fisher's gentle forbearance with what was imperfect and cordial sympathy with what was good in Erasmus, that he exercised so powerful an influence over him. Mr. Mullinger, in considering their relations at Cambridge, says of Fisher : " It would have been perhaps impossible to find in an equal degree, in any one of his contemporaries, at once that moderation, integrity of life, and disinterestedness of purpose which left the bigot no fault to find, and that liberality of sentiment and earnest desire of reform which conciliated far bolder and more advanced thinkers ". And he adds : " Over Erasmus, whose wandering career had not, by his own ingenuous confession, been altogether free from reproach, a character so saintly and yet so sympathising exercised a kind of spell ".* A modern German biographer of Fisher, Dr. Kerker, has very well shown how the opponents of Erasmus rendered good service by refuting his exaggerations and preventing him from having everything in his own way, which was assuredly not always the way of the Holy Ghost, while the Bishop of Rochester and the protectors of Erasmus also did good service to the Church by keeping within it a man who under their guidance was capable of much good, and who might have done incalculable harm had he been rudely repulsed.†

The same author remarks very appositely that Edward Lee, who was a passionate adversary of Erasmus, accusing

---

* *History*, i. 496.   † *Life of Fisher*, ch. xii.

him of every heresy, ended himself, when Archbishop of
York, by yielding in the most cowardly manner to Henry,
and denying the supremacy of the Sovereign Pontiff; while
Fisher, who was lenient in his judgment of the flaws in
Erasmus' Annotations, and defended his substantial orthodoxy and great service to religion, was himself an invincible
martyr of the Catholic faith. Yet Lee was mean and Phari-
saical enough, when the death of Fisher reproached him
with his own recreancy, to attribute it to mere obstinacy of
character, alleging that his partiality for Erasmus had made
him blind to his errors and unjust to his opponents.*

The truth is that Fisher lived not only in a time of transi-
tion but of sifting. It is quite possible that had Fisher and
Colet, Luther and Erasmus, met together at the house of
Sir Thomas More in 1512, they would have conversed on
the state of the Church and of the world with a seemingly
cordial unanimity. They have all written strongly on the
evils of the day, the corruptions of the Roman curia, the
low state of religious orders, the general ignorance, and all
were zealous for reform. But circumstances at last brought
out the real antagonism that then lay hid. Colet indeed
died before the outbreak of heresy, but we have every
assurance, both in his holy and ascetic life, and in his profound piety, that had he lived he would have ranged himself
with More and Fisher. Luther, a man of uncontrolled
temper and sensual temperament, ever passing from one
excess to the other, without distrust of himself, gradually
drifts into rebellion and pride, and then, blinded by evil
passions, learns to hate the Church and to close his eyes to
everything but the things that could feed his hatred. Erasmus has no such strong feelings. He thinks the world is
out of joint, but it is not his business to set it right. He
could laugh and mock at it among men of letters, if admired

* Strype, *Eccl. Mem.*, i. 191; *Letters, &c.*, x. 99.

and applauded in doing so, or lament over it with seeming earnestness with holy men like Fisher. But he would be no martyr: he loved peace. He would neither stir up riot and contention among the populace like Luther, nor endure himself the violence of kings like Fisher.* He was a religious, but he had got himself secularised; a priest, but we have no record that he ever stood at the altar.

More and Fisher were men of prayer, men who not only spoke or wrote about God, but lived in intimate communication with Him. They had a profound sense of the presence of the Holy Ghost in the Church, and therefore deplored so deeply the evil that dishonoured it. But they never confounded the Church, which is God's work, with the evil that is of man's doing. Therefore there are two periods in their lives. While heresy was unknown, their voices were raised to bewail and to rebuke the corruptions in the Church. When heresy began to rail at God's work, their zeal was aroused in its defence. We have now to consider Fisher in the first period of contest.

* Early in Luther's course (5th July, 1521) Erasmus thus wrote to Pace: "By what spirit Luther has written I cannot conceive, but certainly he has brought great disrepute on the cultivators of good literature. Much of his teaching and admonitions was excellent. Would to God he had not spoilt what was good by intolerable evil. But even though he had written all piously I had no mind to risk my life for the truth. All have not strength enough to be martyrs; and I fear that if tumults arise I should imitate Peter. If the pope and the emperor make good decrees, I obey piously; if they make bad ones, I yield safely. I think such a course is allowed to good men, if there is no hope of success (by acting otherwise)."—*Ep.* 583. Later on he spoke more strongly against Luther, but even in his lament over Fisher's death, not long before his own, he repeats the same vile and cowardly sophisms about yielding to the civil power.

CHAPTER VI.

IT was not to satisfy greedy intellectual curiosity that the Bishop of Rochester gave himself so ardently to study. He knew that he was one of those to whom it is said : You are the light of the world. His natural talents, his special opportunities of study at Cambridge, and his position as a bishop, placed him under the obligation of diffusing that light as far as possible. This he did both by example, by preaching, and by writing.

Neglect of preaching was perhaps the greatest evil of the 15th century, and the source of every other. There were innumerable pulpits from which the Word of God was never heard ; others were silent except on the Sundays in Lent.* Very few congregations had any experience of a weekly or a monthly sermon. Such sermons as were preached were often ambitious, far-fetched, ill-judged efforts at oratory. Such compositions could neither come spon- taneously to the preacher's lips nor be easily committed to his memory. Hence a custom prevailed of reading the sermon instead of preaching it.† All this greatly afflicted the Bishop of Rochester, and he set himself to correct it by every means in his power.

Dr. Hall has told us how indefatigably he preached in his

---

* I take pulpit in a wide sense, for of pulpits proper there were very few.

† Erasmus says : "Quosdam de charta concionari, id quod multi frigide faciunt in Anglia ".— *Ep. ad Judocum Jonam.*

own diocese, "which custom he used, not only in his younger days when health served, but also even to his extreme age, when many times his weary and feeble legs were not able to sustain his weak body standing, but forced him to have a chair, and so to teach sitting". In the first year of his episcopate be preached that series of sermons on the Penitential Psalms which we still possess.* They were preached by the Lady Margaret's desire, and in her presence, but whether at Rochester, London, or Cambridge does not appear. They seem to be composed on the model of St. Augustine's tractates on the Psalms. There is little of strict exegetical analysis, yet the interpretations are not trivial or fanciful. Each text serves as a basis for earnest, solid reflections, admirable in themselves, though the reader is perplexed sometimes as to what gave rise to them, or why other moralities might not as legitimately have been drawn. No one can read them without a conviction of the deep piety and fervent zeal of the preacher. A tender and pathetic sermon on Our Lord's Passion has also been preserved. It was preached on Good Friday, and must have occupied two or three hours in delivery, if preached in the form in which it was afterwards published. Of his sermons against Luther I have already spoken.

The best known of his English works are the funeral sermons of Henry VII. and of Lady Margaret, his mother. That of the king was preached in the cathedral church of St. Paul on the 10th May, 1509, his body having been deposited there previous to its interment at Westminster ;

* They were first printed by Pynson in 1505. Other editions appeared in 1508, 1510, 1519, 1528, 1529, some by Wynkin de Worde. They were translated into Latin by Dr. Fen, who also put into Latin a sermon on the Justice of a Christian and a Pharisee. No copy of this sermon in English is now known to exist. Fisher is said by Lord Herbert to have preached before Henry and Catharine after the victory of Flodden.

that of Lady Margaret at Westminster, at her month's mind. She died on 29th June, 1509. They contain no empty flattery ; indeed, at the beginning of that of the king the eulogy is based on the three resolutions his majesty had taken (and made known to several) not long before his last sickness. These were : " 1. A true reformation of all them that were officers and ministers of his laws, to the intent that justice henceforward truly and indifferently might be executed in all causes. 2. Another, that the promotions of the Church that were at his disposition should from henceforth be disposed to able men, such as were virtuous and well-learned. 3. That as touching the dangers and jeopardies for things done in times past, he would grant a pardon generally unto all his people." The sermons are filled with interesting personal details, are very pathetic, and sometimes even eloquent.

There are few European languages that possess sermons published in the vernacular at so early a date.* · The zeal of Fisher to promote preaching in others has been already alluded to. When he was vice-chancellor he obtained a bull from Pope Alexander VI. in 1503, empowering the Chancellor and University of Cambridge yearly to appoint twelve doctors or masters to preach the Word of God in all parts of England, Scotland, and Ireland, both to the clergy and the people, notwithstanding any ordinance or constitution to the contrary.† By his influence with Lady Margaret, in addition to the Divinity professorships founded in Oxford and Cambridge, in the statutes of which preaching was not forgotten,

---

* St. Thomas of Villanova, in Spain, wrote his sermons in Latin, leaving now and then a few words in Spanish, though of course he preached in Spanish. He died in 1555, and his sermons were not published till 1572. St. Charles Borromeo preached to the people in Italian. Possevinus took down his words and translated them into Latin. Luther published a sermon in German in 1523.

† Mullinger, i. 440 ; Lewis, ii. 261.

a chantry,* called the Lady Margaret Preachership), was founded in Cambridge. He also urged Erasmus to write a treatise on preaching. As Erasmus had never been in the pulpit, it may be wished that the bishop had himself undertaken a task for which he was certainly more competent than his friend. The latter, indeed, seems to have felt much reluctance, and yielded at last with so many delays that his work did not appear till shortly after Fisher's death. †

The bishop was modest, without affected humility, and was led to publish by the prompting of others. It was at the request or command of the Lady Margaret that he printed his sermons on the Psalms and his panegyric of Henry VII., and, either from popular request or from a spirit of gratitude, that of Lady Margaret herself. It was by royal command that he published his sermon against Luther. His first work of controversy appeared in 1519, and this also was written by request. A learned Dominican named Jaques Le Fèvre,‡ who was in high esteem among the party of the new learning, or the humanists, had written a dissertation to prove that Catholic popular tradition had attributed to one person what is said in the Gospel of no less than three ; or that three Marys—the converted

---

* The holder had to offer mass for the countess and her intentions. (See *Memoir of Lady Margaret*, p. 94.)

† There is an excellent dissertation on preaching in Bromyard's *Summa Prædicantium* sub voce *Prædicator*. Bromyard was a learned Dominican, who taught in Cambridge at the beginning of the 15th century. I do not think his work was known to Fisher. It has been several times printed, and is well worth reading. Bishop Allcock, the founder of Jesus College, Cambridge, published a book called *Galli-cantus ad Prædicatores*, which I have not seen. In 1528, the Bishop of Ely decreed in synod, " toto clero consentiente," that every parson, vicar, and curate should read every quarter, on a Sunday to be fixed by himself, a part of a book called *Exoneratorium Curatorum*, so as to finish it each year.—Wilkins, iii.

‡ Faber and Fabricius in Latin, Smith in English.

sinner, the sister of Martha, and the woman out of whom
Our Lord cast seven devils—have been erroneously confounded together into one Mary Magdalen. Le Fèvre's
reputation caused the book to be immediately bought up,
and it went into a second edition. The Bishop of Paris,
Etienne Poucher, was then on an embassy in England, and,
in a letter to the Bishop of Rochester, remarked how many
evils might result from rash criticisms, especially at the time
when a great contempt was affected for tradition and for the
ignorance of the Middle Ages, and when novelty was the
fashion. He asked Fisher's opinion on the matter in dispute. Although Fisher had already looked through Faber's
dissertation, and remarked in it many things he disliked,
his respect for Faber's orthodoxy and learning had caused
him to take for granted that he had at least erudition on
his side ; but on his attention being thus called to the
matter, he read the Gospels with minute care, examined the
sacred interpreters of all ages, and then re-read Faber's essay.
The result was not merely a conviction of the accuracy of
the common tradition, but a very unfavourable opinion of
Faber's reasoning powers, and still more of his captious
and contemptuous spirit. He at once composed a thorough
treatise on the subject, under the title *De Unica Magdalena.*
It was printed in Paris, though at first there was some difficulty in finding a publisher, so great was the respect for
Faber. But Fisher's book was bought up, and went into a
second edition, in which he softened the asperity of some
things he had said of Faber, and also replied to another
author named Judocus Clichtovæus.* Erasmus had got

* Referring to the second edition, Erasmus says : " In posteriore
ut stylus est cultior ita minus est stomachi " (21st April, 1519). He
had been rather sore that a humanist should be treated in the style
the humanists were fond of employing towards the "obscurantists ".
He thought it might give a handle to the enemies of classical studies (2nd
April, 1519, *Ep.* 404). One of Erasmus' correspondents, Bilibaldus,
is enraged with Fisher : " Per Deum immortalem ! cui boni nebulones

the book printed, and acknowledged that the victory was with Fisher, yet he did not relish an attack made by a humanist on a humanist, and writes to the Bishop: "I wish your labour had been spent on some other matter, although your work is both pious and elegant. But that commentary, of which you showed me some specimens which greatly delighted me, in which you trace out the order and connection of the Gospel history, would in my opinion have done more honour to your name." * This Concordance of the Gospels has unfortunately not come down to us. The treatise on St. Mary Magdalen has not lost any of its interest.†

Other and fiercer controversies were now at hand. A man of the Bishop of Rochester's position and learning could not be silent amidst the attacks made by Luther and others against the faith of the Catholic Church. I do not propose here to analyse his various works against Luther and Œcolampadius. Though they are monuments of prodigious learning and acumen, considering that they were the first that appeared against the new errors, and the erudition they display was all of Fisher's own gathering, the arguments all the result of his own thought, yet, as manuals of controversy, they have been superseded by later writings which they helped to create. The standard writers, such as Bellarmine and Stapleton, are not slow to acknowledge the debt they owe to Fisher (Roffensis).

The book which gained for Henry the title of Defender of the Faith I do not consider to be Fisher's, but Henry's own. It is attributed to Henry by Fisher himself in such

isti unquam pepercerunt? Quid intentatum reliquerunt ut divam Mariam Magdalenam assertori suo Fabro eriperent, ac cum turpissimis scortis in olidum lupanar detruderent?"—Inter *Ep. Erasmi.*, 561.

* *Ep.* 404.

† The first edition, apparently, is reprinted in the Wirceburg collection of Fisher's works.

terms as to seem to make it impossible that Fisher could have had any large share in it. *

The learning, however, of the bishop was called in to defend his sovereign against the ribald answer of Luther. Hence his book, sometimes called *Against the Babylonian Captivity*, but more properly, *A Defence of the Assertions of the King of England against Luther's Babylonian Captivity.* It was Henry who "asserted" the seven sacraments of the Church against Luther's attacks. Fisher does not directly answer Luther's first work, but Luther's reply to Henry, though in doing so he has often to quote all three. The dispute thus becomes somewhat intricate, and this is the least pleasant of his books to read. It appeared in 1525, in Cologne, having been kept back for a considerable time by some reports of Luther's probable amendment. †

Simultaneously with it appeared another work, called *Defence of the Sacred Priesthood against Luther.* A third

---

* As I have published a special dissertation on this subject, called *The Defender of the Faith*, I do not repeat the arguments here. The matter regards Henry's life, not Fisher's. Since I wrote, the Bishop of Chester has published his *Lectures*. I am glad to confirm my view by his great authority: "Henry's book against Luther, which, whatever assistance he may have received, was in conception and execution entirely his own, was an extraordinary work for a young king".—*Lect.* xi., p. 247.

† It was dedicated to Nicolas West, Bishop of Ely. Luther's reply to Henry was dated 15th July, 1522. Fisher at once began an answer, which he left incomplete, or, at least, unpublished, for nearly two years. In the meantime, he composed another work in defence of the Christian Priesthood against Luther, and printed in Paris his *Lutheranæ Assertionis Confutatio* (by Chevalier, 1523). Then he sent the two other works to Cologne. When they left his hands Luther was not yet married (25th June, 1525), since Fisher nowhere refers to that event. Owing to the keeping back of the book in defence of the king, he in one place alludes to the work on the priest-hood *to be* written, in another as *already* written. Henry did not reply to Luther's attack on him, but when Luther wrote an apology for his attack, the king replied in very strong but dignified language.

work against Luther was published two years earlier in
Paris, called *Lutheranæ Assertionis Confutatio*, in answer to
the articles put forth by Luther when he burnt the pope's
bull.   He had just published this, when Tunstal showed
him a book by Ulrich Wellen, attempting to prove that St.
Peter never was at Rome.   As this, if true, would have
upset many of the arguments by which Fisher had proved
the papal supremacy against Luther, he felt himself obliged
to reply to it, which he did, with much erudition.   Thus,
then, including his elaborate sermon, we have five works of
Fisher's against the errors of Luther.

The style of these Latin works is diffuse; no links are un-
supplied; recapitulations are made and conclusions drawn.
The citations from the fathers are numerous and apposite,
and the explanations of Holy Scripture give proof of long
and deep study.   Fisher often uses Erasmius' version of the
New Testament or his own, instead of that of the Vulgate.*
This he would certainly not have done had the decree of
the Council of Trent then been issued, that "*among Latin
versions* the Vulgate should be taken as authentic in public
disputations".

It is not surprising that Fisher's books, though highly
approved by the learned, were not much read in Germany.
Erasmus, writing on 26th March, 1524, says: "Nothing is
done by means of books against these men" (the German

---

* At the end of the edition of his collected works are some Preca-
tiones, or Psalms, made up of selections from the Psalter put into more
classical Latin.   After these are some translations from the New
Testament.   There is nothing to prove that these are by Fisher, or
(if they are) that they were ever intended to be seen by others.   They
are probably merely exercises of his own.   I give a few words of the
Magnificat: "Magnificat animus meus Dominum, exultatque mea
mens de Deo Servatore meo: qui spectaverit humilitatem ancillæ
suæ, unde me in posterum beatam prædicatura sunt omnia sæcula.
Quoniam mihi magna fecit præpotens ille, cujus et nomen sanctum
est et misericordia perennis erga reverentes eum," &c.

Lutherans); "no one dares even to print anything written against Luther, nor read what has been printed elsewhere". And, on 25th March, 1529, he explains his own reasons for not writing any more, after his book on Free-will: "I saw the pamphlets of Latomus, of Sutor, of Jerome, of Bedda, not only laughed at, but giving confidence to those who were inclined to the new dogmas; and even the books of John, Bishop of Rochester, a man who had every quality of a theologian, utterly neglected".* This is partly explained by the natural love of novelty, partly by the special circumstances of those days. Fisher writes: "If heresies raised their heads so quickly after the shedding of Our Saviour's Blood, while the gifts of the Holy Ghost were still burning in the breasts of many, and the world was made bright with miracles, and if so many were then turned away from the truth, what must we expect now, in the perilous time of which the Apostles prophesied? I think the world was never before so generally inclined to listen to heresy as it is now." †

Besides this, Fisher was at a great disadvantage in contending with a man like Luther. To attack and deny is short and easy, to defend or explain is long and difficult. A proverb says: "Error runs round the world, while Truth is pulling on her boots". Luther was bold, unscrupulous, vehement, and he appealed to national prejudices and evil passions. To take one specimen. Luther writes as follows: "Be certain and never let yourself be persuaded to the contrary, if you wish to hold pure Christian truth, that there is no visible and external priesthood in the New Testament, except what Satan has set up through human lies. Sacrificing masses have been invented to insult the Lord's Testament, therefore nothing in the whole world is so much to be avoided and detested. It is better to be a public bawd

---

* *Ep.* 1033 (" in quo viro nihil desideres "),
† Proœm. of 4th Book against Œcol.

S

or robber than a priest of this sort."* That such language should have been listened to by the descendants of those for whom St. Boniface and the brothers Hewald preached and laid down their lives was marvellous, but it is clear that those who could listen to it would never listen to anything else. A strange delusion or a fierce rage had taken possession of brain and heart. Fisher might exclaim: "O God, who can patiently hear such impious falsehoods cast upon the mysteries of Christ? Who can read such blasphemies without bitter grief and tears if he has but the least spark of Christian piety in his breast?"† But a controversy like this scarcely admitted of calm discussion. When it was stated in such terms, men took their sides at once, and there was war to the death. I do not mean, however, to assert that the bishop's zealous labours were wasted. They bore fruit in England and other countries. When Eck of Ingoldstadt, one of Luther's most strenuous opponents, visited England in 1525, he was surprised to find that Luther was of no account. In the dedicatory epistle to his book, *De Sacrificio Missæ*, he writes: "When last summer I passed over to England to visit the king and the Bishop of Rochester, though tumults and seditions were raging in Germany, I never once heard the name of Luther mentioned except in malediction". Fisher alludes to this visit in his book against Œcolampadius,‡ and I have been fortunate enough to recover a letter hitherto unknown, which brings together these two great theologians. It is a letter addressed by Fisher to the Duke of Bavaria, Prince Wendelin:

"To the illustrious Prince Wendelin, Count Palatine of the Rhine, Duke of Bavaria, my lord and friend in Christ.

---

* "Præstat publicum lenonem aut latronem esse quam hujus generis sacerdotem."—*De Abrog. Missa.*

† Pref. to *Defence of S. Priesthood.*

‡ "Joannes Eckius, quem in Anglia vidisse pergratum fuit."—Prœm. of lib. i.

"You will wonder, excellent prince, at receiving a letter from me, a man unknown to you. I write not so much for myself as for the learned man who is the bearer of this letter. It chanced that he passed over into England, and when I heard who had come, not only was I delighted, but by my persuasion he visited our most illustrious king, and thus it happened that he stayed longer than he had intended. So if he has too long interrupted his lectures in your university, the loss is more than compensated, for your name, which was hitherto not known to us, has now become famous. We have learnt from him and greatly congratulate him [you?] on the fact, that you are a prince entirely Catholic, and that you oppose these Lutheran factions, as a true Christian should do, with all your strength. May God preserve you, and all the princes of Germany who are still orthodox, in the same mind. Wishing your highness health and long life, and eagerly desiring to see you.

"JOHN OF ROCHESTER.

" *From Rochester,* 12 *Kal. Sept.* 1525."*

* I have found this letter transcribed in a contemporary hand in a volume in which Henry's and Fisher's books are bound together, which formerly belonged to the Scotch monastery of Ratisbon, and is now in the possession of the Catholic Bishop of Argyle and the Isles. The copyist writes at the bottom : " The illustrious John Eck brought this letter to our prince ". As the letter is unpublished, I give it in the original.

"Illustri Principi D. Vindelino Comiti Palatino Rheni ac Bavarie duci et domino ac amico nostro Christiano S. D.

"Miraberis optime princeps quod homo tibi incognitus iam ad tuam celsitudinem scripserim. Verum istud feci, non tam mei ipsius caussa quam huius eruditissimi viri qui litteras has ad te nunc attulit, contigit enim ut is in Angliam traiiceret, quem ubi noverimus quis nam esset non solum nobis advenit optatissimus, verum etiam suasu nostro regem nostrum illustrissimum adiit eius visendi gratia, quo factum est ut complures hic dies remoratus sit preter institutum suum. Quare si prelectiones interea suas quas in gymnasio tuo profitetur, diucius quam par esset intermiserit id sane dispendium alio maiori

To return now to the Bishop of Rochester's controversial works. In order to judge his character fairly we must note the great difference between controversy in his day and in our own. Protestants are now born into an inheritance of error, and however novel and ephemeral may be the special form of doctrine of this or that sect, the revolt from the Church as a whole has a prestige of more than three centuries. Such men deserve compassion rather than anger. Those with whom Fisher had to do were all apostate Catholics, many of them apostate priests and religious. Their opposition to Catholic doctrine was a crime, not an error. Fisher knew well how to make this distinction. Luther had said: "The Roman Pontiff never was over all the Churches of the world; he is not now, nor ever will be, I hope. He never was over the Churches of Greece, India, Persia, Egypt, Africa, nor is he now, as he himself loudly and sadly laments." Fisher replies: "Why mention Churches so far off? You might have instanced Churches that we know better, as that of Bohemia and others. But we answer as to all—they withdrew themselves from obedience to the Roman Pontiff, either from malice or from pardonable ignorance. And I would rather believe it is the latter, in the case of some at least, as many of the simpler sort who are led into error by interpreters of Scripture, such as you, or perhaps have never heard any discussion at all on this matter. And such as those I would not easily condemn,

compendio resarcivit, nam Nomen Tuum quod hac tenus ignoravimus hic apud nos iam celebre fecit, per illum enim accepimus de quo ei plurimum gratulamur te principem vere Catholicum esse atque Lutherianorum factionibus, uti verum Christianum decet, totis obsistere viribus, quam tibi ceterisque Germaniæ principibus, qui adhuc in orthodoxa fide persistunt mentem perpetuo servet Deus Optimus Maximus. Fœlix ac diu valeat tua Sublimitas. Ex Roffa 12 Kal. Septembris 1525. Tue Amplitudinis vidende cupidus Joannes Roffensis.

"Clarissimus DD. Joannes Eccius has litteras nostro principi attulit."

if their separation is due to no depravity of their minds, and
if they implicitly believe this truth also, and would believe
it willingly provided they were taught it. But as to those
who have separated themselves maliciously, I assert openly
that they no more belong to the orthodox Church than the
Churches of the Arians, the Donatists, or the like."* Certainly he who thus wrote would be very pitiful and forbear-
ing in dealing with his countrymen, could he now return to
earth.

But he made no pretence of gentleness towards heresiarchs
such as Luther and Œcolampadius.† Luther in challenging
the world had said he would choose his own weapons, and
would fight with the Scriptures only. Fisher replied that
"when a public enemy invades a village he has no choice how
he will fight, for all must rise up to repel him, with the first
weapons that come to hand : sticks, swords, spears, arrows,
or stones. Heretics are not to be admitted to disputation
with choice of weapons. The Apostle does not say : Reject
a heretic after the first and second disputation, but after the
first and second admonition. When that has been made to
no effect, he is an acknowledged enemy, and we must repel
his attack as we choose, not as he chooses."‡

A specimen or two of Fisher's retorts will throw some
light on his own character. Luther writes : " Does not
Paul say : Prove all things, hold fast that which is good ?
and again : If anyone bring another gospel besides that
which has been preached, let him he anathema ? and St.

---

* *Assert. Lut. Confutatio.*   *Contra* Art. 25, col. 544, and again
more fully col. 579.

† " Legat qui volet Hieronymum, legat Augustinum, legat Hilarium
et cæteros qui cum hæreticis digladiantur, non reperiet illos blandis
et mollibus verbis rem agere, sed rigidis et asperis, quemadmodum a
severis Christi religionis propugnatoribus, inimicos veritatis et adver-
sarios fidei tractari decet."—*Contra Œcol.*, Præf.

‡ *Ibid.*, in Procem.

John : Prove the spirits whether they be of God ? Therefore, that man clearly despises all those Apostolic warnings
who admits all the sayings of the fathers without judgment—
the judgment, I mean, of the Spirit, which is only to be
found in the Holy Scriptures." " Well spoken !" says
Fisher. " Therefore, if the writings of the fathers are to be
so carefully examined, who all sought after unity, how much
more diligently are yours to be scrutinised who divide unity.
If he who spoke contrary to St. Paul was to be anathe-
matised, you will incur a tenfold anathema, who in so many
articles differ from the universal Church. If spirits are to
be proved, what kind of spirit must yours be ! He would,
indeed, despise the warnings of the Apostle who should
give heed to your fantastical novelties, in opposition to the
unanimous interpretations of the fathers, whom the Holy
Ghost instructed through the Holy Scriptures." *

Again, Luther says that the Bereans searched the Scriptures
to see if Paul spoke truly. How much more must we
search them to see if the fathers spoke truly. Fisher replies
that there is no similarity between the two cases: "The
Bereans heard a multitude of strange things—that the
Gentiles were now admitted to grace, that the Law had
ceased, the priesthood been transferred, and all this by
Christ's death, whom their own nation had slain. No
wonder they searched the Scriptures, especially when St.
Paul bade them do so, to see if these things were really
foretold. But what then ? We know for certain that we
live in the last times when no change is expected ; we know
that the Holy Ghost resides ever in the Church. Are we
then, because *you* propose some novelties, to set aside the
consent of ages and fly to you, as if some new Spirit had
descended on you ? And even if the doctrine of the fathers
had to be proved from Scripture, does that entitle you to

---

* *Luth. Assert. Conf.*, col. 309.

pass sentence on them, you who twist Scripture as you like, and bend it like a nose of wax?*

Luther says : "I care not a bit that they object against me the length of time that the Roman See has reigned, or the multitude and magnitude of those who conspire to support it. The world used such arguments as these against the Apostles. Yet they could not thereby put down the Gospel Truth, though but recently made known and preached but by a few rude men." Fisher quietly answers : "No, surely, it was not meet that custom should prevail against the Apostles, however long established, when they confirmed what they taught by most evident miracles. So you too, Luther, if you will confirm your doctrine by evident miracles, will perhaps gain over the whole world to believe in you. But in the meantime our doctrines are so established, not only by miracles, but by the words of Christ Himself, and the concordant testimony of ancient fathers, themselves taught by the Holy Ghost, that if we hold not fast to them, we shall indeed be more fickle than the winds, 'ever learning yet never attaining to the knowledge of the truth '."†

Luther, in his self-assumed character of inspired Apostle, justified his own outrageous language towards the Sovereign Pontiff and rejection of General Councils, by saying that St. Paul resisted and blamed St. Peter. Fisher answers : "Everyone may not do what St. Paul did. Show me someone who is St. Paul's equal in his gifts, who has been called like him by Christ, and sent like him to instruct men ; who has so great light of faith and heat of charity and superabundance of wisdom ; who has been enlightened with so many revelations, and proves what he says by most evident miracles. Show me such a man, and I doubt not at all that a council will give heed to him gladly. But not so if an Arius, a Nestorius, a Macedonius, or one like them, stands

---

* *Luth. Assert. Conf.*, col. 309.   † *Ibid.*, col. 580.

out, and, according to the fancies of his own brain, twists the
Scriptures contrary to the teaching of all the fathers.
Certainly no Christian would bear to hear either pope or
council called to task by such a blatant beast (*belua*)." *

These quotations are not intended as specimens of the
general style of Fisher's controversy. They are quite exceptional—a page or two chosen out of thousands. His
general style is serious and majestic. I have given them to
show a side of his character that we might otherwise miss in
the lofty dignity of the chancellor and the bishop, and the
patient endurance of the martyr—his keen sense of the
ridiculous, and his sarcastic contempt for noisy pretension.
The last passage I have quoted with regard to rebuking
superiors may remind the reader of the boldness with
which he himself, in proper time and place, and with proper
self-restraint, had rebuked the pomp and luxury of prelates
and of the papal legate, Wolsey. We shall see him, on
future occasions, raising his voice fearlessly in protest against
the king, when the cause demanded it. I do not, however,
think it right to pass over here the remonstrances addressed
by this holy man to the Sovereign Pontiffs and their court.

Luther had quoted against the authority assumed by the
Roman Pontiffs the words of our Lord : " He that is greater
among you let him become as the younger, and he that is
the leader as he that serveth ".† Fisher replies that this is
merely an exhortation to humility, not a prohibition of
superiority—that on the contrary Our Lord's words pre-
suppose that some will be greater than others, some will
be leaders, others followers; but adds Fisher: " If the
Roman Pontiffs, laying aside pomp and haughtiness, would
but practise humility, you would not have a word left to
utter against them. Yes, would that they would reform the
manners of their court, and drive from it ambition, avarice,

* *Luth. Assert. Conf.*, col. 601.   † *Luke* xxii. 26.

and luxury.   Never otherwise will they impose silence on
revilers like you." *

And in another place : " This is what you aim at.   This
is the real end of all your scribbling.   It is out of mere
hatred of the Romans that you set about your wicked
schemes.   You were grieved to hear of all the troubles
which the Romans inflict on your Germans ; and as you
cannot relieve them by other means, you leave no stone
unturned either utterly to destroy, or at least to diminish, the
authority of the Roman Pontiff.   Yet, however dear your
country may be to you, the religious life of which you have
made profession obliges you to hold dearer still God and
His Scriptures.†   But you strive in vain against God.   You
know the saying of Gamaliel : ' If it is of God, it will stand '.
Yes, the Roman Church will stand, whether you will or no.
You may, indeed, be the founder of a schism ; for St. Paul
predicted that a ' revolt ' would come.   But woe to that
man by whom the revolt comes.   After you have done all,
Luther, the successor of St. Peter will remain ; and if he will
but endeavour to reform the morals of his court, I doubt not
you will greatly repent of all you are doing."‡

Luther concluded one of his invectives thus : " Who will
bring the pope to order ?   Christ only, with the brightness
of His coming.   ' Lord, who has believed our hearing ? ' " §
Fisher replies : " There is no reason to believe your hearing,
since you have heard what you say from no other than the
devil.   It is he who has whispered in your ears that the
pope is Antichrist.   I do not, however, say this as if I were
unwilling that the pope or his court should be reformed, if
there is anything in their life divergent from the teaching of
Christ.   The people (*vulgus*) speak much against them, I

* *Luth. Assert. Conf.*, col. 573.
† This was written about 1522, before Luther had altogether thrown
off the monastic life.
‡ *Ibid.*, col. 579.   § " Quis credit auditui nostro ? " (*Isa.* liii. 1).

know not with what truth. Still, it is constantly repeated that things are so. Would then that, if there is anything amiss, they would reform themselves, and remove the scandal from the souls of the weak. For it is greatly to be feared, unless they do so quickly, that Divine vengeance will not long be delayed. It is not, however, fitting that the emperor or lay princes should attempt such a matter, and reduce them to a more frugal mode of life. The holy emperor Constantine taught this by his example, when he cast into the fire the accusations which bishops were bringing against one another, saying : ' It is not right for me to judge the gods,' meaning the bishops (as in *Exodus : Diis non detrahes*), for they are appointed in God's place judges amongst men. Yet I would not that the popes should trust that all other emperors will follow Constantine's example."*

" Divine vengeance will not long be delayed," was a strange and terrible warning to the Sovereign Pontiff or to his court, from one who would now be called the most Ultramontane of bishops, even when guarded by the words : " It is greatly to be feared ". But when we recall the awful sack of Rome by the Constable of Bourbon, not without the connivance of the emperor, only four years after these words were written, they may certainly be looked upon as prophetic.†

One other treatise completes the list of Fisher's controversial works ; this is his work *On the Truth of Christ's Body and Blood in the Eucharist, against John Œcolampadius.*‡

* *Luth. Assert. Conf.*, col. 653.

† At the conclusion of Fisher's treatise, *Quod Petrus fuerit Romæ*, is a very striking passage, in which he proves God's special providence over the Holy City, in that He chastises it, but never forsakes it. It is quoted at length by Rev. T. Livius, C.SS.R., in his treatise *On the Roman Episcopate of S. Peter*, pp. 244-248.

‡ John Hausschein was his real name ; but Greek and Latin substitutes were the fashion among the Teutons. Some have written of the Bishop of Rochester as Joannes Piscator. Erasmus thus addressed *another* Fisher.

It is the longest and most important of all his writings, and there are many beautiful passages, showing his lively faith and tender love for that great mystery. It has, however, the same defect of method as his works against Luther. He quotes the whole of his opponent's book, making a running commentary. The book of Œcolampadius was short and readable, that of Fisher so long and learned that few would have the patience and very few the inclination to peruse it.

There was a great dissimilarity between the characters of Luther and Œcolampadius. They were probably equally rash and self-sufficient, but Œcolampadius, though he went farther from Catholic truth than Luther, affected moderation and love of peace, and solid argument rather than declamation.

Erasmus wrote to his friend Lupset in England: "Carlstadt here has spread about some book written in German, in which he maintains that in the Eucharist is only bread and wine. This error has taken hold of men's minds more quickly than a flame applied to naphtha. Ulrich Zwingle has supported this opinion in his book, and lately Œcolampadius also, in a book so carefully compiled, so full of argument, that he has given a difficult task to those who would answer him."* In another letter written at the end of 1524, he gives another part of the picture : " Carlstadt has been here. He has put out six pamphlets. Two of the printers were thrown into prison by the magistrates, principally, as I am told, because he denies that the true Body of Christ is in the Holy Eucharist. *This no one tolerates.* The laity are indignant that their God is taken from them, as if God were nowhere but under those signs. The learned are moved by the words of Holy Scripture and the decrees of the Church. This matter will stir up a great tragedy, although

* *Ep.* 790.

we have too many tragedies already. . . . This new Gospel is here giving birth to a new kind of men, impudent, hypocritical, calumnious, liars, sycophants, quarrelsome with one another, seditious, furious, who are so hateful to me that if I knew of a city free from this rabble I would migrate to it. . . . There are many in this town favourable to Luther. Had I foreseen that such rabble would spring up, I would have declared myself an enemy of this faction from the very beginning."*

The book of Œcolampadius, contrasting as it did in tone with these fiercer polemics, pleased the liberal and somewhat sceptical scholar. But he was alarmed when he found himself in danger of being drawn into the controversy. Œcolampadius in his preface had spoken of "our great Erasmus". Erasmus at once protested. Such words, he said, might bring him under the suspicion of the pope, the emperor, the King of England, *the Bishop of Rochester*, the Cardinal of York."†

Two more extracts from the letters of Erasmus will both serve to make known the character of the book that Fisher answered, and, while showing its effect on the mind of Erasmus, will illustrate by contrast its effect on the mind of Fisher. We have no right to doubt the strong asseveration, and even oath, with which Erasmus declared to the Swiss assembled at Baden, on 15th May, 1526, that he had never departed from the Catholic doctrine of the Holy Eucharist : "I call God to witness, who alone knows the hearts of men, and I invoke His anger on me, if ever an opinion has held a place in my mind (with regard to the Eucharist) different from that which the Catholic Church has hitherto unanimously maintained. As to what is revealed to others, let them see to it themselves. No reasonings have ever persuaded me to depart from the prescription of the Church

---

* *Ep.* 715 (10th December, 1524).
† *Ep.* 728 (5th February, 1525).

This is not human fear, it is religious duty and fear of the Divine wrath ".* Yet, in spite of his submission to God's revelation, as declared to him by the Church, he seems to have taken little pains to assimilate it, to penetrate its meaning, its fitness, its harmony, its beauty and sublimity. On the contrary, with a weakness often found in clever men, he rather liked to imagine what could be said on the other side, to listen to difficulties, and dally with objections, until they sapped his piety, if they did not demolish his faith. He writes to his friend Bilibaldus : "In some things regarding the Eucharist, not being very erudite, I should feel hesitation (*subdubitarem*), did not the authority of the Church confirm me. By the Church I mean the consent of the Christian people throughout the world." † And, again, to the same : " The opinion of Œcolampadius would not be displeasing to me, if the consent of the Church were not against it. For I do not see what is the action of a Body that cannot be perceived as a Body,‡ or what would be its utility even if it were perceived, provided that spiritual grace be in the symbols. Yet I cannot depart from the consent of the Church, nor have I ever done so."§ And later on, 19th October, 1527 : " I never said that the opinion of Œcolampadius was the better one. But I said *among my friends* that I could go over to his opinion, if the authority of the Church had approved it ; but I added that I never could differ from the Church. . . . How much the authority of the Church may weigh with others I know not. With me it weighs so much, that I could agree with Arians and Pelagians, if the Church approved their teaching. It is not that the words of Christ are not enough for me ; but surely it is not strange if I take as their interpreter that Church by

---

* *Ep.* 818. † *Ep.* 827.

‡ " Quid agat corpus insensibile ? " perhaps, " *What is the good* of a body that does not fall under the senses ? "

§ *Ep.* 823.

whose authority I believe in the canonical Scriptures. Others, perhaps, may be cleverer or stronger; as for me, I rest safely in nothing so much as in the certain judgments of the Church. Of reasons and arguments there is never an end." *

Such was the state of mind of Erasmus. Of a naturally sceptical disposition, he seems to admit that it would have been a relief to him to have been assured by competent authority that he need not believe in such stupendous and supernatural mysteries as the Divinity of Christ, the Real Presence, the action of Divine grace. He did accept them, and was convinced they were true, and would not be thought for a moment to call them in question. Yet, *among his friends*, he could state plausibly the objections against them, though merely by way of argument; or he could listen to difficulties and admit that they were subtle, and that he could not find the answer, though it doubtless existed. No wonder he was suspected of being sceptical at heart. His was not the case of a neophyte, believing blindly in the hope of one day understanding, and, in the meantime, deploring the ignorance or sensuality that prevented him from sharing the vision and the rapture of the enlightened and the spiritual. His miserable attitude of mind is betrayed in that sneer of his at the people: " The laity are indignant that their God is taken from them, as if God were nowhere but under those signs ".† He knew the people were right. He shared their faith, but, not sharing their devotion, he casts a slur upon it, as if it sprung from ignorance and superstition, rather than from faith.

It is as if a learned Rabbi had sneered at Eli's broken heart when the Ark was taken by the Philistines, or at

---

* *Ep.* 903.

† " Indignantur laici sibi eripi Deum suum, quasi nusquam sit Deus nisi sub illo signo " (*Ep.* 715).

David for panting and yearning after the house of God —
as if God were to be found there only !

My purpose is in no way to depreciate the man whom
Fisher honoured with his admiration and his friendship, or
to show that he was unworthy of either.   Fisher was not a
man to quench the smoking flax, since the spark of faith
and obedience was there.   But the contrast is forced on us
by the collected writings of these two men, between the just
smouldering flax of Erasmus and the clear bright flame of
Fisher.   *He* had no conditional admiration for the impious
negations of heretics, " if only they were true ".   God had
given him understanding and wisdom, as well as faith.   The
plausibilities of Œcolampadius were to him impieties, his
reasoning the merest sophisms, his unction pitiful cant.
It might be a little thing to Erasmus, who seldom if ever
said mass, to have the Presence of the Divine Victim rejected,
but not so to Fisher, whose eyesight was more weakened by
the tears he shed at mass than by poring over books, and
who shortened his sleep to converse with his hidden Love
in the Tabernacle of his cathedral.   I do not, however,
propose to make any extracts here from what he has written
in defence of that most awful but loving mystery.   The
few passages for which I have space are chosen to illustrate
his hatred of hypocrisy.

Œcolampadius, having quoted Our Lord's words, writes :
" We trust that the sense of these words will not be hidden
from us if prayer be joined to the investigation and colla-
tion of the Scriptures.   To pray without searching is to
laugh at God ; to search without prayer is to get involved
in error."   To many Protestants of the present day, to
whom three hundred and fifty years of the method followed
by their first leaders has made everything doubtful, the
thought may well occur : Why should we guess for ever at
a riddle, when we can never know whether we have discovered the right answer?   But when Œcolampadius wrote,

Protestantism was not yet ten years old. It had been assumed that the new method of Scripture-searching would lead to unity. But it was then just beginning to show its first fruits, in the dissensions on the Sacrament of Unity between Luther and Carlstadt. Œcolampadius stepped in as a peacemaker. He addressed, not Catholics, but Protestants, promising them the possession of truth in unity if they would follow his method, or, more correctly, if they would take him as leader and teacher. The outrageous absurdity of the promise was at once apparent to Fisher. "No," he replies, "neither prayer nor study of Scripture, nor both united, will avail you aught; for both must be joined to humility. Œcolampadius thinks that the Doorkeeper, the Holy Ghost, has been so long idle in the Church, that He has not opened to the prayers and searchings of the saints for so many centuries. If, then, he thinks that the Holy Ghost is likely to open specially to him, he is too proud, and the Holy Ghost will laugh at his prayers and searchings." *

Œcolampadius quotes the words of Solomon: "If thou shalt call for wisdom and incline thy heart to prudence; if thou shalt seek for her as money and shalt dig for her as for a treasure, then thou shalt understand the fear of the Lord, and shalt find the knowledge of God". † "See," says Œcolampadius, "how we are exhorted to study. God wishes to be invoked, to be drawn down by prayer; He wishes us to seek and to dig." "Are you not ashamed of all this?" replies Fisher. "Do you think none of our forefathers has done these things? Did not Basil and Chrysostom, Athanasius, Cyril, Cyprian, Jerome, Ambrose, Augustine, and the rest exercise themselves frequently? Are you the only one who has called efficaciously, you the only one who has humbled his heart, the only one who has sought with dili-

* Lib. i., cap. 23.   † *Proverbs* ii. 3, 4.

gence, and dug out with much toil the sense of God's words?
Their prayers, forsooth, were nothing to yours ! Their
humility compared with yours was pride ! Their diligence
and labour was of no account ! Is it not the very height of
pride and self-conceit to yield to such folly for a moment?"*

"We must not blame God but ourselves," wrote Œcolampadius, "if hitherto we have missed the sense of His word;
for do we blame God because the veins of silver have so
long lain hid in the mountains? Or do we blame a wise
man because fools do not understand his parables, especially
if they laugh at him just when he is accommodating his
speech to theirs?"

"Abeas in malam crucem," replied the venerable bishop,
which was the nearest approach to a curse he ever permitted
himself.† "Who finds fault with Christ except yourself?
As for us we adore both the word and the deed of Christ.
Christ came to reveal Himself to little ones, and already
more such have preceded us than there are sands on the
seashore. And are we to think that He has hidden from
all these the true meaning of His principal sacrament, in
order that you may have the glory of discovering it?"‡

Œcolampadius, appealing to his late friends the Lutherans
for a fair hearing, said : "Judge me as you would be judged
yourselves". Though he had ceased to care for the judgment of the Church, Fisher replied as follows : "As for me,
if I saw myself to be such a deadly plague and pest of souls,
as I am certain you are, I would suffer myself to be separated
from the rest of Christians, lest I should infect them more;
or if that did not serve I would give myself up to the judgment of the Church, to suffer for the remission of my sins
whatever she might think right to inflict. Most assuredly

* Lib. i., cap. 31.

† A perfectly classical curse, of which the most literal interpretation would be the Hibernian "High hanging to you".

‡ Lib. i., cap. 31.

9

for the souls you have perverted by your pestilent teaching
—souls redeemed by the precious Blood of Christ—you will
give one day to Him a most rigorous account." *

It is fair to add that though Œcolampadius took no notice
of Fisher's book, it does not seem to have been without its
effect on Erasmus.   We have seen how favourably he was
impressed on first reading the pamphlet of Œcolampadius.
Later on his tone is very different.   He wrote to Conrad
Pelican to say that among the learned he had been accustomed to propose many doubts and difficulties, sometimes
to try them, sometimes for his own instruction, sometimes
for the pleasure of discussion (*animi gratia*).   "But I will
plead guilty to parricide," he says, "if any mortal ever heard
me say, seriously or in joke, that there is nothing in the
Eucharist but bread and wine, or that the true Body and
Blood of our Lord are not there.   Yes, I pray that Christ
be not propitious to me, if such an opinion ever found place
in my mind.   If ever a passing thought of this kind has
touched my soul, I easily shook it off, considering the in-
estimable charity of God towards us, weighing the words of
Holy Scripture, &c.   No human reasons will ever lead me
away from the unanimous judgment of the Christian world.
Those five words, 'In the beginning God made the heaven
and the earth,' weigh more with me than all the arguments
of Aristotle and other philosophers proving the eternity of
the world.   And what have these men now to bring forward
why I should profess their impious and seditious opinion?
Their reasons are as light as straws; such as these: 'He
has removed His Body once for all from us lest it should be
an impediment'; or, 'The Apostles did not wonder, or did
not adore'; or, 'We are commanded to be spiritual,' just as
if Flesh thus set before us could be a hindrance to spirituality.   It is flesh, but unperceived by any of our senses,

* Lib. i., cap. 31.

and yet this itself is a pledge of Divine charity to us, and a solace during our time of waiting." *

Later still he wrote even more strongly : "As regards the Eucharist I see no end to argumentation ; yet no one could ever convince me, nor ever will, that Christ, who is Truth and Charity, would allow His beloved Spouse to cling so long to such an abominable error as to adore a crust of bread instead of Himself. As to the exact words of consecration, I did desire, I allow it, more accurate instruction. But in such little difficulties (*scrupulis*) I am wont easily to acquiesce in the judgment of the Church. The doctrine which gives to all alike the power of consecrating, absolving, and ordaining, I have always looked upon as sheer madness." †

Erasmus, for his health and for facility of printing, had taken up his residence in Basel, before Protestantism had infected it. In 1529, he wrote : "I have grown used to this nest for many years, but for the future I commit myself to the Providence of Christ. I shall do what befits an orthodox man, and care more for piety than health. For to remain here, where it is not allowed to offer sacrifice or to receive the Lord's Body, would be nothing else than to make profession with them. Œcolampadius has possession of all the Churches. Monks and nuns are ordered to go elsewhere, or else to lay aside their sacred habit. The same things are being done in many other cities. In the temples none of the old rites are now performed, except that in some of them a preacher of this sect preaches once (on Sunday), while boys and women sing a psalm in German rhymes. These are the beginnings. I grievously fear that this

* *Ep.* 847. There is much more to the same purpose in this very earnest and eloquent letter.

† *Ep.* 1035, 1st April, 1529. In this letter he says he never dared to go to the holy table without confession, nor would he die without confession to a priest were anything weighing on his conscience.

Pharisaism will end in paganism." * A few weeks previous
to this letter the populace of Basel, instigated by the gentle
and moderate Œcolampadius, after driving away the clergy
who remained faithful, and making a revolution in the
government, stripped the churches of images, altars, and
confessionals, and made a bonfire in the market-place.
Erasmus kept his word.   He went to Fribourg, where he
remained seven years; but having returned to Basel on
business, with the intention of not remaining there, he fell
ill and could not leave, and ended his days without priest,
or any help from the Church, but pronouncing the Holy
Name and calling on the mercy of God.   He died in July,
1536, a year after his friend Fisher.   I cannot but think he
was assisted by the prayers of More, and Reynolds, and
Fisher, of whose blessed deaths he wrote so touchingly
when the news reached him at Basel, as we shall see later on.

Before concluding this sketch of Fisher's controversial
writings, I must give two more passages.   The first will
make clear the ground on which his belief rested, or the
rule by which it was guided.   This was the broad unity of
the Catholic Church.   Revelation was to him historical and
objective, not a matter for conjecture, or discovery, or
private speculation.   He states this in the following words:

"If, then, anyone will attentively consider the solicitude
of Christ for us—if he believes without hesitation that the
Holy Ghost does not reside in the Church to no purpose—
if he reflect on these numerous and most clear testimonies
of the early prelates of the Church, as illustrious by their
lives as by their learning and miracles—if, lastly, he views
the unanimous consent of so many Churches during so many
centuries, without even one dissentient voice, it will surely
be impossible for him to believe that now only at last has
risen upon Luther alone the light of truth, never so much as

* *Ep.* 1033.

suspected by any of the ancient fathers, and the exact contrary of what they all maintained. For if truth has so long
lain hid in darkness, waiting through so many centuries for
its deliverance by Luther, it was to no purpose that Christ
bestowed such care upon our forefathers. It was to no
purpose that the Spirit of Christ was sent to teach them all
truth ; it was to no purpose that they asked for and sought
after truth, seeing that all continued to preach with one
accord to all the Churches a most pernicious falsehood. If
they erred in these first elements of the faith, then in vain
(to use Tertullian's words) have so many thousands of
thousands been baptised ; in vain have been performed so
many works of faith, so many virtues been practised, so
many graces displayed, so many ministries exercised, so
many martyrdoms endured, since all have lived and died
not in faith but in error, for without a right faith could none
of them be pleasing to God." *

The second passage is one in which he expresses, by way
of contrast, what he thought of the strife and contradiction
produced by denying the general faith of Christendom, and
looking for the true sense of God's revelation in the dis-
coveries and combinations of private judgment.

In the preface to his book against Œcolampadius he
exclaims : " May the great and good God be ever blessed,
and His name be ever praised, in that He has so cared for
His Church and so succoured it, in this cruel persecution
which it is now enduring at the hands of heretics ! We
could not have desired, for the confusion and overthrow of
our enemies, anything more fitting than what has happened,
and that no doubt by the great providence of the most
merciful God. Let no one suppose that I say this on
account of the immense slaughter of those who were followers
of Luther s pestilent teaching, though in that too the Almighty

* *De Sacerdotio,* "Congressus primus in fine".

has given a foretaste of His wrath against that execrable sect in which the blood of so many thousands has been shed. not by the sword of any external enemy, but by their own intestine divisions, God taking vengeance on them for their great rebellion against the Church.* Who is so blind as not to see in this great calamity the punishing hand of an angry God? And to whom are the Germans indebted for this but to Luther and his followers? Would that now a. length, late as it is, they would attend to that exhortation in which John Cochlæus, a man most learned and a most zealous defender of the Catholic faith, out of his great zeal and great love for his country, prudently warned them of these dangers that would come on them.

But it is not by any means on account of that miserable slaughter that I have exulted so much. For a greater vengeance has fallen on the authors of these factions, since they have been given up to a reprobate sense—to use the words of St. Paul, "to do those things which are unseemly". What more absurd, or rather more execrable, than that those who have once for all consecrated their chastity to God, and have kept their vow strenuously in the heat of youth, should now when old indulge their obscene lusts? Not only they do this themselves, but exhort others to the same filthiness; so that you may see everywhere not only priests, who seemed to be graver than Cato himself, but monks also marrying nuns, and that publicly without any shame, so that we may rightly say to everyone of them: "You have made for yourself a harlot's forehead, and know not how to blush".† And besides this they abuse the Holy

---

* The war of the peasants in Munster took place in 1525. Erasmus wrote on 24th December, 1525: "Hic longe supra centum millia rusticorum interfecta sunt"; and in the same epistle he speaks of Luther's marriage and of the tragedy ending like a comedy (*Ep.* 781).

† Has not God exercised the same vengeance and given us the same humiliating yet instructive spectacle once more in our own days?

Scriptures to such an extent as to seek to prove from them the necessity of what they have done; as if neither Ambrose, nor Jerome, nor Augustine, nor any of the ancient fathers had been able to observe continence after receiving the holy priesthood. But if they lived chastely, as no doubt they did, then why cannot others also? "There are some," says Our Lord, "who have made themselves eunuchs for the kingdom of God." And with what intention, I ask, did the Lutherans formerly receive the sacred priesthood? Certainly if they did not intend to observe celibacy for the kingdom of heaven, they received the priesthood hypocritically. But if in such a matter they did not fear to dissimulate in the presence of God, how can anyone hope from such hypocrites the fruit of wholesome doctrine, since it is written: "The Holy Spirit of discipline will flee from the deceitful" (*Wisdom* i. 5). But, on the other hand, if they did propose to keep themselves chaste, but were afterwards conquered by the flesh, may we not suppose they have long remained in their filthy state? Surely these were not fitting vessels to receive that Divine Wisdom "who will not enter a malicious soul nor dwell in a body subject to sins" (*Wisdom* i. 4). We may believe then that, not less on account of the impurity of their lives than for the arrogance of their minds, they have fallen into these heresies, and thence into such a reprobate sense as to commit such abominations and teach them publicly.*

Yet it was not even on account of this vengeance of God in abandoning them to a reprobate sense that I exulted. There is a still more evident proof of God's avenging hand. It is related in the Book of Genesis of certain men that they resolved to build a tower, whose top should reach to heaven,

---

* When Fisher wrote this his opponent was not yet married, though Luther had set him the example. But a year afterwards Erasmus writes: "Joannes Œcolampadius hic publice duxit uxorem, puellam sane lepidam ".—*Ep.* 987.

so as to leave their names famous to posterity. The world was then of one tongue, but God so punished their pride as to confound their speech, so that one understood not the other. The same punishment has befallen these factious followers of Luther. They also had conceived in their minds that they would build a new Church, and get fame throughout the world. And in this endeavour it is wonderful how united they were and banded together, so that they seemed to be like one man, with one heart and mind. Nor would they have ceased from their work, had not God, pitying His Church, looked down from on high, and bridled their madness by the strife of tongues. He has brought it about that those who seemed leaders and columns among them understand not each other's voice. They strive with one another, and no one deigns to listen to his neighbour. The followers of Carlstadt have separated from the Lutherans, and they are pouring out insults one against the other. It may be seen, from letters just printed in the name of Luther, how great a controversy rages. Even Melancthon, as I have heard from trustworthy men, is not well agreed with Luther. And now at length another of these leaders comes to the front, named John Œcolampadius, who formerly followed Luther in everything, and now he most vehemently differs from him in many points. . . . Who then does not see that God is fighting for His Church, since He has put confusion in their tongues and turned their arms one against the other, so that thus they defend the Church while attacking their own former allies? . . . Thus it is seen that Christ is faithful to His promise: " Behold I am with you all days, even to the consummation of the world ".

Had Fisher lived but a few years longer he would have seen far fiercer and more numerous strifes than those he mentioned in 1526. But how would he have exulted had he foreseen the spectacle which God has reserved for us?

I do not think I shall be wandering from my subject if I

supplement this chapter by a passage from Sir Thomas More. It bears directly on the writings of Fisher, because in it he refers to and endorses what Fisher had written on the supremacy of the Holy See. It was written by Sir Thomas just after he had read what I have above quoted on certain abuses or defects in the Roman Court, which were the object of popular censure. It will show how perfectly the two friends were agreed in their views on this matter. But I make the quotation for a further reason. Though I am not engaged on the life and martyrdom of Blessed Thomas More, yet those of Fisher are so linked with his, that the one story cannot be told without constant reference to the other. They died almost together, and for the same cause. Now, no one has ever thought that Fisher varied in his views of the pope's supremacy, while it is known by his own words that there had been a certain change or growth in the mind of Sir Thomas. I wish, therefore, to show that this change was effected at an earlier date than is sometimes supposed—that it was, at least in part, the work of Fisher, and that it was complete.

In a letter to Cromwell, Sir Thomas admits that he had at one time thought the pope's supremacy of merely ecclesiastical and not of Divine institution,* though even so no nation was at liberty to withdraw from it, but that he had become convinced of its Divine institution by the king's book against Luther, and by subsequent study. Now, the passage I shall quote was written soon after the appearance of Fisher's first book against Luther in 1523, and shows how thoroughly his vigorous mind grasped the truth when once his attention was properly directed to it.

Even some of More's admirers are wont to deplore the

---

* This was not heresy, for there was no obstinacy. Sir Thomas was not then aware of the explicit teaching of the Church. His studies had been in literature and in law, and he had probably imbibed the error from Erasmus.

answer he wrote under the name of Ross to Luther's scurrility against the king ; while his enemies say that "it is
throughout nothing but downright ribaldry, without a grain
of reasoning to support it, so that it gave the author no
other reputation but that of having the best knack of any
man in Europe at calling bad names in good Latin ".* I
should doubt whether friends or enemies who speak thus
have read the book. That there are some strong passages
in it against Luther I do not deny. He deserved worse ;
but perhaps Sir Thomas might have left him to sink in his
own filth without heaping more on him. In spite of that
the book is a most weighty one, full of excellent reasoning.
The following passage on the supremacy of the pope is
taken from this book, and it will be seen that in 1523 Sir
Thomas More not only held the Divine institution of that
supremacy, but that under the eye of the King of England,
and for his defence, he held also *the deposing power of
the pope* to be of Divine institution.† The passage is as
follows :

"The Rev. Father John Fisher, Bishop of Rochester, a
man illustrious not only by the vastness of his erudition, but
much more so by the purity of his life, has so opened and
overthrown the assertions of Luther, that if he has any
shame he would give a great deal to have burnt his assertions. . . . As regards the Primacy of the Roman Pontiff,
the same Bishop of Rochester has made the matter so clear
from the Gospels, the Acts of the Apostles, and from the
whole of the Old Testament, and from the consent of all

---

* Atterbury (I believe), quoted by Lewis, i. 293.

† In his *Responsio* to Luther's *Apology*, the king says: "I see that
both in England and other places some have replied to what you
wrote against me. Some have treated you according to your deserts,
and handled you after your own fashion, except that they have given
reasons as well as insults, while you give only the latter."—"Aliqui
te ex meritis tuis ornarint, et tuis te tractarint artibus, nisi quod
rationem admiscuere conviciis, quibus tu solis disputas."

the holy fathers, not of the Latins only, but of the Greeks also (of whose opposition Luther is wont to boast), and from the definition of a General Council, in which the Armenians and Greeks, who at that time had been most obstinately resisting, were overcome, and acknowledged themselves overcome, that it would be utterly superfluous for me to write again on the subject.

"I am moved to obedience to that See, not only by what learned and holy men have written, but by this fact especially, that we see so often that, on the one hand, every enemy of the Christian faith makes war on that See, and that, on the other hand, no one has ever declared himself an enemy of that See who has not also shortly after shown most evidently that he was the enemy of Christ and of the Christian religion.

"Another thing that moves me is this, that if after Luther's manner the vices of men are to be imputed to the offices they hold, not only the Papacy will fall, but royalty, and dictatorship, and consulate, and every other kind of magistracy, and the people will be without rulers, without law, and without order. Should such a thing ever come to pass, as it seems indeed imminent in some parts of Germany, they will then feel to their own great loss how much better it is for men to have bad rulers than no rulers at all. Most assuredly as regards the pope, God, who set him over His Church, knows how great an evil it would be to be without one, and I do not think it desirable that Christendom should learn it by experience. It is far more to be wished that God may raise up such popes as befit the Christian cause and the dignity of the Apostolic office : men who, despising riches and honour, will care only for heaven, will promote piety in the people, will bring about peace, and exercise the authority they have received from God against the 'satraps and mighty hunters of the world,' excommunicating and giving over to Satan both those who invade the

territories of others, and those who oppress their own.*
With one or two such popes the Christian world would soon
perceive how much preferable it is that the Papacy should
be reformed than abrogated.   And I doubt not that long ago
Christ would have looked down on the Pastor of His flock,
if the Christian people had chosen rather to pray for the
welfare of their Father than to persecute him, and to hide
the shame of their Father than to laugh at it.

"But be sure, Luther, of this : God will not forsake His
own Vicar.   He will one day cast His eyes of mercy on
him ; nay, He is perhaps now doing it, in allowing a most
wicked son to scourge so painfully his father.   You are
nothing else, Luther, but the scourge of God, to the great
gain of that See, and to your own great loss.   God will act
as a kind mother does, who, when she has chastised her
child, wipes away his tears, and, to appease him, throws the
rod into the fire." †

The great and holy popes whom God raised up for His
Church so soon after these words were written, and the state
of Lutheranism at the present day, both show that the
Blessed Martyr was gifted with a prophetic spirit.   With no
less discernment did he foretell, at the time that he was in
the highest favour of the king, that his own head would fall,
should that monarch think to gain his ends by such an
act. ‡

---

* "Qui auctoritatem, quam acceperunt a Deo, adversus mundi
satrapas et robustos venatores exerceant, diris omnibus persequentes
et tradentes Sathanæ, si quis aut alienam ditionem invadat, aut
male tractet suam."

† Cap. x. (*Opera Th. Mori;* Francofurti, p. 52).

‡ Roper's *Life of More.*

CHAPTER VII

THE DIVORCE.

IN the year 1521, Henry had written as follows in his defence of the Sacraments against Luther:

"'Whom God has joined together let no man put asunder.' Oh! the admirable word, which none could have spoken but the Word that was made flesh! O word, full of joy and fear as it is of admiration! Who would not rejoice that God has so much care of his marriage as to vouchsafe, not only to be present at it, but also to preside in it? Who should not tremble, when he is bound not only to love his wife, but to live with her in such a manner as that he may be able to render her pure and immaculate to God from whom he received her?"

Even in 1521, Henry's infidelities had been such that his ecstatic raptures regarding the marriage tie must have sounded ludicrous to his English readers. But with the whole of his career before us, how marvellous is it to read the following words from the same treatise:

"The heathen were wont by human laws to take wives and cast them off. But in the people of God it was formerly not lawful to separate those who were joined in matrimony. And if God, by Moses, allowed the Hebrews to give a bill of divorce, Christ teaches that the permission was given on account of the hardness of the people, *for otherwise they would have killed the wives that did not please them.* But from the beginning it was not so. And Christ recalled Christians to the original sanctity of marriage."

Doubtless, had Henry been taxed with these words that he had written, he would have replied that God had never joined together what he (the king) had separated, and that his reason for his divorces was that God had never been the Author of those unions which had been broken. It is no business of mine to discuss Henry's matrimonial affairs in general; but as I cannot relate the life and death of Bishop Fisher without investigating to some extent the first of the series of royal divorces, I wish to take note of the Catholic principle laid down by Henry himself. He sought divorce from the pope, not as if the pope could dissolve a valid marriage, but on the ground that his marriage had been null and void from the beginning. I fail to conceive the object of Mr. Froude in importing modern notions regarding marriage and divorce into a history of the 16th century. "The marriages of princes," he says, "have ever been affected by other considerations than those which influence such relations between private persons."*

That is most true, and therefore Pope Julius II. considered himself justified in granting, at the request of Ferdinand and Isabella in Spain, and of Henry VII. in England, a dispensation to Prince Henry to marry the young widow of his brother Arthur, though such a marriage in general is reprobated as unseemly.

But if the marriages of princes are different from those of private persons, their *divorces* stand on the same footing. Reasons of State cannot make lawful for a king what is unlawful for his subjects. Mr. Froude affects to appeal to canon law, and to the principle laid down by canonists, that the pope, as the head of Christendom, can grant extreme dispensations, *dummodo causa cogat urgentissima*—e.g., *ne regnum aliquod penitus pereat*. But this is said of marriage, not of divorce. Mr. Froude assumes that the pope had the

* *History*, i. 134.

power to dissolve Henry's marriage, irrespective of its
validity, if he had had the will; and he complains that the
question of the validity was ever introduced, and accuses
the pope of injustice to Henry, or rather to England, and of
partiality to the emperor, and of forgetfulness of his position
is umpire in matters regarding the welfare of nations. He
blames Henry for allowing the question of the lawfulness of
the marriage *ab initio* to have ever got entangled in that of
its dissolution, thus transferring it from a simple question of
statesmanship to a theme for the subtleties of theologians
and the chicanery of lawyers. But all this is theory not
history.

Henry's contention was not that the pope was omnipotent,
and that he could break what God had bound. It was the
contrary—that the pope was not omnipotent, and that he
had gone beyond his power in trying to remove impediments
which God had placed, and to bind in marriage where God
forbade to bind. Wishing to get rid of his bonds with
Catharine, it never occurred to him to claim a dissolution
on grounds of pure statesmanship; to acknowledge the validity of his marriage, and ask that it should be set aside for the
good of the country. He knew this was impossible. He could
only plead the invalidity from the beginning of his marriage,
and this he could do in but two ways, either by denying the
power of the pope to dispense for such a marriage as his,
and so asking Clement to correct the error of Julius; or he
could plead, not lack of power in the dispenser, but lack of
force in the dispensation. He could allege informalities,
omission of necessary clauses, non-verification of clauses
inserted, deceit and misrepresentation in the petitioners,
error as to facts in the grantor. As a matter of fact he
began by impugning the bull of dispensation, and, failing in
this, he ended by impugning the power of the dispenser.

Happily there is no need for me to relate the history of
these proceedings, and the tedious and unsavoury history of

the divorce. My readers will probably know that history sufficiently or may seek it elsewhere.* I am only concerned with the part taken by the Bishop of Rochester, and the narrative will neither involve us in the history of the king's amours with Anne Boleyn, nor in the complications of foreign diplomacy.

It is unnecessary to enter on the much debated questions as to the time when the thought of a divorce first entered Henry's mind, or the causes which led to it, and whether or not they had any connection in their origin with the person of Anne Boleyn. What seems certain, and now generally admitted, is that, early in the year 1527, everyone knew that a divorce was in agitation, and everyone about the Court knew of the king's passion for Anne. But it does not follow that these two things were connected together in the minds of observers, even of those most intimate with Henry. To them Anne may have appeared but as one of a series, and that she would aspire to marriage and be successful entered into the thoughts of few. Wolsey gave himself earnestly if not cordially to the divorce, but there is no likelihood that he had any intention that Anne should profit by it.† The earlier Catholic writers, such as Hall and Harpsfield and Sander, attribute to Wolsey the very worst motives of personal spite against Catharine, and still more against the emperor, who was nephew to Catharine, and who had

---

* Mr. Pocock's *Records of the Reformation;* Mr. Pocock's Edition of Harpsfield's *History of the Divorce* (Camden Soc., 1878); Mr. Brewer's *Reign of Henry VIII.* (vol. ii.); Mr. Friedmann's *Anne Boleyn* (2 vols., 1884); and of course the *State Papers of Henry VIII.* and the *Kalendars of Letters and Papers.*

† "Wolsey thought that Anne had become Henry's mistress; and as he knew from long experience that in such cases the king was tired of his conquest in a few months, he confidently expected that long before the divorce could be obtained Anne would be cast off. In that case he hoped to make a good bargain by selling the hand of his master to the highest bidder."—Friedmann, i. 50.

thwarted his avaricious and ambitious designs on the arch
bishopric of Toledo and the Papacy. The grossness of his
ambition is flagrant in the State Papers, and his servant and
admirer Cavendish bears witness to his revengeful temper
towards others. Nor do I see how his character gains if we
prefer the view of modern historians, that Wolsey was actu-
ated by views of State policy or of Church policy. Mr.
Froude's view is that "a peremptory conviction" against his
first marriage had been maturing in Henry's mind for years,
together with "a. determined purpose" to marry again, for
the succession to the throne and the welfare of the country,
when "accident precipitated his resolution". The accident
was that the emperor's troops were besieging Rome in the
beginning of May, 1527, and it was thought he was favouring
the Protestant party. "Wolsey caught the opportunity to break
the Spanish alliance, and the prospect of a divorce was
grasped at by him as a lever by which to throw the weight
of English power and influence into the papal scale, to commit Henry definitely to the Catholic cause." * Mr. Brewer's
view seems to be that Wolsey saw Henry so bent on a
divorce, that if he could not get it from the pope he would
cast off the pope's authority, and Wolsey thought it right to
choose the lesser of two evils. If so, he acted both impiously
and foolishly: impiously in choosing an injustice and a scandal
rather than a calamity; and foolishly in thinking that the
pope's authority could be saved by degrading it and making
it a bye-word. In either case he made himself the willing
tool of Henry, and lent himself to "the artifices, the dissimulation, the fraud, and the intimidation that were employed by the king to hunt down a forlorn and defenceless
woman"; and if, as Mr. Brewer says, it is revolting to see
Catharine's "natural protector (Henry) at the head of her
persecutors, armed with the whole power and wealth of his
kingdom. and employing them to gain his end," † it is still

* *History*, i. 124. † *Reign of Henry*, ii. 185.

10

more revolting to see an archbishop and legate of the Holy
See, the "natural protector" of justice and sanctity, co-
operating in the iniquity.   Perhaps the most revolting thing
of all is the frightful hypocrisy practised by king and cardinal.
As the special characteristic of Bishop Fisher in this transaction, as in all others, is simplicity and straightforwardness, and
he opposed this weapon only to the wiles and intrigues of
which he was well aware, it may be well to give here two
specimens of the kind of hypocrisy with which he had to
deal.

Before the opening of the Legatine Court by Campeggio
and Wolsey in England, in May, 1529, to try the question of
the divorce, there came news of the pope's illness and of his
probably approaching death.   Henry thought that if Wolsey
or Campeggio could be elected pope his cause would be
safe.   He wrote therefore on 6th February to his agents in
Rome (Gardiner, Brian, &c.), giving them full commission to
use all his influence in the election.   "If the cardinals present, *having God and the Holy Ghost before them*, consider
what is best for the Church, they cannot fail to agree upon
Wolsey; but as human fragility suffers not all things to be
weighed in just balance, the ambassadors are to make promises of spiritual promotions, offices, dignities, rewards of
money and other things; they are also to show them what
Wolsey will give up if he enters into this dangerous storm
and troublous tempest for the relief of the Church, all of
which benefices shall be given to the king's friends, besides
other large rewards."   Thus the most abominable and
impious simony is proposed, with professions about the
Holy Ghost, that are only not hypocritical, because those to
whom they were addressed must have taken them for
cynical mockery.   Yet all this was written, if not at Wolsey's
dictation, yet with his sanction.*

* The king's letter in *Letters and Papers*, vol. iv., part iii.- n. 5270;
Wolsey's consent, n. 5472.

The second specimen of hypocrisy is the king's mani-
festo to England as to his reasons for bringing the question of his marriage before the Legatine Tribunal. On
8th November, 1528, he held a great assembly of nobles,
privy councillors, with the lord mayor and great merchants
of London. He rehearsed the peace and success the
country had enjoyed hitherto under his reign, but the fear
that, if he should die without legitimate issue, civil discord
might arise like that of the 15th century, which might even
lead to foreign conquest. True, he had a lovely daughter
by the Lady Catharine; but he had lately heard, from
pious and learned theologians, that his marriage with
his deceased brother's widow was forbidden by Divine
law—in fact, this objection had been urged when he was
lately negotiating an alliance for her. The speech had
filled his mind with horror, since it involved a question
of his eternal salvation. *He called God to witness, and
declared on the word of a king,* that this alone had caused
him to ask the opinion of learned theologians throughout
Europe, and the true and equitable judgment of the
legate of the Holy See, in order that henceforth he
might live in lawful marriage with peaceful conscience.
Should it clearly appear that he could continue in his
present marriage, nothing would please him better. He
had been so happy in it, that, were the marriage proved
lawful, he would choose Catharine above all women in
the world. Should it, on the contrary, be found that his
marriage was unlawful and null from the beginning, his fate
would be deplorable. He must, then, separate from the
woman he loved, and his conscience would be torn with
the thought that for twenty years he had been living
in worse than fornication, without any lawful issue to
survive him. These things tortured him day and night;
and, to end his torture, he had sent for the pope's legate.
His hearers would explain this to the people, and he in-

vited all to join their prayers that the truth might be made
manifest.*

The whole speech is one tissue of unmitigated lies. The
hearers had not, as we have, the evidence of the letters
Henry had already written to Anne and his instruction to
his agents in Italy, nor did they know of the clauses he had
got inserted in the conditional bull of dispensation for a
second marriage, in case of the dissolution of the first,
which proved that affinity was the last thing that troubled
his conscience;† but the relations of Henry with Anne,

---

* The original speech, as *written* in Latin, is given in Wilkins, iii.
714. It was, of course, spoken in English.

† On the affinity of Anne Boleyn with Henry, by his relations
with her sister Mary, and on the dispensing clause he purposely got
inserted in the bull, to marry anyone related to him in the first degree
of affinity, *except his brother's widow*, see Friedmann, App. B., vol,
ii., 323, and Mr. Pocock's Preface to the *Records of the Reformation;*
also, Harpsfield, p. 236, and Brewer, ii. 239, &c. As Cardinal Pole's
testimony in this matter is less known, and found in a very rare book,
I here translate it. As a relative and a courtier, Pole must have been
well informed, and he wrote during Anne's life : " At your age of life,
and with all your experience of the world, you were enslaved by your
passion for a girl. But she would not give you your will unless you
rejected your wife, whose place she longed to take. The modest
woman would not be your mistress ; no, but she would be your wife.
She had learned, I think, if from nothing else, at least from the
example of her own sister, how soon you got tired of your mis-
tresses, and she resolved to surpass her sister in retaining you as her
lover. . . .

" Now, what sort of person is it whom you have put in the place
of your divorced wife ? Is she not the sister of her whom first you
violated, and for a long time after kept as your concubine?
(*Quam tu et violasti primum et diu postea concubinæ loco apud
te habuisti ?*) She certainly is. How is it, then, that you now tell
us of the horror you have of illicit marriage ? Are you ignorant of
the law which certainly no less prohibits marriage with a sister of
one with whom *you* have become one flesh, than with one with whom
your brother was one flesh ? If the one kind of marriage is detestable, so is the other. Were you ignorant of this law ? Nay, you
knew it better than others. How do I prove that ? Because, at the

and his determination to marry her, were no longer a secret
to the majority of those whom he addressed. They knew
he was pledging his royal honour to a falsehood, and calling
God to witness to a perjury, when he appealed to the
alarm of conscience as his sole motive for agitating the
question.*

Archdeacon Harpsfield, who in the time of Queen Mary
had access to State papers, and knew well all the circumstances of the divorce, thus sums up his dissertation :
"When I consider this and other premisses, I cannot
be induced to believe that the king, upon conscience only,
and for avoiding God's displeasure (as it was pretended),
but rather to satisfy and serve his bodily pleasures and
appetite, pursued this divorce. And his mind, being thus
depraved and corrupted, and seeking the furthering and
advancement only of his corrupt will, he found like doctors
and like prophets, who, preferring his sensual appetite and
their own worldly advancement before God's blessed will,
accommodated their answer to his carnal corrupted desire.
For, as the Prophet Ezechiel writeth to such as have filthy,
corrupt cogitations in their hearts, and yet pretend to seek
and search and understand God's pleasure, and to be
directed by the same, God sendeth false prophets to make
them a suitable answer, to feed and maintain their corrupt

very time you were rejecting the dispensation of the pope to marry
your brother's widow, you were doing your very utmost (*magna vi
contendebas*) to get leave from the pope to marry the sister of your
former concubine."—*De Unit. Eccl.*, lib. iii.

* The king pretends, in this speech and elsewhere, that the first
suggestion to his mind of doubt as to the lawfulness of his marriage
was a question proposed by the Bishop of Tarbes as to the legitimacy
of Mary, when discussing a treaty of marriage. Mr. Froude, though
admitting that the subject had been maturing in Henry's mind for
years, says : "The gangrene was torn open by the Bishop of Tarbes"
(*History*, i. 124). Mr. Brewer says : "This was a *political figment*
arranged between the king and Wolsey " (*Reign of Henry*, ii. 163).

humours, as it chanced (the more the pity) to this king also." *

Henry, however, was not left without some true prophets, and amongst them the principal was he whom the Lady Margaret had at her death begged to watch over him. Leaving all other phases of this history aside, I will now relate the part taken by, or rather forced on, the Bishop of Rochester. The plan of divorce first concerted between Wolsey and the king was this. A collusive suit was instituted against the king by Wolsey, as legate, and Warham, as Archbishop of Canterbury, on 17th May, 1527. As guardians of public morality, they cited the king to appear before them, to answer for having lived for eighteen years in incestuous intercourse with his brother's widow. Henry personally appeared on his defence, and then appointed a proctor to continue the farce, while one of his devoted servants, Dr. Wolman, pleaded against him. This was all done secretly, but the archbishops dared not take the decision on themselves, and questions were addressed by them to a number of the most learned bishops in England regarding the lawfulness of marriage with a brother's widow, which it was hoped they would answer as the king desired. But the king was disappointed. Most of them answered that such a marriage, with a papal dispensation, would be valid. The answer of the Bishop of Rochester has been preserved, and, as it contains the pith of all the books he subsequently wrote on the subject, I will give it in a literal translation. It is addressed to Cardinal Wolsey, and, after the salutation, continues: "Having now consulted all the mute teachers (as they say) whom I could get in my hands, and diligently sorted their opinions, and

---

* Harpsfield's *Pretended Divorce*, p. 258. The passage referred to is *Ezech.* xiv. 3-10, which is most apposite to this whole history. It is quoted and shown to be apposite by Cardinal Pole, in the third book of his answer to Henry, called *De Unitate Ecclesiæ*.

weighed their reasons, I find, just as I lately wrote to your Eminence, - that there is great divergence between them. Some assert that the matter in hand is prohibited by Divine law ; others, again, strongly maintain that it is in no way repugnant to Divine law. After weighing impartially over and over again the reasons on both sides, I think I perceive an easy reply to all the arguments of those who assert that it is prohibited by Divine law, but no easy reply to those of the other side. So that I am now thoroughly convinced that it can by no means be proved to be prohibited by any Divine law that is now in force, that a brother marry the wife of his brother deceased without children.

" If this is true, and I have no doubt that it is most certainly true, who can deny, considering the plenitude of power which Christ has conferred on the Sovereign Pontiff, that the pope may dispense, for some very grave reason, for such a marriage ?

" Even if I granted that the reasons on either side were evenly balanced, and that the difficulties on each side could be solved with equal ease, I should nevertheless be more inclined to give the power of dispensation to the Pontiff, for this reason that the theologians of both sides grant that it belongs to the plenitude of the pontifical office to interpret ambiguous places of Holy Scripture, having heard the judgment of theologians and jurists. Otherwise to no purpose Christ would have said : ' Whatsoever thou shalt loose on earth shall be loosed in heaven, and whatsoever thou shalt bind on earth shall be bound in heaven '. Now, as it is most evident that by their very acts the Sovereign Pontiffs have more than once declared that it is lawful in the case mentioned to dispense in favour of the second brother, this alone would powerfully move me to give my assent, even if they alleged no reasons or proofs. From these premisses no scruple or hesitation remains in my mind about the matter. I wish your eminence long life and happiness."

The above letter was written from Rochester, in May and enclosed by Wolsey in a letter sent by him to the king on 2nd June, 1527.[*]

However secretly these proceedings were carried on, they soon got generally rumoured and came to the ears of the queen. She asked an explanation of the king, who pleaded the torment of his conscience at his probable state of mortal sin, and declared that he only sought light and peace. He even asked her to choose a separate residence till the matter should be decided. This she declined, and demanded to have counsel given her both in England and elsewhere ; but the king pressed the importance of secrecy upon her.[†] Both he and Wolsey seem to have suspected that she gained her information from Fisher, which was not the case.

It had been determined that Wolsey should go on an embassy into France, and he visited Rochester on his way. Nine hundred horsemen rode with the cardinal, besides a multitude of attendants. They started on 3rd July, 1527, and the first night rested at Sir John Wiltshire's, near Dartford. There Wolsey was met by the Archbishop of Canterbury. Wolsey told him that the queen had discovered the collusive suit, and that the king had assured her they were only " searching out the truth, on occasion of doubts moved by the Bishop of Tarbes. Which fashion and manner liked my Lord of Canterbury very well." From the whole context of this communication of Wolsey to the king it would seem that Warham was overreached, and persuaded of the good faith of the whole proceedings. And as he had been originally averse to the marriage in the time of Henry VII., it was not difficult to convince him that the case might be reopened.

The next day the cardinal slept at Rochester, in the

---

* Pocock, *Records*, i. 9; *State Papers*, i. 189. Also, but abridged, in *Letters and Papers*, iv., part ii., n. 3148.
† Friedmann, i. 53; Brewer, ii. 193, 204.

bishop's palace; "the rest of his train," says Cavendish, "in the city, and in Stroud on this side of the bridge ".* The day after the cardinal reached Faversham, and thence wrote to the king a long account of his interview with Warham and Fisher.† He had begun by talking with Fisher on the calamities of the Church, and what plans were devised for the pope's release, "as well in prayer and fasting as other good deeds," he added, to please the bishop. "After which communication I asked him whether he had heard lately any tidings from the Court, and whether any man had been sent unto him from the queen's grace. At which question he somewhat stayed and paused; nevertheless in conclusion he answered how truth it is that of late one was sent unto him from the queen's grace, who brought him a message only by mouth, without disclosure of any particularity, that certain matters there were between your grace and her lately chanced, wherein she would be glad to have his counsel, alleging that your highness was content she should so have. Whereunto, as he saith, he made answer likewise by mouth, that he was ready and prone to give her his counsel in anything that concerned and touched only herself; but in matters concerning your highness and her, he would nothing do, without knowledge of your pleasure and express commandment, and herewith dismissed the messenger.

"After declaration whereof, I replied and said, ' My lord, ye and I have been of an old acquaintance, and the one hath loved and trusted the other; wherefore, postponing all doubt and fear, ye may be frank and plain with me, like as I, for my part, will be with you '. And so I demanded of him whether he had any special conjecture or knowledge what the matter should be wherein the queen desired to have his advice. Whereunto he answered, that by certain

* *Life of Wolsey*, p. 69 (Morley's edition, 1885).
† *State Papers*, i. 196; Brewer's *Reign of Henry*, ii. 193-198.

report and relation he knew nothing; howbeit, upon conjecture arising upon such things as he had heard, he
thinketh it was for a divorce to be had between your
highness and the queen. Which to conject he was specially
moved, upon a tale brought unto him by his brother from
London, who showed, that being there in a certain company,
he heard say that things were set forth, sounding to such a
purpose; whereupon calling to remembrance the question I
moved unto him by your grace's commandment,* with the
message sent unto him from the queen, he verily supposed
such a matter to be in hand. And this was all he knoweth
therein, as he constantly affirmeth; without that ever he
sent any word or knowledge thereof, by his faith, to the
queen's grace, or any other living person."

Wolsey then began to pretend to be very confidential.
The king, he said, had bid him reveal his secret to Fisher,
upon oath of secrecy, and obtain his opinion through Wolsey.
He then told the story about the Bishop of Tarbes, and how
the bishop's objections were to be discussed by Wolsey in
France in this very embassy.† "And thus declaring the
whole matter unto him at length, *as was devised with your
highness in York Place*, I added that, by what means it was
not yet apprehended, an inkling of this matter is come to the
queen's knowledge; who being suspicious, and casting
further doubts than was meant or intended, hath broken
with your grace thereof, after a very displeasant manner,
saying that by my procurement and setting forth, a divorce
was purposed between her and your highness." He then
went on, according to his own account, to calumniate the

---

* The theological doubt to which he had given a written answer.

† Mr. Brewer remarks that the matter was never mooted in France,
and considers the whole thing a pure fiction. However, the Venetian
ambassador, Venier, writes that the Bishop of Tarbes made his
objection *by Wolsey's advice*, who wanted to marry the king to the
French king's sister.

queen as making the matter public. "And I assure your
grace, my Lord of Rochester, hearing the process of the
matter after this sort, did greatly blame the queen, as well
for giving so light credence in so grave a matter," as for her
imprudent want of secrecy, which might endanger peace and
imperil the succession to the Crown. The good bishop even
wished to show her fault to the queen, "considering that
the thing done by your grace was so necessary and expedient
and the queen's act so perilous. Howbeit I have so persuaded
him that he will nothing speak or do therein, or anything
counsel her, but as shall stand with your pleasure; for, he
saith, although she be queen of this realm, yet he acknow-
ledgeth you for his high sovereign lord and king."

Thus the king and Wolsey, by tricks and lies, sought to
blind the man they most feared, depriving the queen of her
counsellor, and persuading him that the king was only intent
on assuring the legitimacy of his daughter against objections,
while the queen by her indiscretion was imperilling it. The
cardinal went on to discuss the difficulties in the bull of
dispensation granted by Julius. But on this head he could
not get much from the bishop; who, after all, probably saw
through the whole deceit.

It is almost a pleasure to know that the king was trying
in secret to outwit Wolsey himself, and by means of his
envoy, Dr. Knight, to carry his point with the pope, then in
captivity.* But with the negotiations with the pope which
filled the next year Fisher is not connected, and they must
be passed over here. One thing only it is important
to remark. Though the original grounds of seeking a
divorce were that Pope Julius had gone beyond his powers
in dispensing for Henry's marriage, and this was the final
issue on which Henry's creature, Cranmer, pronounced the
divorce, yet there was no possible or impossible exercise of

* Brewer, ii. 220.

papal authority which was not conceived and proposed during the course of the negotiations by the king and his advisers, and which would not have been admitted without question if in favour of his own passions. He would have accepted a dispensation to commit bigamy, or he would have sent Catharine into a nunnery, and taken a vow of chastity himself, on condition of being presently dispensed, if by such a pretext the marriage could have been dissolved.*
He would have played fast and loose with the pope's jurisdiction, asking him, in the same breath, to declare it limited as regards the impediment arising from affinity with Catharine, and unlimited as regards affinity with Anne. Mr. Friedmann is severe but is accurate when he says: "Machiavelli would have turned with disgust from so miserable a liar. Henry was a liar to his own conscience. He was a thoroughly immoral man, and he dared not own it to himself. He tried by all kinds of casuistic subterfuges to make his most dishonest acts appear pure virtue, to make himself believe in his own goodness." † And though Bishop Stubbs has a higher estimate of Henry's character and ability than Mr. Friedmann, yet in this respect their judgments do not much differ: "I seem to see in him," writes the bishop, "a grand, gross figure, very far removed from ordinary human sympathies, self-engrossed, self-confident, self-willed; unscrupulous in act, violent, and crafty, but justifying to himself, by his belief in himself, both unscrupulousness, violence, and craft". ‡ Bishop Stubbs would

---

* Brewer, ii. 312. Henry even assured the queen that if she should enter religion the pope could not dispense the king to marry again, since he had no power to do it; and at the very time he was urging the pope to such a stretch of power (*Ibid.*, p. 317).

† *Anne Boleyn*, i. 17.

‡ *Lectures on Mediæval and Modern History*, p. 290. M. Du Boys, in his *Catharine d'Aragon*, has probably summed up Henry's character best of all, when he calls him a compound of Nero and Tartuffe.

explain this portent as the result of uncontrolled, uncontradicted, irresponsible power long exercised. There is perhaps a more secret but more profound cause that should be added—hypocritical and sacrilegious communions. Towards the beginning of July, 1528, when the terrible " sweating sickness " was carrying off its victims by thousands, Henry sent Anne away, and went to confession. " This day, his highness, like a gracious prince, hath received his Maker at the friars (at Greenwich), which was ministered to his highness by my Lord of Lincoln." Thus wrote one of his attendants to Wolsey. " I hear he has made his will and taken the Sacraments, for fear of sudden death," wrote the French ambassador.* Yet he did not put a stop to his vile correspondence with Anne, nor interrupt his unjust and sacrilegious projects in case he should escape. During the following years, when he was living in open adultery, he interrupted none of his usual communions at Christmas, Easter, and Whitsuntide.† I mention these things, because they are passed over by historians as trivial, though in all probability they are the turning-points in men's lives and in the history of nations.

It is more than insinuated by some that the pope was as double-dealing and reckless of justice as either king or cardinal, and that if he did not grant the divorce, it was from calculations of self-interest and fear of the emperor. Were this the case, the issue would show the overruling Providence of God in not allowing an unworthy pope to do an unworthy thing. But I can see no proof of the fact alleged. He was explicitly threatened over and over again by the king, by Wolsey,‡ by Parliament, by the king's

* Brewer, ii. 273.

† The Privy Purse expenses mention the offerings made on these occasions.

‡ One specimen may suffice. Wolsey wrote : " I cannot conceal my fears lest his majesty, relying on the Divine and human rights

agents, that to refuse the king's demand was to lose
England for ever.   He did at last refuse, saying that if
England was to be lost, it was better that it should be lost
by justice than by injustice.   But for nearly six years he
dallied with the king, and protracted the suit by every
possible device that was not criminal.   It may be that, had
he followed a different policy, and taken decided and
strong measures from the beginning, he would have served
justice better, and even saved England to the Church.
There were many who thought so then, and the Bishop of
Rochester (as will be seen later on) was among the number.
But the matter was uncertain, and it was a question of
policy.   The pope was in hopes that by mild answers and
by delay he might weary out the king.   He even encouraged hopes that he knew were fallacious.   He appeared
to entertain propositions that he knew were absurd, and
allowed them to be discussed by theologians.   But that he
either did anything or promised anything that was simply
illicit has not been proved.   Sir Gregory Casale, Henry's
agent in Italy, wrote to his brother Vincent, then in England :
" I hear you have told Wolsey that, if the pope's fears were
removed, he would do everything for the king, *licita et
illicita*.   But, if you remember rightly, I told you the pope
would do all that *could be done ;* but there are many things
the pope says *he cannot do*."   The English ambassadors also
reported a saying of the pope's that " though the king's
cause might be in his *Pater Noster*, it had no place in his
Creed," meaning (I suppose) that, however much he might

belonging to him as a Christian, should he find that he is frustrated
of the grace of the Apostolic See and the clemency of the Vicar of
Christ, by the favour of Cæsar, to whom it in no way belongs to
oppose such holy purposes, will take measures and seek remedies,
which may give occasion not only to this kingdom, but to other
Christian princes also, to diminish and slight the authority and
jurisdiction of the Apostolic See " (Burnet's *Collect.*, p. 16).   This is
one of the earliest and mildest of the threats.

wish and pray for the king's prosperity, he could not promote it by sacrificing any point of Catholic faith or discipline.*

To return to Fisher. After Wolsey's insidious interview with him in July, 1527, more than fifteen months passed before his name appears again in connection with this matter. He was watching its progress with great anxiety, praying and studying, but the king's spies were watching him lest he should lend assistance to the queen. At last the pope's legate Campeggio arrived in England in October, 1528. His first endeavour was to reconcile the king to his present marriage; and as the king had called in question the validity of the dispensation of Pope Julius, by which he had contracted marriage, Campeggio in the pope's name offered to grant a new dispensation, so that by renewal of consent the marriage might be revalidated in case it were invalid. But in spite of Henry's professions of love for Catharine this would not have served his purpose. He therefore threw his conscientious scruples on the uncertainty of the pope's power to grant any such dispensation, as being contrary to the law of God. Campeggio writes: "He told me plainly he wanted nothing more than a declaration whether this marriage was valid or not, he himself always assuming its invalidity; and I believe if an angel descended from heaven, he would not be able to convince his majesty to the contrary".† Wolsey also, though he was one of the judges who was to hear evidence and pronounce impartially, was equally determined, and sought to determine his colleague, not by arguing the merits of the case, but by reasons of State. "In my last conversation with his lordship," writes Campeggio, "he said and repeated it many times in Latin: 'Most reverend lord, beware lest, in like manner as the greater part of Germany, owing to the harshness and severity

---

* *Letters and Papers*, iv. 2333, 2370.   † Brewer, ii. 298.

of a certain cardinal, has become estranged from the Apostolic See and the Faith, it should be said that another
cardinal has given the same occasion to England with the
same result '." * The legate had also an interview with the
queen. She was very prudent. "She concluded the conference," he writes, "by saying she was a lone woman and
a stranger, without friend or adviser, and intended to ask
the king for counsellors." †

It was considered certain that, if allowed to choose, the
queen would select the Bishop of Rochester in the first
place, nor could the king in decency refuse her request. As
he had therefore tried to gain over the bishop by means of
Wolsey, he now attempts the same thing by means of Campeggio. It has been always held that, even after a marriage
has been validly contracted, if before its consummation one
of the parties should make solemn profession in a religious
order, the contract is dissolved. Some canonists were seeking in this fact a solution for Henry's difficulties. They
seem to have argued that if an unconsummated marriage of
certain validity could be thus broken, a marriage of doubtful
validity (as they assumed this to be), even though it had lasted
for twenty years, might be set aside by papal dispensation,
if Catharine would take a vow of chastity in some religious
order. Though this scheme was rejected by all theologians
when it came to be seriously discussed, it must have been
entertained for a time by Campeggio. "I do not despair,"
he writes, " of success in persuading the queen to enter some
religion, though I see it is difficult, and more than doubtful.
. . . As the Bishop of Rochester is in her favour, and I
believe she will choose him as one of her counsellors, with
the king's consent, I had a long interview with him on the
25th, ‡ and exhorted him to adopt this course for many
reasons. When he left me he seemed to be satisfied with

* Brewer, ii. 299.   † *Ibid.*, p. 302.
‡ Sunday, 25th October 1528.

what I had urged. God grant that the best counsels may prevail."* Campeggio, however, was mistaken, or else the bishop, on reflection, saw the matter in another light.

The queen asked for counsellors. The king appointed the Archbishop of Canterbury, the Bishops of Rochester,† Bath, and London, the queen's confessor, Thomes Abel, and others. Warham, the Archbishop of Canterbury, was a man of high character, of great learning, and a distinguished canonist, but he was not a fit counsellor for the queen, having opposed the marriage originally, and having taken action against it in instituting the collusive suit. He stood also in great dread of the king's anger. The Bishop of London, Cuthbert Tunstal, was also a man of great eminence, and he seems to have been faithful though somewhat timid. The conduct of Clerk, Bishop of Bath and Wells, was vacillating. Thomas Abel, the queen's confessor, proved his character and courage when he laid down his life for the faith in 1540. To these were soon added Standish, the Bishop of St. Asaph's, a Franciscan, whose attack on clerical immunity had gained him the king's favour in 1515, and West, Bishop of Ely, a man of great piety and charity as well as learning. The queen had never shown the least disposition to accept the plan proposed to her by Campeggio, and she was encouraged in this resolution by her counsellors, especially by Fisher.‡

Eight months more passed before the cause was brought into the Legatine Court. The reasons of this delay I may pass over. The interval was spent by the Bishop of Rochester in a profound study of the whole question of im-

* Brewer, ii. 302.

† I do not understand why Mr. Brewer says (p. 339, note) that Fisher was not one of the counsellors. He himself quotes, at p. 303, Campeggio's words that he was appointed. See also the words of the Duke of Norfolk, quoted *infra*, p. 165. The bishop also distinctly asserts it (Lewis, ii. 403).

‡ Brewer, ii. 306.

pediments of marriage in Scripture, in history, and in canon
law.   On this we have his own testimony.   Some years
later, when Fisher was imprisoned, the officials who were
sent to Rochester to seize his goods for the king came
upon some letters of a mysterious nature, which suggested
to the ingenuity of some of the privy councillors no less
than forty interrogations.*   I extract all that is of importance.   The bishop says he never addressed the Lady
Catharine in private, except in the time the king commanded
him to give her counsel. † To the question how many
books he had written concerning the king's matrimony and
divorce, he says : " I am not certain of the number, but I
think seven or eight.   The matter was so serious, both on
account of the importance of the persons concerned, and on
account of the injunction given me by the king, that I
devoted more attention to examining the truth of it, lest I
should deceive myself and others, than to anything else in
my life."   It should be noted that by the word " book " in
those days was not meant a printed book, or even a written
book of any great size.   Any treatise of a few sheets was
called a book.   The bishop enlarged or rewrote his disser-
tations according as new books appeared on the other side.
To the question : How many copies have been made of
them, and in whose hands are they ? he replies : " I do not
know, nor was I very careful about the others, but only of
the two last written by me, and which contained the pith of
the former ones.   One of these the Archbishop of Canterbury now hath."   (This was Cranmer, as the bishop is writing
in 1534.)   " I never sent nor consented to the sending of

---

* The questions are given in *Letters and Papers*, viii. 859, and the
answers (abridged) in English.   The answers however, in Latin, are
given in full by Lewis (ii. 403), but without the questions.

† " Ego nunquam clanculo sum allocutus dictam D. Katherinam
citra id temporis, quo Regia Majestas in mandatis mihi dederat, ut
essem illi in consiliis in ipsius negotio."

any of these books over the sea. I never counselled Abel, or consented to the publishing of his book, neither had he any book of mine, to my knowledge."

It would seem that some spiritual letters addressed by the bishop to the queen had come into the hands of Henry; being probably stolen from the queen by some of his spies in her service. Not only had he the abominable meanness and impiety to read these, he even put infamous constructions on them, showed them to his council, and allowed Cromwell to found on them a series of interrogations addressed to the bishop : " Whether he wrote any letter to the Lady Catharine, as if she despaired of the mercy of God ? Whether the cause of the despair was that she committed perjury, and, as some say, received the Host that she was never carnally known by Prince Arthur ? " The bishop replies : "The king knows right well that by his own consent the Lady Catharine sent for me more than once, on account of certain scruples of conscience, and that long before this business was begun. To allay her scruples I used many words *viva voce*, and afterwards wrote some letters. I never heard from her that she despaired of mercy or had committed perjury ; but whatever I may have written, it was with the purpose that she should lay aside scruples and strengthen her mind in hope and confidence in the promises of Christ."

This document, to which too little attention has been paid, sinks Henry to the level of King Wenceslas and other violators of sacramental secrecy ; and, on the other hand, since it is certain that Henry's hatred towards Fisher was founded on the confidence given to him by the queen, it places the Bishop of Rochester with St. John Nepomucen and other martyrs of the sacrament of penance.*

* With regard to the books mentioned in the text, Fisher says he wrote seven or eight. Some were printed in Spain; one by Michael de Eguia in 1530 (Brunet), one at Alcala (Compluti) in August, 1530;

To complete what can be said of Fisher's relations with
the queen, I will here give Chapuys' account of the queen's
reference to it in June, 1531. At that date the king was
striving to induce the queen to retract her appeal to the

De Causa Matrimonii Ser.-Regis Angliæ Liber, Joanne Roffensi
episcopo auctore (84 pages in Latin). Vaughan, an envoy of Cromwell, writes to him from Antwerp, 3rd August, 1533, that he has been
inquiring as to the author and publisher there of a Latin book against
the king's cause. He has been told that the book was written by the
Bishop of Rochester, and delivered by him to the Spaniards in England, who finished the draft, and that friars Peto and Elstow of Canterbury are conveyers of the same into England. He suggests that the
bishop's house should be searched, as the first copy will be probably
found there. He adds that the bishop delivered his copy to the Spaniards, who transcribed it in haste, *unknown to the bishop*, and that it
is intermingled with Greek and Spanish (*State Papers*, vii. 372, and
Letters and Papers, vi. 934). There is frequent reference to Fisher's
writings on this subject in the correspondence of the imperial ambassador. On 6th February, 1530, he writes : " Since my last the Bishop
of Rochester has finished revising the book which he lately wrote, and
which he sent to your majesty. Since then he has written another,
which the queen has forwarded at the request of the bishop, to be
examined at leisure, though he fears to be known as the author " (*Letters*, iv. 6199). On 27th November, 1530, he writes again that the king's
party were going to circulate in England the votes of the universities
in favour of the king. " If they do, it will be better to get attestation
of the votes in favour of the queen, and circulate some books, as
Fisher's were circulated in Spain. Some thought he would be annoyed,
and feared the king's displeasure; but the king has shown himself
quite indifferent. I have commissioned May to get the bishop's two
later books printed, and will distribute them at the opening of Parliament." On 4th December, 1530, he writes : " The Bishop of Rochester
has written another book in favour of the queen, now sent ". MS.
copies of some of these treatises are in the Record Office, the British
Museum, and Cambridge University Library. The library of St.
John's College, Cambridge, possesses one of his printed books. But
his most important and latest treatise, written in answer to the official
book which came out in 1530 in favour of the king, with the suffrages
of certain universities, was translated into English (with some abridgment) by Archdeacon Harpsfield, and makes the first part of his
Treatise on the Divorce. This treatise was first printed in 1878 for
the Camden Society, with the excellent notes of Mr. Pocock.

pope, and to allow her cause to be tried elsewhere. He
sent to her the principal members of his council. They
were quite unsuccessful in their mission. Among other
things, the Duke of Norfolk told her that she had no reason
to complain of partiality in England, for she had had the
most complete counsel, as the Archbishop of Canterbury, the
Bishops of Durham,* Rochester, and others. The queen
replied that they were fine counsellors, for when she asked
advice of the Archbishop of Canterbury, he replied that he
would not meddle in these affairs, saying frequently : " Ira
principis mors est " ; the Bishop of Durham said he dared
not, for he was the king's subject and vassal ; Rochester
told her to keep up her courage, and that was all the counsel
she got from them. Such is the account given by Eustace
Chapuys, the imperial ambassador, and he probably heard it
from the queen herself.† Words spoken in warmth by a
woman ill-treated and insulted, and then taunted with the
generosity of her persecutor, must not be pressed beyond
their meaning. There is every reason indeed to think that
Warham and Tunstal were but faint-hearted defenders or
counsellors ; but this cannot be said of Fisher. From the
day the question was mooted in the spring of 1527 till the
eve of Henry's marriage with Anne Boleyn he did not cease
to defend the queen's cause by his pen and in the pulpit.‡
Nor can the queen have forgotten his bold defence of her
rights before the Legatine Court in 1529. This must be
now related.

After long delays Cardinals Campeggio and Wolsey
opened their court in the great hall at Blackfriars, on the
last day of May, 1529, citing the king and queen to appear

· * Tunstal had been translated to Durham in 1530.

† *Letters and Papers*, v. 287.

‡ When, however, he saw the case hopeless, and that he could not
advance the queen's cause, he ceased to give advice, except in matters
of conscience, as he admits in his answer to Question 21. (Lewis, ii.
405.)

on the 18th June.   On that day the king appeared by
proxy, the queen in person, and protested against the jurisdiction of the court.   The cardinals promised to decide on
the validity of the appeal on the 21st.   Both king and
queen appeared.   The event has been made famous by
Shakespeare, who gathered his account from the chroniclers.
But I will transcribe the more authentic account, written
only a few days after the event by eye-witnesses.   Ludovico
Falier, the Venetian ambassador, wrote, on the 29th : "The
cardinal judges assembled in a hall, on a raised platform,
the queen having preceded them, followed by the king, who
was the first to seat himself under a canopy of gold brocade
on the right, the queen being on the left, under another
canopy on a lower level.   The king then said a few words
to the judges in English, to the effect that he would no
longer remain in mortal sin, as he had done during the last
twenty years, and that he should never be at case until the
rights of this marriage were decided, requesting the judges
to despatch the case.   Cardinal Wolsey replied that, although
he had received infinite benefits from his majesty, and was
declared suspected, yet, as this case had been committed to
him and Cardinal Campeggio by the pope, he would judge
it according to such reason as his poor ability supplied,
saying that he was unworthy to judge such a case, but
would, nevertheless, not omit to do what appeared to him
just.   The queen then rose, and, throwing herself on her
knees before the king, said aloud that she had lived for
twenty years with his majesty as his lawful wife, keeping her
faith to him, and that she did not deserve to be repudiated
and thus put to shame without a cause, and she besought
the said judges to show her favour.   The queen said
nothing more ; and the king sent for his privy councillors,
with whom he remained for half-an-hour, after which the
judges prorogued the term until the 22nd.   On that day,
two bishops appeared as advocates and proctors for the

queen, namely, the Bishop of Rochester and the Bishop of
Bath, saying that, to prevent the king falling into mortal sin,
they would defend the rights of the queen, and show that
she was his legitimate and true wife; and they presented
the writ of appeal, rejecting the judges as suspected, so that
nothing farther was done."*

On the very day of this famous scene, Cardinal Campeggio
wrote to Salviati in Rome, not, indeed, a full description of
what had happened, for that was not his scope, but an
account of the queen's appeal. He says that she knelt,
although the king twice raised her up, and asked permission,
as it was a question which concerned the honour and conscience of herself and of the house of Spain, to write and
send messengers to the emperor and to his holiness.† All
communication hitherto had been refused her. Cavendish,
in his *Life of Wolsey*, writing many years later, and from
recollection, not only amplifies the queen's speech, but puts
into the mouth of the king, after the queen's departure from
the court, a long declaration of the queen's virtue and his
own esteem and love for her. But this seems to be a
reminiscence of the speech I have given above, which he
made to the citizens of London in the same place (Blackfriars) at the first arrival of the legate. Cavendish also
refers to this occasion a somewhat sharp contention between
the Archbishop of Canterbury and the Bishop of Rochester
in the king's presence, which cannot be an invention of his
own, though it is not recorded by any other writer, and probably took place on some other occasion. The king,
according to Cavendish, declared that, in moving this
question, he was following the advice given to him by all
his prelates. "'That is truth, if it please your highness,'
quoth the Bishop of Canterbury; 'I doubt not but all my

* *Cal. of Venetian State Papers*, iv. 482.
† The letter is in the Appendix to Mr. Gairdner's edition of
Mr. Brewer's Introductions, in *Reign of Henry*, ii. 491.

brethren will affirm the same.' 'No, sir, not I,' quoth the Bishop of Rochester; 'ye have not my consent thereto.' 'No! ha' thee!' quoth the king; 'look here upon this, is not this your hand and seal?' and showed him the instrument with seals. 'No, forsooth, sire,' quoth the Bishop of Rochester, ' it is not my hand nor seal.' To that quoth the king to my Lord of Canterbury, 'Sir, how say ye, is it not his hand and seal?' 'Yes, sir,' quoth my Lord of Canterbury. 'That is not so,' quoth the Bishop of Rochester, 'for, indeed, you were in hand with me to have both my hand and seal, as other of my lords had already done; but then I said to you that I would never consent to no such act, for it were much against my conscience; nor my hand and seal should never be seen to any such instrument, God willing, with much more matter touching the same communication between us.' 'You say truth,' quoth the Bishop of Canterbury; 'such words ye said to me; but at the last ye were fully persuaded that I should for you subscribe your name, and put to a seal myself, and ye would allow the same.' 'All which words and matter,' quoth the Bishop of Rochester, 'under your correction, my lord, and supportation of this noble audience, there is nothing more untrue.' 'Well, well,' quoth the king, 'it shall make no matter; we will not stand with you in argument herein, for you are but one man.' And with that the court was adjourned."* Such is Cavendish's account. The dialogue is his own composition, a quarter of a century after the occurrence, but that there was an altercation of this sort cannot be doubted. There exists at the present day an instrument with Fisher's signature and seal, but dated at a later period (1st July), in which he, with the other bishops, states that the king had consulted them on the divorce, and that they considered that he had great reasons for his scruples.† This

---

* *Life of Wolsey*, p. 121 (ed. Morley).   † Rymer, xiv. 301.

is probably the document which Fisher repudiated as regards himself.

Cavendish tells another tale of an altercation between the Bishop of Rochester and Cardinal Wolsey. When many witnesses had been heard on both sides regarding the facts of Catharine's first marriage, someone observed that in such condradictions no man could know the truth. " 'Yes,' quoth the Bishop of Rochester, 'I know the truth.' 'How know you the truth?' quoth my lord cardinal. 'Forsooth, my lord,' quoth he, 'I am professor of the Truth. I know that God is Truth itself, nor He never spake but truth, who saith : What God hath joined together, let not man put asunder. And forasmuch as this marriage was made and joined by God to a good intent, I say that I know the truth, the which cannot be broken or loosed by the power of man upon no feigned occasion.'. 'So much doth all faithful men know,' quoth my lord cardinal, 'as well as you. Yet this reason is not sufficient in this case, for the king's counsel doth allege divers presumptions, to prove the marriage not good at the beginning; *ergo*, say they, it was not joined at the beginning, and therefore it is not lawful.' "

The cardinal, however, knew well the bishop's meaning that the whole trial was a piece of elaborate hypocrisy. Henry's pains of conscience and scruples about his state of mortal sin and his desire to arrive at truth, and Wolsey's affectation of justice and impartiality, were known, not only to Fisher, but to all men, to be lies, and Fisher's heart sickened at the cruel and impious farce.

Cardinal Campeggio, however, though he had a part to play, was an upright judge and an admirer of honesty. In one of his letters he bears the following testimony to the boldness of the Bishop of Rochester's advocacy. He writes to Salviati in Italy on the 29th June, 1529 : " Yesterday the fifth audience was given. While the proceedings were going on as usual, owing to the queen's contumacy, the Bishop of

Rochester made his appearance, and said, in an appropriate
speech, that in a former audience he had heard the king's
majesty discuss the cause, and testify before all that his only
intention was to get justice done, and to relieve himself of
the scruple that he had on his conscience, inviting both the
judges and everyone else to throw some light on the investigation of the cause, because on this account he found his
mind much distressed and perplexed. If, on this offer and
command of the king, he (the bishop) did not come forward
in public and manifest what he had discovered in this matter
after two years' most diligent study [he would be guilty].
Therefore, both in order not to procure the damnation of
his soul, and in order not to be unfaithful to the king, or to
fail in doing the duty which he owed to the truth, in a
matter of such great importance, he presented himself before
their reverend lordships to declare, to affirm, and with
forcible reasons to demonstrate to them that this marriage
of the king and queen can be dissolved by no power,
human or Divine, and for this opinion he declared he
would even lay down his life. He added that the Baptist
in olden times regarded it as impossible for him to die
more gloriously than in the cause of marriage ; and that
as it was not so holy at that time as it has now become
by the shedding of Christ's Blood, he (the bishop) could
encourage himself more ardently, more effectually, and
with greater confidence to dare any great or extreme peril
whatever. He used many other suitable words, and at
the end presented the book which had been written by
him on the subject.

"After him the Bishop of St. Asaph's (Standish), of the
Minorite order, spoke, and expressed nearly the same opinion, but with less polished eloquence and in briefer terms,
and he offered several comments. Then followed a doctor,
called the dean of the arches, president of the court of Canterbury (Peter Ligham), who alleged various arguments from

the sacred canons in favour of the marriage, which were not very cogent.

"The Cardinal of York replied to all of them, that in the first place he was surprised they had attacked them (the legates?) without warning; next, that they stood and sat there to hear all things connected with the cause, and to do for the sake of justice whatever the Divine Wisdom should inspire them to do. The proceedings then continued. On account of her non-appearance, the queen was pronounced contumacious, but she was cited to appear once for all. They determined to examine witnesses respecting her. . . .

"This affair of Rochester was unexpected and unforeseen, and consequently has kept everybody in wonder. What he will do we shall see when the day comes. You already know what sort of a man he is, and may imagine what is likely to happen." *

In a letter written by the cardinal's secretary the scene is also related, but he adds, not prophetically : " As this man (the bishop) is a man of good fame, the king can no longer persist in dissolving the marriage; for this man being adverse to it, the kingdom will not permit the queen to suffer wrong ".†

The French ambassador also, the Bishop of Bayonne, wrote to Francis I. on the same day : "The cause was called on again yesterday, when the king's proctor appeared, and the queen was a second time put in default for non-appearance. The Bishop of Rochester, however, who is accounted one of the best and most holy divines in England, especially in his opposition to these last heresies of Luther, was there with other counsellors, but not as her proctor, only to remonstrate with the judges, offering to prove that she had a good cause by a little book which he had made thereon

---

* Theiner, p. 585, and *Letters, &c., of Henry VIII.*, vol. iv., part iii., n. 5732.

† Lœmmer, *Mon. Vat.*, p. 33, and *Letters, &c.*, n. 5734.

jointly with his companions, which he then presented,
enlarging upon the queen's cause with many wise words.
A rather modest answer was made by the judges, that it
was not his business to pronounce so decidedly in the
matter, as the cause was not committed to him."*

The statement of the bishop that he was ready to suffer
death like St. John Baptist, which so startled the Legatine
Court and the world, gave great offence when it was reported
to the king, as it naturally suggested a comparison between
him and Herod Antipas. There is still in the Record Office
a Latin MS. of considerable length, composed by the king
himself as an address to the legates in answer to the Bishop
of Rochester's speech. "The arrogance of its tone," writes
Mr. Brewer; "the bitter sarcasms levelled at the motives
and attainments of the bishop; the resentment, ill-concealed,
at his untimely protest, show how profound was the king's
displeasure. The Latin vocabulary is ransacked for its
choicest epithets of vituperation, and the whole style of the
reply rather resembles the invective of an irritated and angry
controversialist than the calm rebuke and dignified bearing
of majesty." This MS. has been in the bishop's hands, a
copy of it having been probably submitted to him by the
king, and his annotations are written on the margin. They
show how little he was intimidated by the roar of the lion.

"Men sometimes fail," writes the king, "even the wisest,
in their projects; but I never thought, judges, to see the
Bishop of Rochester taking upon himself the task of accusing me before your tribunal—an accusation more befitting
the malice of a disaffected subject than the character and
station of a bishop. I had certainly explained this to
Rochester some months ago" (Fisher in the margin,
"*nearly a year ago*"); "and not once only, that those scruples
of mine respecting my marriage had not been studiously

---

* *Letters, &c.,* iv. 5741.

raked up or causelessly invented. Until the present time Rochester approved of them, and thought them so grave and so momentous that, without consulting the pope respecting them, he did not think I could recover my tranquillity of mind." (Fisher in the margin, "*I did not say so, but the cardinal would have been glad if I had said so*".)* "When the pope, moved by the judgment of his cardinals and others, considered that the reasons urged were sufficient, and the doubts were such as were worthy the consideration of the ablest judges—when he left the whole decision of the cause to your religious determination, and sent you, Campeggio, here at great expense, for no other purpose than to decide this cause, what, are we to suppose, could have instigated Rochester to press forward thus imprudently, and thus unseasonably declare *his* opinion after keeping silence for many months?" (Fisher, "*I was obliged to this by the protestation of the king and the cardinal*".) "If, after a study of many years he had clearly discovered what was just, true, and lawful in this most weighty cause, he should have admonished me privately again and again,† and not have publicly denounced with such boldness and self-assertion the burthensome reproaches of my conscience. It was his duty, as a religious and obedient prelate, to acquiesce in the sentence of his holiness, who had sent judges here, admitting the necessity of the case, rather than thus accuse the pope of levity, as if the cause which he had remitted here for decision was so clear, easy, and obvious, that it was folly to call it in question." (Fisher, "*It is not obvious to all, but only to those who are compelled to study it*".)

"But, judges, in this bishop we look for those require-ments in vain. Two most pernicious counsellors have taken

---

* Has not Cavendish, perhaps, put Warham's name instead of Wolsey's in the dialogue concerning Fisher's hand and seal at p. 168.

† Had Henry's marriage been unlawful, Fisher would not have failed to admonish him.

possession of him, and agitate all his thoughts—unbridled
arrogance and overweening temerity." (Fisher, "*Arrogance,
temerity*".) "How else can we account for his assertion
that by solid and invincible arguments he will immediately
place the naked truth of this cause, without disguise, before
the eyes of all men, and defend it even to the flames?"
(Fisher, "*I said nothing of that*") "adding that he had
better reasons for resisting the dissolution of this marriage
than John the Baptist had formerly in the case of Herod.
Monstrous assertion, devoid of all modesty and sobriety!"
(Fisher, "*What more do I assert than the cardinal, who
[affirmed that] he would be burnt or torn limb from limb
sooner than act contrary to justice?*") "Why talk of fire and
flames, and his readiness to submit to them, when he must
be fully convinced of my clemency and anxiety to defend
and not oppress the truth? What is the meaning of that
comparison of his, in which he endeavours to assimilate
his own cause to that of John the Baptist, unless he held
the opinion that I was acting like Herod, or attempting
some outrage like that of Herod?* I, judges, never
approved of the impiety of Herod, certainly not that which
the Gospel condemns in him, wherein we learn by the
words of the Baptist that he had taken his brother's sister
to wife."+

"Whatever Fisher may think of me, I have never been
guilty of such cruelty. Let him say if ever I have passed a
severe sentence upon those who did not seem favourable to

---

* The event was to show whether Fisher was mistaken.

+ Fisher writes *non intelligo*, as well he might; but we must suppose Henry meant "his brother's widow," not "his brother's sister".
Yet she was not a widow. Herod's brother was still alive, and
Henry did imitate Herod in adultery, taking another woman while his
own wife was living, and that woman being in the same degree of
relationship to himself that he affected to hold in horror in his lawful
wife.

this divorce. and did not rather show them the highest favour in proportion to their deserts."*

The king was fond of repeating this boast, yet there were few who took a prominent part in favour of the injured queen who did not i. t victims at last to the king's revenge. But the circumstances of Fisher's death bear so close a resemblance to those of the Baptist's, that it is strange even Henry did not observe and seek to avoid it. Both were cast into prison, and left there to linger at the will of a tyrant; both at last were beheaded, and both by the revenge of impure women. But what Herod did reluctantly, Henry did with cruel deliberation.

There is a passage in Fisher's defence of the king's book against Luther which shows that the martyrdom of St. John Baptist had long been to him a familiar subject of contemplation. "One consideration," he writes, "that greatly affects me to believe in the sacrament of marriage is the martyrdom of St. John Baptist, who suffered death for his reproof of the violation of marriage. There were many crimes in appearance more grievous for rebuking which he might have suffered, but there was none more fitting than the crime of adultery to be the cause of the blood-shedding of the Friend of the Bridegroom, since the violation of marriage is is no little insult to Him who is called the Bridegroom." †

These words were written at the end of 1524 or beginning of 1525. At that time no thought of divorce had as yet, in all probability, entered the mind of Henry; and Anne Boleyn, Fisher's Herodias, was then unknown. Whether, in June, 1529, it was merely a reminiscence of this passage that made him speak as he did, or a prophetic anticipation of his own end, we cannot know.

---

* Mr. Brewer's Translation (*Reign of Henry VIII.*, vol. ii., p. 348). The king proceeds to argue for his own view at great length. His MS. contains 95 pages. —*Letters, &c.*, iv. 5729.

† *Assertionum Regis Angliæ Defensio*, xii. 9.

But if the reader will turn back to the inventory given in Chapter iii., of the furniture of the bishop's house at the time of his imprisonment in 1534, he will find that on the altar of his private oratory there was standing a somewhat strange piece of furniture—the head of John the Baptist! This would probably be represented as it was carried in the dish by the daughter of Herodias, and, according to the custom of those days, would be coloured. This emblem of royal tyranny and saintly constancy Fisher kept ever before him when offering the Holy Sacrifice. Had God given him any presentiment of the kind of death by which he should glorify Him? Or was the use of this head merely suggested to him by the train of thought he had followed in his book and in his speech? This is uncertain. But he was well aware of the danger of the course he had entered on in opposing the king's passions. The Archbishop of Canterbury, a worthy yet somewhat weak charactered man, used to repeat, "The anger of a king is death to man".[*] When this same word was quoted by the Duke of Norfolk to Sir Thomas More, he replied: "Is that all, my lord? Then in good faith the difference between your grace and me is but this, that I shall die to-day and you to-morrow."[†] The same thoughts must have been also in Fisher's mind. Dr. Hall tells us he had been accustomed to keep on his altar a skull, to remind him of natural death, but in the latter years it seems he had replaced this by the sacred head of the Baptist. He thus kept in mind not only, like Warham, that the anger of a king may threaten death to his subjects, but that they who lose their lives for the King of kings shall find them again to life everlasting.

I shall not pursue the history of the divorce as it dragged on through another three years and a half. After the advocation of the cause to Rome, Fisher watched the

---

[*] Prov xvi. 14.   [†] Roper's *Life of More.*

negotiations and the progress of the king's infatuation with
the deepest and most painful interest. continuing to write, to
preach, and to protest.   Never had king a more faithful
subject, a more holy bishop, a more loving and watchful
father.   Never was fidelity repaid with more cruel injustice.
love with more bitter hate.

CHAPTER VIII

"WHAT Rochester will do we shall see when the day comes. You already know what sort of man he is, and may imagine what is likely to happen." Thus wrote Cardinal Campeggio on the feast of St. Peter and St. Paul, June 29th, 1529, the day after the unexpected speech mentioned in the last chapter. The bishop was now to be forced into public strife, both as a peer of Parliament and a member of the Church's synods, and to show himself as bold and fearless in debate as he was later on in suffering and martyrdom. The day foreseen by Campeggio 'soon came. On the 23rd July, the day on which judgment in the king's divorce suit was expected, the legates had suspended their Court until October. But already, on July 19th, the legatine powers were revoked, and the cause drawn to himself in Rome by the Sovereign Pontiff. The king's orator at Rome had threatened the pope that to do so would involve the "ruin of the Church and the loss of England and France"; but the pope had nevertheless accepted the queen's appeal. Wolsey, forgetting his duty as a bishop and a cardinal of the Holy Roman Church, had written insolently on the 27th July: "It shall never be seen that the king's cause shall be ventilated and decided in any place out of his own realm, but that if his grace should come at any time to the Court of Rome, he would do the same with such a main and army royal as should be formidable to the pope and to all Italy".* The words, though mere bluster, were a

* *State Papers*, vii. 193.

cowardly and shameful reminder of the infamous sack of Rome by the emperor's troops two years before. In a few months the king's rage and disappointment spent them-selves, not on the sack of Rome, but on the disgrace and spoliation of Wolsey himself and the clergy in England.

On the 19th October, Wolsey ceased to be chancellor ; a writ of Præmunire* was issued against him, and he was in danger not only of loss of goods and liberty, but even of a charge of treason and loss of life. Du Bellay, the French ambassador, wrote : " The Duke of Norfolk is made head of the Council ; in his absence, the Duke of Suffolk ; above all is Mademoiselle Anne. It is not as yet known who is to have the seal. I verily believe that the priests will not touch it any more, *and that in this Parliament they will have terrible alarms.*"†

A Parliament had been summoned, the first with the exception of a short session in 1523 that had met for four-teen years. From the words just quoted it is evident that the rumour had gone out that its work was to be one of menace and revenge. It was to be the king's instrument to punish or subdue the English clergy, who were generally opposed to the divorce, and to menace the pope into com-pliance with the king's will. It cannot be denied that, in its various sessions,‡ it was an eventful Parliament, perhaps

---

* As we shall have much more of this word, it may be said here, for readers not familiar with English history, that there were several statutes called Præmunire, aimed at those who referred any matter *belonging to the king's courts* to any foreign jurisdiction, meaning that of the pope. The penalties were terrible. Other offences were gradually included, and made a breach of the statute. The word is a corruption of *præmoneri*, and derived from the first words of the writ *Præmoneri facias.* Obtaining legatine authority, and conferring benefices by virtue of it, were among Wolsey's lesser offences ; but the most important to notice here, since both clergy and laity were involved in them.

† *Letters and Papers,* iv. 2678.

‡ This Parliament lasted until the spring of 1536, after Fisher's death.

the most eventful in English history. But as to its character and composition very different estimates have been made. Mr. Froude lauds it to the skies as imbued with the new spirit of reform; bold and independent, representing all that was noblest in English society; free in its discussions and its acts. Dr. Hall (the biographer of Fisher) is much nearer the truth when he thus describes it: " In this Parliament the Commons House was so partially chosen, that the king had his will almost in all things that himself listed. For whereas in old time the king used to direct his brief or writ of Parliament to every city, borough, and corporate town within the realm, that they (from) among them should make election of two honest, fit, and skilful men of their own number, the same order and form of the writ was now observed, but then with every writ there came also a private letter from some one or other of the king's council, requiring them to choose the persons named in their letters, who, fearing their great authority, durst commonly choose none other. So that whereas in times past the Commons House was usually furnished with grave and discreet townsmen, apparelled in comely and sage furred gowns, now might you have seen in this Parliament few others than roystering courtiers, serving-men, parasites, and flatterers of all sorts, lightly apparelled in short cloaks and swords, and as lightly furnished either with learning or honesty. So that when anything was moved against the spirituality or the liberty of the Church, to that they hearkened diligently, giving straight their assents in anything the king would require."*

This description is in accordance with the contemporary and unsuspected evidence of Dr. Hall's namesake, the chronicler, who asserts that "most part of the Commons were the king's servants".

Mr. Brewer, from a careful examination of all historical

---

* This passage is not given by Baily. It is from Hall's MS. Life.

evidence, concludes: "There is no ground for imagining that this Parliament differed much from other Parliaments assembled by the Tudors, in the mode of its election, in the measures it passed, or in its exemption from the dictation and interference of the Crown. The choice of the electors was still determined by the king or his powerful ministers, with as much certainty and assurance as that of the sheriffs. Independence of discussion prevailed so far and in such questions as the Crown thought good, no further and no more. As Henry required no grants of money from his Parliament, as he was now engaged in no war, was exacting from the clergy, by the Act of Præmunire, a larger sum than he could ever have expected from Parliament, he was independent of its decisions. To him, as to others of his race, Parliament was nothing better than a court to register the king's decrees, and assume a responsibility for acts the unpopularity of which he did not care to take upon himself." *

Mr. Froude admits that the "petition against the clergy," in which he founds especially the supposed greatness of this assembly, was drawn up before it met by the Crown lawyers, and presented in the first week of the session. To accept a Government scheme is no proof of servility on the part of a legislative assembly, but it is certainly not one of originality or independence.

This memoir has of course no farther concern with the Parliament and its measures than to explain the action of the Bishop of Rochester. Parliament met on 3rd November, 1529, and almost immediately the Commons adopted a "bill of complaints" against abuses on the part of the clergy,

---

* Mr. Brewer has much more to show that this vaunted Parliament was altogether servile and commonplace, but his brilliant Introductions end at this period. He discussed its constitution, but "left to another occasion," which never came, the examination of its acts.

which was presented to the king, and by him sent to the bishops for their answer. Both petition and answer are printed at great length by Mr. Froude, who considers them of surpassing importance and epoch making.* Mr. Brewer's estimate is very different. "The Parliament of 1529," he writes, "instead of any burning questions, any heroic assertion of spiritual freedom or the rights of conscience, directed its first attention to mortuary fees, to fines for pro- bates taken by the ecclesiastical courts, to regulations for executors, to pluralities and the like." Perhaps the truth may be found somewhere between these two views. Cer- tainly the grievances enumerated, even if they were all true and unexaggerated, were no worse or rather far less serious, than would be the case if a similar bill of complaints were drawn up against our modern land-system, or our modern administration of law and justice. But as a proposed reform at the present day might betoken either a fair or a hostile spirit, be conservative or revolutionary, so was it then. The bishops in their answer complain especially of the animus of the petitioners, of the vagueness of the accusations in them- selves, and of the general or universal character that was given to them.

The Commons petitioned against the great exactions of the parochial clergy in taking corpse-presents or mortuaries: "They would let dead men's children die of hunger or go a-begging, sooner than give them in charity the cow which the dead man owed, though he had but one ". † Very similar things have been said of modern landlords. Whether or not the complaint is true in either case must be proved

---

* This historian, however, has given the answer of the bishops to another complaint made in 1532, as if it were to the minor complaints of 1529. The sequence of events in this Parliament and in Convoca- tion will be found in a paper drawn up by Bishop Stubbs, and printed in the Report of Commissioners on the Eccles. Courts in 1883, p. 74.

† This is Fox's abridgment, given also in Wilkins, iii. 740.

from other evidence than the fact that the accusation is made. It was complained that "priests were stewards of bishops and abbots, so that poor husbandmen could have nothing but of them, and had to pay dearly for it ". So in our own day, men rail against the landlords' middle-men, and agents: "Holders of great benefices," it was said, "having their living of their flocks, lay in the court, in lords' houses, and spent nothing on their parishioners". This grievance sounds like a complaint against our modern absentee landlords. And again it was alleged that while "one priest, being but little learned, had ten or twelve benefices, and was resident on none, many well-learned scholars had neither benefice nor exhibition". These are specimens of the complaints made; and so far as they were well founded they proved, not the need of new laws, but the neglect to execute laws already made and well-known. The Commons were not satisfied with mere complaints; in a few days, they passed and sent to the Upper House a series of bills, which were certainly encroachments on the legislative powers of the Church.

There exists no official and authoritative record of the debates of this Parliament. When, therefore, chroniclers and historians give us a speech, we know that it is the composition of the historian, not of the orator. The substance may be accurate, but the words cannot be so. Hall, the chronicler, reports that the Bishop of Rochester thus addressed the Peers: "My lords, you see clearly what bills come hither from the Common House, and all is to the destruction of the Church. For God's sake, see what a realm the kingdom of Bohemia was, and when the Church went down, then fell the glory of the kingdom. Now, with the Commons is nothing but down with the Church! and all this meseemeth is for lack of faith only."

Dr. Hall, the biographer, gives a far longer speech, but with the wise introduction: "The bishop said, *in effect*, as followeth ". It is therefore needless to quote the discourse he puts in the bishop's mouth. The substance is not different from that already given, though the charge against the Commons is, of course, less bluntly put.* Dr. Hall continues : " This speech being ended, although there were divers of the clergy that liked well thereof, and some of the laity also, yet were there some again that seemed to mislike the same, only for flattery and fear of the king. In so much as the Duke of Norfolk reproved him, half-merrily and half-angrily, saying that many of those words might have been missed; adding further these words : ' I wis, my lord, it is many times seen that the greatest clerks be not always the wisest men '. But to that he answered as merrily again, and said that he could not remember any fools in his time that had proved great clerks. But when the Commons heard these words spoken against them, they straightway conceived such displeasure against my Lord of Rochester, that by the mouth of Mr. Audley, their Speaker, they made a grievous complaint to the king of his words, saying that it was a great discredit to them all to be thus charged that they lacked faith, which, in effect, was all one to say they were heretics and infidels; and, therefore, desired the king that they might have some remedy against him. The king, therefore, to satisfy them, calling my Lord of Rochester

* Baily simply says, " He spake as followeth," and then gives a speech in many respects different from Hall's version. Historians in those, and even in later days, imitating the Ancients, thought themselves at liberty to compose speeches for their heroes. One of the most singular examples of this style of composition occurs in Lord Herbert's account of this very debate. He has concocted a long speech, and put it in the mouth of an unnamed member of Parliament as an answer to the bishop's complaints. The speech is mentioned by no other historian—it has not the slightest *vraisemblance*. It is merely the deism of the next century. The style also is altogether unlike that of the year 1529. It is, in fact, a synopsis of Lord Herbert's own views on religion, and was never spoken in Parliament. Lord Herbert has many other such speeches.

before him, demanded why he spake in that sort. And he answered again that, being in council, he spake his mind in defence and right of the Church, whom he saw daily injured and oppressed among the common people, whose office was not to deal with her, and therefore said that he thought him-self in conscience bound to defend her all that he might. The king, nevertheless, willed him to use his word tem-perately, and so the matter ended, much to the discontenta-tion of Mr. Audley and divers others of the Common House."

As on this incident a double charge, of moral cowardice and want of veracity, has been recently made against the holy bishop, it will be necessary to dwell somewhat longer on the facts than their intrinsic importance merits. Mr. Froude never disguises his contempt and hatred of the Catholic clergy, but the great and universal estimation in which the name of Fisher is held stood awkwardly in his way. He has therefore seized every opportunity of a sneer either at his intellect or his moral character. The following words are a specimen :

Having related the bishop's speech and the complaint of the Commons, he says that the Bishop of Rochester and other prelates were summoned by the king. "It would have been well for the weak, trembling old men if they could have repeated what they believed, and had maintained their right to believe it. . . , But they were forsaken in their hour of calamity, not by courage only, but by prudence, by judg-ment, by conscience itself. The Bishop of Rochester stooped to an equivocation too transparent to deceive any-one—he said that ' he meant only the doings of the Bohe-mians were for lack of faith, and not the doings of the Commons House'—'which saying was confirmed by the bishops present'. The king allowed the excuse, and the bishops were dismissed ; but they were dismissed into ignominy, and thenceforward, in all Henry's dealings with them, they were treated with contemptuous disrespect. For Fisher himself we must feel only sorrow. After seventy-six years of a useful and honourable life, which he might have hoped to close in a quiet haven, he was launched suddenly upon stormy waters, to which he was too brave to yield, which he was too timid to contend against; and the frail vessel, drifting where the waves drove it, was soon piteously to perish." *

The popularity of Mr. Froude's history requires careful study of this appreciation. Mr. Froude is fertile and sometimes very happy in his metaphors, but that with which he concludes the above passage is singularly ill-chosen. The body and earthly fortunes of the venerable bishop became, no doubt, the sport of the storm of Henry's tyranny; but since his soul remained immovable as a rock, whatever compassion we feel is mingled with admiration. But Mr. Froude, by first picturing him in the presence of the king as "a weak, trembling old man," for which he has no historical authority; by then representing him as "stooping to equivocation" to escape the king's anger; and, lastly, by describing him as one "too brave to yield and yet too timid to contend against the stormy waters," turns his reader's compassion from the feeble body of a martyr to the inconstant, cringing soul of a victim of folly and misfortune. And what is the ground for all this? The mere fact has been handed down by the chroniclers that the Commons complained to the king that they had been called infidels, and that Fisher explained that he had not called them infidels, but warned them by the analogy of the Bohemians against such attacks against the Church as lead to heresy and ruin. Mr. Froude is willing enough to grant that it was the spirit of heresy (as understood by Fisher) that was moving the Commons. "The words," he says,

"of which Fisher had made use were truer than the
Commons knew; perhaps the latent truth of them was the
secret cause of the pain which they inflicted." But he
thinks it cowardice and mean dissimulation that Fisher did
not urge the charge home when it was complained of.
Surely we are all familiar in the present day with parliamentary apologies, when the form of offensive words is
withdrawn while the substance is maintained. Is this
called stooping to equivocation? or does the skill or the
clumsiness of the apology enhance its guilt? Does the
man who withdraws or explains what he has said "in a
manner too transparent to deceive anyone" (to use Mr.
Froude's account of Fisher's explanation)—does such a
man deserve at once "to be dismissed into ignominy and
thenceforth to be treated with contemptuous disrespect"?
If his accusation has been vile and false, and he is convicted
of slander, and refuses to retract except in form, no doubt
he deserves to be scouted by honest men. But if he has
said the truth, and maintains it, while putting it in a less
galling form, he is worthy of all esteem. The Bishop of
Rochester was evidently not seeking to excuse himself but
his accusers. They had warmly repudiated the notion that
they were "infidels and no Christians—as ill as Turks
and Saracens"; this was the interpretation their Speaker
put on the Bishop's words about "lack of faith". They
claimed to be most orthodox Catholics. Was he then to
urge on them that they were no Catholics, and no better
than Turks or Saracens? Surely that would have been the
method most likely to irritate them into real infidelity or
heresy. Of course, therefore, he gladly admitted their
protestation, and explained his own words, not by pitiful
equivocation, but in all truth and charity, to have meant no
more than a warning not to walk in the steps of heretical
nations.

Nor is there any historical authority whatever for Mr.

Froude's assertion—for he does not give it as a conjecture—
that the supposed cowardice or shuffling of the Bishop of
Rochester and the other prelates gave rise in the mind of
the king to contempt, or in any way changed his attitude
towards them. Whatever it may have been before, favourable or unfavourable, this incident, so far as we know, had
no influence upon it. As to Fisher, Henry well knew his
boldness and constancy, and he was destined to have many
a future proof that he was no " reed shaken by the wind ".

There is, indeed, something comical in this picture of
perhaps the greatest liar of a lying age turning with disdain
from a bishop who " stoops to equivocation "; unless, indeed, his scorn was aroused by the transparency of the
apology, and the ignorance of the bishop in the arts of
deception. But the whole passage is worthy of a historian
who defends the conduct of Cranmer in taking, before his
consecration, the usual oath to the pope, while making a
protest beforehand which invalidated all its principal articles.
There are historians who strain at gnats in the conduct of
those they dislike, and swallow camels in the defence of
their heroes.

The fate of the measures which had given occasion
to the warm expostulation of the Bishop of Rochester
gives a good illustration of one of the methods by which
the king secured his ends. He followed the old maxim :
Divide et impera. He set the lower clergy against
the higher, and the higher against the lower, and the laity
against both. " The bishops," writes a modern historian,
" were willing to enforce discipline on the lower clergy ; the
lower clergy were willing to reduce the profits of probate
which went to the officials of the bishops ; but the lower
clergy would defend their trade and their benefices, and the
bishops could not allow the profits of their courts to be
touched. . . . Both agreed in regarding the discussion of
these things in Parliament as an attack, as indeed they were,

on the Church itself. . . . Fanning the flames of dissension, the king suggested that the Commons should pass the two most obnoxious bills, strike a blow at the bishops by the bill on probate, and at the parochial clergy by the bill against mortuaries. The other points—non-residence, plu- ralities, and trading—were decided likewise. The lords spiritual, by their majority in the Upper House, rejected the bills ; the Commons insisted on pressing them. The king suggested a conference in Star Chamber of eight members from each House. The lay lords on the committee voted with the Commons, and by this contrivance the bill was passed. This little trick shows that it was not by force alone that the Parliament was manipulated to pass the king's bills. More, as chancellor, must, in this business, as in 1523, when he was Speaker, have acted as the king's agent, but the burden was already too heavy for his back." *

That the Bishop of Rochester not only opposed the measures in Parliament, but appealed against them after- wards, and thereby was brought into serious trouble with the king, we learn, not from his biographers or from English historians, but from foreign sources. On 29th October, 1530, Ludovico Falieri, the Venetian ambassador, writes from London to the Senate : " The king has caused the arrest of three bishops, accusing them of having bestowed benefices contrary to the orders, and a process is being formed : but these bishops were of the queen's faction, so the king chooses to be revenged on them. They are as follows : The Bishop . . ."† The rest of the MS. is mutilated, but fortunately the missing names are supplied by another document. On 22nd November, 1530, the Mantuan ambassador, Segismund, wrote to the Marquis of Mantua from Augsburg that he " had seen a letter from

---

* *Lectures on Mediæval and Modern History*, by Dr. Stubbs, Bishop of Chester (1886), p. 276.

† *Venetian State Papers*, iv.

England stating a prohibition in that kingdom for anyone to hold more than one church-benefice. Three bishops— namely, Rochester, Bath, and Ely—disputed this order, and *appealed to the Apostolic See.* The king, enraged at this, issued an edict imposing heavy penalties on such as appeal to Rome on this account ; and, as authors and chief cause of this disobedience, he had the three bishops arrested." *

This was more than two years before the Act of Parlia· ment against appeals to Rome, and the edict as well as the arrest were exercises of the merest arbitrary power. We have no record of the result of the " process " of which the Venetian ambassador speaks, nor of the length of time during which the arrest continued. Apparently it was not long, since we find the bishop active in Convocation, as well as perfectly undaunted, not many months after. The incident, however, serves to show the futility of the boast made by the king's ambassadors to the pope (as they wrote 11th March, 1533), that the queen was quite wrong in refusing to have the trial of her cause in England, as a place suspect, because so impartial was the king that he showed no displeasure towards her counsellors.† As regards the matter itself on which the bishops had appealed to Rome, Fisher was the last man in England to encourage the abuses of pluralism ; but the matter was one of ecclesi astical competence.

* *Venetian State Papers,* iv. 634.   † *Letters and Papers,* vi. 226.

PARLIAMENT was prorogued in December, 1529, and did not meet in 1530, nor did Convocation continue its sittings. The king, however, was anxious that no suspicion of heterodoxy should be connected with his proceedings against the clergy. The bill of complaints, which the Commons had first accepted from the Government, was very explicit in profession of the Catholic faith, and even affected to lament that the uncharitable conduct of the bishops gave a handle to heretics and assisted the spread of pernicious books. The king had, therefore, desired the clergy to investigate this matter, and a committee of Convocation was appointed, and in May was ready with its report. It is probable, from former proceedings in a similar matter, that the Bishop of Rochester had a share in this work, but we have no record of the proceedings. A long list of errors contained in the new books was drawn up. The archbishop and the commissioners presented it to the king at Westminster, on 24th May, 1530, and it was published by a royal proclamation. " The king, our sovereign lord, of his most virtuous and gracious disposition, considering that this noble realm of England hath, of long time, continued in the true Catholic faith of Christ's religion, and that his noble progenitors, kings of this his said realm, have before this time made and enacted many devout laws, statutes, and ordinances for the maintenance and defence of the said faith against malicious and wicked sects of heretics and Lollards, who, by perversion of

Scripture, do induce erroneous opinions, sow sedition among Christian people, and finally disturb the peace and tran- quillity of Christian realms, as lately happened in some parts of Germany . . . his highness, like a most gracious prince, of his blessed and virtuous disposition, willeth now to put in execution all good laws, statutes, and ordinances ordained by his most noble progenitors, kings of England, for the protection of religion." *

Some have seen in this proclamation an act of royal supremacy, a prelude to the claim of Supreme Head of the Church in England that the king would put forth the next year.† There is, however, nothing unusual in the language. The claim implied is that of being Defender of the Faith, not its Interpreter ; Protector of the Church, not her Master; Vindicator and Executor of her laws, not Legislator over her. The pompous and exaggerated style, however, that is used, which is the character of all documents of that age, explains how " Head of the Church " might be an ambiguous phrase, capable of an orthodox meaning, though suggestive of something dangerous and heretical. The document will serve as an introduction to that question of the royal supremacy that is henceforth to occupy us, both in this and future chapters.

It will be enough to state in the most summary manner the events which led to the debate in Convocation of this matter in the spring of 1531. Cardinal Wolsey's failure to carry through the divorce in England so excited the king's anger against him, that his enemies, who were many, brought about his dismissal from office, which in those days was almost certainly followed by impeachment for some real or supposed breach of law, and total ruin. When prosecuted in 1529, under the statute of Præmunire, for seeking and

---

* Wilkins' *Concilia*, iii. 737. The archbishop's decree at p. 727.
† Dr. Hook in his *Archbishops of Canterbury*, vi., ch. ii., p. 340.

exercising the office of legate, and in that capacity super-
seding the ordinary jurisdiction and tribunals in England.
he had thought it safest to plead guilty and throw himself
on the king's mercy; and after yielding into the king's
hands the greater part of the vast wealth he had acquired,
he received a qualified pardon. His enemies, and especially
Anne Boleyn, were dissatisfied, and, in 1530, brought about
his arrest on a charge of high treason. His death, on Novem
ber 26, 1530, on his journey towards London, placed him
beyond the king's anger. But the proceedings against the
late legate had suggested to plotting brains a plan of humiliation of the clergy and enrichment of the king. This was
to convict them as a body under the same statute of Præmunire, for having acknowledged the legatine authority. It
is one of the strangest facts in English history that such a
project should have been conceived and carried out. It is
evident that if the clergy were technically guilty of breach of
the statute, so was the whole nation; moreover, everything
had been done, not only with the consent of the king, but
by his desire and influence. It appears, however, that the
weak and servile judges, in spite of some resistance and
much repugnance, were literally bullied by the king into a
declaration of the law, according to his desire.* The laity
were pardoned, but a writ was issued against the clergy.
The penalty of conviction was confiscation of all their goods
and imprisonment at the king's pleasure. Had they made a
united stand against this absurd and tyrannous charge, it
would have been impossible to have gone on with it. They
weakly and foolishly offered the king an enormous sum by
way of compromise, or to purchase a pardon. A modern
historian, after acknowledging that " Wolsey's legatine

---

* As to the king's power of overbearing men by brutal language,
we have frequent testimony in Chapuys' letters; and he specially
alludes to the king's having constrained the judges on this occasion.
(See *Letters, &c.*, vi. 1445, 1460.)

faculties had been the object of the general dread of the clergy," is cynical enough to add : " But their punishment, if tyrannical in form, was equitable in substance, and we can reconcile ourselves without difficulty to an act of judicial confiscation ".* It is only when we read language like this in the 19th century that we can understand the state of mind of the king and his advisers in the 16th. We may add to what is found in our English histories on this subject the appreciation made at the time by a clever and very observant witness. Chapuys writes to the Emperor Charles V., 23rd January, 1531 : " Nothing has yet been said in the estates concerning the affair of the queen They have been occupied with police arrangements against plague, and also what is considered to be the principal cause of this assembly, to exact a composition from the clergy, who heretofore acknowledged the legation of the cardinal, and whom the king, as I wrote to your majesty, pretends to be liable to a confiscation in bodies and goods. Though the clergy knew themselves innocent, seeing that it was determined to find fault with them, they offered of their own accord 160,000 ducats, which the king refused to accept, swearing that he will have 400,000, or that he will punish them every one with extreme rigour, so that they will be obliged to pass it, though it will compel them to sell their chalices and reliquaries.

" About five days ago it was agreed between the nuncio† and me that he should go to the said ecclesiastics in their congregation, and recommend them to support the immunity of the Church, and to inform themselves about the queen's affair, showing them the letters which the pope has written to them thereupon, and offering to intercede for them with the king about the gift with which he wishes to charge them.

* Froude, *History*, i. 296.

† Baron John De Burgo was papal nuncio, a Sicilian. He arrived in London in September, 1530

On his coming into the congregation, they were all utterly astonished and scandalised, and, without allowing him to open his mouth, they begged him to leave them in peace, for they had not the king's leave to speak with him, and if he came to execute any Apostolic mandate, he ought to address himself to the Archbishop of Canterbury, their chief, who was not then present. The nuncio accordingly returned without having public audience of them, and only explained his intention to the Bishop of London, their proctor, who said he would report it. But he will beware of doing so without having the king's command, for he is the principal promoter of these affairs.*

"The Bishop of Rochester lately sent to me, to say that the king had made new attempts to suborn him and others who hold for the queen, telling him many follies and false-hoods; among other things, that the pope had promised Cardinal Grammont that, whatever show he made of pro-ceeding against the king, he would favour him to the utmost of his power, and that his holiness was in secret a great enemy of your majesty, because you wished to compel him to convoke the council. . . . The nuncio had also heard something of these *canards*, and at my request he explained to the bishop the truths about them. Next day, the king sent for the bishop early, to know what had passed between them, and the bishop replied it was nothing, but that the nuncio had expressed to him the desire the pope had to convoke the council, and had requested him to do his best to promote it, both with the king and the clergy. Of this answer he apprised the nuncio, in order that if he were examined their answers might correspond." †

It is probable that these rumours that the Sovereign Pontiff was really on the king's side, and would favour him

---

* Stokesley was then Bishop of London. He was altogether a king's man.
† *Letters and Papers,* v., n. 62.

in the end,—rumours industriously and plausibly circulated
by the king and his agents,—were to no small extent the
cause of that weakness on the part of the clergy which
surprises us so much on this occasion.   We need not perhaps give much attention to the complaints so frequently
and strongly made by Chapuys of the pope's dilatoriness
and weakness.   The envoy's office was to watch the queen's
interests, and he could see only from her point of view.
Chapuys' opinion is, however, shared by Mr. Gairdner,
who writes: "Apart from all questions of morality, the
disobedience shown by the king to the Holy See was such
as might well have justified a sentence of excommunication,
if the papal authority intended still to make itself respected.
But Clement was not the sort of pope who could be expected to bring kings to a sense of duty.   He was not
made of the same stuff as a Hildebrand or a Boniface, and
during the whole progress of this unhappy question he
contrived more and more to weaken his own authority, till
it was finally repudiated altogether." *

Whether the conduct of the pope was or was not weak
and temporising beyond the limits of right or prudence, the
rumours and fears that it was so explain the yielding spirit
of the English clergy, while they increase our respect for the
undaunted attitude of Fisher.   Whether, however, even he
was not, on the present occasion, borne down by the general
feeling of his brother prelates to undue compliance, admits
of question.   There exists no official and detailed record
of the debates in Convocation, and they are not reported in

---

* *Letters and Papers*, Introd. to vol. v., p. 10.   It may, however, be
said in answer to this, that the times did not admit of a Hildebrand
or a Boniface.   St. Pius V. has been equally blamed for being too
firm towards Henry's daughter Elizabeth, and for forgetting that the
days of Hildebrand were gone by.   It is easy to make these reasonings when a policy has been unsuccessful.   Perhaps it was God's will
to show that both mild measures and strong measures were tried in
vain on " a wicked and adulterous generation ".

the same manner by different authors. That which will now be given is from Hall's MS., and he had better chances of correct information than those from whom the accounts hitherto known have been derived.*

He first relates how a proposal was made early in the Convocation to suppress small monasteries, in order to compensate the king for his great expenses in prosecuting his divorce, and how the zeal of the Bishop of Rochester frustrated this plan for a time. This affair has been reported and discussed in a former chapter, and may now be passed over.† Next he gives the story of the Præmunire and the grant of £100,000 by the southern Convocation to the king. He then continues : " But yet the pardon was not accomplished very hastily, for before the full performance thereof a new and strange demand was made to the clergy in their Convocation, such a one as hath not in any Christian prince's days been heard of before ; and that was, that they should acknowledge the king to be their supreme head. This request, although it was very monstrous and rare, yet notwithstanding the matter was sore urged, and the king's orators omitted no time nor occasion that might help forward their purpose, sometime by fair words, and sometime by hard and cruel threatenings, among which Mr. Thomas Audley was a great doer (who, after such time as blessed Sir Thomas More gave over the office of lord chancellor, succeeded him in that place). ‡

" When this matter was come to scanning in the Convocation house, great hold and stir was made about it, for among them there wanted not some that stood ready to set forward the king's purpose,and for fear of them many others durst not

* Baily's account, which has hitherto passed as Hall's, differs in many particulars.

† See Chap. ii.

‡ Hall does not mean that he was then chancellor. Sir Thomas did not resign until May, 1532. Audley was Speaker in 1531.

speak their minds freely; but when this holy father saw what
was towards, and how ready some of their own company were
to help forward the king's purpose, he opened before the
bishops such and so many inconveniences by granting to
this demand, that in conclusion all was rejected, and the
king's intent clean overthrown for that time.

" Then the king hearing what was done, and perceiving
that the whole Convocation rested upon this worthy bishop,
he wrought by sundry means to bring the matter about.
And yet doubting that with overmuch haste and rigour at the
beginning he might easily at the first overthrow all his intent,
he sent his orators at another time to the Convocation house,
who in their own names moved the clergy to have good consideration of this gentle and reasonable demand, putting
them in mind what danger and peril they stood in, at this
present, against his majesty, for their late contempt in
accepting the legatine power of the cardinal, whereby they
had also deeply incurred the danger of the law; that their
lands and goods were wholly at his highness's will and
pleasure, which notwithstanding he hath hitherto forborne
to execute, upon hope of their good wills and conformities
to be showed to him again in this matter.

" Then the king sent for divers of the bishops and certain
others of the chief Convocation to come to him at his palace
of Westminster; to whom he proposed with gentle words his
request and demand, promising them in the word of a king that
if they would among them acknowledge and confess him for
supreme head of the Church of England, he would never by
virtue of that grant assume unto himself any more power,
jurisdiction, or authority over them than all other the kings
of the realm, his predecessors, had done before; neither
would take upon him to make or promulgate any spiritual
law, or exercise any spiritual jurisdiction, nor yet by any
kind of mean intermeddle himself among them, in altering,
changing, ordering, or judging of any spiritual business.

' Therefore having made you,' he said, ' this frank promise,
I do expect that you shall deal with me as frankly again,
whereby agreement may the better continue between us.'
And so the bishops departed with heavy hearts to talk
further of this matter in the Convocation among themselves,
but still it stuck sore among them upon certain inconveniences before showed by my Lord of Rochester, who
never spared to open and declare his mind freely in defence
of the Church, which many others durst not so frankly do,
for fear of the king's displeasure, although they were for
the most part men of deep wisdom and profound learning.

" Then came the king's counsellors again from the king
to know how the matter sped, seeming as though they had
not known what was said or done in the Convocation house
before their coming. So hotly they followed this matter
once begun, for many causes. The king having indeed
a further secret meaning than was commonly known to
many, which in few years broke out, to the confusion of the
whole clergy and temporality both. These counsellors then
repeated unto the Convocation the king's words which he
himself had spoken to some of them ; saying, further, that if
any man would stick now against his majesty in this point,
it must needs declare a great mistrustfulness they had in his
highness' words, seeing he had made so solemn and high
an oath. With this subtle and false persuasion the clergy
began somewhat to shrink, and for the most part to yield to
the king's request, saving this holy bishop, who utterly
refused to condescend thereunto, and, therefore, earnestly
required the lords and others of the Convocation to consider and take good heed what mischiefs and inconveniences
would ensue to the whole Church of Christ by this un-
reasonable and unseemly grant made to a temporal prince,
which never yet to this day was once so much as demanded
before, neither can it by any means or reason be in the
power or rule of any temporal potentate. ' And, therefore,'

said he, 'if ye grant to the king's request in this matter, it
seemeth to me to portend an imminent and present danger
at hand; for what if he should shortly after change his
mind, and exercise in deed the supremacy over the Church
of this realm ?   Or what if he should die, and then his
successor challenge continuance of the same ?   Or what if
the crown of this realm should in time fall to an infant or
a woman that shall still continue and take the same name
upon them ?   What shall we then do ? whom shall we sue ?
or where shall we have remedy ? '   The king's counsellors
to that replied and said, that the king had no such meaning
as he doubted, and then alleged again his royal protestation
and oath made in the word of a king.   And further (said
they), though the supremacy were granted to his majesty
simply and absolutely, according to his demand, yet it must
needs be understood and taken, that he can have no further
power or authority by it than *quantum per legem Dei licet*,
and then if a temporal prince can have no such authority
and power by God's law (as his lordship had there declared)
what needeth the forecasting of all these doubts ?   Then at
last the counsellors fell into disputation among the bishops
of a temporal prince's authority over the clergy, but thereunto my Lord of Rochester answered them so fully, that they
had no list to deal that way any further, for they were in
deed but simple smatterers in divinity, to speak before such
a divine as he was, and so they departed in great anger,
showing themselves openly in their own likeness, and saying,
that whosoever would refuse to condescend to the king's
demand herein was not worthy to be accounted a true and
loving subject.

"The lords and other of the Convocation seeing this kind
of threatening persuasion, besides many other false practices,
and fearing the report of the counsellors to be made to the
king (whom they knew and perceived to be all cruelly bent
against the clergy), grew at last to a conclusion, and so, after

sundry days' argument in great striving and contention, agreed in manner fully and wholly among them to condescend to the king's demand, that he should be supreme head of the Church of England, and to credit his princely word so faithfully and solemnly promised unto them.

"My Lord of Rochester, perceiving this sudden and hasty grant, only made for fear, and not upon any just ground, stood up again, all angry, and rebuked them for their pusillanimity in being so lightly changed and easily persuaded; and being very loth that any such grant should pass from the clergy thus absolutely, and yet by no means able to stay it, for the fear that was among them, he then advised the Convocation that, seeing the king, both by his own mouth and also by sundry speeches of his orators, had faithfully promised and solemnly sworn, in the high word of a king, that his meaning was to require no further than *quantum per legem Dei licet*, and that by virtue thereof his purpose was not to intermeddle with any spiritual laws, spiritual jurisdiction, or government more than all other his predecessors had always done before. If so be that you are fully determined to grant him his demand (which I rather wish you to deny than grant), yet, for a more true and plain exposition of your meaning towards the king and all his posterity, let these conditional words be expressed in your grant: *Quantum per legem Dei licet*. Which is no otherwise (as the king and his learned council say) than themselves mean.* But then the counsellors (who by that time were returned to the Convocation house for speed of their business), hearing of my Lord of Rochester's words, cried upon them with open and continual clamour to have the grant pass absolutely, and to credit the king's honour in

---

* Augustine Scarpinelli, representative of the Duke of Milan, writes from London, 19th February, 1531, that the clergy first proposed another clause: "Quantum per leges canonicas liceat," and that this was refused by the king.—*Venetian State Papers*, iv. 656.

giving them so solemn a protestation and oath. But after
this time nothing could prevail; for then the clergy
answered, with full resolution, that they neither could nor
would grant this title and dignity of supremacy without
these conditional words: *Quantum per legem Dei licet.*
And so the orators departed, making to the king relation of
all that was done, who, seeing no other remedy, was of
necessity driven to accept it in this conditional sort, and
then granted to the clergy pardon for their bodies and
goods, so that they should pay him a hundred thousand
pounds, which was paid to the last penny."

Such is Hall's account of the part taken by Fisher. It
has all appearance of authenticity. But however the debates may have been conducted, the result arrived at was
that which he states. The date of this important document is the 11th February, 1531.

It must not be understood that any doctrinal decree was
drawn up, affirming the headship of the king. The title
merely came in a parenthesis of a long address of gratitude
on the part of the clergy. In this they take no notice of
their having done wrong in owning the legatine authority,
but merely ask for a discharge from any forfeitures incurred
by the statutes of Provisors or by breach of other penal laws;
and they make their gift a benevolence and a mark of gratitude to his majesty for his zeal in writing against Luther,
in suppressing heresy, and checking insults against the
clergy. In this address, then, after the words, "of the
English Church and clergy," comes the following parenthesis: "Of which we recognise his majesty as the singular
protector, the only and supreme lord, and, so far as the law
of Christ permits, even the supreme head".[*]

To understand the sense in which this title was thus

---

[*] "Ecclesiæ et cleri Anglicani, cujus singularem protectorem
unicum et supremum Dominum, et quantum per Christi legem licet,
etiam supremum caput, ipsius majestatem recognoscimus."

claimed and granted, the reader must put from his mind
the controversies which arose regarding the king's supremacy
a few years later. Baily, unfortunately, bearing all these in
mind, and wishing to represent the Bishop of Rochester as
anticipating and rejecting the royal supremacy, gives a long
speech addressed by him to the Convocation. The heads
of this speech are the following : (1) A warning, lest in trying
to save their goods the clergy should cut themselves off
from the Church ; (2) that supremacy could only mean the
power of the keys (which were given to Peter, not to kings)
and the feeding of Christ's flock (also committed to Peter,
not to kings); (3) that the grant of the supremacy would
be the same as to renounce the See of Rome and the unity
of the Church, with other consequences, which he enume-
rates under five heads ; (4) he goes on to contrast this new
claim with the conduct of Christian emperors ; (5) lastly,
he states a dilemma—either the Church of Rome is the
true Church, and then we must be in communion with her,
or she is "a malignant Church" (*Ecclesia malignantium*),
and then it will follow that England never was Christian,
&c., &c.

Mr. Lewis, another of Fisher's biographers, has laboured
much in examining and refuting this speech. We may
spare ourselves the pains of following this discussion, since
not one word of all this speech was ever spoken by Fisher.
It is a pure invention of Baily's. It has no resemblance to
anything in Hall. It is a piece of controversy belonging to
the 17th century, and in no way whatever regards the
title of Supreme Head as it came before Convocation in
1531. In Baily the whole matter turns on the renunciation
of the See of Rome. In the debates of the Convocation not
one explicit mention was made of the See of Rome. The
question before the minds of the clergy was that of the
legislative powers, privileges, and immunities of the English
Church. They feared an encroachment on these in the

name of the royal prerogative, "lest perhaps," as the Lower
House stated, "after a long lapse of time terms used in
this article in a general sense be drawn to an improper and
unlawful one ". *

A clear proof that the question before the minds of the
clergy had as yet no explicit bearing on the authority of the
Holy See is in the protestation of Bishop Tunstal, and the
letter addressed to him by the king. When the matter
came before the northern Convocation, the Bishop of
Durham not only could not consent to the new title, but
required that his protest should be recorded in the acts.
He does not allege that there is encroachment on the papal
supremacy, but that there is ambiguity, which will be taken
advantage of by heretics to reject episcopal jurisdiction and
censures, and to appeal to the king's courts. He concludes
his protestation thus : " Supreme Head of the Church ·
carries a complicated and mysterious meaning ; for this title
may either relate to spirituals or temporals, or both. Now
when a proposition is thus comprehensive and big with
several meanings, there is no returning a single and
categorical answer. And therefore, that we may not give
scandal to weak brethren, I conceive this acknowledgment
of the king's supreme headship should be so carefully expressed as to point wholly upon civil and secular jurisdiction." †

There is also an answer drawn up by the king, or by
some theologian writing for him and in his name. In this
he meets objections that Tunstal must have stated in a
private letter of explanation of his conduct. The letter has
not reached us, but its contents are known from the answer.
The bishop had said that Christ, the Supreme Head of the

* " Ne forte post longævi temporis tractum termini in eodem articulo
generaliter positi in sensum improbum traherentur." (See Atterbury,
Rights of Convocation, 82.)

† Collier's Translation ; original in Wilkins, iii. 745.

whole Church, had lodged the spiritual and temporal jurisdiction in different subjects. The king replies that the texts
cited to prove obedience due to princes comprehend all
persons, both clergy and laity, and the Scripture makes no
exemption as to matter of obedience. If princes may punish
those who violate their own temporal laws, *a fortiori* they
should punish those who violate Divine laws. Again, all
spiritual things in which liberty and property are concerned
are necessarily included in the prince's power. Of course
no one denies that preaching and administering sacraments
belong to priests only, but kings must see that priests do
their duty. Our Lord, though a priest, submitted to Pilate's
jurisdiction (!), and St. Paul appealed to Cæsar. As to
clerical exemption, "some criminal causes," he says, "are
reserved to our courts, and some by our permission remitted
to the ordinaries. Murder, felony, and treason we reserve
to our correction; as for other instances of misbehaviour,
we leave the clergy to be punished by their respective
bishops." Convocations are called by royal writ; bishops
make homage and oaths of allegiance; the royal licence and
assent is required in election of abbots. Since, then, the
prince's authority is previous to the execution of their
office, why should spiritual persons scruple to call him
Head, with respect to that power which is derived from
him?* There is no need to examine here the force of the
royal arguments. The point to be carefully borne in mind
is that, as yet, the papal supremacy had not explicitly
entered into the question. Even though Henry were
supreme head over the clergy in England, it did not follow
that there should be no appeal over him to the supreme
visible head of Christendom, even in temporal matters.
And if his headship consisted in repressing vice in the

---

* I have not cared to give the document in full. My argument is
negative : that there was no question as to papal supremacy at that
time. The king's letter is given by Wilkins, iii. 762.

clergy, and obliging them to preach the Catholic faith and administer the Catholic sacraments, it did not follow that the pope had no authority to decide in questions of faith, or jurisdiction in matters spiritual. It is mere anachronism to import these anti-papal consequences into the present discussion. It has been done by Baily in his ill-timed zeal to enlist Fisher as a champion against Elizabethan and Jacobian theories; it was done by the Protestant Bishop Andrews, who, in his answer to Bellarmine, asserted that, five years before this title was made law, Bishop Fisher had subscribed it in synod,* as if Convocation had in 1531 given the title in the same sense in which it was afterwards given in Parliament, when Fisher died rather than assent to it. The same misstatement was made by Cranmer when he was accused, in Queen Mary's reign, that he had been the first to set up the king's supremacy against that of the pope. He replied "that it was Warham gave the supremacy to Henry VIII., and that he had said he ought to have it before the Bishop of Rome, and that God's word would bear it". But other testimony is needed than that of Cranmer, or his reporter Foxe, before such a charge can be received against Archbishop Warham as that of having cast aside the supremacy of the Holy See. He died on 22nd of August, 1532; and one of the acts of his last sickness was to dictate a protest that "he neither intended to consent, nor with a clear conscience could consent, to any statute passed, or hereafter to be passed, *in the Parliament* (that met first in 1529) derogatory to the rights of the Apostolic See, or to the subversion of the laws, privileges, prerogatives, pre-eminence, or liberties of the Metropolitan See of Canterbury".† Had he considered that the title to which he had consented *in Convocation* was contrary to the

---

* *Responsio ad C. Bellarm.*, Apol., p. 23 (*apud* Lewis, ii. 72).
† Wilkins, iii. 746.

rights of the Holy See, he would no doubt have retracted when on the point of passing before the tribunal of Christ.

It is not meant by these remarks to justify this title or the conduct of those who granted it at the claim of Henry VIII., even with a saving clause, as they imagined. My object is to ascertain its precise import, and to explain how it could have been granted by men like Warham and Fisher. I am glad here to be in entire agreement with Mr. Froude, who writes : " It is creditable to the clergy that the demand which they showed most desire to resist was not that which most touched their personal interests. In the preamble of the Subsidy Bill, under which they were to levy their ransom, they were required by the council to designate the king by the famous title, which gave occasion for such momentous consequences, of 'Protector and only Supreme Head of the Church and Clergy of England'. It is not very easy to see what Henry proposed to himself by requiring this designation at so early a stage in the move-ment. The breach with the pope was still distant, and he was prepared to make many sacrifices before he would even seriously contemplate a step which he so little desired. . . It is certain only that this title was not intended to imply what it implied when, four years later, it was conferred by Act of Parliament, and when virtually England was severed by it from the Roman communion."*

Yet, on the other hand, although the title of Supreme Head, when first claimed by the king and first conceded by the clergy, was not meant or understood to be a denial of the higher rights of the Holy See, it would seem that the king meant to assert his supremacy with regard to the

* *History*, i. 4. Dr. Hook, who is altogether an asserter of the antiquity of the royal supremacy, admits nevertheless that " the royal supremacy was not at the time of the Convocation regarded as incon-sistent with the legitimate claims of the papacy ".—*Archbp. of Cant.* (Cranmer), vol. vi. 424.

English Church, in case "the great affair" of his divorce should come before any ecclesiastical tribunal in England. The ultimate appeal should be to himself. He meant also to prepare the way for resistance to the Holy See, should a decision be given against him in Rome. The word, Supreme Head, was sufficiently vague and capable of an orthodox interpretation, otherwise he could not have hoped to get it acknowledged by the clergy. But in its vagueness lay its danger. It might in time be made to mean anything and to cover every assumption of authority, disciplinary or doctrinal. The bishops knew this, and therefore held back. The clause they introduced was little more than a bolt without a ward, when they did not define what "the law of Christ allowed" and what it forbade Dr. Lingard says that "it is plain that the introduction of the clause served to invalidate the whole recognition, since those who might reject the king's supremacy could maintain that it was not allowed by the law of Christ". This is true ; but, on the other hand, what was there to prevent the advocates of that supremacy from pushing it to any extreme on the same grounds that it was not forbidden to do so by the law of Christ ? And this is what really happened, and was foreseen as likely to happen ; and some better safeguard should have been provided than an elastic or disputable clause.

The question, however, as it regards the Bishop of Ro-chester, is this : "Was it better that, by himself consenting to adopt the obnoxious title, with a clause that made it tolerable, he should lead the clergy (as he did) to refuse the title un-qualified, or that he should have stood aloof and taken the utmost consequences for himself, thereby leaving the clergy to give a title without the clause to indicate its dangerous character ? We dare not accuse him of weakness in yielding. We believe that he chose what seemed best to him in the dilemma. His conduct, however, was eagerly seized on by the king. Cuthbert Tunstal, Bishop of

Durham, was on the queen s side in the matter of the divorce, and he had urged the king to conform his conscience to that of the greater number. When, therefore, in 1531, Tunstal wrote to the king his objections to the title of Supreme Head, the king retorted on him his own argument by asking him why he did not conform his conscience to that of so many learned divines as sat in the Convocation of Canterbury, and amongst others mentioned the Bishop of Rochester as learned both in divinity and canon law.*

Probably the foresight of the use that would be made of his name was one cause of the anxiety, or perhaps alarm of conscience, that took possession of him as soon as the document was signed, and of which we have evidence in the following letter. The obnoxious clause had been carried in Convocation on 11th February, 1531. On the 21st Chapuys tells the emperor: " If the pope had ordered the lady to be separated from the king, the king would never have pretended to claim sovereignty over the Church ; for, as far as I can understand, she and her father have been the principal cause of it. The latter, speaking of the affair a few days ago to the Bishop of Rochester, ventured to say he could prove by the authority of Scripture that when God left this world He left no successor nor vicar.

"There is none that does not blame this usurpation, except those who have promoted it. The chancellor (More) is so mortified at it that he is anxious above all things to resign his office. *The Bishop of Rochester is very ill with disappointment at it.* He opposes it as much as he can ; but being threatened that he and his adherents should be thrown in the river, he was forced to consent to the king's will."†

---

* *Letters and Papers*, vol. v., App., n. 9 ; or Wilkins, iii. 762.

† *Letters and Papers*, vol. v., n. 112.

This illness of the holy bishop was not caused by fears for himself, but by "disappointment". He had not checked but only retarded the yielding of his brethren. He foresaw the consequences. Yet his labours had not been altogether lost. He had succeeded in fixing the proverbial wisp of hay on the horns of the dangerous title. The bull had broken into the Church's paddock in spite of him. But to those inclined to draw too near he could say: *Habet fœnum in cornu.*

And, indeed, scarcely had the concession or compromise been made by the clergy than a reaction set in. A protest was signed by numerous priests of both provinces against any encroachments on the liberty of the Church, or any act derogatory to the authority of the Holy See. Chapuys wrote on 22nd May:

"SIRE,—Four days ago the ecclesiastics of the archdiocese of York and the diocese of Durham have sent to the king a great protest against the sovereignty which he would claim and usurp over them. Those of the archdiocese of Canterbury [he means the province] have also published a protest, of which I send a copy to M. de Granvelle. The king is greatly displeased."

This protestation, which is preserved in the archives of Vienna, is signed by Peter Ligham in his own name and that of the clergy of Canterbury, by Robert Shorton, Adam Travis, Richard Featherstone, Richard Henrison, Thomas Petty, John Quarr, Rowland Philips, William Clyffe, archdeacon of London; J. Fitzjames, for the clergy of Bath and chapter of Wells; Thomas Parker, for the clergy of Worcester; Robert Ridley, for the clergy of London; Ralph Swede, for the clergy and chapter of Coventry and Lichfield; John Rayne, for the clergy of Lincoln; and, what is to be noted as regards the influence of Fisher, by Nicolas Metcalf, archdeacon of Rochester and master of St. John's, Cambridge; Robert Johanson, for the clergy and chapter of Rochester; John Willo, for the clergy of Rochester.*

The name at the head of this list is that of a great friend of Fisher. Peter Ligham, the dean of the arches, wrote to the Bishop of Rochester on 12th October, 1532, from Canterbury :

"I thank you for your venison. The king left Canterbury on Thursday last at 12 noon, and reached Calais on Friday about 10 in the morning. I was named by the prior of Christ-church to be his vicar-general and master of the preroga-tive, but the king will none of me, saying that he heard I was a good priest, but he would have more experience of me whether I were *plene conversus* or (*i.e.*, ere) I should have any such room. I am well content. I am very desirous to hear how our good, gracious queen doth, and where she is, for I have not heard of her grace this many days, nor how her cause doth at Rome." †

This shows how the king kept in his memory the names of those who opposed his will. To dissent from his judg-ment and be true to conscience was to renounce all hope of preferment, even when it exposed to no severer penalties.

---

* We owe this information to Mr. Friedmann, *Anne Boleyn*, i. 142. The document is neither in the *State Papers* nor in the *Kalendars of Letters and Papers*.

† *Letters and Papers*, vol. v.. n. 1411.

CHAPTER X.

D R. HALL has given us very few biographical details of the holy martyr during the years 1531, 1532, and 1533. His name, however, appears at intervals in public documents and in the letters of ambassadors. These detached notices will be given here in chronological order.

In the letter of Chapuys quoted at the conclusion of the last chapter, mention is made of a threat of throwing the bishop and his adherents into the river, if they continued their opposition. Though this may have been no more than a burst of insolence on the part of one of the great nobles of the council, the threat, which in itself sounds more of the Bosphorus than the Thames, was probably made in those very words. About a year later * the Earl of Essex told Peto and Elstow, the undaunted Franciscan friars of Greenwich, that they deserved to be put into a sack and thrown into the Thames, which elicited the famous answer from Elstow that the road to heaven was as near by water as by land.

Threats like these may account for the suspicions, which fell on members of the king's council and Court, when, shortly after the debates of Convocation just related, the

---

* This event is sometimes erroneously given in 1533. It took place at Easter, 1532. (See letter of Chapuys, vol. v. 941.) The best account is in Harpsfield's *History of the Divorce* (Camd. Soc.), p. 204. He heard the details from Elstow himself.

bishop narrowly escaped being poisoned. The affair occurred on the 18th February.

Chapuys, writing to the emperor on 1st March, 1531, says
that the King of England, addressing the House of Lords on
the previous day, had "called their attention to the matter
of the Bishop of Rochester's cook, a very extraordinary case.
There was in the bishop's house about ten days ago some
pottage, of which all who tasted, that is, nearly all the
servants, were brought to the point of death, though only
two of them died, and some poor people to whom they had
given it. The good bishop, happily, did not taste it. The
cook was immediately seized, at the instance of the bishop's
brother, and, it is said, confessed he had thrown in a
powder which, he had been given to understand, would only
hocus the servants, without doing them any harm.* I do
not yet know whom he has accused of giving him this
powder, nor the issue of the affair. The king has done well
to show dissatisfaction at this ; nevertheless, he cannot
wholly avoid some suspicion, if not against himself, whom I
think too good to do such a thing, at least against the lady
and her father.

"The said Bishop of Rochester is very ill, and has been
so ever since the acknowledgment made by the clergy, of
which I wrote. But, notwithstanding his indisposition, he
has arranged to leave this to-morrow by the king's leave. I
know not why, being ill, he is anxious to go on a journey,
especially as he will get better attendance of physicians here
than elsewhere, unless it be that he will be no longer a
witness of things done against the Church, or that he fears
there is some more powder in reserve for him.

"If the king desired to treat of the affair of the queen,

---

* An anonymous letter from Ghent in the Venetian Archives also
mentions that the cook, when racked, declared that he had only
thrown in a purgative powder, out of jest.—*Venetian State Papers,*
iv. 668.

the absence of the said bishop, and of the Bishop of Durham (late of London), would be unfortunate."*

Dr. Hall, who relates this affair, mentions that the bishop had, "by overlong sitting and reading in his study that forenoon, more than his accustomed hour, no great stomach to his dinner," and put it off till evening, bidding his household dine without him. He says that the poison had been thrown into the gruel by "a certain person of a most damnable and wicked disposition," who was an acquaintance of the bishop's own cook, and had called upon him, and, while the cook was gone to the buttery to fetch him some drink, took advantage of his absence to mix the poison in some yeast. Chapuys seems to have thought that Richard Roose, the poisoner, was the bishop's own cook. The Act of Parliament leaves the matter uncertain, merely mentioning his name, and that he was by occupation a cook, and from Rochester. The case was deemed too atrocious to be treated in the ordinary course of justice; and instead of being brought to trial and condemned to death for a felony, the murderer was by special Act of Parliament adjudged guilty of high treason!

The Act of Parliament passed for this case is so curious that it deserves to be known:† "The king's royal majesty, calling to his most blessed remembrance that the making of good and wholesome laws, and due execution of the same against the offenders thereof, is the only cause that good obedience and order hath been preserved in this realm; and his highness having most tender zeal to the same, among other things considering that man's life above all things is chiefly to be favoured, and voluntary murders most highly to be detested and abhorred, and specially, of all kinds of

---

* *Letters and Papers*, vol. v., n. 120.

† It is not in the statutes at large, but is given in full in the great edition of the *Statutes of the Realm*, printed 1810 28. The Act is 22 Henry VIII., ch. 9.

murder, poisoning, which in this realm hitherto (Our Lord
be thanked) hath been most rare, and seldom committed or
practised: And now in the time of this present Parliament,
that is to say, in the 18th day of February, in the twenty-
second year of his most victorious reign (1531), one
Richard Roose, late of Rochester, in the county of Kent,
cook, otherwise called Richard Cook, of his most damnable
and wicked disposition, did cast a certain venom or poison
into a vessel replenished with yeast or barm, standing in the
kitchen of the reverend father in God, John, Bishop of
Rochester, at his place in Lamehyth Marsh [Lambeth], with
which yeast or barm and other things convenient, porridge
or gruel was forthwith made for his family there being,
whereby not only the number of seventeen persons of his
said family, which did eat of this porridge, were mortally
infected and poisoned, and one of them, that is to say,
Burnet Curwen, gentleman, thereof is deceased, but also
certain poor people which resorted to the said bishop's place
and were there charitably fed with the remains of the said
porridge and other victuals, were in likewise infected, and
one poor woman of them, that is to say, Alice Trippit,
widow, is also thereof now deceased: Our said sovereign lord
the king, of his blessed disposition inwardly abhorring all
such damnable offences, because that in manner no
person can live in surety out of danger of death by that
mean, if practice thereof should not be eschewed, hath
ordained and enacted by authority of this present Parliament, that the said poisoning be adjudged and deemed as
high treason; and that the said Richard Roose, for the said
murder and poisoning of the said two persons (as is aforesaid), by the authority of this present Parliament, shall stand
and be attainted of high treason.

"And because that detestable offence now newly practised
and committed requireth condign punishment for the same,
it is ordained and enacted by authority of this present

Parliament that the said Richard Roose shall be therefore
boiled to death, without having any advantage of his clergy;*
and that all future poisonings shall be deemed high treason,†
and similarly punished by boiling."

If anything can add to the brutality of this act, it is the
horrible manner in which it was carried out The chronicler
of the Grey Friars thus writes: "This year was a cook
boiled in a cauldron in Smithfield, for he would have
poisoned the Bishop of Rochester, Fisher, with divers of his
servants, and he was locked in a chain, and pulled up and
down with a gibbet at divers times till he was dead". ‡

Dr. Hall relates another attempt on the bishop's life, or
at least an attempt to frighten him: "Shortly after this
dangerous escape there happened also another great danger
at the same house in Lambeth; for suddenly a gun was shot
through the top of his house, not far from his study, where
he accustomably used to sit, which made such a horrible
noise over his head, and bruised the tiles and rafters of the
house so sore, that both he and divers other of his
servants were suddenly amazed thereat. Whereupon
speedily search was made whence this shot should come,
and what it meant, which at last was found to come from
the other side of the Thames, out of the Earl of Wiltshire's
house, who was father of the Lady Anne. Then he perceived that great malice was meant towards him, and, calling
speedily certain of his servants, said : 'Let us truss up our
gear, and be gone from hence; for here is no place for us

* *Sine privilegio cleri*, or "without benefit of clergy," in our old
laws, means that they could not plead the clerical state, or *education*,
in being able to read, in favour of exemption from capital punishment.

† We can form some conception how coining was deemed high
treason, but how poisoning a subject was high treason to the monarch
is bewildering. The Act was repealed in the next reign, and poisoning became felony.

‡ *Grey Friars' Chronicle*, p. 194, in second vol. of *Monumenta
Franciscana* (Rolls Series).

to tarry any longer'; and so immediately departed to Rochester."

Chapuys says that the bishop was to leave London on 2nd March. Dr. Hall is very sparing in dates, and cannot always be trusted for the sequence of events, though he doubtless reports accurately the facts themselves, as he had learnt them from the bishop's friends. He inserts here the sum the bishop expended on the reparation of the Bridge of Rochester, and praises the zeal with which he gave himself to preaching and works of mercy. "But above all this," he says, "he bestowed no small labour and pain in repressing of heresies, which by this time were very much increased and far spread in this realm. And although by his continual travail he brought many heretics into the way again, yet among other heretics his most labour was with one John Frith, a very obstinate and stubborn wretch, whom he could not reclaim and bring to any conformity, and therefore was justly, by order of law, condemned, and after burned in Smithfield."

The Anglican Church historian, Collier, writes as follows: "Fox charges Fisher with the death of Frith, Tewkesbury, and Bayfield. But this is more than appears; for these men were tried before Stokesly, Bishop of London, neither was Fisher one of the assessors." * In theory, certainly, the Bishop of Rochester held that formal and dogmatising heretics, admonished and relapsed, might be put to death by the civil power, after the judgment of the Church.† But there is no record that he had any part in such condemnations, or that his zeal was exercised otherwise than in reclaiming by argument.‡

Indeed, the time of his own troubles had begun. Chapuys

---

* Vol. iv., p. 277.   † *Luth. Assertionis Confut.*, Art. 33.

‡ Hitton, a Lutheranising priest who was burnt at Maidstone, was, according to Sir Thomas More, examined by the Bishop of Rochester, as well as the Archbishop, but he was in the jurisdiction of the latter.

writes, on 9th October, 1531, that Parliament has been prorogued until after All Saints (1st November). "The lady [*i.e.*,
the king's mistress] fears no one here more than the Bishop of
Rochester, for it is he who has always defended the queen's
cause; and she [*i.e.*, Anne] has therefore sent to persuade
the bishop to forbear coming to this Parliament, that he
may not catch any sickness, as he did last year; but it is of
no use, for he is resolved to come and to speak more boldly
than he has ever done, should he die a hundred thousand
times."*

The same ambassador writes again on the 11th January,
1532 : "Respecting the Bishop of Rochester, I will inform
him as soon as possible of the paragraphs in your majesty's
letter that concern him.   This will be done in writing and
through a third person, as there is no other means at
present of communicating with that prelate, for he has
lately sent me word that, should we meet anywhere in
public, I must not appear to know him, or make any
attempt whatever to speak.   He himself would do the
same, and begged to be excused if he took no notice of me
until the present storm had blown away.   As I have sure
means, without the least danger, of maintaining the bishop
in his good intentions, I will omit no trouble to keep him to
his purpose." †

On 22nd January he writes again: "On the 13th, the
session of Parliament began. . . . The assembly is numerous, being attended by almost all the lords, temporal as
well as spiritual.   Only the Bishop of Durham (Tunstal),
one of the queen's good champions, has not been called in;
no more has Rochester, as I have been informed, though
this last has not failed to come, and is actually in town."
He then continues, in cipher: "Intending to tell the king
the plain truth about the divorce, and speak without dis-

---

* *Letters and Papers*, vol. v., n. 472.
† *Spanish Calendar*, vol. iv., part ii., ii. 883.

guise (rudement). No sooner did the king hear of this bishop's arrival, than he sent him word he was very glad at his coming, and had many important things to say to him. The bishop, fearing lest the communication which the king said he had to make should be for the purpose of begging him not to speak on the subject, seized the moment when the king was going to mass, attended by the gentlemen of his household, to make his reverence and present his respects—thus avoiding, if possible, the said communication. The king received him more graciously, and put on a better mien than ever he had done before, deferring the conversation till after the mass; but the good bishop, owing to the above fears, prudently retired before mass was over.

"I have faithfully transmitted to the said bishop your majesty's last message; he has begged me not only to thank you most sincerely, but to offer his unconditional services in this affair of the queen, requesting me at the same time not to write about him, or mention him in my despatches, unless it be in cypher." *

As the *Lords' Journals* were not kept between 1515 and 1534, we have unfortunately no help from them as to the action of the bishop in Parliament. There is an important reference to him in the proceedings of the Convocation in May of this year, 1532, which, while it proves his absence (probably from illness), shows also the esteem in which he was held. Complaints had been made by the Commons that some of the legislation enacted by the clergy was contrary to the king's prerogative and the statutes of the realm, and the clergy were asked for an explanation. The answer was drawn up by Gardiner, Bishop of Winchester, and displeased the king. The negotiations were long; but as the subject of this memoir had little part in them, it need only be said here that the king ultimately made three demands: (1) That no future constitution should be made without

* *Spanish Calendar*, vol. iv., part ii., n. 888.

the king's approval; (2) that all former canons should be
submitted to the judgment of a commission of thirty-two
persons, sixteen of the clergy and sixteen of the laity, all to
be appointed by the king; (3) that such constitutions as
should be found unobjectionable should have the royal
assent given to them.   It thus began to appear what was
meant by the Supreme Headship.   The Church was to
surrender that legislative power given to her by her Divine
Founder—" Teach them to observe all things whatsoever I
have commanded you "—or to exercise it at the will or
caprice of a king.

Collier says : " The Convocation were much perplexed at
their receiving this message from the king, and, after some
time spent in consultation, it was resolved to send four of
the Upper and six of the Lower House to the Bishop of
Rochester, by whose advice they seemed disposed to govern
themselves, and to wait for this prelate's resolution they
adjourned for three days " (*i.e.*, until Monday, 13th May).
Dr. Wake, however, remarks that from the wording of the
Acts the prorogation was made before the thought occurred
of seeking the Bishop of Rochester's help; and a committee
was then formed to go to his " lodging," not for his private
advice, but to debate with him.*   In any case, the incident
proves the bishop's illness, which kept him at his house in
Lambeth, and the opinion entertained of his wisdom.   No
record of the interview exists, nor do we know what was
his advice.   Collier continues : " Fisher's principles were
not likely to put the clergymen upon any measures acceptable to the Court.   The king, therefore, being informed
to whom the matter was referred, sends for the Speaker
of the House of Commons, and complains the clergy
were but half his subjects." †   The result of the con-

* Wake's *State of the Church*, p. 487.

† He refers to the oath of obedience to the Sovereign Pontiff taken
before consecration by bishops.

tention was that the clergy promised not to legislate for the future without the royal assent. As to the canons already existing, though they refused the king's demand, "not to attempt, claim, or put in ure (*i.e.*, use) any of the old canons without leave from the Crown," they agreed that they should be revised by the king and the proposed commission, "so that whichsoever of the said constitutions . . provincial or synodal, shall be thought and determined by your grace ar.¹ by the most part of the said thirty-two persons not to stand with God's laws and the laws of the realm, the same to be abrogated and taken away by your grace and the clergy. And such of them as shall be seen by your grace and by the most part of the said thirty-two persons to stand with God's laws and the laws of the realm, to stand in full strength, your grace's most royal assent and authority once impetrate fully given to the same." In their preamble they sought to limit this concession to the king's life-time, by putting it on personal grounds. "We, your most humble subjects . . . having our special trust and confidence in your most excellent wisdom, your princely goodness, and fervent zeal to the promotion of God's honour and the Christian religion, and also in your learning far exceeding in our judgment the learning of all other kings and princes that we have read of, and doubting nothing but that the same shall still continue and daily increase in your majesty." Alas for the vain hopes of man! We know what was the future wisdom of the Defender of the Faith, and we know how far the limitation to his life-time held good. This Act was rightly called the Submission of the clergy. It was passed by Convocation on 15th May, 1532, and was incorporated without these idle and delusive limitations in an Act of Parliament in the spring of 1534.*
The Bishop of Rochester cannot be shown to have had any

---

* 25 Henry VIII., c. 19.

share in this disgraceful surrender of the Church's Divine
rights to an earthly tyrant.*

There were three stages in the fall of the ancient Church
of England.   Her clergy were first subservient, then
schismatical, and lastly heretical.   As yet there was no
question of formal schism.   The pope's name was no more
mentioned in this discussion in 1532 on the submission of
the clergy than it had been in 1531 on the king's headship.
Things were, indeed, moving more speedily in Parliament.
While the clergy were debating on their dependence or
independence in making laws, an Act had been passed by
the two Houses suppressing the Annates or first-fruits paid
to the Holy See by bishops on the occasion of obtaining
bulls of consecration, palls, &c.   There was in these
nothing of a simoniacal character.   They were paid by all
bishops-elect equally, and were not bribes to the Sovereign
Pontiff to promote one rather than another.   In fact, the appointment to bishoprics had for a considerable time been
entirely vested in the Crown; the election of chapters and
confirmation by the pope following as a matter of course.
And when the Annates were no longer paid to the Holy See
they continued to be paid to the Crown; but the Parliament
of 1532, wishing to influence the conduct of the pope in the
matter of the divorce, suppressed the Annates, without,
however, making the law absolute.   It was left to the king
to make negotiations with the Sovereign Pontiff.   The
first-fruits of the bishoprics were claimed by the Holy See as
a tax, and went principally to the support of the cardinals.
It was not denied that confirmation of election to bishoprics
should be sought from the pope, or that some subsidy

* See Collier, vol. iv., pp. 188-198; Hook's *Warham*, vi. 403-415.
Clerk, Bishop of Bath and Wells, dissented; the Bishops of London,
Lincoln, and St. Asaph agreed only conditionally.   The Bishops of
Bath and Lincoln were two of the deputation sent to consult with
Fisher.   There were many dissentients in the Lower House.

should be paid. This was fixed at five per cent. of the first year's income, or the rateable value of the bishopric. The schismatical character of the Act appears in this, that should the pope refuse to grant bulls on these new terms, or pursue his claim by spiritual censures, these were to be despised, the consecrations were to be made by the archbishop, and spiritual functions exercised, without any regard to the authority of the Holy See. Still there was no repudiation of the supremacy of the Church of Rome. Parliament as yet only claimed the right to resist exorbitant demands and to despise unjust censures. As usual, subserviency to the king, the power near at hand, armed with material scourges, was allied to insolence towards the pope, the power far off, armed only with spiritual weapons. Those who can see in this a mark of national greatness, or an exercise of manly and Christian vigour, must have their judgment strangely distorted.

While holding out threats of loss of income to the pope, in order to purchase a venal judgment in his favour,* Henry tried to perplex prelates and people at home by a great show of politeness to the pope's nuncio. The king's object was to persuade the opponents of the divorce that the pope really favoured his cause, and the Bishop of Rochester told the imperial ambassador, on 15th February, 1533, that the king's policy was so far successful that the partisans of the queen were becoming intimidated and perplexed.†

It was not easy to intimidate the holy bishop. By a letter of the same ambassador, written on the 20th June, 1532, we find that he had no sooner somewhat recovered from the illness which had kept him from Convocation than

---

* This is euphuistically called by Rev. Joseph Hunter in his Introduction to *Valor Ecclesiasticus* (prepared for the Government) " strengthening the king's hands in his negotiations concerning the divorce " (p. ii.).

† *Letters and Papers*, vi. 160.

he publicly denounced in a sermon the great iniquity which was now imminent. "About twelve days ago the Bishop of Rochester preached in favour of the queen, and has been in danger of prison and other trouble. He has shut the mouths of those who spoke in the king's favour, but the treatment of the queen is not improved."* The sermon must have been preached in London to be spoken of in such terms; but whether in the presence of the king or not, or in what church, or on what occasion, Chapuys does not say.

Owing to the plague, Parliament had been prorogued in the spring of 1532. It met again in February, 1533. The Lower House, as we have seen, had been well packed, and could be trusted. It was important to eliminate the independent element from the Upper House. On February 15, 1533, Chapuys tells the emperor that the three prelates who sided with the queen will be excused from this Parliament, and that the king has himself appointed their proctors. These prelates were no doubt Fisher of Rochester, Clerk of Bath and Wells, and either Tunstal of Durham or West of Ely. Fisher, however, came. Warham, the Archbishop of Canterbury, had died in the preceding August. Cranmer had been nominated as his successor, but was not yet consecrated.

In spite of a bold opposition by the Bishop of Rochester, an Act was at once passed against appeals to Rome in cases of wills, marriages, tithes, and the like. This was another step on the road to schism, but still it was not yet a formal rupture. It was not a denial of the pope's supremacy in the Church. It had nothing to do with questions of doctrine; its real object was to obstruct the queen's appeal to the Holy See, and to pave the way for Cranmer's sentence of divorce. The king had long been cohabiting with Anne Boleyn, in spite of the formal injunc-

---

* *Letters and Papers*, vi. 1109.

tion and threatened excommunication by the pope. He was now secretly married to her, or rather had gone through the ceremony. The cause was still being pursued by him in Rome ; but to render Anne's expected issue legitimate,* it was necessary to hasten proceedings to get a legal declaration that, his former marriage having been null, he had been free to marry. For this purpose the willing judge had been chosen in the person of Cranmer, and the statute against appeals in matrimonial cases put the case into his hands. The bulls arrived from Rome for his consecration on 26th of March, and he was consecrated on the 30th. He assembled Convocation, and the question of the king's affinity was laid before the clergy with a foregone conclusion. Chapuys writes to the emperor, 31st March, 1533 :

" The king was only waiting for the bulls of the Archbishop of Canterbury in order to proceed to the decision of his marriage ; which having arrived within these five days, to the great regret of everybody, the king was extremely urgent with the synod here [the Convocation], for the determination of his said affair, so that those present could scarcely eat or drink, and using such terms to them that no one dared open his mouth to contradict, except the good Bishop of Roches-ter.† But his single voice cannot avail against the majority, so that the queen and he now consider her cause desperate. It is expected that the new marriage will be solemnised before Easter, or immediately after."

He then goes on strongly to blame the pope's dilatoriness or timidity in not having excommunicated Henry ; and adds : " His holiness will be among the first to repent this, for he will lose his authority here, which will be not a little

---

* The Princess Elizabeth was born on 7th September, 1533.

† The opposition of Fisher, and warm disputes between him and Stokesley, Bishop of London, are mentioned by Jocelyn, *Antiq. Britan.*, p. 327. (See also Lewis, ii. 98.)

scandal to Christendom and prejudice to the queen. For among other things contained in the libel exhibited in Parliament against the pope's authority, it is expressed that no one shall appeal from here to Rome on any matter, temporal or spiritual, on pain of confiscation of body and goods as a rebel . . . which clause directly applies to the queen." *

The king had determined to have the Bishop of Rochester out of the way during the public farce of Queen Catharine's citation and divorce by Cranmer, and the coronation of Anne Boleyn, lest one voice at least should be heard in indignant protest.

Cranmer was consecrated 30th March, and Fisher was arrested on 6th April.

The imperial ambassador thus communicates these proceedings to Charles V. on 10th April : " Last Sunday, being Palm Sunday,† the king made the Bishop of Rochester prisoner, and put him under charge of the Bishop of Winchester ; which is a very strange thing, as he is the most holy and learned prelate in Christendom. The king gave out in Parliament that this was done because the bishop had insinuated that Rochford had gone to France with a commission to present an innumerable sum of money to the Chancellor of France and the Cardinal of Lorraine, to persuade the pope by a bribe to ratify this new marriage, or at all events to overlook it and proceed no further. . . . The real cause of the bishop's detention is his manly defence of the queen's cause." ‡

Carlo Capello, the Venetian ambassador, who had taken the place of Ludovico Falieri, wrote from London to the Senate on 12th April, 1533 : " On the Monday in Passion week Parliament assembled. They decreed that the marriage

---

* *Letters and Papers*, vi., n. 296, and *Spanish Calendars*, iv. 1057.

† *Paques Fiories :* wrongly translated Easter Sunday by Mr. Gayangos, but rightly by Mr. Gairdner.

‡ *Letters and Papers*, vi. 324 ; *Spanish Calendars*, 1058.

of Queen Catharine with the king is null, and that he may
marry; and they have abolished the appeal to the pope.
. . . They have also abrogated the dispensations for holding
a plurality of benefices with cure of souls, and for marriage
and other things. They have prohibited obedience to papal
monitions and interdicts. The Bishop of Rochester, having
publicly opposed these measures, was arrested on Palm Sunday (6th April) and given in custody to the Bishop of
Winchester; and three days ago he was sent to reside at
a place of his, and not to go more than a mile beyond it." *

It is from another letter of Chapuys that we learn the
length of this imprisonment. He writes on the 16th June
that Tunstal of Durham has incurred the king's anger for
his opposition to the title of Supreme Head, and to the
divorce, in the northern Convocation; "and were it not
that the king cannot find a man more competent to govern
the country adjoining Scotland, he would have been put in
prison, like the Bishop of Rochester, who has not been at
liberty till within these three days, and this only at the intercession of Cromwell ".†

Caiphas, then, being now high priest, and the Easter
festival approaching, Fisher, like his Divine Master, wit-
nessed a good confession before the powers of the earth.
At the risk of liberty and life he cleared his conscience both
in Parliament and Convocation. In reading his biographers
I have often wondered where he was and how he acted at
Catharine's divorce and Anne's coronation. The letters
just quoted make all clear. He was neither in his own
diocese nor in London when Cranmer, on 12th April,
craved permission of Henry to inquire into the validity of
his marriage with Catharine, on the 23rd May gave sentence

---

* *Venetian State Papers*, iv. 870. No mention of this second
arrest, any more than of the first in 1530, has been made by English
historians or biographers of Fisher.

† *Letters and Papers*, vi. 653: *Spanish Calendars*, iv. 1081.

against it, and on the 28th declared valid the marriage
between Henry and Anne. It must have been a pain to
the saintly prisoner to be unable to celebrate the Easter and
Whitsuntide festivals, yet he would doubtless have preferred
imprisonment to the ignominy of his time-serving host or
jailor; for on the feast of Pentecost, which that year fell on
1st June, was celebrated with immense pomp the coronation
of Anne Boleyn, at which "the Bishops of London and
Winchester (Stokesley and Gardiner) bore up the laps of
her robe," while she was crowned and communicated by
Cranmer. *

The bishop returned to his diocese with a sad heart on
his release on 13th June, and prepared himself for the worst.
On 11th July the pope annulled the proceedings of Cranmer,
and on 8th August a brief of censure was issued against him,
as well as against Henry and Anne. The king at once
appealed to the next General Council, the meeting of which
he was resolved by all means to prevent. What was now to
be Fisher's course? What did he consider his duty under
these circumstances? The recent publication of the letters
of the imperial ambassador answers these questions, and
puts before us a very serious problem with regard to the
holy martyr, not hitherto discussed by biographers or
historians. Chapuys thus writes to the emperor on 27th
September, 1533:

"Since my last letters there has been nothing new about
the treatment of the queen and princess, nor about the
affairs of Scotland; nor do I see any appearance of their
[*i.e.*, the king and his council] obeying the censures of the
pope, unless they be accompanied with the remedies of
which I have before written". These remedies were an
armed invasion of England by the emperor's troops, which
would be met, as Chapuys thought, by an immediate and
almost general rising in England against the king. He

* *Letters and Papers*, vi. 601.

adds : "And as the good bishop of Rochester says, who has sent to me to notify it, the arms of the pope [*i.e.*, spiritual censures] against these men, who are so obstinate, are more frail than lead, *and that your majesty must set your hand to it*, in which you will do a work as agreeable to God as going against the Turk ".*

And on 10th October he writes : "The queen has charged me to beg you to press the pope to proceed at once to the execution of the sentence, through all the most rigorous terms of justice possible, without forgetting to solicit the definition of the principal case ; and she fully believes that if you and the pope hold the reins firm without any relaxation, these men will be brought to reason ; for with all their show of boldness, they are in great fear, and will be all the more so if the pope, in whom they have some hope, stand firm. For the love she bears her husband she dare not speak of any other remedy but law and justice ; but the good and holy bishop [of Rochester] *would like you to take active measures immediately*, as I wrote in my last ; *which advice he has sent to me again lately to repeat.* The most part of the English, as far as I can learn, are of his opinion, and only fear that your majesty will not listen to it. . . . Were it not for the fear which the king has that his people are so prone to rebellion, and that his subjects would treat him as the German peasantry did their lords, he would long since have declared himself Lutheran." †

That the bishop really sent these messages to Chapuys there can be no doubt, for the ambassador's despatches are always accurate and truthful. And there is as little doubt that in sending such messages, provocative of foreign invasion, he was doing a thing for which, had it been discovered, he would have been adjudged guilty of high treason

* *Letters and Papers*, vi., n. 1164 ; *Spanish Calendars*, iv. 1130.
† *Ibid.*, n. 1249. The king of England just at this time was seeking an alliance with the Lutheran princes.

But is high treason always criminal before God or man?
Surely those who glory in the Revolution of 1688, and who
reckon among patriots the nobles and prelates who invited
the Prince of Orange to invade England and dethrone his
father-in-law, can lay down no such absolute rule as would
prove *a priori* that the conduct of Fisher was a crime.
Constitutional lawyers, like Blackstone, may reason that, by
actions subversive of the constitution, King James II. had
virtually renounced his authority and abdicated his throne,
and that its vacancy was declared by the united senate of
the whole nation; but even supposing this true, yet to make
that declaration possible, individual statesmen had first to
judge the cause themselves, and to invite and bring about,
by treasonable means, an armed invasion of the country.
The address of the Earls of Shrewsbury and Devonshire,
the Bishop of London, and the other conspirators of 1688,
to William is almost verbally what the Bishop of Rochester
might have said to Charles V. They stated that, "of the
common people, nineteen parts out of twenty longed most
anxiously for a change; and that the nobility and gentry,
though they did not express themselves with equal freedom,
were animated with the same sentiments; that if the prince
were to land with a force sufficient to promise protection to
his friends, he would in a few days find himself at the head
of an army double in number to that of the king," &c. *

I must refer to the State Papers of Henry VIII., and to
the comments of their able and candid editor, Mr. Gairdner,
for the proofs that such was exactly the state of England at
the period when Fisher made his appeal to the emperor.
He was not alone. Many noblemen, and some of the very
councillors least suspected by Henry, were sending to
Chapuys similar messages.† Henry had violated his oath,
had violated the constitution, was destroying the Church he

---

* Lingard, *James II.*, chap. iv.
† See Mr. Gairdner's Introductions to vols. viii., ix.

had sworn to protect, was bringing heresy and schism into a country in which they were hitherto unknown, was cutting off that country from the rest of Christendom, had incurred the solemn censures of the Sovereign Pontiff, then recognised even by the general law of Europe.*

But I have no thought of drawing a parallel between the conduct of the saintly Bishop of Rochester and that of the nobles who committed treason against James by inviting the Prince of Orange. They wished to dethrone the king; Fisher's only wish was to deprive him of his evil counsellors and oblige him to observe his coronation oath. They wished to change the succession. The efforts of the Bishop of Rochester, on the contrary, were directed to preserve the rights of Henry's lawful successor, the Princess Mary, cruelly sacrificed to the passions of her unnatural father. He appealed, also, not to France or Scotland, but to the head of the Holy Roman Empire, who was the acknowledged arbitrator of Europe, and vindicator of the unity of Christendom, even in countries which were outside the Empire's bounds.† Henry had admitted this when, on the visit of the emperor to London in 1522, he had allowed the following words to be put up over the Council Chamber of the Guildhall, where they were both entertained :

" CAROLUS, HENRICUS, VIVANT, DEFENSOR UTERQUE HENRICUS FIDEI, CAROLUS ECCLESIÆ ". ‡

If ever it can be lawful for subjects to appeal to foreign aid against a monarch, it was assuredly a righteous and godly

---

* On 12th July, the pope, in a brief, declared the king to have already incurred excommunication, but suspended the censure till the close of September. The brief was published in Dunkirk (Froude, ii. 129). So also Sanders and Pocock; but Mr. Gairdner shows that the term fixed was the end of *October*, and the brief was issued on 11th July (*Letters and Papers*, vi., Append. 3).

† See Dr. Bryce's *The Holy Roman Empire*, chap. xv.

‡ Selden's *Titles of Honour*, part i., chap. v.

appeal that the holy bishop made at that moment, against
him who had been guilty of treason to his Church, 'yranny
towards his people, adultery to his wife, and was bringing
on the land danger of civil war or foreign conquest by dis-
turbing the succession to the Crown.   It was the deliberate
judgment of one who had been privy councillor to Henry
VII. and to Henry VIII., and who by universal assent was
the most learned and holy prelate at that day in the Catholic
Church, that by invading England, not to conquer it. but to
enable its people to combine and assert their rights, the
emperor would have done as holy an action as by a crusade
against the Turks.

Appendix to Chapter X.

It is curious how the considerations which, according to Lord
Macaulay, converted even the Tories to the doctrine of lawful resistance to tyranny, may be applied to this period of Henry's life.   How
few words in the following extract require to be changed if they are
applied to 1533 instead of 1688 : " The prosecution of the bishops,
and the birth of the Prince of Wales " [write *Princess Elizabeth*],
" had produced a great revolution in the feelings of many Tories.   At
the very moment at which their Church was suffering the last excess
of injury and insult, they were compelled to renounce the hope of
peaceful deliverance.   Hitherto they had flattered themselves that
the trial to which their loyalty was subjected would, though severe,
be temporary, and that their wrongs would shortly be redressed without any violation of the ordinary rule of succession.   A very different
prospect was now before them.   As far as they could look forward they
saw only misgovernment, such as that of the last three years, extending
through ages.   The cradle of the heir-apparent of the Crown was surrounded by Jesuits " [write *Protestants*].   " Deadly hatred of that
Church of which he [*she*] would be one day the head would be
studiously instilled into his [*her*] infant mind, would be the guiding
principle of his [*her*] life, and would be bequeathed by him [*her*] to
his [*her*] posterity.   This vista of calamity had no end." *

If it be objected that Henry's measures were sanctioned by Parliament, while James's were opposed, it may be answered that Henry's
Parliament did not represent the nation.   It was notoriously com-

* Macaulay's *James II.*, chap. ix.

posed of men who were virtually the king's nominees, and those who were not considered sufficiently pliant had been excused attendance. Now, that the opposition of such a Parliament would be of no weight was admitted by the revolutionists of 1688, since in their invitation to the Prince of Orange they urged that "the enterprise would be far more arduous if it were deferred till the king, by remodelling boroughs, had procured a Parliament on which he could rely".* Hence, according to them, it was the real feeling of the country, not the votes of an obsequious Parliament, which should have weight.

Lord Campbell is not writing on ecclesiastical questions, but on arbitrary taxation, when he says : "Against such an arbitrary sovereign as Henry, with such tools as Audley, the only remedy for public wrongs was *resistance* ".† The same eminent writer and politician has admitted the gravity of the circumstances in which Fisher would have promoted resistance, in the following words : " Instead of considering Sir Thomas More disloyal or morose " (in refusing to be present at Anne's coronation) " we ought rather to condemn the base servility of the clergy and nobility, who yielded to every caprice of the tyrant under whom they trembled, and now heedlessly acquiesced in a measure which might have been the cause of a civil war as bloody as that between the houses of York and Lancaster ".‡

In tracing these analogies I am merely stating an *argumentum ad hominem*, and by no means pledging the Blessed John Fisher to any theory of resistance to tyranny. We have his conduct and his words before us on this occasion. We know little of his political views. He probably agreed with Blessed Thomas More, whose words, quoted at p. 140, Henry had once read without displeasure.

* Macaulay's *James II.*, chap. ix.   † In his *Life of Audley*.
        ‡ In his *Life of More.*

CHAPTER XI.

THE HOLY MAID OF KENT.

THE next great trouble of the bishop arose from an attempt by Cromwell to connect him with a conspiracy, or supposed conspiracy, to stir up popular feeling against the king and his proceedings, by means of the visions and revelations of a nun named Elizabeth Barton.* It seems impossible at this distance of time, with the documents which have come down to us, and which are all on one side, to decide whether there was anything true and supernatural in these revelations; and if not, how much was delusion and how much conscious imposture. Even in the time of Dr. Hall there were different versions of the nun's character, so that he says: "For my own part, I will not for certain affirm anything, either with her or against her, because I have heard her diversely reported of, and that

* The principal sources for the history of this affair are the following: (1) The Act of Attainder for treason of Dr. Bocking and others, and for misprision of treason of the Bishop of Rochester and others, 25 Henry VIII., cap. 12 (March, 1534). This Act is incredibly verbose. It is to be found in the great edition of the Statutes printed in 1817 and in Hall's *Chronicle*. (2) The statements contained in it are derived from the confessions and answers to interrogations made by Cranmer, Cromwell, and their agents, and by other members of the Council. Some of these were printed by Mr. Wright in his volume on the Suppression of the Monasteries. (3) Many new documents are contained in vols. vi. and vii. of the *Letters and Papers* of Henry VIII. I have read all the documents carefully, and extracted whatever regards Fisher. Of course I have read Mr. Froude's picturesque pages, but I have preferred authentic documents to his mixture of theory, real evidence, and hostile narratives, indistinguishable except to those who have carefully examined the sources.

of persons of right good fame and estimation". Fortunately, in order to relate the history of the Bishop of
Rochester, and to form a judgment on his conduct, there is
no need to enter into the various details that have come
down to us regarding this nun, nor to form any opinion as
to the nature of her revelations. It will be enough to give
the outline of her story, without reference to the bishop, and
then the points by which he was entangled in it.

Elizabeth Barton was born in 1506, in the parish of
Aldington, near Romney-Marsh, in Kent.* At the age of
fifteen she was servant-maid to Thomas Cobbe in that parish,
and subject to some fits of sickness, seemingly hysterical.
Richard Master, the rector or parson of Aldington, is accused,
in the Act of Attainder, of being her instigator in these
trances, in which she was supposed to receive Divine communications. He is said to have been moved by cupidity
to get up pilgrimages to Our Lady of Court-up-Street,† the
name of a hamlet in the neighbouring parish of Lymne,
where there was a small and neglected chapel of the Blessed
Virgin, within which Elizabeth was, or pretended to have
been, cured. The only basis, apparently, for these charges
against the good priest was the desire of Cromwell to malign
the clergy. Master may have been a dupe, but there is
nothing to show that he was a knave. The Act of Attainder
says that the chapel of Court-up-Street was "within the said
parish" of Aldington, which is not true. So he had no
special, or at least personal, motive for magnifying and en-
riching it.‡ In any case he did his duty in laying the

---

* See the Map, p. 59.
† In the Act of Attainder always written Courte at Strete, in other
documents it is Courte-up-Strete, Courte-of-Streate, Cortopstrete,
Cortoppe Strete, with other variations according to each scribe's fancy.
‡ Canon Jenkins, in his recent *Diocesan History of Canterbury*,
says, very gratuitously, that Master encouraged the girl "to begin a
course of prophecies," with a view to the restoration of the chapel
(p. 250).

matter before his diocesan, the Archbishop of Canterbury, Warham. The girl's revelations were in perfect harmony with the faith, her exhortations all tended to virtue, and her life was without reproach; the archbishop, therefore, without passing any judgment, merely bade her pastor watch the case, and report again. By an (alleged) command of the Blessed Virgin, she became a nun at the age of sixteen, in the Benedictine house of St. Sepulchre, in Canterbury; and as the fame of her sanctity, visions, and miracles spread, she came to be known as the Holy Maid of Kent. Though a professed nun, she was allowed to leave her monastery from time to time, as was not unfrequently the case before the Council of Trent restored the discipline of strict enclosure; and we hear of her as visiting the chapel at Court-up-Street, the nuns at Syon, near Isleworth, and the Charterhouse monks at Shene, the archbishop, and even the king.

In the meantime the archbishop had commissioned the prior of Christchurch, Canterbury, and two of his monks, Richard Bocking, D.D., and William Hadley, B.D., to go to Court-up-Street and witness the trances, and report to him on them. Dr. Bocking was then appointed by the archbishop to be her confessor, an appointment which cost him his life.

When the question of the king's marriage with Catharine of Aragon and the divorce became the talk of the country, the revelations of the nun began to assume a personal and political character. She circulated evil things of Cardinal Wolsey, both before his fall and after his death, and still more about the conduct of the king, and prophesied his dreadful fate if he persisted in his evil ways. One witness says that she stated that "an angel bade her go to the king, that infidel prince, and command him to amend his life, not to usurp the pope's rights, to put down the new learning; and to say that, if he married Anne, the vengeance of God should plague him"; and that she asserted that she had

shown ..ll this to the king: that two or three months later
the angel bade her go again to the king, and say that "since
her last being with him, he had more highly studied to bring
his purpose to pass; and that if he did not take back his
wife." [here the witness dare not relate the threat, but says:
"It is so naughty a matter that my hand shaketh to write it,
and something better unwritten than written"].* Other
witnesses are not so nervous, and tell us that she spread
about, and even gave out that she had told it to the king
himself, that if he married Anne he should not live six
months after (or one month according to another version),
and that from the time of his marriage he would cease to be
king in the sight of God, &c.†

It was asserted that in these and similar matters she was
the political tool of Dr. Bocking and others of the queen's
party, and that there was a conspiracy, by means of writings
and printed books containing her prophecies, and by means
of sermons that should be preached when the Holy Maid
should give the word, to stir up the people to disaffection
towards the king, and so imperil his life.

Arrests having been made and the materials of accusation
got together in the autumn of 1533, the accused were not
brought to trial, but, by a more easy and summary process,
were indicted and attainted in Parliament in January, 1534,
some of treason and others of misprision‡ of treason. Those
attainted of treason were: Dr. Bocking and John Dering,
Benedictine monks of Canterbury; Hugh Rich and Richard
Risby, Observant Franciscans; Richard Master, parson of
Aldington; and Henry Gold, parson of Aldermary, London; and the nun, Elizabeth Barton. These were all

---

* *Letters and Papers*, vi. 1.466.
† Nos. 1470, 1468.
‡ Misprision, from the French *mépris*, "contempt," means the
bare knowledge and concealment of treason without any degree of
assent thereto

executed at Tyburn on 21st April, 1534, after long imprisonment.

Those attainted of misprision of treason were: The
Bishop of Rochester; his chaplain, John Adeson; Thomas
Abell,* chaplain to Queen Catharine, and one of her de-
fenders, by writing; Thomas Lawrence, registrar to the
archdeacon of Canterbury; Thomas Gold and Edward
Thwaytes, laymen.

Before relating Fisher's share in this matter, it may be
well to repeat that it is not necessary to form any judgment
for or against Elizabeth Barton, so far as the bishop is
concerned. Certainly, if we could rely on the depositions
that have come down to us, her visions were intrinsically
improbable and her prophecies unfulfilled. But we must
remember that we have only the case as got up by Cromwell. If, without irreverence, we may imagine a Jewish
Cromwell plying St. Peter and the other Apostles with
interrogations, in their moment of fear and weakness, he
would doubtless have been able to procure a strange caricature of Our Lord's sayings and doings. And though the Holy
Maid of Kent may have been a weak visionary or a cunning
impostor, and, in truth, when we compare the evidence of the
various witnesses, it is hard to refrain from the opinion that
she was a little of both, yet it is not right to decide the
matter, as most historians do, by declaring the imposture
proved, and appealing to the confession of the chief impostor. The Act of Attainder throughout speaks, indeed,
of the "false-cloaked hypocrisy and feigned revelations
and miracles" of the nun, and of her having "confessed all
her falsehood before divers of the king's counsellors, and
that these were manifestly proved, found, and tried most
false and untrue". But this may, for all we know, be
merely equivalent to the attainder of the Jewish tribunal:

* Thomas Abell, afterwards a martyr, is one of those who were
beatified with Fisher.

"What need we any further testimony? For we have ourselves heard it from His own mouth." That Elizabeth Barton ever confessed herself an impostor, we have no convincing proof. Cranmer, indeed, writes to a friend of his on the Continent: "Now she hath confessed that she never had a vision in her life, but feigned them all";* but this can be only decisive to those who have some trust in Cranmer's truthfulness. One of Cromwell's correspondents, Dr. Gwent, writes: "She confessed to Cranmer many mad follies"; he explains, however, his meaning, by adding that Cranmer got her to acknowledge these "follies" by pretending to believe in them, so that the nun's confession was not one of imposture.† Though Blessed Thomas More, in his letter to Cromwell, calls her a lewd nun and a "huswife," and speaks of her "detestable hypocrisy" and her "confession," it is not clear that he is not merely assuming the truth of Cromwell's got-up case. It must, however, be admitted that a great weight of evidence is apparently against her.‡

To turn now to the Bishop of Rochester. He has been accused of great credulity.§ But credulity and superstition are vague terms. It will be well to see what were his general principles and what his conduct in this instance.

There is a remarkable passage on the subject of private revelations in one of Fisher's treatises against Luther, that can hardly fail to interest the reader, because it contains his judgment about the famous Savonarola: "How can Luther (he asks) be so certain, as he says he is, that all his doctrines come from heaven, unless it has been evidently revealed to him? Nay, even so, such revelations are in general deceitful. They are thought to have emanated

* Cranmer's *Letters*, 273.
† *Letters and Papers*, n. 967.
‡ Hall, the chronicler, gives her speech on the scaffold. *If it is authentic*, it is decisive against her.
§ Lewis, ii. 112.

from God, while in reality they proceed from the evil spirit.
Does not St. Paul say that Satan transforms himself into an
angel of light ?   And we read that a certain spirit said to the
Lord : I will go and be a lying spirit in the mouth of all the
prophets of Achab.   And in our own times there was a man,
not without learning, Jerome of Florence, who boldly and
repeatedly (*constanter*) predicted to the Florentines many
things as about to take place, and thereby was held in
the greatest esteem of people and princes.   However, as
after his death none of those things took place which he had
foretold, by that token it is now certain that his prophecies
did not come from God.   For Jeremias writes : 'The prophet that prophesied peace, when his word shall come to
pass, the prophet shall be known whom the Lord hath sent
in truth'.*   So that, as it seems, Jerome (Savonarola) was
himself under a delusion,† although he was an eminent man,
and venerable in word and life, so far as human judgment
can decide, nor did he ever swerve a hair's-breadth in doctrine from the orthodox fathers, except that he despised
the excommunication pronounced against him, and taught
others to despise it.   Now, if a man so great and so Catholic
could be misled by revelations, what surety can we have as
to the revelations made to Luther ?   Although he (Jerome
Savonarola) might have seemed to have received great
offence at the hands of the Supreme Pontiff, Alexander, he
yet never spoke against his authority, but only against its
abuse.   He possessed the greatest moderation (*modestia*),
humility, patience, and charity.   He never inveighed
against the pontifical dignity, but only against the Pontiff's
life and conduct.   He never presumed that anything should
be taught contrary to the common faith of the Catholic
Church.   Whereas Luther is not ashamed to root up the

* *Jerem.* xxviii. 9.

† Fisher adds, in a marginal note, that Pico della Mirandola excuses him, and that the Florentines still hold him in great veneration.

Church's doctrines, to despise the maxims of the fathers, to call the best and holiest popes impostors, to make nought of the authority which Christ gave to St. Peter, to insult and outrage excellent kings, to infect the people with the most pernicious heresies, to fill heaven and earth with lies, and is yet brazen-faced enough to boast that he is certain that all his doctrines have come to him from heaven." *

Such were Fisher's principles as to revelations. Was, then, he himself the victim of feigned revelations? Or did he forget in practice the caution he had taught? The reader shall judge for himself by contemporary evidence.

When Cromwell was himself attainted all his papers were seized, and thus even his private memoranda have been carefully preserved. From them it is clear that the thought of connecting Fisher with Dame Elizabeth Barton's seditious or treasonable revelations emanated from him. On one occasion, in October, he notes down that he is to speak to the king of "the Bishop of Rochester's saying to Rysby," one of the friars accused of treason ; a little later, that he is to ask "whether the bishop is to be sent for". And in his notes of matters to be brought before the next Parliament we find the following : "To declare the names of all offenders accused with the nun. To cause indictments to be drawn for them in treason and misprision." †

The letters of Chapuys will tell us the course of events, so far as they were public, and the rumours that were afloat. On November 12, 1533, he writes to the emperor : "The king has lately imprisoned a nun who had always lived till this time as a good, simple, and saintly woman, and had many revelations. The cause of her imprisonment is that

* *Assertionum Regis Angliæ Defensio*, cap. i., n. 6. In another work, Fisher writes in a similar manner of Savonarola, showing that he had nothing in common with Luther, who called him a saint (*Assert. Luth. Confutatio*, Art. 33).

† *Letters and Papers*, vi. 1370, 1381, 1382.

16

she had had a revelation that in a short time this king would
not only lose his kingdom, but that he should be damned,
and she had seen the place and seat prepared for him in
hell. Many have been taken up on suspicion of having
encouraged her to such prophecies to stir up the people to
rebellion. It seems as if God inspires the queen (*i.e.*, the
deposed Queen Catharine) on all occasions to conduct herself well, and avoid all inconveniences and suspicions ; for
the nun had been very urgent at divers times to speak with
her and console her in her great affliction, but the queen
would never see her. Yet the council do not desist from
making continual inquiry whether the queen has had any
communication with her. She has no fear for herself, as
she never had any, but she fears for the Marquis and
Marchioness of Exeter and the good Bishop of Rochester,
who have been very familiar with the nun."*

On the 20th November Chapuys writes again : "The
king has assembled the principal judges and many prelates
and nobles, who have been employed three days, from
morning till night, to consult on the crimes and superstitions
of the nun and her adherents ; † and at the end of this long
consultation, which the world imagines is for a more important matter, the chancellor [Audley], at a public audience,
where were people from almost all the counties of the
kingdom, made an oration how that all the people of this
kingdom were greatly obliged to God, who by His Divine
goodness had brought to light the damnable abuses and
great wickedness of the said nun and of her accomplices,
whom for the most part he would not name, who had
wickedly conspired against God and religion, and indirectly
against the king, whom he lauded to the skies as a prince

---

* *Letters and Papers*, vi. 1419 ; *Spanish Calendars*, iv. 1149.

† Cromwell, in a letter to Fisher, speaks of "the great assembly of
the lords of this realm as has ever been seen many years to meet out
of Parliament " before whom the question had been brought.

without a peer ". The reader will remark that all this was done long before the attainder, and before any legal trial of the accused. Chapuys continues : " He praised also the general devotion to the king of the whole realm, who knew him to be rightly divorced from the queen, whom he called princess-dowager, and that the most lawful marriage he had made with this lady (Anne Boleyn) was not for his own gratification, but to procure a lawful successor in the kingdom ; and that they must not treat as of any account whatever a certain invalid sentence said to have been given by the pope against the king, because his holiness had been induced to pass it by improper means, and especially by the diabolic plot of the said nun, who had written to him a thousand false persuasions, which she authorised in a spirit of prophecy and Divine revelation in case he did not give sentence.

" Up to this point no one dared to say a word, or make the slightest sign of pleasure or displeasure. But on the chancellor proceeding to say that the nun and her accomplices, in her detestable malice, desiring to incite the people to rebellion, had spread abroad and written that she had a Divine revelation that the king would soon be shamefully driven from his kingdom by his own subjects, some of them began to murmur and cry that she merited the fire. The said nun, who was present, had so much resolution that she showed not the least fear or astonishment, clearly and openly alleging that what the chancellor said was true." *

" At the end he declared that the late Archbishop of Canterbury and many other great personages were mixed up in these affairs ; and many were still alive who were infected, whom the world would know hereafter. Many believe that

---

* From the mention of the nun's fearlessness it would appear that she admitted the fact of her having promulgated these revelations and adhered to their Divine origin, not that she admitted an imposture.

those who have the said nun in hand will make her accuse many unjustly in order to take vengeance on the queen's party, and get money from them, which is the thing he (*i.e.*, the king) thinks most of in this world. The said nun has been almost entirely under the keepership of Cromwell or his people, and is continually treated as 'a great lady,'* which strongly confirms the above-named suspicion.

" The chief business still remains, for the king insists that the said accomplices of the nun be declared heretics for having given faith to her, and also be guilty of high treason for not having revealed what concerned the king; consequently their goods should be confiscated. To which the judges during the last three days will not agree, as being without any appearance of reason, even as to the last, since the nun a year ago had told the king of it in person. It is to be feared, however, that they will do that which the king desires, as they did when they condemned the cardinal for having received his legateship." †

Four days later, 24th November, Chapuys returns to the subject : " Yesterday the nun was placed upon a high scaffold before the cathedral of this city [at St. Paul's Cross], where she, two good and religious Observants, two Augustinian monks, two secular priests, a hermit, and a respectable layman, waited all the time of the sermon ; and for their vituperation the preacher, who was a monk lately made bishop, in order to support the 'lady's' party, repeated all that the chancellor had said against them, further affirming

---

* " *Grosse dame.*" According to M. Littré the word may bear in old French the sense I have given to it. Mr. Gairdner translates *grosse* "stupid," but with a note of interrogation. Would not the context indicate that she was well treated, in order to encourage her to stand to her revelations, and so involve more accomplices ? It was certainly thus that Cranmer "dallied with her, as if he did believe her every word," according to his own official, the dean of the arches. (See n. 967.)

† *Letters and Papers,* vi. 1445 ; *Spanish Calendars,* iv. 1153.

that the nun, by her feigned superstition, had prevented the
Cardinal of York from proceeding to give sentence for the
divorce, as he had resolved ; and this had been one of the
greatest calamities of this kingdom, as much for the present
as for the future. To her other accomplices who were there
the preacher imputed levity and superstition for sticking to
such things, and disloyalty for not revealing them. He
attributed to the two Observants especially, that under the
shadow of the said superstition they had suborned and
seduced their companions to maintain the false opinion and
wicked quarrel of the queen against the king. And as the
principal matter of his harangue he confined the rest of his
discourse to a justification of the king's quarrel, impugning
the first marriage, exhorting the people with great vehemence
never to listen to the contrary."*

"It is said on the two next Sundays the nun and the
above-mentioned persons will play the same part in the
comedy, for it hardly deserves any other name, and that
afterwards they will be taken through all the towns in the
kingdom, to make a similar representation, in order to efface
the general impression of the nun's sanctity ; because this
people is peculiarly credulous, and is easily moved to
insurrection by prophecies, and, in its present disposition,
is glad to hear any to the king's disadvantage. The king
has not yet prevailed on the judges to make the declaration
against those who have practised against him with the said
nun, in the form that I last wrote.† He is go'ng to have
the affair discussed with them on Friday ; and although
some of the principal judges would sooner die than make

* This courtly preacher was John Capon or Salcote, Abbot of
Hyde (Winchester), and nominated Bishop of Bangor. The Protestant writers of the day say that the accused all confessed their
guilt and fraud on this occasion. Chapuys says nothing of this ;
yet he had no reason to omit it, were it really so.

† That is, the declaration that they were guilty of heresy and treason.

the said declaration, yet, when the king comes to dispute, there is no one who will dare contradict him, unless he wishes to have 'beast' or 'traitor' thrown at his head. So that it seems as if he had made a total divorce, not only from his wife, but from good conscience, humanity, and gentleness, which he used to have."*

It must be noticed, since it bears on the administration of justice in those times, that not one of the persons thus placed in public ignominy had been convicted or tried for any crime, while the king is bullying his judges to consent beforehand to a capital sentence against them, and Cromwell is arranging for their attainder by Parliament. Cromwell's agents sought out more evidence. Lee and Bedyll write to him, on 10th December, from Canterbury: " We intend to return home shortly, for we find not so great matters here as we expected. The crafty nun† keeps herself very secret here, and showed her merchandise more openly when she was far from home. If she had been as wary elsewhere as here, she might have continued longer in her falsehood."‡ Cranmer writes, at the same time (13th December), from Canterbury, to the king: "The feigned revelations of the false nun of St. Sepulchre's, now that they are declared to the people, are had in great abomination, and everyone seems glad that they are exposed. I have examined the prior and convent of my church (Christchurch), and find them as conformable as any. They greatly regret that any of their congregation should have caused slander, and brought them under your displeasure, when only a few consented to these revelations, almost all being Dr. Bocking's novices. The prior and brethren are much dismayed, and have desired me to mediate with you.

---

* *Letters and Papers*, vi. 1460 ; *Spanish Calendars*, iv. 1154.

† Here is a further proof that she had made no confession, in the sense of acknowledgment, of imposture.

‡ *Letters, &c.*, 1512.

Think they will offer £200 or £300 for their pardon."* This last clause certainly justifies Chapuys' view, that greed for money was urging on the king to these prosecutions. £300 was a large sum, equivalent to at least £3000 in our own day. His new archbishop is getting him this bribe from his frightened subjects, whom he had sworn to protect. They are guilty of no offence, yet they have to buy off his displeasure. Cromwell also was making something by these transactions, as was his custom. Richard Master, the rector of Aldington, and Elizabeth Barton's first confessor, being in prison, and thinking that Cromwell had got him a pardon, sends his benefactor two gold royals, pleading his poverty that he can do no more.† Yet the poor man remained in prison, and was hung, drawn, and quartered notwithstanding.

But the king was to get neither offer of money nor apology from the Bishop of Rochester. In the month of December, 1533, the bishop fell very ill, and during his illness had to undertake the correspondence with Cromwell, the king, and the House of Lords that will now be given, and which certainly shows no sign of a sick or weakened mind. Cromwell sent a message to him, by his brother Robert, that if he would write an humble letter to the king, asking pardon and submitting himself, he would not be further troubled.‡ We may judge what this meant by an example. A letter of the kind, from the prior and monks of Christchurch, Canterbury, is in existence. They declare that they would have had intolerable sorrow and despair but for the common fame of the king's benignity. The temerity and furious zeal of one of their number, Dr. Bocking, had led him to slander the king's present marriage ; of which crime the writers desire to be purged, as no other among them has impugned it,

---

* *Letters and Papers*, n. 1519. † *ibid.*, 1660.
‡ It is Cromwell himself who reminds the bishop of this in his letter printed by Burnet.

though it is true that some of them, especially of the
younger sort, were informed by the said doctor of the
counterfeit revelations of the nun.   They would not be so
presumptuous as to impugn the Archbishop of Canterbury's
sentence, and the opinion of the most famous clerks of
Christendom. *   This letter, probably drawn up for them
by Cranmer, together with the *douceur* of two or three
hundred pounds mentioned by him in his letter already
given, had its effect, not merely in obtaining their "pardon,"
but also in compromising them in the matter of the divorce.
already condemned by the Sovereign Pontiff.   Mr. Bruce
has remarked that Cromwell's desire in sending the message
to the bishop by his brother was to entrap him.   " Had he
adopted this course, he would have destroyed his freedom
of action, and have rendered himself incapable of offering
any future opposition to the measures of the Court."   Mr.
Southey, in his *Book of the Church,* asserts that "the bishop's
persistence in refusing to do this was plai· 'y a matter of
obstinacy, not of conscience".   To which Mr. Bruce replies:
" It is indeed extraordinary that a man is to be denounced
as obstinate because, at the summons of a Secretary of
State, upon a promise of pardon, he did not acknowledge
himself guilty of an undefined offence, of the commission of
which his own conscience did not accuse him ". †

Instead of writing a hypocritical letter to the king, Fisher
replied to Cromwell's message, in a letter that has not come
down to us, but of which we know the substance by Cromwell's answer.   He declared that his motive in communicating at all with Elizabeth Barton had been to make trial
whether her revelations were from God.   He had heard
much of her holiness, and her director was in repute for
virtue and learning; Archbishop Warham had spoken to
him about the nun's visions and revelations; such revela-

* *Letters and Papers,* vi. 1469.   † *Archæologia,* vol. xxv.

tions were not to be rejected beforehand, since the Holy
Scriptures say: "The Lord God doeth nothing without
revealing His secrets to His servants the prophets".*

In his reply, the secretary read the bishop a severe
lecture on his conduct, his imprudence, his prejudices, and
partisanship in everything regarding the deposed queen;
that he had not taken the proper means to ascertain the
truth; and, in conclusion, that since, instead of asking
pardon, he defended himself, he must now not look for
mercy, and that if the matter came to a trial, his own confession in this letter, besides the witnesses that were against
him, would be sufficient to condemn him. He therefore repeats his advice to write a letter of submission to the king.
As the bishop had spoken of his conscience, the secretary
concludes by saying that it was thought he had written and
said as much as he could, and many things, as some very
probably believed, against his conscience; that it was
reported that at the last Convocation he spake many things
he could not well defend, and therefore it was not greatly
feared what he could say or write in that matter more.†

To this the bishop replied from his sick-bed as follows:
"After my right humble commendations, I most entirely
beseech you that I no farther be moved to make answer
unto your letters, for I see that mine answer must rather
grow into a great book, or else be insufficient, so that ye
shall still thereby take occasion to be offended, and I
nothing profit. For I perceive that everything I writ is

---

* *Amos* iii. 7. Although the bishop's letter is not in existence,
Mr. Froude calls it "ridiculous," and blames him for being "unable
to see that the exposure of the imposture had imparted a fresh
character to his conduct, which he was bound to regret" (*History*, ii.,
ch. vii).

† Cromwell's letter is very long. It is printed in substance in
Lewis, ii. 114-117, and in full in Wright's *Suppression of Monasteries*
(Camden Society), p. 27.

ascribed either to craft, or to wilfulness, or to affection, or to unkindness against my sovereign ; so that my writing rather provoketh you to displeasure than it furthereth me in any point concerning your favour, which I most effectually covet. Nothing I read in all your long letters that I take any comfort of, but the only subscription wherein it pleased you to call you my friend ; which undoubtedly was a word of much consolation unto me, and therefore I beseech you so to continue, and so to show yourself unto me at this time.

" In two points of my writing methought ye were most offended, and both concerned the king's grace. That one was where I excused myself by the displeasure that his highness took with me when I spake once or twice until him of like matters. That other was where I touched his great matter. And as to the first, methink it very hard that I might not signify unto you such things secretly as might be most effectual for mine excuse. And as to the second, my study and purpose was specially to decline that I should not be straited to offend his grace in that behalf, for then I must needs declare my conscience, the which (as then I wrote) I would be loth to do any more largely than I have done. Not that I condemn any other men's conscience. Their conscience may save them, and mine must save me. Wherefore, good master Cromwell, I beseech you for the love of God be contented with this mine answer, and to give credence unto my brother in such things as he hath to say unto you. Thus fare you well.

" At Rochester, the 31 day of January [1534],
    " By your faithful beadman,
        " JO. ROFFS." *

Three days before writing this letter the bishop had received a summons to attend Parliament, and had written the following excuse :

* B. M., *Cleop.*, E. vi. 161. Printed by Lewis and Bruce.

"MASTER CROMWELL,

"After my right humble commendations, I beseech you to have some pity of me, considering the case and condition I am in; and I doubt not if ye might see in what plight that I am, ye would have some pity upon me. For in good faith, now almost this six weeks I have had a grievous cough, with a fever in the beginning thereof, as divers other here in this country hath had, and divers have died thereof. And now the matter is fallen down into my legs and feet, with such swelling and ache that I may neither ride nor go [*i.e.* walk], for the which I beseech you eftsoons to have some pity upon me, and to spare me for a season, to the end the swelling and aches of my legs and feet may assuage and abate; and then, by the grace of Our Lord, I shall with all speed obey your commandment. Then fare ye well.

"At Rochester, the 28 day of January,

"By your faithful beadman,

"JO. ROFFS." *

Cromwell in reply promised to obtain for him leave of absence, but in all probability informed him that a bill of attainder was about to be introduced against him as a participator, or as involved by misprision, in Elizabeth Barton's treasonous frauds. Parliament met on 15th January, 1534, and on 21st February the bill was read for the first time in the House of Lords, and a second time on the 26th. The bishop was still very ill and unable to appear before Parliament for his own defence. From his sick-bed he wrote the two following letters, to the king and to the lords, contrasting in the most marked manner, by their frank and noble, though respectful, tone, with the verbose, cringing, and slavish effusions with which petitioners generally approached their sovereign in those days of hypocrisy and arbitrary power:

* R. M., *Vespas.*, F. xiii., f. 154*b*. Printed by Lewis and Bruce.

"To the King's Most Gracious Highness,

"Please it, your gracious highness, benignly
to hear this my most humble suit, which I have to make
unto your grace at this time, and to pardon me that I come
not myself unto your grace for the same.   For, in good
faith, I have had so many perilous diseases, one after
another, which began with me before Advent, and so by
long continuance hath now brought my body into that
weakness, that without peril of destruction of the same
(which I dare say your grace for your sovereign goodness
would not), I may not as yet take any travelling upon me.
And so I wrote to Master Cromwell, your most trusty
counsellor, beseeching him to obtain your gracious licence
for me to be absent from this Parliament, for that same
cause, and he put me in comfort so to do.

"Now, thus it is (most gracious sovereign lord), that in
your most high court of Parliament is put in a bill against
me, concerning the nun of Canterbury, and intending my
condemnation for not revealing of such words as she said
unto me touching your highness.   Wherein I most humbly
beseech your grace, that without displeasure I may show
unto you the consideration that moved me so to do, which,
when your most excellent wisdom hath deeply considered,
I trust assuredly that your charitable goodness will not
impute any blame to me therefore.

"A truth it is, this nun was with me thrice in coming
from London by Rochester, as I wrote to Master Cromwell,
and showed unto him the occasions of her coming, and of
my sendings until her again.

"The first time she came unto my house, unsent for of
my part, and then she told me that she had been with your
grace, and that she had shown unto you a revelation which
she had from Almighty God (your grace, I hope, will not
be displeased with this my rehearsal thereof); she said

that *if your grace went forth with the purpose that ye
intended, ye should not be King of England seven months
after.*

"I conceived not by these words, I take it upon my soul,
that any malice or evil was intended or meant unto your
highness, by any mortal man, but only that they were the
threats of God, as she then did affirm.

"And though they were feigned, that (as I would be
saved) was to me unknown. I never counselled her unto
that feigning, nor was privy thereunto, nor to any such
purposes, as it is now said they went about.*

"Nevertheless, if she had told me this revelation, and had
not also told me that she had reported the same unto your
grace, I had been verily far to blame, and worthy extreme
punishment, for not disclosing the same unto your highness, or else to some of your council. But since she did
assure me therewith, that she had plainly told unto your
grace the same thing, I thought doubtless that your grace
would have suspected me that I had come in to renew her
tale again unto you, rather for the confirming of my opinion
than for any other cause.

"I beseech your highness to take no displeasure with
me for this that I will say. It sticketh yet (most gracious
sovereign) in my heart, to my no little heaviness, your
grievous letters, and after that your most fearful words, that
your grace said unto me, for showing unto you my mind
and opinion in the same matter, notwithstanding that your
highness had so often and so straitly commanded me to
search for the same before. And for this cause I right

---

* Everywhere the bishop expresses himself on the subject of the
"Holy Maid" with the greatest caution. He speaks hypothetically
of her being an impostor. To have defended her then would have
been worse than useless; to treat her as certainly guilty would have
been unjust, unless he were convinced, as Sir Thomas More seems
to have been, that she had confessed to fraud.

loathe to have come unto your grace again, with such a tale
pertaining to that matter.

"Many other considerations I had, but this was the very
cause why that I came not unto your grace. For, in good
faith, I dreaded lest I should thereby have provoked your
grace to farther displeasure against me.

"My Lord of Canterbury also, which was your great
counsellor, told me that she had been with your grace, and
had shown you this same matter, and of him (as I will
answer before God) I learned greater things of her pretended visions than she told me herself. And, at the same
time, I showed unto him that she had been with me, and
told me as I have written before.

"I trust now that your excellent wisdom and learning
seeth there is in me no default for not revealing of her words
unto your grace, when she herself did affirm unto me that
she had so done, and my Lord of Canterbury, that then was,
confirmed also the same.

"Wherefore, most gracious sovereign lord, in my most
humble wise, I beseech your highness to dismiss me of this
trouble, whereby I shall the more quietly serve God, and
the more effectually pray for your grace. This, if there
were a right great offence in me, should be to your merit to
pardon, but much rather, taking the case as it is, I trust
verily you will so do.

"Now, my body is much weakened with many diseases
and infirmities, and my soul is much inquieted by this
trouble, so that my heart is more withdrawn from God, and
from the devotion of prayer, than I would. And verily,
I think that my life may not long continue. Wherefore,
eftsoons, I beseech your most gracious highness, that by
your charitable goodness I may be delivered of this business,
and only to prepare my soul to God, and to make it ready
against the coming of death, and no more to come abroad
in the world. This, most gracious sovereign lord, I

beseech your highness, by all the singular and excellent endowments of your most noble body and soul, and for the love of Christ Jesus, that so dearly with His most precious Blood redeemed your soul and mine. And during my life I shall not cease (as I am bound), and yet now the more entirely, to make my prayer to God for the preservation of your most royal majesty.

"At Rochester, the 27th day of February.

"Your most humble beadman and subject,

"JO. ROFFS."*

The second letter is to the House of Lords:

"MY LORDS,

"After my most humble commendations unto all your good lordships, that sit in this most high court of Parliament, I beseech in like manner to hear and to tender this my suit, which by necessity I am now driven to make unto all your lordships in writing, because I may not, by reason of disease and weakness, at this time be present myself before you without peril of destruction of my body, as heretofore I have written to Mr. Cromwell, which gave me comfort to obtain of the king's grace respite for my absence till I be recovered. If I might have been present myself, I doubt not the great weakness of my body, with other manifold infirmities, would have moved you much rather to have pity of my cause and matter, whereby I am put under this grievous trouble.

"So it is, my good lords, that I am informed of a certain bill that is put into this high court against me and others concerning the matter of the nun of Canterbury, which thing is to me no little heaviness, and most especially in this piteous condition that I am in.

---

* Lewis, ii. 336.

"Nevertheless, I trust in your honours' wisdom and consciences, that you will not in this high court suffer any act of condemnation to pass against me till my cause may be well and duly heard. And, therefore, in my most humble wise, I beseech all you, my lords, in the way of charity, and for the love of Christ, and for the mean season, it may please you to consider, that I sought not for this woman's coming unto me, nor thought in her any manner of deceit. She was the person, that by many probable and likely conjectures, I then reputed to be right honest, religious, and very good and virtuous. I verily supposed that such feigning and craft, compassing of any guile or fraud, had been far from her. And what default was this in me so to think, when I had so many probable testimonies of her virtue?

"*First*, The bruit of the country, which generally called her *the Holy Maid*.

"*Secondly*, Her entrance into religion upon certain visions which was commonly said that she had.

"*Thirdly*, For the good religion and learning that was thought to be in her ghostly father, and in other virtuous and well-learned priests that then testified of her holiness, as it was commonly reported.

"*Finally*, My Lord of Canterbury that then was, both her ordinary and a man reputed of high wisdom and learning, told me that she had many great visions. And of him I learned greater things than ever I heard of the nun herself. Your wisdoms, I doubt not, here see plainly that in me there was no default to believe this woman to be honest, religious, and of good credence.

"For sithen [*i.e.*, since] I am bound by the law of God to believe the best of every per· n until the contrary be proved, much rather I ought so to believe of this woman, that had then so many probable testimonies of her goodness and virtue.

" But here it will be said, that she told me such word as was to the peril of the prince and of the realm. Surely I am right sorry to make any rehearsal of her words, but only that necessity so compels me now to do. The words that she told me concerning the peril of the king's highness were these : she said that she had her revelation from God, that if the king went forth with the purpose that he intended, he should not be King of England seven months after ; and she told me, also, that she had been with the king and shown unto his grace the same revelation.

" Though this was forged by her or any other, what default is mine, that knew nothing of that forgery ? If I had given her any counsel to the forging this revelation, or had any knowledge that it was feigned, I had been worthy great blame and punishment. But whereas I never gave her any counsel to this matter, nor knew of any forging or feigning thereof, I trust in your great wisdoms that you will not think any default in me touching this point.

" And as I will answer before the throne of Christ, I knew not of any malice or evil that was intended by her, or by any other earthly creature unto the king's highness : neither her words did so sound that by any temporal or worldly power such thing was intended, but only by the power of God, of whom, as she then said, she had this revelation to show unto the king.

" But here it will be said, that I should have shown the words unto the king's highness. Verily, if I had not undoubtedly thought she had shown the same words unto his grace, my duty had been so to have done. But when she herself, which pretended to have had this revelation from God, had shown the same, I saw no necessity why that I should renew it again to his grace. For her esteemed honesty, qualified, as I said before, with so many probable testimonies, affirming unto me that she had told the same unto the king, made me right assuredly to think that she

17

had shown the same words to his grace. And not only her own saying thus persuaded me, but her prioress's words confirmed the same, and their servants also reported to my servants that she had been with the king. And yet besides all this, I knew it not long after, that so it was indeed. I thought, therefore, that it was not for me to rehearse the . nun's words to the king again, when his grace knew them already, and she herself had told him before. And surely divers other causes dissuaded me so to do, which are not here openly to be rehearsed. Nevertheless, when they shall be heard, I doubt not but they will altogether clearly excuse me as concerning this matter.

"My suit, therefore, unto all you, my honourable lords, at this time is, that no act of condemnation concerning this matter be suffered to pass against me in this high court before that I be heard, or else some other for me, how that I can declare myself to be guiltless herein.

"And this I most humbly beseech you all, on your charitable goodnesses, and also if that peradventure in the meantime there shall be thought any negligence in me for not revealing this matter unto the king's highness, you, for the punishment thereof which is now past, ordain no new law, but let me stand unto the laws which have been heretofore made, unto the which I must and will obey.*

"Beseeching always the king's most noble grace that the same his laws may be ministered unto me with favour and equity, and not with the strictest rigour. I need not here to advise your most high wisdoms to look up to God, and upon your own souls in ordaining such laws for the punishment of negligences, or of other deeds which are already past, nor yet to look upon your own perils which may

* Lord Chancellor Campbell calls a bill of attainder "that commodious instrument of tyranny which obviated the inconvenient requirements of proofs and judicial forms" (*Life of Audley*). Fisher was therefore protesting in favour of freedom and constitutional right.

happen to you in like cases. For there sits not one lord here but the same or other like may chance unto himself that now is imputed unto me.*

"And therefore eftsoons I beseech all your benign charities to tender this my most humble suit as you would be tendered if you were in the same danger yourselves : And this to do for the reverence of Christ, for the discharge of your own souls, and for the honour of this most High Court : And finally for your own sureties, and others that hereafter shall succeed you, for I verily trust in Almighty God that, by the succour of His grace, and your charitable supportations, I shall so declare myself, that every nobleman that sits here shall have good reason to be therewith satisfied. Thus Our Lord have you all, this most honourable court, in his protection. Amen."†

The only result of these solemn appeals, not for mercy, but for justice, was that the bill was read a third time on 6th March. The entry in the *Lords' Journal* of that date is as follows : " A bill, written on paper, concerning the due punishment of Elizabeth Barton, nun and hypocrite (*monacellæ et hypocritæ*), formerly called the Holy Maid of Kent, with her adherents, was thrice read. Their lordships thereupon thought it fit to find whether it was according to the king's will, that Sir Thomas More, and the others named with him in the said bill, with the exception of the Bishop of Rochester, who is laid up with illness, and whose answer is already known by his letters, should be required to appear before their lordships in the Star Chamber, that it may be heard what they can say for themselves."

Hence it appears that the name of Sir Thomas More had been up to this time on the bill, and was afterwards struck

---

* Prophetic words. It was Cromwell who contrived these bills of attainder, and who was himself doomed to death by the same instrument of tyranny.

† Lewis, ii. 332.

off.* The bishop's letter, asking to be heard, was considered as equivalent to his having been heard.†

On the 12th of March, the bill was engrossed on parch-ment, and passed the Lords. It was expedited through the Commons, and returned to the Lords on the 17th. On the 20th, it was delivered to the chancellor, for what cause does not appear. He brought it back on the 21st, and it seems that the royal assent was given to it on 30th March, accord-ing to the practice then usual, when the king attended to put an end to the session.

The exact terms of the Act were these: "In considera-tion of which premises . . . be it enacted . . . that John, Bishop of Rochester" (and others), "shall be convict and attainted of misprision and concealment of treason, as persons that have given such credit, counsel, and constant belief to the said principal offenders" (viz., those attainted of treason), "whereby they have taken courage and bold-ness to commit their said detestable treasons and offences. And that the said Bishop of Rochester" (and others) ". . . shall suffer imprisonment of their bodies at the king's will, and forfeit to the king's highness all their goods, chattels, and debts" (due to them) "which they had on the 16th January, or at any time since the said day, And that such benefices and spiritual promotions as the said John Adeson and Thomas Abell had on the 16th January shall from the 20th March, 1533" (*i.e.*, 1534) "be void in the law . . . as

* More had written earnest exculpatory, but not apolegetic, letters to Cromwell, and to the king. The latter is dated 5th March. (See *Letters, &c.*, vii. 287-289.)

† Only three bishops are recorded in the *Lords' Journals* as present in this Parliament. The Bishop of Rochester's name is on the lists, though without the P signifying "present" until the 21st February, when the bill of attainder against him was introduced. From that date his name is omitted. Chapuys twice mentions how the king "packed" this Parliament, and countermanded those likely to oppose him (*Letters, &c.*, vii. 83, 296, 373).

if the said John Adeson and Thomas Abell were dead of their natural deaths."

Nothing is said of making void the bishopric of Rochester.

Chapuys wrote to the emperor on 25th March : "The good Bishop of Rochester, who is the paragon of Christian prelates, both for learning and holiness, has been condemned to confiscation of body and goods. All this injustice is in consequence of his support of the queen."*

It is remarkable that the pope's final decree in favour of the validity of the marriage between Henry and Catharine was given on 23rd March, and was, thererefore, simul taneous with the attainder of the great champion of that marriage.

It is painful to an Englishman, even after three centuries and a half, to think that the Peers of this nation, together with the Commons and the sovereign, should, on the most frivolous pretexts, and without a trial or hearing the accused in his own defence, have passed such a sentence on a bishop who was the glory of their episcopate. " It is needless,' writes Mr. Bruce, " to dwell upon the manifest injustice and breach of constitutional form which distinguished the whole of this proceeding. It was the opening of a fearful tragedy, the turning of a page in our history, which reflects equal disgrace upon the malignity of the king and the cold-hearted suppleness of his advisers. That the king could obliterate the memory of former kindnesses, and close his heart against the entreaties of an infirm man, who had long served his father and himself, whose pretended fault had been committed without fraud, and was followed by no evil consequences, and who, in his extreme age, declares that he merely sighs 'to prepare his soul to God and make it ready against the coming of death, and no more to come abroad

* *Letters and Papers*, vii. **373.**

into the world,' is a proof how rapidly he was descending into the state of ferocious tyranny which distinguished the after portion of his life."*

It does not appear, however, that on account of this attainder the bishop was imprisoned or forfeited his goods, "although, as I have heard," says Dr. Hall, "he was after fain to redeem himself with payment of three hundred pounds for a fine, which was one whole year's revenue of his bishopric ; for the king meant not to spoil his goods, which he knew to be of small value, but rather thirsted after his life, knowing him to be a great stop and hindrance of all his licentious proceedings". The bishop's Protestant biographer, or rather slanderer, Mr. Lewis, takes another view of the matter. " The king, it seems, willing to try what he could do with the bishop *by fair and gentle means*, was pleased, it is said to mitigate the rigour of the law, and to pardon his lordship on his paying a fine of £300, which favour was obtained for him by the mediation and intercession of the new queen." Mr. Froude, with his usual taste, says : "Fisher found mercy thrust upon him, till by fresh provocation the miserable old man forced himself upon his fate ".

There is no need to have recourse to the apocryphal mediation of Anne Boleyn, nor to the still more apocryphal benignity of the king, to explain this mystery. Another Act had been passed in the same session of Parliament, and it afforded an easier and more effectual means to accomplish the ruin of the bishop than the Act of Attainder. This was the Act of Succession, by means of which the bishop was placed in the dilemma of taking an oath such as the king desired, or of being guilty of misprision of treason by refusing it. The king therefore had the choice of two weapons against the bishop, and he naturally chose the

* Mr. Bruce in *Archæologia*, vol. xxv., p. 70.

latter. **If he** could get him to take the oath, it would be a complete humiliation of the bishop, and a thorough triumph for the king and for Anne Boleyn. If he should refuse the oath, he would be even more in the king's power than he now was. This must be explained in the next chapter.

CHAPTER XII

THE king's divorce from Catharine and marriage with Anne involved a change in the succession to the Crown. It had become necessary to set aside the Princess Mary as illegitimate, and to fix the inheritance on the king's offspring by Anne Boleyn. This was done by an Act of 25th Henry, chap. 22 (March, 1534).* The preamble of the Act recites the importance of providing for the succession to the Crown, the illegality and invalidity of the marriage between Henry and Catharine, the validity of the divorce pronounced by Cranmer, the validity and lawfulness of the marriage contracted by the king with Anne. The Act then goes on to limit the succession to his and her issue, making it high treason to oppose this succession, and misprision of treason to speak against it. It then continues as follows :

"Be it further enacted that all the nobles of the realm, spiritual and temporal, and all other subjects arrived at full age, at the will of the king, may be obliged to take corporal oath, in the presence of the king or his commissioners, that they shall truly, firmly, and constantly, without fraud or guile,

* The Act, going beyond the immediate purpose, declares that there is no power residing with anyone to dispense with the Levitical impediments, and that any marriages hitherto contracted with such dispensations, on pretence of the pope's dispensation, must be dissolved by the ecclesiastical courts. This is the first in a long series of blundering legislation on marriage by the civil power, founded on no principle and issuing in utter confusion.

observe, fulfil, maintain, defend, and keep, to their cunning, wit, and uttermost of their powers, the whole effect and contents of the present Act".

Then after mentioning persons from whom, and circumstances in which, the taking of the oath must be exacted, the Act concludes :

"And if any persons, being commanded by authority of this Act to take the said oath afore limited, obstinately refuse that to do, in contempt of this Act, they become guilty of misprision of treason".

The Act, however, had not indicated the precise form of the oath to be taken. A form was drawn up by the commissioners, who were the Lord Chancellor (Audley), the Archbishop of Canterbury (Cranmer), and the Dukes of Norfolk and Suffolk, to whom were afterwards added the secretary (Cromwell) and the Abbot of Westminster. The oath given in the *Lords' Journals* is as follows :

"Ye shall swear to bear your faith, truth, and obedience, alonely to the king's majesty, and to the heirs of his body . . . according to the limitation and rehearsal within this statute of succession . . . and not to any other within this realm, *nor foreign authority, prince or potentate ;* and in case any oath be made, or hath been made by you, to any other person or persons, that you thus do repute the same as vain and annihilate ; and that to your cunning, wit, and uttermost of your power, without guile, fraud, or other undue means, ye shall observe, keep, maintain, and defend this Act, and all the whole contents and effects thereof, and all other Acts and Statutes made since the beginning of this present Parliament, in confirmation or for the due execution of the same, or of anything therein contained. And thus ye shall do against all manner of persons, of what estate, dignity, degree, or condition soever they be, and in nowise do or attempt, nor to your power suffer to be done or attempted,, directly or indirectly, any thing or things, privily or apertly to the let, hindrance, damage, or derogation thereof, or of any part of the same, by any manner of means, or for any manner of pretence or cause. So help you God and all saints." *

But though this formula is placed in the *Lords' Journals* as if it had been authorised and used in March, 1534, it is in reality taken from an Act passed in December of the same year, and called "An Act ratifying the oath that every of the king's subjects hath taken, or hereafter shall be bound to take"; and this Act recites the above formula with the introduction: "The tenour of which oath hereafter en- sueth".† What form of oath was taken by the two houses we do not know. But we know that, as it were in virtue of the Act of Succession, the king immediately began to exact from the clergy an explicit renunciation of the pope's autho- rity. Rowland Lee, who was consecrated by Cranmer on 19th April, 1534, nine months before the Act of Supremacy was passed, swore as follows: "I acknowledge and recognise your majesty immediately under Almighty God to be the chief and supreme head of the Church of England, and claim to have the bishopric of Chester ‡ wholly and only of your gift, &c. So help me God, all saints, and the holy evangelists." § Of course no bulls were asked from the pope for this man's appointment. A little later the bishops all took a new oath to the king, and repudiated that which all (Rowland Lee, Goodrich, and Salcot excepted) had taken to the pope. "From this day forward I shall swear, pro- mise, give or cause to be given to no foreign potentate . . . nor yet to the Bishop of Rome whom they call the pope,

---

The *Lords' Journals*, vol. i., p. 82.

† 26 Henry VIII., c. 2. Given only in the *Statutes of the Realm*, not in *Statutes at Large*.

‡ The diocese of Lichfield and Coventry was often called Chester. In 1537, a distinct diocese of Chester was erected by royal authority.

§ Burnet, vi. 291 (ed. Pocock).

any oath or fealty, directly or indirectly . . . but at all times, and in every case and condition, I shall . . . maintain . . . the quarrel and cause of your royal majesty and your successors. I profess the Papacy of Rome not to be ordained of God by Holy Scripture," &c.* Other examples of oaths exacted from the clergy and religious orders will be given later on. It was necessary to say thus much by anticipation, in order to make clear the use of the words succession and supremacy, as they will occur henceforth. Burnet, and after him Lewis, the biographer of Fisher, call it "a calumny, that runs in a thread through all the historians of the Popish side," to have confounded these words, and to have asserted that men were put to death for refusing the "oath of supremacy". Lewis maintains that there was no *oath* of supremacy, but simply an Act declaring the supremacy, the violation of which Act was treason, and punished by death; that there was an oath of succession, but that the refusal of this oath was merely misprision of treason, punishable by imprisonment. This is correct enough if we merely look to Acts of Parliament. But if we interpret those Acts by the royal proclamations that accompanied them, and the public Acts of the nation, we shall see that "the Popish historians" speak correctly. The oath of succession was made into an oath of supremacy; and the Act of Supremacy, though it did not name the pope, nor gave any right to exact an oath, was really enforced by an oath of supremacy, the refusal of which was fatal. All this will appear more clearly as we proceed. In the meantime it may be mentioned that Lord Campbell (but on what authority I know not) gives the following as the form proposed to More (and Fisher): "To bear faith and true obedience to the king and to the issue of his present marriage with Queen Anne; to acknowledge him the head of the Church of England, and to

* Gardiner's oath. Foxe, v. 70; Wilkins, iii. 780.

renounce all obedience to the Bishop of Rome, as having no more power than any other bishop". The Lords and Commons present at the conclusion of the session on 30th March took the oath, whatever it was, publicly in presence of the king. Fisher, as has been said, was ill in Rochester.

The sentence of the Sovereign Pontiff declaring the validity of the king's marriage with Catharine had been given on the 23rd March (1534), but was not published for a few days. The news, therefore, had not reached England when Chapuys wrote on 4th April: "The king has prorogued Parliament to November, at which time they are again summoned to complete the ruin of the Churches and Churchmen, as I am informed on good authority. And for a conclusion of this last session, the king has declared that those present at the said Parliament should individually sign the statutes and ordinances made against the queen and princess, and the others passed in favour of his mistress and her posterity. The process of signing has been a thing unused hitherto, and has been resorted to to confirm the iniquity of the ordinances, the future observance of which the king has reason to doubt. What the king has got passed against the pope and the authority of the Holy See he has not exactly required them to confirm, but only conditionally, in case between this and the feast of St. John (24th June) it be in his power to annul it in whole or in part, which is a lure to his holiness to consent to his desire, and the king has no little hope of doing so, both by means of the French king and of the bravadoes he employs." *

But on Holy Saturday, the very day on which Chapuys had written the letter just quoted, the news of the sentence reached England, and the king celebrated his Easter festival by ordering the preachers to say the very worst they possibly could against the pope; "in which," says Chapuys, "they

* *Letters and Papers*, vii. 434.

have acquitted themselves desperately, saying the most outrageous and abominable things in the world". The king
also commanded that the statutes made in Parliament, which
he had suspended and reserved *in pectore* till St. John's Day,
should be immediately published.*

Though the Act of Succession was not one of those held
in suspense, the exasperation of the king made him more
eager to enforce it, and more pitiless towards all who should
dare to refuse the oath. Speaking of this crisis, Mr. Froude
says: "The Tudor spirit was at length awake in Henry. . . .
In quiet times occasionally wayward and capricious, Henry
reserved his noblest nature for the moments of danger, and
was ever greatest when peril was most immediate. Woe to
those who crossed him now, for the time was grown stern,
and to trifle further was to be lost. . . . Convocation, which
was still sitting, hurried through a declaration that the pope
had no more power in England than any other bishop. Five
years before, if a heretic had ventured so desperate an
opinion, the clergy would have shut their ears and run upon
him : now they only contested with each other in precipi-
tate obsequiousness. . . . The commission appointed under
the Statute of Succession opened its sittings to receive the
oaths of allegiance. Now more than ever was it necessary
to try men's dispositions, when the pope had challenged

---

* *Letters and Papers*, vii. 469 The Act of Parliament held in
suspense was the Act against Peter's Pence and other tributes to the
Holy See. It was declared that the pope had hitherto " beguiled "
the English nation, and they would no longer be beguiled. However,
they would still submit to the impositions, if the pope would pronounce in favour of the king. Mr. Froude puts it according to his
peculiar fashion : " The pope had received these revenues as the
supreme judge in the highest court in Europe, and he might retain
his revenues, or receive compensation for them, *if he dared to be
just*". In 1532, the Statute against Annates had similarly been left
to the discretion of the king to make absolute or permanent. (See
Mr. Gairdner, Preface to vol. vi., p. vii., and to vol. vii., p. xx.)

their obedience.   In words all went well : the peers swore
bishops, abbots, priors, heads of colleges, swore with scarcely
an exception—the nation seemed to unite in an unanimous
declaration of freedom (!).   In one quarter only, **and** that a
very painful one, was there refusal." *

In some such language as the above did the Babylonian
historians record how the nobles, magistrates, judges, captains,
and chief men came to adore the golden statue that king
Nabuchodonosor had set up, and how from a certain quarter
whence it was most "painful," from the favoured three,
Sidrach, Misach, and Abdenago, alone there came refusal.

Of this refusal Sir Thomas More has given an account in
a letter to his daughter Margaret, written a few days after
the occurrence.   We have no such authentic detail of the
refusal of the Bishop of Rochester.   Yet from More's letter
and other sources we may gather the following facts.

He had celebrated the Easter festival for the last time in
his diocese on April 5th.   It would seem that his health
was sufficiently improved to allow him to travel to London ; †
and he was summoned to appear before the commissioners
at Lambeth.   Dr. Hall gives a minute and affecting account
of his farewell to his episcopal city, derived in all probability
from the testimony of eye-witnesses, such as Dr. Phillips
or Mr. Buddell, with whom Hall was intimate.‡   "The
Archbishop of Canterbury's letter," he says, " being once
known and heard of in his house, cast such a terror and fear
among his servants, and after among his friends abroad in the

---

* *History*, ii., ch. vii.

† Dr. Hall (and after him Baily) says that he was present at the
close of the session and openly refused the oath, that this was at first
passed over and he was allowed to return to Rochester, and was
summoned to London "after four days".   This seems to be a
conjecture, as Dr. Hall was evidently unacquainted with the bishop's
illness and absence from Parliament.   It is clear from the *Lords'
Journals* that he was not in London at the close of the session.

‡ See the Preface.

country, that nothing was there to be heard but lamentation and mourning on all sides. Howbeit the holy man, nothing at all dismayed therewith (as a thing that he daily and hourly looked for before), called all his family before him, and willed them to be of good cheer and to take no care for him, saying that he nothing doubted but all this should be to the glory of God and his own quietness."

Hall then tells of the instructions the bishop gave his steward as to rewards to his household, and of his bequest of a hundred pounds to Michael House at Cambridge, which was afterwards paid, and of his gifts to the poor of Rochester. He reserved a small sum for his own wants. "The next day he set forward on his journey towards Lambeth, and passing through Rochester, there were by that time assembled a great number of people of that city and country, about to see him depart, to whom he gave his blessing on all sides as he rode through the city bareheaded. There might you have heard great wailing and lamenting, some crying that they should never see him again. Some others said, 'Woe worth they that are the cause of his trouble'; others cried out upon the wickedness of the time to see such a sight; everyone uttering their grief to others as their minds served them.

"Thus passed he till he came to a place in the way called Shooter's Hill, nigh twenty miles from Rochester, at the top whereof he rested himself, and descended from his horse; and because the hour of his refection was then come (which he observed at due times), he caused to be set before him such victuals as were thither brought for him of purpose, his servants standing round about him. And so he came to London that night. And this precise order of diet he used long before, because the physicians thought, and he feared himself, to be entered into a consumption." *

* Cardinal Pole, in a passage to be quoted presently, says that the bishop swooned from weakness during this journey.

It was on Monday, the 13th April, 1534, that the bishop
appeared before the commissioners.   Baily says that at
Lambeth he met Sir Thomas More, who welcomed him
with the words : "Well met, my lord, I hope we shall meet
in heaven" ; to which the bishop replied : "This should be
the way, Sir Thomas, for it is a very strait gate we are in".
Sir Thomas, however, does not mention this meeting with the
bishop, nor is there a word about this salutation in Dr. Hall,
who was Baily's sole authority.   We may therefore class it
among Baily's many inventions.   Dr. Hall says that the
bishop found at Lambeth Sir Thomas More and Dr.
Wilson, sometime the king's confessor, who both had refused the oath a little before his coming.   From Sir
Thomas' letter to his daughter we know that Dr. Wilson,
after refusing the oath, was led off directly to the Tower, so
that the bishop could not have spoken with him if Wilson
refused the oath before his coming.   And it is probable that
he held no conversation with Sir Thomas.   Sir Thomas
had been the very first called, and, having refused the oath
as offered and been remanded for a time, waited "in an
old burned chamber that looketh into the garden," until the
others, who had been summoned, and who were all
ecclesiastics of London and Westminster, "had played their
pageant (as Sir Thomas expresses it), and were gone out of
the place," when he was recalled, and on his second refusal,
he was committed for four days to the custody of the abbot
of Westminster, while the king consulted with his council
what order should be taken with him. *   On Friday Sir
Thomas was committed to the Tower, and on the same day
wrote to his daughter: "What time my Lord of Rochester was
called in before (the commissioners) that cannot I tell.   But
at night I heard that he had been before them, but where
he remained that night, and so forth till he was sent hither,
I never heard."

* Roper's *Life of More.*

Dr. Hall writes that when the Bishop of Rochester was equired by the commissioners to take the oath, he asked to ee and consider it, and that for this purpose he was remanded for a few days to his own house in Lambeth Marsh. He there received visits from many friends, and amongst thers from Mr. Seton and Mr. Brandsby, fellows of St. ohn's, Cambridge, who came as a deputation from the ollege to beg him to confirm their statutes under his seal.* He replied that he would first read and consider them once nore. "Alas!" said they, "we fear the time is now too short or you to read them, before you go to prison." "Then," aid he, "I will read them in prison." "Nay," said they, "that will hardly be brought to pass." "Then," said he, "let God's will be done, for I will never allow under my eal that thing that I have not well and substantially viewed nd considered." Wherefore these two fellows departed without their purpose.†

"The day being at last come," continues Dr. Hall, "when his blessed man should give answer before the commissioners, whether he would accept the oath or no, he presented himself again unto them, saying that he had perused he same oath with as good deliberation as he could, but hat, being framed in such sort as it is, by no means he could ccept it with safety of his conscience. Nevertheless (said e), to satisfy the king's majesty's will and pleasure, I am ontent to swear to some part thereof, so that myself may rame it with other conditions and other sort than it now

---

* He was still chancellor of the university.

† Baker in his *History of St. John's* mentions that Cranmer had been amending the bishop's statutes, and that the bishop's seal was lesired, as that of the last surviving executor of Lady Margaret. This will explain his caution. The college afterwards sought leave o interview him when in the Tower for the same purpose, but probably were either refused leave to see him, or he refused to give his sanction; for the revised statutes did not receive his seal. (See Baker p. 101.)

standeth, and so both my own conscience shall be thereby
satisfied and his majesty's doings the better justified and
warranted by law.   But to that they answered that the king
would by no means like of any kind of exceptions or conditions, 'and therefore' (said my Lord of Canturbury) 'you must
answer directly to our question whether you will swear the
oath or no'.   'Then,' said my Lord of Rochester, 'if you
will needs have me answer directly, my answer is, that
forasmuch as mine own conscience cannot be satisfied, I
do absolutely refuse the oath.'   Upon which answer he was
sent straight away to the Tower of London."

Hall does not give the form of oath, nor does he explain
what points the bishop could accept, and what he felt
constrained to refuse.   We have, however, the bishop's own
explanation in a letter, written about nine months later, to
Cromwell, which will be quoted in full in its place.   In this
he says: "I was content to be sworn to that parcel concerning the succession; and I did rehearse this reason,
which I said moved me.   I doubted not but the prince of
any realm, with the consent of the Nobles and Commons,
might appoint for his succession royal such an order as was
seen unto his wisdom most according . . . albeit, I refused
to swear to some other parcels."*   His objections, therefore, were religious, not political, nor even of personal
loyalty to the queen and princess.   He admitted the power,
however he might regret its exercise, of the nation, represented by king and Parliament, to deprive the legitimate

---

* Sir Thomas was also willing to swear to the succession, but in
what way we do not know.   He says: "The bishop was content to
have sworn in a different manner to what I was minded to do" (*Eng.
Works*, 1453).   Yet Stapleton says that Sir Thomas admitted the
power of Parliament to make or depose a king.   That is, of course,
a very different question, and we know nothing of the bishop's views
regarding it.   He merely says that the king *and* Parliament may
change the succession.

Princess Mary of her inheritance, and to give it to the bastard daughter of Anne Boleyn. I say bastard, because Fisher would not admit the invalidity of Henry's marriage with Catharine, and held that Elizabeth was the fruit of open adultery. But he could not take the oath for more than one reason. Whether it contained the explicit rejection of the pope (as Lord Campbell supposes), or the implicit rejection (as in the form found in the *Lords' Journals*), it was schismatical and heretical. But, independently of the pope's supremacy in general, the oath proposed to him required the admission, not only of the new succession, but of the reasons for it given in the preamble of the Act of Parliament. To accept this preamble regarding the illegitimacy of Mary and legitimacy of Elizabeth, after the decision just given by the pope, was an act of rebellion, and a repudiation of all living authority in the Church to declare the Divine law of marriage.

Sir Thomas More had said : " Though I would not deny i.e., refuse] to swear to the succession, yet unto that oath that was there offered me I could not swear, without the jeoparding of my soul to perpetual damnation ". Though some authors have asserted that both Fisher and More were aware of circumstances that would have made a marriage between Henry and Anne impossible, even though the marriage of the former with Catharine had been null, yet it is certain that the difficulties of Sir Thomas did not lie in these supposed circumstances alone (if at all), since he declared to the commissioners that his conscience was grounded on the general consent of Christendom, which could not be outweighed by the council of one realm. His objections, therefore, arose from public principles, not personal facts.

On the same day on which the two illustrious recusants were sent to the Tower, the Archbishop of Canterbury wrote the following letter to the Secretary of State, Cromwell.

"RIGHT WORSHIPFUL MASTER CROMWELL,

"After most hearty commendations, &c. I doubt not
but you do right well remember that my Lord of Rochester
and Master More were contented to be sworn to the Act
of the king's succession, but not to the preamble of the
same. What was the cause of their refusal I am uncertain, and they would by no means express the same.
Nevertheless, it must needs be either the diminution of
the authority of the Bishop of Rome, or else the reprobation of the king's first pretensed matrimony. But if
they do obstinately persist in their opinions of the preamble, yet meseemeth it should not be refused, if they
will be sworn to the very Act of Succession, so that they
will be sworn to maintain the same against all powers
and potentates.

"For hereby shall be a great occasion to satisfy the
princess dowager and the Lady Mary, which do think that
they should damn their souls if they should abandon and
relinquish their estates. And not only it should stop the
mouths of them, but also of the emperor and other their
friends, if they give as much credence to my Lord of
Rochester and Master More speaking or doing against them,
as they hitherto have done, and thought that all should have
done, when they spake and did with them.

"And, peradventure, it should be a good quietation to
many other within this realm, if such men should say that
the succession comprised within the said Act is good and
according to God's laws. For then, I think, there is not one
within this realm that would once reclaim against it. And
whereas divers persons, either of a wilfulness will not, or of
an indurate and invertible conscience cannot, alter from
their opinions of the king's first pretensed marriage (wherein
they have once said their minds, and percase have a persuasion
in their heads that if they should now vary therefrom their

fame and estimation were distained for ever), or else of the authority of the Bishop of Rome; yet, if all the realm with one accord would apprehend the said succession, in my judgment it is a thing to be amplected and embraced. Which thing, though I trust surely in God that it shall be brought to pass, yet hereunto might not a little avail the consent and oaths of these two persons, the Bishop of Rochester and Master More, with their adherents, or, rather, confederates.

"And if the king's pleasure so were, their said oaths might be suppressed, but [*i.e.*, except] when and where his highness might take some commodity by the publishing of the same. Thus Our Lord have you ever in His conservation.

"From my manor at Croydon, the 17th day of April.
"Your own assured ever,
"THOMAS CANTUAR."*

The last clause about *suppressing* the exact nature of the oath to be taken by More and Fisher is worthy of Cranmer, to whom oaths were what cards are to the juggler. It was to be given out (such was the scheme) that they had yielded, so as to induce others to yield; but occasionally it might "suit the king's commodity," as when dealing with persons of similar scruples, to reveal and use the modified form. Roper did not know of this letter, but it entirely justifies what he asserts in the life of his father-in-law, Sir Thomas More, that "albeit in the beginning they (the Government) were resolved that with an oath not to be acknown [*i.e.*, acknowledged] whether he had to the supremacy been sworn, or what he thought thereof, he should be discharged. Yet did Queen Anne by her importunate clamour so sore exasperate the king against him, that, con-

* Lewis, ii. 354; Burnet, i. 255. Also (in abridgment) in Gairdner, *Letters and Papers* vii. 499.

trary to his former resolution, he caused the said oath of
the supremacy * to be ministered to him."

The plan of Cranmer recalls the "wicked pity," as the
Holy Scriptures name it, of those who proposed that the
venerable Eleazar should eat lawful flesh while pretending
to eat pork in obedience to the king.†   The reply of
Eleazar—"It doth not become our age to dissemble "—
would have been the reply of More and Fisher had the
suppression of their mitigated oath been proposed to them.
Indeed, More had told the commissioners, as he himself
relates, that even if an oath strictly confined to the succession were allowed him, he must carefully examine the
wording of it.   "I thought and think it reason, that to mine
own oath I look well myself, and be of counsel also in the
fashion [of it], and *never intended to swear for a piece, and
set my hand to the whole oath.*"

The account which Mr. Froude gives of the transaction
is as follows : "It was thought that possibly an exception
might be made, yet kept a secret from the world ; and the
fact that they had sworn under any form might go far to
silence objectors and reconcile the better class of the disaffected.   This view was particularly urged by Cranmer,
always gentle, hoping, and illogical.   For, in fact, secrecy
was impossible.   If More's discretion could have been
relied upon, Fisher's babbling tongue would have trumpeted
his victory to all the winds.   Nor would the Government
consent to pass censure on its own conduct by evading the
question whether the Act was or was not *just.*   If it was not
just, it ought not to be maintained at all ; if it was just,
there must be no respect of persons."   Mr. Froude is un-

---

* The editors of Roper, as well as Lewis, correct this word supremacy, as if it were erroneously used instead of succession.   But Roper
uses it purposely.   It was the royal supremacy *involved* in the oath
of succession as proposed which made More and Fisher refuse it.

† 2 *Machabees* vi. 21-24.

doubtedly right in saying that Fisher would not have allowed it to go out, to the scandal of the world, that he had taken an oath which he considered it a deadly sin to take. And the same may be affirmed with equal certainty of the Blessed Thomas More. He had discretion enough, but none of that sort.

But Mr. Froude is certainly wrong in saying that the rejection of Cranmer's proposal was due to a sense of justice and respect for the law. The Act of Succession had not prescribed any formula of oath, and it was on that very ground that More and Fisher claimed to reject the oath drawn up by the commissioners, and to take an oath such as would satisfy the Act and not offend their own consciences. Cromwell's answer to Cranmer's letter does not deny the power of the king to be satisfied with another oath, but asserts the inexpediency of yielding to the demand.

" My lord, after mine humble commendation, it may please your grace to be advertised that I have received your letter and showed the same to the king's highness, who, perceiving that your mind and opinion is that it were good that the Bishop of Rochester and Master More should be sworn to the king's succession, and not to the preamble of the same, thinketh that if their oaths should be taken it were an occasion to all men to refuse the whole, or at least the like. For, in case they be sworn to the succession, and not to the preamble, it is to be thought that it might be taken not only as a confirmation of the Bishop of Rome's authority, but also as a reprobation of the king's second marriage. Wherefore, to the intent that no such things should be brought into the heads of the people by the example of the said Bishop of Rochester and Master More, the king's highness in no wise willeth but that they shall be sworn as well to the preamble as to the Act. Wherefore, his grace specially trusteth that ye will in no wise attempt or move him to the contrary ; for, as his grace supposeth, that

manner of swearing, if it shall be suffered, may be an utter
destruction of his whole cause, and also to the effect of the
law made for the same."

From the king's answer it appears that he differed from
his archbishop as to what was "for his commodity," but
that neither of them took any account of what was just.[*]

Some time in the month of April the venerable prisoner
received a visit from Rowland Lee, the royal chaplain who,
according to Harpsfield, had secretly married Henry and
Anne, and who was now, in reward for his obsequiousness, made by Henry (according to a late Act of Parliament, without the confirmation of the pope), Bishop
of Lichfield and Coventry. He wrote a hasty letter to
Cromwell, saying "that the bishop continued as he left
him; that he was very ready to take his oath for the
succession and to swear never to meddle more in disputation of the validity or invalidity of the marriage of the king
with the lady dowager, but could go no further. But as for
the case of the prohibition Levitical his conscience is so knit
that he cannot send it off from him whatsoever betide him.
Yet he will and doth profess allegiance to our sovereign lord
the king during his life." Lee added that "truly the bishop
was nigh going [*i.e.*, dying] and doubtless could not continue
unless the king and his council were merciful to him, he
being already so wasted that his body could not bear the
clothes on his back".[†]

From the Act of Attainder it appears that the oath was
again tendered on the 1st May and again refused. According
to justice the bishop ought to have been brought to trial

---

[*] Mr. Lewis applauds the appeal of "the wise and charitable
archbishop" (ii. 140), and the "good archbishop" (p. 141). Mr.
Froude speaks of the "mild and tender-hearted man" (ii. 319, note).
In this instance, however, there is not a word implying kindness to
More or Fisher, but merely craft and expediency.

[†] Cotton MSS. *Cleopatra*, E. vi., p. 165.

and convicted of refusing the oath, before the penalties of
refusal were inflicted on him. But this course would have
been inconvenient, since he might have pleaded that he had
not refused any oath imposed by law. Roper says that
"whereas the oath . . . was by the first statute in few
words comprised, the lord chancellor and Mr. Secretary
did of their own heads add more words to it, to make it
appear to the king's ears more pleasant and plausible, and
that oath, so amplified, caused they to be ministered . . .
which Sir Thomas More perceiving said unto my wife : ' I
may tell thee, Meg, they that have committed me hither for
refusing of this oath, not agreeable with their statute, are
not by their own law able to justify mine imprisonment.
And surely, daughter, it is great pity that any Christian
prince should, by a flexible council, ready to follow his
affections, and by a weak clergy, lacking grace constantly to
stand to their learning, with flattery be so shamefully
abused.'" It may perhaps be thought that this was merely
a petulant complaint of the late chancellor, and that it could
not have been maintained before the judges. It is, however,
a strong confimation of More's contention, that his imprisonment was illegal as well as unjust, that in the next session
of Parliament a retrospective Act was passed declaring the
proffered oath valid, and that instead of the usual process of
law an Act of Attainder was adjudged an easier and surer
process.

Mr. Bruce writes as follows : " The penalty inflicted by
the statute attached on the refusal to take an oath of a
particular description ; the amplified oath was not such an
oath, and therefore that penalty did not attach upon the
refusal to take it. An objection so entirely technical one
would have thought beneath the notice of the king's unscrupulous advisers ; but they seem to have been influenced
by the common weakness of endeavouring to give their
injustice the sanction of legal form ; and as soon as Parlia-

ment assembled (*i.e.*, in November, 1534), a bill was passed
to remedy the defect (26 Henry VIII., c. 2).   After reciting
the former statute, and that the Lords and Commons upon
the last prorogation had taken, not the oath directed by the
statute, but 'such oath as was then devised,' it was declared
that they meant and intended that all the king's subjects
should be bound to accept the same oath, 'the tenour' of
which, but not a copy of it, was then given in the form of an
oath; and it was enacted that this new oath should be
adjudged to be the very oath that the Parliament meant and
intended should be taken, and upon the refusal to take
which the penalties denounced by the former oath accrued.

"A more atrocious and blundering instance of *ex post
facto* legislation than this can scarcely be pointed out.
Here are three oaths : one described by the former statute,
a second which was taken by the Parliament at its prorogation, and a third contained in this last Act of Parliament.
All these oaths are different, and yet it is declared that the
Parliament meant the second when they legislated concerning
the first; that they meant the third when they took the
second; and it is enacted that penalties imposed for not
taking the first have been incurred by refusing to take the
third.

"In this manner it was imagined that an appearance of
legality was given to the confinement of Fisher and his
fellow-prisoner.   It seems probable, however, that the second
was the one tendered to them, and if so the statute after all
left them untouched."*

Lord Campbell also, in his *Life of Sir Thomas More*,
says that the imprisonment was illegal, and the attainder
was "for an alleged offence, created by no law".

It was likewise enacted in this statute, passed in the next
session, to explain this oath of succession,† that the com-

---

* *Arch.*, vol. xxv., p. 23.   † 26 Henry VIII., c. 2.

missioners appointed to receive this oath, or any two of them, should have power to certify into the King's Bench. by writing under their seals, every refusal that should here-after be made before them of the oath, and that every such certificate should be as available in the law as an indictment of twelve men lawfully found of the said refusal. Why this process was not followed as regards the bishop does not appear. He had been attainted once, by Act of Parliament, of misprision of treason in the affair of the nun of Kent ; he had been already imprisoned during seven months, as if undergoing the legal penalty of refusal of an oath, which refusal was, by the statute, misprision of treason, punishable by forfeiture of all goods to the king, and imprisonment at the king's pleasure. Yet a special Act was now passed, attainting him by name on the very same plea. " Foras-much as John, Bishop of Rochester, Christopher Plummer, late of Windsor, Nicolas Wilson, Miles Willyn, Edward Powell, and Richard Featherstone (otherwise called Richard Featherstone Hawgh),* contrary to the duties of allegiance, intending to sow sedition, murmur, and grudge within the realm, among the king's loving and obedient subjects, by refusing the oath of succession since the 1st May . . . be it enacted that the above be attainted of misprision of treason, and shall suffer the penalties. The sentence to take effect, as regards loss of goods, from 1st March last." They are to forfeit all their lands, manors, &c. " And that also the see and bishopric of the Bishop of Rochester, and all other benefices and promotions spiritual, which the same Bishop of Rochester (and the others) hath, shall be, at the 2nd day of January next coming, and not before, void and destitute of bishop and other incumbency, as though they and every one of them were naturally dead. This attainder shall not ex-

* Edward Powell and Richard Featherstone were hanged at Smithfield, together with Thomas Abel. on 30th July, 1540, and are counted amongst the Blessed.

tend to the forfeiture of, or to any manors, &c., whereof
they or any of them be possessed in the right of the said
bishopric, or other spiritual benefice."[*]

Why the penalty for refusing an oath on 1st May should
take effect from 1st March I cannot conjecture. But the
king had not waited for this attainder. On the 27th April,
1534, ten days after the bishop's committal to the Tower,
commissioners were sent to Rochester and Halling to take
an inventory and make a seizure of the bishop's goods. I
have already given the principal items in describing the
bishop's episcopal life and poverty.[†] There exists also in
the Record Office an inventory of the bishop's plate. It
consists of "chalices, salts with the portcullis on them, two
nutts with a gilt cover, and a little standing masser, a little
flat book with a gilt cover, and the French king's arms on
the inside, cruets, altar basins, &c., with portcullis, a mitre
set with counterfeit stone and pearl, with the appurtenances,
cups, flagons, basins; in all 2020 oz. troy weight, of which
1112 oz. is in gilt plate, 114 oz. parcel gilt, and 794 white
silver".[‡] It must be admitted that this was a slender outfit
for a bishop in those days, especially since by far the greater
part consisted of church plate.[§] The portcullis, the well-
known Lancastrian badge, shows that most of these things
were presents of the Countess of Richmond, the saintly
grandmother of the robber king.[||]

* 26 Henry VIII., c. 22, in large edition of *Statutes of the Realm.*
† See p. 62.   ‡ *Letters and Papers,* viii., n. 888.

§ Dr. Hall, however, relates that when the bishop's troubles were
drawing near, his house at Halling was robbed one night, and all his
plate stolen. A part only was recovered that had been hidden in a
wood. He mentions the equanimity with which the bishop took his
loss.

|| In Lady Margaret's will mention is made of legacies to the
bishop of "gilt pots," weighing 126 oz., and a gold "salt," with
pearls and sapphire, weighing 8 oz. (*Memoir of Lady Margaret,*
p. 133).

Dr. Hall writes as follows: "The king sent down Sir Richard Moryson, of his Privy Chamber, and one Eastwick, with certain other commissioners, to make a seasin of all his moveable goods they could there find. Being come to Rochester, they entered his house, and first turned out all his servants ; then they fell to rifling of his goods, whereof some part was taken to the king's use, but more was em-bezzled to the uses of themselves and their servants. Then they came into his library of books, which they spoiled in most pityful wise, scattering them in such sort as it was lamentable to behold, for it was replenished with such and so many kind of books as the like was scant to be found again in the possession of any one private man in Christen-dom. And of them they trussed up thirty-two great pipes, besides a number that were stolen away. And whereas before he had made a deed of gift of all these books and other his household stuff to the College of St. John's, in Cambridge, the poor college was now defrauded of their gift, and all was turned another way.*

" And where(as), likewise, a sum of money of £300 was given by one of his predecessors, a bishop of Rochester, to remain for ever to the said See of Rochester, in custody of the bishop for the time being, for any sudden occasion that might mischance to the bishopric, the same sum, with £100 more laid to it, was found in his gallery, locked in a chest, and from thence carried clean away by the commissioners.

" Among all other things found in his house, I cannot omit to tell you of a coffer standing in his oratory, where commonly no man came but himself alone, for it was his secret place of prayer. This coffer being surely locked, and standing always so near unto him, every man began to think that some great treasure was there stored up. Wherefore,

---

* Even the furniture of Lady Margaret, in the rooms occupied by the bishop in St. John's College, was seized, and never recovered. (See Baker's *History of St. John's*, p. 103.)

because no collusion or falsehood should be used to defraud
the king in a matter of so great a charge as this was thought
to be, witnesses were solemnly called to be present. So the
coffer was broken up (*i.e.*, open) before them ; but when it
was open they found within it, instead of gold and silver
which they looked for, a shirt of hair and two or three
whips, wherewith he used full often to punish himself, as
some of his chaplains and servants would report that were
there about him, and curiously marked his doings. And
other treasure than that found they none at all. But when
report was made to him in his prison of the opening of that
coffer, he was very sorry for it, and said that if haste had not
made him to forget that and many things else, they should
not have found it there at that time."*

* Baily has transcribed the above, adding, however, a few details
not found in my copy of Hall's MS., as that the £100 had been
given by the bishop, and the inscriptions on the chest that it was the
Church's treasure, and on the money bag, *Tu quoque fac simile.*

BELL TOWER.

CHAPTER XIII

W E have now to consider the bishop's manner of life and sufferings in prison, and to many of the readers of this memoir acquaintance with the scene of these sufferings will add greatly to the interest of the narra-tive. The bishop's palaces at Rochester, Halling, and Lambeth have perished, but the Tower of London still exists, and within its walls the Bell Tower, in which he was imprisoned for fourteen months, and the Chapel of St. Peter ad Vincula, in which his sacred dust awaits its glorious resurrection.

There is no place in England so crowded with memories of every kind as the Tower of London : memories of strife and triumph, of glory and misery, of crime and sanctity.* It was for centuries a mighty fortress, a royal palace, and a State prison. The White Tower, or great central keep, from which the whole pile derives its name, was built by one of Fisher's predecessors in the See of Rochester, Gundulf, who had been monk at Bec, and was the friend of Lanfranc and St. Anselm. It had stood unchanged for four hundred and fifty years when Fisher's eyes last rested upon it, and stands unchanged still, now that another three centuries and a half have passed over it. In 1509, the bishop had sat within

---

* See *History and Antiquities of the Tower of London*, by John Bayley (1830); *Notices of the Historic Persons Buried in the Chapel of the Tower*, by D. C. Bell (1877); and a very interesting article in the *Month*, for December, 1874, by Rev. J. Morris, S.J.

its walls at the council table of the youthful king, and from
it he rode forth in the magnificent coronation procession of
Henry and Catharine.   In doing so he must have passed
close under the wall of the Bell Tower, which was to be
the place of his imprisonment, and which stands at the
south-west corner of the inner ward, not far from the
entrance gate.   This was one of thirteen towers that
strengthened the inner ramparts.   It was called the Bell
Tower, from a small wooden turret in its roof containing the
alarm bell of the garrison.   Built up against it was the
house of the lieutenant.   The Tower is circular, and the
walls are from nine to thirteen feet thick, with narrow
windows or loopholes.   The bishop was confined, not in
the vaults or dungeon, but in the upper story.   "The
apartment is spacious and airy, and it was perhaps the
best prison in the Tower, and was used for prisoners of
distinction; and as the only mode of ingress or egress was
through the lieutenant's house, he was enabled to guard
them very vigilantly." *

The bishop's prison house is little changed since he
inhabited it.   The same rough stone walls, merely white-
washed; the same flagged floor; the same apertures for
door and windows, though the glass is very different from
the rough glazing of the 16th century.   But how different the prospect from the windows.   From that to the
south we have a view of the Pool below London Bridge,
filled with great steamers and the commerce of the whole
world.   From another opening to the west there is a view of
Tower Hill.   The Church of All Hallows is still there, but
almost hidden by great warehouses.   On its north side is a
station of the underground railway.   The cruel scaffold is
gone, and a cab-stand occupies its place.   Instead of the
old London of the reign of Henry, with its ninety thousand

---

* Mr. Doyne C. Bell, *The Chapel in the Tower*, p. 64.   The Bell
Tower is now part of the Queen's or Governor's House.

inhabitants within the walls and forty thousand dwellers in
the suburbs, we look out towards the homes of five millions,
a million and a half more than the population of all England in the days of Fisher.   But in that room, and looking
from those windows, modern London disappears, and we
seem to stand by the aged bishop as he watches the
Carthusians dragged on hurdles through the mud towards
Tyburn, and thinks of his own death soon to follow, or
gazes towards old London Bridge, with the knowledge that
the head that gazes will before long be fixed upon a pole
above the battlements, to strike fear of treason into the
passers-by.   But we see the traitor-bishop lift his eyes to
heaven, and his thoughts are of the Beatific Vision.

That the Bishop of Rochester was confined in this Tower
has been the constant tradition of the place itself, and is
explicitly stated by Dr. Hall.   Describing the bishop's
death, his biographer says : " The lieutenant came to him in
his chamber in the Bell Tower ".*

* It is to be regretted that a recent writer, who is generally very
accurate, while admitting the above fact, and giving a ground plan
of the bishop's prison-house and a view of it as it now stands, has
added in a note : " Bishop Fisher was also confined in the White
Tower; in one of the dungeons below is an inscription, almost
obliterated, in which his name can be read ; it was probably cut out
by one of his servants " (Mr. Bell, *Chapel in Tower*, p. 65).   There
is indeed an inscription of the following words : " Vestibus sacris in
cubiculo carceris mei inventis hic includor.   R. Fisher ; " *i.e.*, "Sacred
vestments having been found in my prison cell, I am shut up here ".
But (1) no event of this kind is recorded of the bishop ; (2) it savours
much more of the days of Elizabeth, when mass was a crime ; (3) it
is evidently written by the prisoner himself ; (4) the bishop would
have signed his name Roffensis, not Fisher ; (5) the initial is R., not
J.; and (6) if Fisher's servant could write English (which is doubtful),
he certainly could not write Latin.   Mr. Hepworth Dixon, who has
given the whole inscription wrong, says it was made by a "Jesuit father
who was concerned in the Powder Plot ".   No Jesuit father named
Fisher was concerned in that plot.   Father Morris thinks the name
is really Ithell, as is clear on a rubbing being made of the surface.
(See article on the Tower in *Month*, Dec., 1874.)

19

The great infirmities of the bishop at this period of his imprisonment have been described by Cardinal Pole in the following words: " As to the Bishop of Rochester, who survived the long misery of his prison, who, that considered his age, the delicacy of health which belonged to him, and the leanness of his body, could have believed that he could last even one month in prison? Most certainly, when I left England, three years ago,* I thought that even if he should use the greatest possible care about his health, in his own house, considering what he suffered, he could not live another year. And I heard afterwards, that when he was summoned to London to be imprisoned, on the journey he swooned away for some time from weakness. And now, since he has been able to exist for fifteen months in the squalor of that noisome prison, who does not see the hand of God, above the powers of nature, prolonging his life, O king, for your great disgrace, that he might perish by your sword rather than by natural death?" †

The cell I have described was not incommodious as a prison-house, but assuredly it was no fit dwelling-place for an old and infirm man, especially during the winter months. If the thickness of the stone walls and the smaliness of the windows gave some coolness in the great heats, they rendered the room damp and cold and dark in the long winter. The proximity of the lieutenant's house did not imply either warmth from his fires or dainties from his table. A most pathetic letter has been preserved, written by the bishop to Cromwell on the 22nd December, 1534, after he had been eight months in prison. This precious relic of his martyrdom shall be given in the very words and spelling of the original:

" After my most humbyl commendations, whereas ye be content that I shold wryte unto the King's Hyghnesse, in

---

* He is writing in 1535, shortly after the bishop's death.
† De Unitate Eccl., lib. iii.

gude faithe I dread mee that I kan not be soo circumspect
in my wryteing but that sume worde shal escape me wherewith his grace shal be moved to sum further displeasure
againste me, whereof I wold be veray sorry. For as I wyll
answer byfore God, I wold not in any manner of poynte
offend his grace, my dutey saved unto God, whom I muste
in every thyng prefer. And for this consideration I am full
loth and full of fear to wryte unto his highnesse in this
matter. Nevertheless, and if then I conceyve that itt is
your mynde that I shal soo doo, I wyll endevor me to the
best that I kan.

" But first here I must beseeche you, gode Master Secretary, to call to your rememberance that att my last beyng
befor yow, and the other Commyssionars, for taking of the
othe concernyng the King's most noble succession, I was
content to be sworne unto that parcell concerning the succession. And there I did rehcars this reason, which I sade
moved mee, I dowted nott but the prynce of eny realme,
with the assent of his nobles and commons, myght appoynte
for his succession royal such an order as was seen unto his
wysdom most accordyng ; and for this reason I sade, that I
was content to be sworne unto that part of the othe ass
concerning the succession. This is veray trowth, as God
help my sowl att my most neede. All be itt I refused to
swear to sum other parcels by cause that my conscience
wold not serve me so to do.

" Furthermore, I byseche yow to be gode master unto me
in my necessite ; for I have neither shirt nor sute, nor yett
other clothes, that ar necessary for me to wear, but that bee
ragged and rent to shamefully. Notwithstanding I might
easily suffer that, if thei wold keep my body warm. Butt
my dyett allso, God knoweth how slendar it is at meny
tymes, and noo in myn age my sthomak may nott awaye but
with a few kynd of meates, which if I want I decaye forthwith, and fall in to coates [coughs] and diseases of my

bodye, and kan not keep myself in health. And ass our
Lord knoweth, I have nothyng laft un to me for to provide
any better, but ass my brother of his own purs layeth out
for me to his great hynderance. Wherefoor, gode master
secretarye, eftsones I byseche you to have sum pittee uppon
me, and latt me have such thyngs ass ar necessary for me in
myn age, and specially for my health.

"And allso that it may pleas you by yo hygh wysdom,
to move the Kyng's Highnesse to take me unto his gracious
favor agane, and to restore me unto my liberty, out of this
cold and paynefull emprysonment; whearby ye shall fynd
me to be your pore beadsman for ever unto Allmighty God,
who ever have you in his protection and custoody.

"Other twayne thyngs I mustt allso desyer uppon yow :
thatt oon is, that itt may pleas yow that I may take some
preest with in the Towr, by the assyngment of master leve-
tenant,* to hear my confession againste this hooly tyme ;
the other is, that I may borow sum bowks to styr my devotion mor effectuelly thes hooly dayes for the comforth of my
sowl. This I byseche yow to grant me of your charitie.
And thus our Lord send you a mery Christenmass and a
comforthable to your harts desyer.

"At the Tour, the 22d day of December.

"Yo pore Beadsman,

"JO. ROFFS."†

This letter suggests several questions as to the treatment
of State prisoners, both with respect to body and soul, in the
days of Henry VIII. There is no reason to think that
Fisher experienced exceptional hardships or privations ; but
the lot of all prisoners was bitter indeed. Were they utterly
without means or friends, they would no doubt have had

---

* Sir Edmund Walsingham was then lieutenant of the Tower, and
Sir Thomas Kingston was constable or chief governor.

† Cotton MSS. *Cleopatra*, E. vi., f.172. Often printed, but with
incorrect spelling, as by Lewis, ii. 330.

breaa and water given them sufficient to preserve life, but they would have been left in foul rags in a foul dungeon. Governors and jailors lived on their perquisites, and prisoners were fleeced without redress. When Sir Thomas More entered the Tower, the porter (in the presence of the lieutenant) demanded of him his upper garment. The cheerful knight feigned to misunderstand him. " Mr. Porter," quoth he, "here it is," and took off his cap and delivered it to him, saying, " I am very sorry it is no better for thee." " No, sir," quoth the porter, " I must have your gown." * Thus he was taught what he had to expect, until he bestowed his last fee and his clothes on his executioner.

We have heard the Blessed Fisher describe his forlorn condition, cold, nakedness, and monotonous and slender diet. Yet even for this he had to pay an enormous price. A document has been preserved in which are memoranda of the charges of certain persons in the Tower. Amongst others is the following entry: "The Bishop of Rochester for 14 months after 20s. le week, £56.—Sir Thomas More, for 3 months unpaid, after 10s. le week, and his servant 5s. le week, £9." † Taking account of the difference in value of money, it would seem from this that the poor bishop, the whole of whose income had been confiscated, had to pay for his somewhat more commodious prison-house, and for his scanty diet, with that of his servant Richard Wilson, from ten to twelve pounds sterling a week in modern value. From a deposition of this servant, that will be mentioned presently, and that of the bishop himself, it appears that this money was paid for him by his brother Robert; and

* Roper's *Life of More*.

† British Museum, Cotton MS. *Titus*, B. i., fol. 165. In the time of Richard II. the fees were fixed, for a duke at 5 marks a week, for an earl at 40s., for a baron or a bishop at 20s., for a knight at 10s. See Mr. W. H. Dixon's *Her Majesty's Tower*, ch. viii. ; but Mr. Dixon erroneously supposes that these charges were defrayed by " the Government ".

when his brother died in the spring of 1535, by a Mr.
Thornton and another (whose name is now illegible).* Mr.
White, the bishop's brother-in-law, also states that he had
received communications concerning the bishop's diet from
his servant. George Gold, the lieutenant's servant, mentions
also that he was accustomed to go to William Thornton's
house in Thames Street for the bishop's diet. An excellent
Italian gentleman, named Antonio Bonvisi, a Florentine
merchant long resident in London, and who for years had
been a most intimate friend of Sir Thomas More, not only
supplied the late chancellor with food, but was equally charitable to the bishop—viz., sending a quart of French wine
every day and three or four dishes of jelly, "until a quarter
of a year ago," the evidence being given on 7th June, 1535.

Perhaps this cessation was occasioned by the bishop's
illness, for in the same precious depositions John Pennoll,
who had been the bishop's falconer, states that in the Lent
he carried a letter from Fisher about his disease to Mr.
Bonvisi, who consulted Mr. Clement, a physician, another
of More's friends and one of his household. Clement sent
back word that Fisher's liver was wasted, that he should
take goat's milk and other things. He also carried another
letter to Dr. Tre—— concerning physic, and others to Mr.
White, to desire him to seek relief for the bishop.†

When interrogations were administered to Fisher himself,

* Mr. Friedmann says that this charge was defrayed by the king
(*Anne Boleyn*, ii. 342). If that was the case, the contributions of
friends were for *extras*. But is it credible that the king should pay
at such a rate for lodging a prisoner in his own fortress and the insufficient rations supplied by the lieutenant ?

† The above details are gathered from depositions of a number of
witnesses examined regarding the conduct of More and Fisher. They
are contained on twenty-one mutilated papers, which have been put
together and read with the greatest difficulty by Mr. Gairdner. They
will be frequently quoted, as they contain most precious details. We
are most grateful to Mr. Gairdner for his labour. (See *Letters and
Papers*, viii., n. 856.)

regarding his correspondence, he replied "that he wrote oftentimes letters touching his diet to him that provided his diet, as to Robert Fisher while he lived, and to Edward White, and a letter to my Lady of Oxford for her comfort, and letters of request to certain of his friends that he might pay Mr. Lieutenant for his diet, to whom he was in great debt, and he was in great need. He received money of each of them according to his request, and no other answer." This statement was made by him on the 12th June, ten days before his death.* Sir Thomas More also, in a similar deposition, which will be quoted presently, acknowledges that the bishop and he had sent each other little presents of meat and drink by their servants, when they happened to receive some dainties from their friends.

It is not without suspicion that there may be some error that I give the following extract from Dr. Hall: " The good bishop," he writes, and he is alluding to the last weeks of his life, "chanced at the present to be sick and feeble, that he kept his bed in great danger of his life; wherefore the king sent unto him divers physicians to give him preserva-tives, whereby he might the rather be able to come to his public trial and cruel punishment, which the king above all things desired, in so much so that he spent upon him in charge of physic the sum of forty or fifty pounds ".

If the king's physician really attended the bishop, the circumstance would have been known to many, and it is one unlikely to have been invented either by Dr. Hall or his informants. We may therefore accept this much of the statement The sum spent is doubtless a guess, and seems exaggerated.† The time may also have been earlier. Dr.

---

* These depositions are printed by Lewis (ii. 407) more fully than in *Letters, &c.*, n. 858.

† It is, however, to be noted that the lieutenant's charge given above is for 56 weeks, whereas he was in prison 61 weeks. Perhaps, then, during 5 weeks his diet had been provided by the physicians.

Hall has just mentioned the execution of the second band of Carthusians as having taken place on the 19th June, and he is evidently placing the illness between the issue of the commission on the 2nd June and the trial on the 17th. As Bonvisi ceased to send his usual supplies of food about the end of February, and as we know from George Gold's deposition that about that time the bishop became very ill, I should conjecture that this would be the illness referred to by Dr. Hall, and that as the king's physicians were now at last supplying the wants of the sufferer, his friend Bonvisi henceforth confined his supplies to Sir Thomas.

These details are all that have been handed down to us regarding the holy martyr's bodily sufferings in the Tower; and though there were no chains or torture, no noisome underground dungeon, no starvation on mouldy bread and filthy water, such as we read of in the acts of many martyrs, yet, when we remember the bishop's great age, his previous long and almost fatal illnesses, his "wasted liver" and dropsy, his want of exercise, and that he was left in tattered clothes without fire throughout the winter, it must be admitted that it was only by a special providence of God that he did not succumb to sickness during those long months of agony, and so lose the crown of perfect martyrdom.

But it was not the "close, filthy prison," or "to be shut up among mice and rats," to use Mistress More's description of life in the Tower, that pressed most hardly on the bishop's soul. He was deprived of all external helps and consolations of religion. It seems somewhat strange that Hall makes no allusion whatever either to the presence or absence of sacred rites, during his imprisonment or at his death. The reason most probably is that there was nothing singular in his case. As a prisoner and a condemned criminal (for so the law regarded him) he would, of course, be precluded from officiating either as a bishop or as a simple priest. To assist at the Holy Sacrifice offered by another is a privilege

ST. PETER'S AD VINCULA.

indeed; but it is one that need not be denied to the most guilty, unless by his contumacy he has been cut off by the Church from sacred rites for a time; and monastic prisons were generally so contrived that the prisoner could see the priest celebrating at some altar within the church.* But I do not find that this humane provision was imitated in any State prison of that age. There were in the Tower two churches, both still existing; but the beautiful Norman Church of St. John, within the White Tower, was reserved for the royal family, or for the officials of the place; that of St. Peter ad Vincula was the parish church of the garrison and other residents in the Tower district. Masses were daily offered in both, but not even on Sundays or festivals were the wretched prisoners brought from their cells and dungeons to kneel before the altar. Occasionally, indeed, a greater liberty was granted, and a prisoner of distinction might roam on parole or under guard through certain parts of the enclosure; and in such rare cases the governor might allow him to assist at mass. This liberty was granted to Sir Thomas More, occasionally at least, at his first coming to the Tower. His daughter, Margaret Roper, writes, when this liberty had been restricted, that she "cannot hear what moved them to shut him up again. She supposes that, considering he was of so temperate mind that he was content to abide there all his life with such liberty, they thought it not possible to incline him to their will, *except by restraining him from the church* and the company of his wife and children. She remembers that he told her in the garden [of the Tower] that these things were like enough to chance shortly after." †

If the bishop ever enjoyed a similar liberty he was certainly jealously watched that he should have no communica-

---

* See Taylor's *Index Monasticus,* Introd., p. vi. He instances Norwich and Worcester, Canterbury, Gloucester, and St. Alban's.

† More's *English Works,* p. 1446.

tion with **Sir** Thomas; nor is it anywhere stated that they even once met, though they managed to exchange letters. It seems indeed very probable that, owing to previous open opposition to the king and the anger he felt towards the bishop, no such indulgence was ever granted to him. Permissions, like that granted to Sir Thomas More, must have been very rare. Thomas Howard, the third Duke of Norfolk, who was the uncle of the two queens, whose headless trunks were laid in the Tower chapel, and who was one of Fisher's bitterest enemies in the Privy Council, came himself as prisoner to the Tower in the last year of the tyrant. He then became a petitioner for a grace he had little cared to grant to others, "that he might have a ghostly father sent to him, and that he might receive his Maker," and that he might have mass, and be bound upon his life to speak no word to him that shall say mass; "which he may do," says the duke, "in the other chamber, and I to remain within".* Even this great nobleman was not suffered to leave his prison for the church.

From a letter of Sir William Kingston, constable of the Tower, to Cromwell, we learn that a barbarous and unchristian custom, that had been reprobated by the Church, of not allowing criminals to receive communion before execution, had again established itself in England. "Sir, the time is short, for the king supposes the gentlemen do die to-morrow, and my Lord of Rochford, with the residue of the gentlemen" [*i.e.,* the four others condemned with him to death on a charge of adultery with Anne Boleyn], "is as yet without Dr. Abbynge" [the confessor], "which I look for; but I have told my Lord of Rochford that he must be in readiness to-morrow to suffer execution, and so he accepts it well, and will do his best to be ready" [*i.e.,* to make his confession and his peace with God]. "Notwithstanding, he

---

* This is the only instance in which hearing mass is even alluded to in all Mr. Baily's records of distinguished prisoners in the Tower.

would have received his rights, *which hath not been used*, *and in especial here."* To receive one's rights* was the usual phrase in that age for receiving holy communion, especially at Easter or before death, when it was *right*, or a duty, to receive.

Anne Boleyn made a still bolder petition. Though she had been reported as a favourer of the new Protestant tenets during life, as more favourable to her guilty career, in the presence of death she looked for help to the faith of her days of innocence. Sir William Kingston writes : "And then she desired me to move the king's highness that she might have the Sacrament in the closet by her chamber. that she might pray for mercy". It is not likely that a boon like this was granted ; but she at least received other helps. "The king's grace showed me," says Kingston, "that my Lord of Canterbury shall be her confessor, and he was here this day, and *not* on that matter." "The queen hath much desired to have here in the closet the Sacrament, and also her almoner for one hour." And, in another letter : "Sir, her almoner is continually " [*i.e.*, continuously] "with her, and has been since two of the clock after midnight ". "This morning she sent for me, that I might be with her as she received the Good Lord, to the intent I should hear her confessions " [*i.e.*, professions] "touching her innocency."†

I have given these various incidents regarding other illustrious prisoners as the only commentary I could make on the petition of our holy bishop in the letter above quoted : "That I may take some priest within the Tower, by the assignment of Master Lieutenant, to hear my confession against this holy time," *i.e.*, Christmas. Whether he was allowed to receive communion then, or at Easter, or before his death, we cannot now discover. What sort of con-

---

* Not rites—debita scilicet vel jura, non ritus sacri.
† The letters are in Ellis' *Collection*, first series.

fessor was assigned him before his execution we shall see presently.

From a casual remark of his servant Wilson, we learn that the bishop was not deprived of his porteous or breviary, even when other books were taken from him. " I came to my master while he was saying evensong," are his words, and he is speaking of the month of May, 1535.*

In the letter above quoted, the bishop asks leave to have some books to stir up his devotion. We know that Sir Thomas was allowed books, and that they were all taken from him, together with his writing materials, when his correspondence with Fisher was discovered. He then closed his shutters, and, sitting all day long in a darkened room, gave himself, not to melancholy, but to the contemplation of the joys of heaven. When the lieutenant remarked the closed shutters, Sir Thomas jestingly said that the shop may be shut when the goods are gone. There is no similar record, either of indulgence or restraint, regarding the bishop. In the treatises he wrote there are many quotations from Scripture, and several short sayings of the fathers, but I have found no quotations but such as a man like Fisher might easily have in his memory. As he was led out to execution he took up the New Testament. That consolation, therefore, had not been denied him. That he had any other books we have no proof. The request that he made to Cromwell at Christmas for the use of a few books, "to stir his devotion," seems to indicate that he had none, or very few.

He was allowed to write a few letters asking food or money, since that was in his jailor's interest. It is pleasant to know that his old friend Erasmus, hearing of his im-

---

* *Letters and Papers*, viii. 856 (19). The words, however, are not conclusive, since the bishop would certainly know vespers by heart, and would have said them even had he no book at hand. Yet it seems unlikely that he would have been deprived.

prisonment, wrote to him. The letter passed through the lieutenant's hands and was delivered.* So was that from his college. He distinctly denies any other correspondence except with his fellow-prisoner, the history of which will be given in another chapter.

Both of these noble martyrs during the earlier part of their captivity were allowed the use of pen and paper, and both spent their solitary hours in composing works that have come down to us. We may trust that they will be in future more widely read than they have been hitherto. Sir Thomas More wrote his *Dialogue of Comfort against Tribulation*, a treatise which, for sound theology, deep knowledge of Holy Scripture, force of reasoning, wit, pathos, and eloquence, has few equals in Christian literature. The nineteenth and twentieth chapters of the third book treat of imprisonment, and in a life of the Blessed More would deserve to be transcribed at length ; but in a life of Blessed Fisher, I must forbear quotation from a work he never read. One page, however, may be appropriately given here, having been inspired by the building itself in which they were both confined. The Tower was a palace as well as a prison, and, in writing his *History of Richard III.*, Sir Thomas had had occasion to study some part at least of its dreadful tragedies, and had at a later period of his life been eye-witness or sharer in its pageants. With the memory of these strange vicissitudes now vividly recalled by every tower and bastion, he writes as follows :

" ANTONY.—Oh ! cousin Vincent, if the whole world were animated with a reasonable soul, as Plato had weened it were, and that it had wit and understanding to mark and perceive all thing : Lord God ! how the ground, on which a prince buildeth his palace, would loud laugh his lord to scorn, when he saw him proud of his possession, and heard him boast himself that he and his blood are for ever the

---

* In his deposition, Lewis, ii., **App. 40.**

very lords and owners of that land! For then would the
ground think the while in himself: Oh! thou silly, poor
soul, that weenest thou wert half a god, and art amid thy
glory but a man in a gay gown : I that am the ground here,
over whom thou art so proud, have had an hundred such
owners of me as thou callest thyself, more than ever thou
hast heard the names of. And some of them that proudly
went over my head lie now in my belly, and my side lieth
over them ; and many one shall, as thou doest now, call
himself mine owner after thee, that neither shall be sib to
thy blood, nor any word bear of thy name.

" Who aught [owned] your castle, cousin, three thousand
years ago ?

"VINCENT.—Three thousand, uncle! Nay, nay, in anything
Christian or heathen, you may strike off a third part of that
well enough, and as far as I ween half of the remnant too.
In far fewer years than three thousand it may well fortune
that a poor ploughman's blood may come up to a kingdom,
and a king's right royal kin on the other side fall down to
the plough and cart, and neither that king know that ever
he came from the cart, nor that carter know that ever he
came from the crown.

"ANTONY.—We find, cousin Vincent, in full authentic
stories, many strange chances as marvellous as that, come
about in the compass of very few years in effect. And be
such things then in reason so greatly to be set by, that we
should esteem the loss so great, when in the keeping our
surety is so little ? " *

The books written by the bishop of Rochester during his
captivity are three in number. One is called *A Spiritual
Consolation*, and is addressed to his sister Elizabeth, who
was a Dominican nun at Dartford in Kent. He tells her
that nothing helps more to a virtuous life than to stir up the
soul by meditation, when it is without devotion and in-

* *Dialogue of Comfort,* book iii., ch. vi.

disposed to prayer or good works. The meditation he sends her is, he says, a manner of lamentation and sorrowful complaining made in the person of one that was hastily overtaken by death. It is a forcible and pathetic piece, but most certainly in no way represented the state of soul of the holy writer, nor (we may well presume) of his sister. He therefore wrote for her a second treatise called *The Ways of Perfect Religion.* In this he begins by a curious comparison between the labours of a hunter in quest of game and of a man in pursuit of holiness or of God. A nun rises at midnight but went to bed in good time and returns to bed ; the hunter rises early and lies down late ; he is often up all night. The nun fasts till noon, the hunter till night. The nun singeth all the forenoon ; the hunter hallooeth all the day long. The nun sits long in the choir ; the hunter runs over the fallow, leaps hedges, creeps through bushes. Would to God that religious would seek Christ with as little concern for worldly honours, riches, pleasures, as the hunter seeks his game ; that their comfort were to converse of Christ as his is to speak of the hare. The love of game makes all things pleasant to the hunter. Love of God should make their life a paradise for the religious ; without love it would be weary. He then draws up a series of ten considerations moving to the love of God.* The third treatise is in Latin, and is on the Necessity of Prayer, as also on its Fruits and Method. †

The comparison with the hunter in the second of these treatises derives some interest from a tradition that the bishop in his earlier days had been fond of field sports or at

* Both these treatises have been reprinted by the Early English Text Society.

† I do not know on what grounds Mr. Lewis conjectures that it was first written in English and put into Latin by another hand. I have nowhere seen any allusion to an English original. An English *translation* was printed in London in 1577, and again in Paris in 1640, according to Lowndes. This has been lately reprinted.

least of coursing.* Coursing was in that age not thought
inconsistent with the gravity of the episcopal character, and
it may give some support to the tradition that among the
servants examined by the Privy Council, as to what messages
they had carried to and from the bishop while in the Tower,
was one who had been his falconer. It should, however, be
remarked that a falconer was not a mere attendant on a
sportsman. He was a purveyor of birds for the table.† If
ever the bishop allowed himself a few hours' recreation in
such ways, it must have been in the spirit of St. Augustine,
who meditated on beauty and order while looking on a cock-
fight;‡ or like St. Francis Borgia, who, when at the emperor's
court, turned hawking into a spiritual exercise. To judge
from the bishop's exhortation to his sister, the ardour of
huntsmen had been to himself a spur to episcopal zeal.

* Harl. MS. in British Museum, n. 7047, p. 207.

† Though hawking was not a prohibited sport, yet it was decreed
in a provincial synod in 1530, in which the Bishop of Rochester took
part, that if anyone in holy orders, or beneficed cleric, should lead
dogs or carry hawks *through any town* he should be suspended *ipso facto*
for a month. (Wilkins, iii. 721.)

‡ See the metaphysical dialogue on the subject in his treatise *De
Ordine*. St. Augustine's scholar was at a loss to find *order* in a
cock-fight, whereas the saint saw a beautiful order. Perhaps it is
needless to say that the fight came about in the order of nature, and
was not got up as a sport.

CHAPTER XIV

THE NEW SUPREMACY.

SINCE the bishop's imprisonment matters had proceeded rapidly in the direction of schism. When Henry found that his last hopes of a decision in his favour in Rome were at an end, and that the formal censures of the Holy See would fall on him if he persisted in his present marriage with Anne, he at once published an appeal (as has been already said) to the next General Council. Such a proceeding had, by bulls of previous popes, been declared illegal and schismatical. It was, however, the only course now open to the king, unless he was willing to go over to the Lutherans or Calvinists. For that the country was not prepared, and Henry became the author or upholder of a theory that still finds favour among a few. This theory is, that as a venerable bridge might by some convulsion be shattered arch from arch, and yet each arch remain entire by the cohesion of the mortar; so the Catholic Church may, by the passions of princes or of peoples, be rent into several separate national Churches, each national Church retaining, and able to retain indefinitely, all Catholic truth and worship. Or, to use the words of Mr. Froude, " that it was possible for a national Church to separate itself from the unity of Christendom, and at the same time to crush or prevent innovation of doctrine; that faith in the sacra-mental system could still be maintained, though the priest-hood by whom those mysteries were dispensed should minister in gilded chains. This was the English historical theory, handed down from William Rufus, the second Henry, and the Edwards; yet it was a mere phantasm, a thing of words and paper fictions." *

Forced, then, upon this royal theory, Henry set about reducing it to practice. As in the days of Rufus and Henry II., there were Court bishops ready to go all lengths with the king against St. Anselm and St. Thomas of Canterbury, so now against Blessed John of Rochester. The king and his Privy Council drew up the following programme:

"To send for all the bishops of this realm, and specially for such as be nearest to the Court, and to examine them *apart*, whether they by the law of God can prove or justify, that he, that is now called the Pope of Rome, is above the General Councils, or the General Councils above him; or whether he hath given unto him, by the law of God, any more authority within the realm than any other foreign bishop ".

The king seems to have been quite satisfied as to what the answer would be from these bishops, examined each apart, in the way he so well understood, to which Fisher alludes so significantly, and which we have heard Chapuys describe so graphically. So, without waiting for the judgments of the bishops on these important questions, the king and council, as if all the bishops of Christendom had decided that the pope was a mere usurper, thus go on with their programme:

"To devise with all the bishops of their realm, to set forth, preach, and cause to be preached *to the king's people* (1) that the said Bishop of Rome, called the pope, is not in authority above the General Council, but the General Council is above him and all bishops; and that he hath not, by God's law, any more jurisdiction within this realm than any other foreign bishop, being of any other realm, hath. And that such authority as he before this hath

* *History of England*, i., ch. 2.

usurped within this realm is both against God's, and also against the General Council's, which usurpation of authority only hath grown to him by the sufferance of princes of this realm, and by none authority from God."

Determinations were then made that this new view of the pope's power should be preached Sunday after Sunday at St. Paul's Cross—by all the bishops in their dioceses, by all the religious orders, by all parsons, vicars, and curates ; that the late Act of Parliament against appeals should be affixed to every church door in England, as well as the king's appeal to a General Council, "to the intent the falsehood, iniquity, malice, and injustice of the Bishop of Rome may thereby appear to all the world ; and also to the intent that all the world may know that the king's highness, standing under those appeals, no censures can prevail, neither take effect against him and his realm ".

Before proceeding further with the king's doings, I must set by the side of this programme of 1534 the king's own words to Luther in 1521 :

"Greece herself, he wrote, though the empire had been transferred thither, yielded to the Roman Church in whatever regarded the Primacy, except *in times of some violent schism.*[*]

"St. Jerome shows clearly what judgment he formed of the authority of the Roman See, since, though he was not himself a Roman, yet he openly declares that it is enough for him if the Pope of Rome approves his faith, whoever else may find fault with it.

"Now, as Luther so impudently lays down that the pope has no right whatever over the Catholic Church, even by human law, but has acquired his tyranny by mere force, I greatly marvel that he should deem his readers so credulous or so stupid as to believe that an unarmed priest, alone, and without followers—and such he must have been in Luther's supposition before he obtained the power which he invaded

[*] " Præterquam dum schismate laborabat."

—could ever even have hoped to acquire such an empire,
being without rights and without title, over so many bishops
who were his equals, and over so many and far separated
nations.   Nay, more than this, how can anyone believe
that all peoples, cities, provinces, and kingdoms were so pro-
digal of their property, their rights, and their liberty as to
give to a foreign priest, to whom they owed nothing, more
power than he himself ever dared to hope for ?   But what
matters it what Luther thinks ?   In his anger and envy he
does not know himself what he thinks, but shows that his
science has been clouded and his foolish heart darkened,
and that he has been given up to a reprobate sense, to do
and say what is unseemly.   How true is the saying of the
Apostle : If I should have the gift of prophecy and know all
mysteries and all science, and if I should have all faith so
as to move mountains, and have not charity, I am nothing.
And how far from charity this man is is evident from this,
not only that in his madness he destroys himself, but still
more that he endeavours to draw all others with him to
perdition, since he strives to turn all from their obedience to
the Sovereign Pontiff. . . .

"He does not consider that, if it is provided in *Deutero-
nomy* (xvii. 12) that he that will be proud and refuse to
obey the commandment of the priest, who ministereth at
that time to the Lord and the decree of the judge, that man
shall die ; *what horrible punishment he must deserve, who refuses to obey the highest priest of all, and the supreme judge on
earth.* . . . Yet Luther, as far as in him lies, disturbs the
whole Church, and seduces the whole body to rebel against
its head, to rebel against whom is like the sin of witchcraft, and
like the crime of idolatry to refuse to obey (1 *Kings* xv. 23).

"Wherefore, since Luther, hurried along by his hatred,
casts himself into destruction, and refuses to be subject to
the laws of God, setting up his own instead, let us, on the
other hand, the followers of Christ, be on our guard, LEST

(as the Apostle says) BY THE DISOBEDIENCE OF ONE MAN MANY BE MADE SINNERS.''

If it be said by anyone that Henry had grown in knowledge and in wisdom during the thirteen years since he thus wrote, I will let the king himself reply: "Formerly (says the king) Luther wrote against the Bohemians that they sinned damnably who did not obey the pope. Having written those things so short a time before, he now embraces what he then detested. The like stability he hath in this, that after he preached in a sermon to the people that 'excommunication is a medicine, and to be suffered with patience and obedience,' he himself, being for very good cause, a while after, excommunicated, was so impatient of that sentence, that, mad with rage, he breaks forth into insupportable contumelies, reproaches, and blasphemies ; so that by his fury it plainly appears that those *who are driven from the bosom of their holy mother the Church are immediately seized and possessed with furies and tormented by devils*. But I ask this : he that saw these things so short a while since, how is it that he becomes of opinion that then he saw nothing at all ? What new eyes has he got? Is his sight more sharp after he has joined anger to his wonted pride, and has added hatred to both ?"

Yet when the papal nuncio in 1533 expostulated with the king on the inconsistency of his conduct, he had the effrontery, in the very same breath, both to affirm that deeper studies had convinced him of the very contrary of what he had formerly written, and to hint that deeper studies still might lead him once more to his former conclusions—all would depend on the conduct of the pope.*

---

* " Il estoit bien vray quil avoit autresfoys compose livres a la faveur du pape, mais quil avoit depuis mieulx estudie, et trouvoit le contraire de ce quil avoit escript, et quil pourroit estre que lon luy donneroit occasion destudier plus avant, reconformer ce quil avoit escript, veullant innuyr quil ne tiendra sinon que le pape luy veuille complaire."—Letter of Chapuys (*Spanish Calendars*, iv. 1057).

From this slight digression we return to the proceedings of 1534. By Act of Parliament an oath with regard to the new succession to the Crown could be required from all, and commissioners had been appointed to demand it, especially from the clergy. This oath, as it was administered even to the laity, comprised an affirmation with regard to the two marriages of Henry, and thus, indirectly at least, touched on the papal authority, and for that reason had been refused by Fisher. But now, by an exercise of mere arbitrary power, in addition to and in conjunction with the oath of succession, an explicit declaration was required from all the clergy, both secular and regular (under penalty of imprisonment), rejecting the whole jurisdiction and authority of the Sovereign Pontiff.* It is for this reason that the oath of succession came to be popularly spoken of as "the oath of supremacy". The oath of supremacy, strictly speaking, belongs to a later period of Henry's reign and to the reign of Elizabeth. The Act of Supremacy passed at the end of this year, 1534, required no oath. But since the oath of succession indirectly involved the question of supremacy, since in its exaction from the clergy it was supplemented by explicit negations of the pope's authority, and since it was followed up so quickly by the Act regarding the royal supremacy, it was inevitable that it should be thought of and spoken of as an oath denying the supremacy of the Sovereign Pontiff.† It is important to bear all this in mind if we would trace the progress of the schism, and appreciate the various degrees of responsibility incurred, or the state of men's minds at each step in the great catastrophe.

---

* 25th June, 1534. See *Letters and Papers*, vii. 876.

† Thus, in the evidence of John Leek against the Blessed John Hall, given on 20th April, 1535, but referring to the spring of 1534, he says: "He advised Hall not to go to Hounslow before the commissioners to take oath to renounce the papacy and acknowledge the king's supremacy".—*Letters and Papers*, viii. 565.

It has been already said that when first the admission of the king's headship in the Church was required of Convocation, no allusion whatever was made to the pope, nor was any definition made as to what was involved in the term. It was merely brought into a parenthesis of an address of thanks, and was then guarded by a qualifying clause. It is probable that even then Henry and his advisers foresaw the consequences they might one day draw from it. But they kept these in the dark, since, if the pope favoured Henry in his divorce suit, they had no intention of proceeding further in the road of schism. There was one, however, who, with sure instinct, penetrated the design. This was the injured queen. Convocation had used the perilous title on 11th February, 1531. At the beginning of June of that year, the Dukes of Norfolk and Suffolk, and many earls and bishops, were sent to the queen, urging her not to persist in her appeal to Rome, but to allow her cause to be tried elsewhere. In a letter of 6th June, Chapuys relates how she had had several masses of the Holy Ghost celebrated, on the morning before the interview, to ask for light and strength. The messengers of the king pressed her with many arguments, and sometimes in unseemly language. Her replies were both modest and spirited. "As to the Supremum Caput" (for they had urged the new title), "she considered the king as her sovereign, and would therefore serve and obey him. He was also sovereign in his realm, as far as regards temporal jurisdiction ; but as to the spiritual, it was not pleasing to God either that the king should so intend, or that she should consent, *for the pope was the only true sovereign and vicar of God*, who had power to judge of spiritual matters, of which marriage was one. As to electing any other judge but the pope, it was no use to speak of it, for she would never consent, not for any favour that she expected from his holiness, because hitherto he had shown himself much more partial to the king than could be ex-

pressed. But as the king in the first instance had recourse
to the pope, who held the place and puissance of God upon
earth, and, consequently, of the Truth—for God was true,
and Eternal Truth—she wished that truth and justice should
be seen and determined by the minister of the Sovereign
Truth."*

What the bishops had foreseen as possible, and tried to
guard against, the queen saw as imminent, and protested
against it. But the substitution of the royal for the pontifical authority was as yet a State secret from the people.
Even the "Statute of Appeals," of March, 1533, seemed to
them a question of legal procedure, and did not touch on
questions of faith or morals. It was still to the successors
of St. Peter that the commission was given: "Feed My
sheep, feed My lambs". But now, in 1534, Christ's flock,
which He purchased with His most precious Blood, has
become "the king's people," and it is from his lips the
bishops receive instruction as to what shall be taught.

In April, 1534, commissioners were appointed to require
submission from all friars and monks. The required for-
mulas were signed, alas! almost without resistance. Hilsey,
one of the commissioners, writes with diabolical glee, on
21st June, to Cromwell, that "he has not met many who
have refused the oath of obedience, but some have sworn to
it with an evil will, and slenderly taken it".† This man was
Fisher's successor as Bishop of Rochester, but was not
elected till after the martyr's death, who was thereby spared
the anguish of seeing his beloved flock given over to a cruel
wolf.‡ The shame, however, of the cowardice of his clergy
was not spared him. Cranmer visited Rochester on 10th

---

* *Letters and Papers*, v. 287.

† *Ibid.*, vii. 869. Surely it is *diabolical* to rejoice in outraged consciences, false swearing, and cowardly hypocrisy.

‡ John Hilsey, a Dominican, was elected on 7th August, 1535.
The see was declared vacant by forfeiture, not by death.

June, and by his influence Lawrence Mereworth, the prior
of the cathedral church of St. Andrew, the sub-prior, and
eighteen monks set their signatures and seal to a form in
which they declared "that the Bishop of Rome, who, in
his bulls, usurps the name of pope, and arrogates to himself
the principality of Supreme Pontiff, has no greater jurisdiction given him by God in this kingdom of England than
any other foreign bishop. . . . Also, that we will cling only
to our aforesaid lord, the king, and to his successors, and
maintain his laws and decrees, renouncing for ever the laws
and decrees and canons of the Bishop of Rome, which
shall be found contrary to the Divine law and Holy Scripture, or contrary to the laws of this kingdom."* Cranmer
visited the diocese of Rochester by royal authority in July,
and received the adhesion of forty priests of the deanery of
Malling, thirty of that of Dartford, forty-five of that of
Rochester, and three of the collegiate church of Cobham.†
The bishop must have learnt all these facts from his brother
Robert.

There had been one gleam of light since the bishop's
imprisonment. The master and fellows of St. John's
College, at Cambridge, had written to him a very affectionate and sympathising letter. It appears that it was
presented by the master, Dr. Nicolas Metcalf, and some of
the fellows personally. They speak of him in terms of most
filial reverence; and they write, "more because they are
ashamed to be silent, than because they know what is fit for
them to say, but they judge it base and wicked in the present
condition of affairs not to signify their affection for him and
declare their solicitude on his behalf. When all others who
bear the Christian name, or love their country, lament at

---

* *Letters and Papers*, vii. 1025. The forms of subscription of the
various monasteries are given in Rymer.

† *Ibid.*, vii. 1025. As the diocese contained only ninety-nine
parishes, nearly all the clergy must have taken the oath.

this time his troubles and distress, they snould be very ungrateful did they not feel a still greater grief." After many holy words, they conclude by saying, that "whatever wealth they had in common, if they could spend it all in his cause, they should not yet equal his beneficence to them, but they entreat him to use whatever is theirs as his own ".*

This letter and visit were no doubt consoling to the venerable founder; yet they must have increased his grief when he heard, a few weeks later, that those who had reminded him so piously that "if he pleased men he would not be the servant of Christ," had, from sheer fear of displeasing Henry, both taken the oath and renounced all allegiance to the Sovereign Pontiff.† It is, however, said that the visit was repeated more than once, and that there are several things entered upon the college books for the bishop's use and service while in the Tower.‡

What better tidings reached him from his diocese, from either clergy or laity, to show him that all his labours had not been in vain, we do not know, but, having mentioned the servility both of Rochester and Cambridge, I am tempted, before continuing the narrative of the bishop's troubles, to give two scraps of history, which, though they were never known to him, will show us that all was not mere slavish timidity in the England of 1534.

The following letter has by some means got into our Record Office. Probably the writer fell into some trouble on account of it. It is a letter from Elizabeth George, a good lady of Dartford, in Kent, to her son, John George, a friar, residing in Cambridge:

---

* The letter, which is in Latin, is printed by Lewis, ii. 356.

† Cambridge subscribed the declaration on 2nd May, 1534. On 3rd June, all the scholars in Cambridge took the oath in St. Mary's Church. (Cooper's *Annals of Cambridge*, i. 368.)

‡ Baker's *History of St. John's*, p. 102.

"I send you my blessing if you do well; but then you must change your condition. I hear of you very well, more than I am well content with, for I hear that you are of the new fashion, that is to say, a heretic. Never none of your kindred were so named, and it grieves me to hear that you are the first. I heard also of the letters you sent to the nuns of Detford * [Dartford] and another to your 'bener'. I am sorry for it, but you are not, or you would be ashamed .o write to such discreet persons, especially to those who have had to bring you up. I do not marvel at it, for you keep in your company that same Bull that you cannot thrive. Also, I hear in what favour you are with your prior, which grieves me much. And you send me word you will come over to me this summer, but come not unless you change your conditions, or you shall be as welcome as water into the 'schepe'. You shall have God's curse and mine, and never a penny. I had rather give my goods to a poor creature that goeth from door to door, being a good Christian man, than to you, to maintain you in lewdness and heresy

" By your mother,
" ELIZABETH GEORGE."†

From the nature of the case, few such evidences of the faith and loyalty of the people have come down to us as this letter. It shows how fidelity to Our Lord brought the

---

* Unfortunately, these poor nuns, of the Order of St. Dominic, whether by this man's persuasion, or for other inducement, took the oath of succession, which included a rejection of the authority of the Holy See, and acknowledgment of the king as supreme head, in the form in which it was tendered to them. In this, however, they merely followed all the bishops, except their own, and nearly all the clergy, secular and regular. Their declaration is dated 14th May. 1534. The bishop's half-sister, Elizabeth Wright, was among them. —*Letters and Papers*, vii. 665, 921.

† *Letters and Papers*, vii. 667.

sword into families, dividing even between mother and son,
in the sense in which He had Himself predicted.   Another
glimpse at popular feeling may, perhaps, be excused as not
altogether foreign to the subject of this memoir, since the
scene is in Cambridge.   The metaphorical sword in this
case takes the material form of a cudgel.

Henry Kylby, having got into trouble, gives the following explanation.   He is servant to Mr. Patchett, of Leices-
ter.   His master and he had ridden to London, and were
on their way home.   On Saturday, 2nd May, they reached
Cambridge, and put up at the White Horse, where they
remained over Sunday.   The very day they arrived the
university had subscribed the declaration just mentioned,
and of course it must have been the whole subject of talk
on the Sunday.   On Monday evening, when he was dress-
ing his master's horse, he fell into communication with the
hostler, who told him there was no pope, but a Bishop of
Rome, to which he replied there was a pope, and that
whoever held the contrary were strong heretics.   Then the
hostler answered that the king's grace held of his part.
Kilby replied that then was both he a heretic and the king
another, and said also that this business had never been if
the king had not married Anne Boleyn ; and therewithal
they multiplied words, and waxed so hot in their communication, that the one called the other knave, and so fell
together by the ears, "so that I brake the hostler's head
with a faggot-stick," says Kilby.*

It would have been well for more learned heads than that
of the hostler of the White Horse had they been broken
before they used brain and tongue in perverting truth in
themselves and others.   But to proceed with public events.
Parliament met again in November, 1534.   It passed the
following Acts, which must be given at length, since they
were the cause of the bishop's martyrdom.

* *Letters and Papers,* vii. 754

Chapter one says : " Albeit the king's majesty justly and rightfully is, and ought to be supreme head of the Church of England, and so is recognised by the clergy of this realm in their convocations ; yet, nevertheless, for corroboration and confirmation thereof, and for increase of virtue in Christ's religion within this realm of England, and to repress and extirpate all errors, heresies, and other enormities and abuses heretofore used in the same ; be it enacted, by the authority of this present Parliament, that the king, our sovereign lord, his heirs and successors, kings of this realm, shall be taken, accepted, and reputed, the only supreme head in earth of the Church of England, called Anglicana Ecclesia, and shall have and enjoy annexed and united to the imperial crown of this realm, as well the title and style thereof, as all honours, dignities, immunities, profits, and commodities to the said dignity of supreme head of the said Church belonging and appertaining.

" And that our said sovereign lord, his heirs and successors, kings of this realm, shall have full power and authority, from time to time, to visit, repress, redress, reform, order, correct, restrain, and amend all such errors, heresies, abuses, offences, contempts, and enormities, whatsoever they be, which by any manner of spiritual authority or jurisdiction ought to be or may lawfully be reformed, repressed, ordered, redressed, corrected, restrained, or amended, most to the pleasure of Almighty God, the increase of virtue in Christ's religion, or for the conservation of the peace, unity, and tranquillity of this realm, any usage, custom, foreign laws, foreign authority, prescription, or any other thing or things to the contrary hereof notwithstanding."

By the thirteenth chapter of the same year it was made high treason for any person after the first day of February next coming (*i.e.*, February, 1535, *new style*) " maliciously to wish, will, or desire by words or writing, or by craft imagine, invent, practise, or attempt any bodily harm to be done or committed to the king's most royal person, the queen's, or their heirs apparent, or deprive them or any of them of their dignity, title, or name of their royal estates, or slanderously and maliciously publish and pronounce, by express writing or words, that the king our sovereign lord should be heretic, schismatic, tyrant, infidel, &c.".

In the same session Parliament, as has been already said, attainted of misprision of treason the Bishop of Rochester and Sir Thomas More for refusing to swear to the Act of Succession.

The statutes of this reign were nearly all of Government initiation, and the independence of Parliament went no farther than some slight resistance or modification. There was a good deal of hesitation at making hasty words treason, and the word " maliciously " had been purposely introduced to exempt from the awful penalties of high treason words uttered incautiously, or words spoken soberly and as the result of conviction, but with no purpose of rebellion or sedition. The precaution was in vain, as we shall see.

The statute deserves attention from another point. The Government in this Evolution (as it has been justly called)* of ecclesiastical bills felt that they had reached a point where the expressions against which they guard, " heretic, schismatic, tyrant," were likely to burst spontaneously from the lips of Englishmen. The precaution was itself a kind of impeachment of the king.

And this new sense of royal dignity, which forbade a whole nation to give to the conduct of its ruler its inevitable qualification, was accompanied by an insolent and licentious speaking of the supreme ruler of Christendom that was not only tolerated, but provoked by the king. It was well understood that the way to gain his favour was to know no bounds

* See the excellent lecture on " The Reign of Henry VIII." by Dr. Stubbs, the present Bishop of Chester, in his *Lectures on the Study of Mediæval and Modern History* (1886), p. 254.

of ribaldry towards the Sovereign Pontiff.* The statute was quickly followed in the spring of 1535 by energetic measures to insult and vilify the person, to repudiate the authority, and to banish if possible the name of the pope from the land which owed both its Christianity and its civilisation to the Holy See.

Chapuys writes to Charles V. on 28th January, 1535: "The king has added to his titles that of Sovereign Head of the Church of England on earth, and it is proposed to burn all the bulls and provisions hitherto granted by the Holy See. With this view, on Sunday last an Augustinian friar,† who has been appointed by the king general of all the mendicant orders, in reward for having married the king and the lady, preached a very solemn sermon maintaining that the bishops and all others who did not burn all their bulls obtained from the Holy See, and get new ones from the king, deserved very severe punishment, and that without that they could not discharge any episcopal duty; that the sacred chrism of the bishops would be inefficacious, as made by men without authority, seeing that they obeyed the bishop or idol of Rome, who was a limb of the devil; and that to-morrow or after it would be a question whether to re-baptise those baptised during that time. This language is so abominable that it is clear it must have been prompted by the king or by Cromwell, who makes the said friar his right-hand man in all things unlawful.

"Cromwell does not cease to harass the bishops, even the good ones like Winchester [Gardiner] and some others, whom he called lately before the council, to ask them if the king could not make or unmake bishops at pleasure, who

* As early as 17th March, 1534, Chapuys could write about the sermons preached in the king's presence: "The invectives of the German Lutherans against the pope are literally nothing in comparison with the daily abuse of these English preachers". — *Spanish Calendars*, v. 26.

† Dr. George Brown, afterwards Archbishop of Dublin.

were obliged to say Yes, else they should have been deprived
of their dignities, as the said Cromwell told a person who
reported it to me, and said the council had been summoned
only to entrap the bishops." *

In the disputes with which England now rang there seems
to have prevailed the utmost confusion of thought and of
language. Two different questions—(*a*) that of the power
of a Catholic king over the clergy and laity of a Catholic
nation, and (*b*) that of the Bishop of Rome over both king
and people of the same nation, with the respective spheres
of their authority and their mutual relations—questions difficult and delicate enough for jurists and statesmen—were
cast upon an uneducated people, and a scarcely half
educated clergy. And these questions were further
complicated by the ambiguity of the metaphorical term
Supreme Head. It would be amusing to collect from contemporary documents instances of the blundering solutions
that were current, were not the matter so serious in its own
nature and its consequences. When St. Paul gave instructions to St. Timothy, "that he might know how he ought
to behave himself in the house of God, which is the Church
of the living God, the pillar and ground of the truth," he
expressed his own reverential awe, and inspired that of his
disciple, by the thought that the Church is nothing less than
the result of the Incarnation and its permanence among
men. "Evidently great is the Mystery of piety, which was
manifested in the flesh, was justified in the Spirit, appeared
to angels, hath been preached to the Gentiles, is believed in
the world, is taken up in glory." † This great "mystery of
piety," and the way the Holy Ghost would have it treated,
was to be the subject of roadside talk and ale-house jests.

Such talk and jests could scarcely be sillier than the
conclusions of some who laid claim to education. Cop.

* *Letters and Papers*, viii. 121.
† I *Tim.* iii. 15, 16

pinger and Lache, two monks of Syon, under the influence of Cromwell and Stokesley, Bishop of London, accept the royal supremacy, and then, by orders of the same, write a letter to the Charterhouse monks, justifying their action and inviting imitation. "As to the king being head of the Church of England, next and immediately under God," argue these wise men, "if there is any Church in England, the king is supreme. St. Paul bids all the Church to be obedient unto his grace, *quia superior potestas.* St. Peter bids all the Church be subject to his grace, as to the most precellent person among them." So, according to this version of the lesson they are repeating, not only Henry, but Herod and Nero were supreme heads. They go on : "Though it seems that the king does in the spirituality what other princes did not before, the truth is that in this doing he does not break the law of God ; for doctors grant that the Bishop of Rome may license a layman to be judge in a spiritual cause ; and if he may, it is not against the law of God that our prince as judge directs spiritual causes ". This was no doubt intended as an *argumentum ad hominem,* an overthrowing of the schoolmen by their own weapons. The pope, they say, may delegate one not in holy orders to act in his name ; *ergo,* the king may thrust the pope aside, and judge doctrine and persons according to his own fancies.*

Mr. Thomas Bedyll, one of the Privy Council sent to reason with the Bishop of Rochester, proceeded more summarily : The king is the head of the people ; the people are the Church. *Ergo.* Even Richard Wilson, the bishop's servant, who overheard this syllogism, was not satisfied, and told his master so.†

A certain Mr. Morris, a layman, agent to the Bishop of Winchester, was interrogated as to his sentiments by Cromwell. His answers were found satisfactory. The bishop

* *Letters and Papers,* viii. 78.   † *Letters, &c.,* viii. 856.

had told him that the pope's power was human in its origin, though scholars had sought afterwards Scripture-texts to uphold it ; that if it had been sanctioned by General Councils, why, so had the prohibition of blood ; but such decrees with time become obsolete ; that an Act of Parliament discharges the conscience ; and so in conclusion, from these episcopal premisses, Mr. Morris concluded that " he thinks the Holy Ghost is as much present at an Act of Parliament as ever He was at any General Council ". *

The arguments of the prelates, if not more solid, were at least more subtle than the above. Tunstal of Durham, who had at first protested against the title of Supreme Head in the northern Convocation, had afterwards yielded assent to the title, even with the new meaning as conferred by Act of Parliament. It was the wont of the king to compromise his half-hearted adherents ; so Tunstal received orders to compose, along with Stokesley of London, a letter or treatise on the supremacy, for the conversion of Reginald Pole. They thus develop and defend the metaphor of Supreme Head :

" And whereas ye think that the king cannot be taken as supreme head of the Church, because he cannot exercise the chief office of the Church, in preaching and ministering of the sacraments, it is not requisite, in every body natural, that the head shall exercise either all manner of offices of the body, or the chief office of the same. For albeit the head is the highest and chief member of the natural body, yet the distribution of life to all the members of the body, as well to the head as to the other members, cometh from the heart, and is minister of life to the whole body, as chief act of the body. . The office deputed to the bishops in the mystical body is to be as eyes to the whole body ; and what bishop soever refuseth to use the office of an eye in the mystical body, to show unto the body the right way of

* *Letters* viii. 592.

living, shall show himself to be a blind eye. And if he shall take other office in hand than appertaineth to the right eye, shall make a confusion in the body, taking upon him another office than is given to him by God. Wherefore if the eye will take upon him the office of the whole head, it may be answered unto it : It cannot be, for it lacketh brain.

" And examples show likewise that it is not necessary always that the head should have the faculty or chief office of administration. You may see in a navy by sea, where the admiral, who is captain over all, doth not meddle with steering or governing of every ship, but every master particular must direct the ship, to pass the sea, in breaking the waves. . . . And likewise many a captain of great armies, which is not able, nor never could, peradventure, shoot or break a spear by his own strength, yet by his wisdom and commandment only, he achieveth the wars and attaineth the victory. . . . By all which it may appear that Christian kings be sovereign over the priests, as over all other their subjects, and may command the priests to do their offices as well as they do other ; and ought by their supreme office to see that all men by all degrees do their duties, whereunto they be called, either by God or by the king. And those kings that do so chiefly, do execute well their office.

" So that the king's highness, taking upon him, as supreme head of the Church of England, to see that as well spiritual men as temporal do their duties, doth neither make innovation in the Church, nor yet trouble the order thereof ; but doth as the chief and best of the kings of Israel did, and as all good Christian kings ought to do." *

Had Henry, indeed, claimed no more than to see that the Church's laws were carried out, he might have pleaded precedent, not only among Jewish, but among Catholic

* This treatise was published in 1560, immediately after Tunstal's death. by Reginald Wolf; and is reprinted in full in the Appendix to Knight's *Erasmus.*

kings, some of whom the Church has ranked among her saints In that sense there would have been no "innovation" in the right claimed, though there would have been novelty in the title.   And it seems probable that, by thus explaining the title, Tunstal wished to prevent innovation. But Henry was neither so insane, on the one hand, as to claim the right to say mass and give absolution, nor so childish, on the other hand, as to insist so strongly on the new title merely that he might fulfil an ancient and uncontested duty.   He meant to be master, especially in the matter of the divorce, though his caprice was to show his mastery against Protestants as much as against the pope.

Tunstal soon found, what he ought to have foreseen, that the head included both eyes and mouth; or, in other words, that the royal supremacy included the power of discerning and defining the doctrine of the faith and sacraments; and that, if the king did not himself preach from a pulpit, he preached by royal proclamations, and by the Acts of his obsequious Parliaments.*   The fundamental changes introduced under Edward, always in virtue of the royal supremacy, opened the eyes of Tunstal and others to its true nature.   The logic of facts was a more efficient teacher than that of words.   Having discovered the error into which they had fallen as to the royal supremacy, they were led to reconsider the whole subject, and to look more deeply into the provisions made by Jesus Christ for the unity of His Church.   They thus saw the fallacy of their objections to the authority of the Holy See.   Some of the bishops who refused to admit the supremacy of Elizabeth were taunted with their fickleness and inconsistency, since they had so easily admitted and warmly defended that of her father. So far as they were inconsistent, it was with the inconsist-

* One of his very first Acts as " visitor " of the universities, in the place of the pope, was to abolish all study of canon law, and revolutionise theology.

ency of a sincere repentance. But in reality the change of principles was not so great as it might appear. They had been always firmly attached to the Catholic faith and to the unity of the Church. Owing either to the false principles which had become current since the great schism, to the want of deep theological studies at the universities, or to the contempt of ancient ways that then prevailed among the disciples of the Renaissance, the importance of the supremacy of the Holy See for the maintenance of unity was less felt than in former ages in England. Tunstal and others considered it to be of merely ecclesiastical institution, like the patriarchal and metropolitan authority, and, in their exaggerated spirit of nationalism, thought that it might be set aside and replaced by that of Catholic kings. The acts of the sovereigns of England, father, son, and daughter, were the best practical refutation of these theories.*

It must not be thought that I am excusing the conduct of the English bishops. I would merely observe that the

---

* A biographical work like this is not a place for controversy not strictly belonging to the subject. I do not feel at liberty, therefore, to examine at length the theory of Henry's claim to supremacy recently put forward by Dean Hook, Canon Dixon, and others. They maintain that it was an ancient right of the Crown of England (and of all Christian kings), and Canon Dixon asserts that it had no primary opposition to the supremacy of the pope. I have tried to show how far this is true and how far false. As to the novelty of the claim as made by Henry, I will be satisfied with the following quotations. Mr. Brewer says : " Opposition to papal authority was familiar to men; but a spiritual supremacy, an ecclesiastical headship, as it separated Henry VIII. from all his predecessors by an immeasurable interval, so it was without precedent and at variance with all tradition. Fools could raise objections ; the wisest could hardly catch a glimpse of its profound significance " (*Introductions*, vol. i., p. 107). Mr. Gairdner writes that the period from January to July, 1535, "is a very marked period in the history of the reign—the very crisis of royal supremacy, and *of a totally new order in the Church*" (Preface to vol. viii., p. 1). The competency of both these writers to form a correct judgment regarding the times of Henry will not be questioned.

question was not so clear to them as it is to us, after the
multiplied experience of three centuries and a half. But
bishops who, as Tunstal truly said, are eyes in the body to
see and make known the way, are bound to see far ahead;
or if they cannot do this, they are at least bound to keep to
the ancient ways, even though the new ways may seem to
them more commodious and likely to lead to the same
goal. I have dwelt on the perplexities and confusion of
thought of clergy and laity, in order to show by contrast the
perspicacity of Fisher. But the chief condemnation of the
blind guides of England at this crisis was that Fisher's
writings were quite recent and widely spread, and he himself survived to enforce their teaching by his example.
Henry feared the influence of his books, and by a proclamation at the beginning of 1535 required their suppression.
Stokesley of London writes to Cromwell on 16th January:
"I would have sent you my books of the canon law and
schoolmen favouring the Bishop of Rome; but as I am
informed by those to whom you have declared the king's
proclamation in this behalf, *it is not meant but of the Bishop
of Rochester's books and sermons*, and of those who have
lately written in defence of the said primacy against the
opinion of the Germans, I do not send them until I know
your further pleasure. I shall send them and all other
books, rather than keep unawares any that maintain that
intolerable and exorbitant primacy." * This is a fair specimen of the eagerness of these servile courtiers to obey, and
even to anticipate, the wishes of their master, though coming to them only through the arbitrary interpretations of his
lay vicar-general.

Some Anglican writers boast of the unanimity with which
this statute was received. That few dared oppose it at first
must be admitted. Whether the conduct of its advocates is
worthy of admiration may be judged by a few instances. Row-

* *Letters and Papers*, viii. 55.

land Lee writes to Cromwell on 7th June, 1535 : "Yester-night I received the king's letter for preaching against the usurped power of the Bishop of Rome. That no dissimula-tion might appear in me, or anything contrary to my promise, I will send for my horses and repair to my diocese, and in my own person, *though I was never heretofore in pulpit,* and by others, will execute this declaration." *

Edward Lee, Archbishop of York, a learned man and once an opponent of Erasmus, was somewhat suspected by Henry of being papistically inclined. On 14th June, 1535, he writes to the king to vindicate himself. He had for-bidden the collect *Pro papa* on Good Friday, and made the deacon omit the pope in the *Exultet* on Holy Saturday ; he had himself preached in the Cathedral of York before the lord mayor, and taken for his text " Uxorem duxi, ideo non possum venire," explaining the injuries done to the king by the Bishop of Rome.† Unfortunately, we have not the sermon to judge of the application of this strange text. It would seem like a sly joke : "I have married Anne Boleyn, and therefore must make a schism ".

The same archbishop writes to Cromwell on 1st July, 1535: " I send you a copy of a book which I have conceived as a brief declaration of the king's title of Supreme Head, and that the Bishop of Rome has no jurisdiction here by the law of God. It shall be spread abroad so that curates and others who can perceive and utter it may read it to their audiences." He complains that he does not know twelve secular priests in his diocese who can preach. Those who have the best benefices are not resident. Only a few friars can preach, and none of any other religious order.‡

In these words lies perhaps the real reason of the quick spread of schism and heresy in England. Non-resident pastors and non-preaching clergy must have left the flock in

---

* *Letters and Papers*, viii. 839.   † *Ibid.*, viii. 860.

‡ *Ibid.*, viii. 963.

the densest ignorance, and an easy prey to a wolf in sheep's
clothing, or in his own.   Unfortunate people ! the only time
they listened to these dumb dogs was when they were forced
by the royal lash to bark at the Vicar of Christ.   Almost the
solitary example of zeal and activity in the pulpits of England
in those evil days was on this occasion of the introduction
of heresy.   The Bishop of Chichester, Robert Sherburn,
writes to Cromwell, on 29th June, 1535: "On Sunday,
13th June, he preached the Word of God (!) openly in his
cathedral, and published the king's most dreadful commandment as to the union of the supreme head of the Church of
England to the imperial Crown, and the abolition of the
Bishop of Rome's authority.   He has also sent forth his
suffragan to preach and publish the same.   By this time
every abbot, prior, dean, parson, &c., in his diocese has
received similar orders."*   He had also had 2000 copies
printed of a declaration of the king's supremacy to be read
to the people.†

At the beginning of this very year, Chapuys, in a letter
to the emperor, 14th January, 1535, mentions that "sermons
and farces" against the pope's authority are the order of the
day.‡   Jokes, however, were also made about Henry on the
Continent.   In one caricature he was represented as standing between Christ, Moses, and Mohamed, with the words
underneath, *Quo me vertam nescio* (I know not to which to
betake myself).§   At least he was determined to allow no
hesitation in his bishops.   Their master should be the king,
and his will their will.   Chapuys writes to Granvelle, on 11th
July, 1535: "The Bishop of London (Stokesley), *who never
preached in his life*, on account of his stammering and bad
speaking, preached this morning in the cathedral by the
king's order.   Cromwell was present.   The whole of the
sermon was to invalidate the king's marriage, and to deny

* *Letters and Papers*, viii. 941.   † *Ibid.*, viii. 963.
‡ *Ibid.*, viii. 48.   § *Ibid.*, viii. 33.

the authority of the pope and those who favoured it—even those who suffered death in its defence. The other bishops must do the same, or it will cost them their benefices and their lives."* When the Bishop of London thus stammered out his first sermon, the blood of Fisher and More was scarcely dry beneath the scaffold on Tower Hill.

I am not writing a history of the Church of England in the reign of Henry, except in so far as it is necessary to understand the life and death of one great bishop. I shall not, therefore, inquire what may be said in behalf of the religious orders, the inferior clergy, or the people at this crisis. Only for the people I would remark that, being without books or newspapers, or those means of information now universal, they were more dependent on the pulpit than we can well imagine, and that this one source of knowledge was poisoned for them. This was remarked by Chapuys in a letter of 4th February, 1534 : "Every day new tracts and books are published against the authority of the Apostolic See. . . . Were it only a question, by such books and writings, of bespattering the pope and the authority of the Holy See, the measure after all would not be so important ; for the English people, knowing as they do that all this proceeds from passion, malice, and revenge, do not attach much faith to it, but are, on the contrary, very angry with the king for doing so. The worst is that some preachers from the pulpits—wherefrom nothing should be said that is not absolutely holy and edifying—are, under cover of religious charity and devotion, inculcating on the minds of simple persons the theories propounded in such writings ; whence it is to be feared that, unless the venomous root be promptly pulled up, everything here will go to ruin and perdition."† This was written at the very commencement of the preaching campaign.

---

* *Letters and Papers,* viii. 1013.   † *Spanish Calendars,* v. 9.

For the oishops, at least, it would be hard to find any plausible defence, excuse, or palliation. What Fisher knew they should have known ; what he did they were able to do, and were bound to do, even though it were to shed their life-blood, to defend the unity of the Church. But it is most certain that, had they all been dauntless as he was, not even the audacity and obstinacy of Henry could have pre-vailed against a united episcopate ; for the clergy and religious orders would have stood firm at their example and encouragement, and the people would have rallied to their defence. For the sins of the country God permitted it to be otherwise ; yet, in His merciful providence, He chose for the Church's champions, representatives of both clergy and laity, the two men who deservedly stood highest in public esteem both in England and in Europe. If More and Fisher will stand up in judgment against their faithless and servile contemporaries, they stand up now by way of contrast, to confirm the faith of Catholics, and to give to hesitating Protestants a proof of the sanctity of the cause for which such men were willing to die.

And, since attempts have been made of late years to represent Henry as merely claiming an ancient right of the Crown of England, and Fisher and More as obstinate and contumacious in refusing the claim, I will quote the judg-ment of a lord chancellor who was certainly not biassed in favour of the Church, nor inclined to diminish the rights of the State. Lord Campbell remarks, upon the saying of Sir Thomas More, "that after seven years' study he never could find that a layman could be head of the Church". "Taking this position (that the king is head of the Church) to mean, as *we* understand it, that the sovereign, representing the civil power of the State, is supreme, it may be easily assented to. But in Henry's own sense that he was substituted for the pope,* and that all the powers claimed by the pope in ecclesiastical affairs were transferred to him, and might be lawfully exercised by him, it is contrary to reason, and is unfounded in Scripture, and would truly make any church 'Erastian' in which it is recognised." He adds therefore that he cannot agree with Hume that it is a pity More (and Fisher) did not die for a better cause.

* Dr. Stubbs, the present Bishop of Chester goes further. He says that Henry from the beginning wished to be the king, the whole king, and nothing but the king; but that afterwards " he wished to be, with regard to the Church of England, the pope, the whole pope, and something more than pope " (*Lectures on Med. and Mod. History*, p. 264).

CHAPTER XV.

ROYAL SNARES.

LET us return from this ignominious survey of the English Church outside the Tower walls to its two most illustrious representatives within their enclosure. Lady Alington, Sir Thomas More's stepdaughter, having interceded for him with the chancellor, Audley, he made great pretence of sympathy, and, referring to Sir Thomas' refusal of the oath, said "he marvelled that More was so obstinate in his own conceit, in what everybody went forth withal, except the blind bishop and he". He then told her a fable about a country where rain fell which made all whom it wetted fools. Some persons concealed themselves in caves till the rain was past, thinking afterwards to rule the fools, but the fools would have none of that, but would have the rule themselves. When the wise men saw this they wished they had been in the rain too. "After telling this story," writes Lady Alington, "he laughed very merrily, and I was abashed at his answer, and see no better suit than to Almighty God."

When More heard this he said that as a lord chancellor ought to be a wise man, he was afraid that by proposing such a tale, some drops of rain must have entered the cave also. As for him his name was Morus,* and he had not the ambition of the wise men to rule, as he had proved by resigning his chancellorship.

"Many," Sir Thomas goes on to say, "call the taking of

* In Greek, a fool.

the oath a trifle and the refusing an over great scruple. He does not believe, however, that everyone who says so thinks so. But whether they do or not, does not make much difference to him, even if he saw the Bishop of Rochester himself swear the oath. Although he reckons that no one in this realm is meet to be compared with the bishop in wisdom, learning, and long approved virtue, he (More) was clearly not led by him, for he refused the oath before it was offered to the bishop. And also the bishop was content to have sworn in a different manner to what More was minded to do. He never means to pin his soul at another man's back, for he knows not where he may hap to carry it. There is no man living of whom he can be sure while he is alive." *

Even from the beginning of their long captivity fears had been entertained by many that worse things were meant to follow. "It is feared," writes Chapuys to Charles, "that the king will put to death the Bishop of Rochester and Mr More, late chancellor, who, as I lately wrote, are confined in the Tower with others for refusal to swear." † This was written on 23rd April, 1534, only a few days after their committal. From the Act of Attainder we find that on the 1st of May the commissioners again proposed the oath, and that it was again refused. Dr. Hall relates that the king made many efforts to gain over the venerable confessor by means of more courtly bishops, and as he declares that he learnt this from their own lips, his account must be given in full. "There came to him at several times Bishop Stokesley of London, Bishop Stephen Gardiner of Winchester, Bishop Tunstal of Durham, with certain other bishops, to persuade

---

* More u *English Works*, p. 1437. More might well decline to trust his soul even to his fellow-sufferers; for Dr. Nicolas Wilson, formerly the king's confessor, and afterwards parson of St. Thomas the Apostle, had refused the oath with More and been committed to the Tower. More and he had studied the question together. But Wilson's courage failed under captivity, and he took the oath.

† *Letters and Papers*, vii. 530.

him to yield to the king's demand. And yet no doubt but most of them did this against their stomachs, and rather for fear of the king's displeasure, in whom they knew was no mercy, than for any truth they thought in the matter. For I have credibly heard say, that Bishop Stokesley, all his life after, when he had occasion to speak of this business, would earnestly weep and say : 'Oh ! that I had holden still with my brother Fisher and not left him when time was'. And for this the Bishop of Winchester, myself have divers times heard him, sometimes in the pulpit openly and sometimes in talk at dinner among the lords of the council, and some-times in other places, very earnestly accuse himself of his behaviour and doings in that time.

"I have also heard the right reverend and learned father, Doctor Thomas Harding, sometime his chaplain and ghostly father, say that oftentimes in much of his secret talk among his chaplains, he would so bitterly accuse himself of his doings in that and such like business of those days, that at last the tears would fall from his eyes abundantly. And, finally, in the days of King Edward the Sixth, being con-vented before the king's commissioners, and there greatly urged to proceed yet further according to the fruits of that time, he not only retracted, before them all, his former doings, but also suffered himself to be deprived of his great dignity and living, with sharp imprisonment in the Tower of London, the space of five years and more, minding there to have recovered the thing which he before had lost, I mean the blissful state of martyrdom, if God had been so pleased ; or else in place thereof to continue a godly confessor, remaining a perpetual prisoner all the days of his life, for a just and true deserved penance of his offence. Howbeit, shortly after, in the reign of this most noble and virtuous Queen Mary, all fell out otherwise. For after God had once placed her in the government and crown of this realm, she not only restored the ancient and Catholic religion throughout the same realm,

but also delivered him out of prison, with the Bishop of
Durham before named, and divers others who lay there in
like sort, and almost the like space that the Bishop of
Winchester did.* These bishops, I say, persuaded thus
continually with this holy man, sometime one and sometime another, but all in vain; for by no means would he be
won to swear one jot from that which, by his learning, he
knew to be just and true.

" At another time there came to him, by the king's
commandment, six or seven bishops at once, to treat with
him in like sort as the others had done severally before; and
when they had declared their intent and cause of their
coming, he made answer again, *in these or like words :* ' My
lords, it is no small grief to me that occasion is given to deal
in such matters as these be. But it grieveth me much more
to see and hear such men as you be persuade with me
therein, seeing it concerneth you in [your] several charge
as deeply as it doth me in mine; and, therefore, methinketh,
it had been rather our parts to stick together in repressing
these violent and unlawful intrusions and injuries daily offered
to our common mother the Church of Christ, than by any
manner of persuasion to help or set forward the same. And
we ought rather to seek by all means the temporal destruction
of these ravening wolves that daily go about worrying and
devouring everlastingly the flock that Christ committed to
our charge, and the flock that Himself died for, than to
suffer them thus to range abroad. But alas ! seeing we do
it not, ye see in what peril the Christian state now standeth.
We are besieged on all sides and can hardly escape the
danger of our enemy. And seeing the judgment is begun

* I have remarked in the Preface that the above passage proves
that Dr. Hall was a Catholic in the time of Queen Mary—that he was
intimate with Gardiner and others of the Privy Council. Therefore,
what he is about to relate of the conversation of Fisher in the Tower
may be considered authentic.

at the house of God, what hope is there left, if we fall, that
the rest shall stand? The fort is betrayed even of them
that should have defended it. And, therefore, seeing the
matter is thus begun, and so faintly resisted on our parts, I
fear we be not the men that shall see the end of this misery.
Wherefore, seeing I am an old man, and look not long to
live, I mind not, by the help of God, to trouble my conscience in pleasing the king in this way, whatsoever become
of me, but rather here to spend out the remnant of my old
days in praying to God for him.'*

"And so their communications being ended the bishops
departed, some of them with heavy hearts, and after that
day came no more to him. But within a little space after
these bishops were thus gone, his own man that kept him in
the prison, being but a simple fellow, and hearing all this
talk, fell in hand with him about this matter, and said:
'Alas! my lord, why should you stick with the king more
than the rest of the bishops have done, who be right well
learned and godly men? Doubt you not he requireth no
more of you but only to say he is head of the Church, and
methinketh that is no great matter, for your lordship may
still think as you list.' The bishop perceiving his simplicity, and knowing he spake of good-will and love towards
him, said unto him again, in the way of talk: 'Tush, tush,
thou art but a fool and knowest little what this matter
meaneth, but hereafter thou mayest know more. But I tell
thee that it is not for the supremacy only that I am thus
tossed and troubled, but also for an oath [meaning the oath
of the king's succession], which if I would have sworn I
doubt whether I should ever have been questioned for the
supremacy or no. But, God being my good Lord, I will
never agree to any of them both, and this thou may'st say

* Baily has invented a short speech of Fisher to the bishops which
has no resemblance whatever to the above. It is also given, copied
from him, by Lewis, vol. ii., ch. xxxiv., n. 6.

another day thou heard'st me speak, when I am dead and gone out of this world.' " *

In discussing the force of certain Acts of Parliament, as well as with regard to the last scene in the bishop's life, his arraignment and trial for high treason, I shall gladly quote the words of Lord Chancellor Campbell.† They will carry greater weight in legal matters than those of Dr. Hall, while they entirely sustain the latter both in many parts of his narrative and in his appreciations of persons and events. "The Parliament," says this eminent writer, "which had answered Henry's purposes so slavishly that it was kept on foot for six years, met again on the 4th November, and proceeded to pass an Act of Attainder for misprision of treason against More and Fisher, Bishop of Rochester, the only surviving minister of Henry VII., and the son's early tutor, counsellor, and friend, on the ground that they had refused to take the oath of supremacy,‡ for which alleged offence, created by no law, they were to forfeit all their property and to be subject to perpetual imprisonment. But this was insufficient for the royal vengeance; and soon after, not only was an Act passed to declare the king supreme head of the Church,§ but authority was given to require an oath

* Whether Richard Wilson reported his master's words correctly may be doubted. It is true, however, that the validity of his marriage was the king's point of honour, and on this point he was ever urged by Anne Boleyn. The supremacy was an afterthought, and no one would have been more loyal to the pope than Henry had the divorce been granted.

† Lord Campbell deals indirectly with Fisher in his *Life of More*, and more directly in his *Lives of Audley* and *Rich*.

‡ Lord Campbell rightly here uses the word supremacy instead of succession, although he had previously himself found fault with the biographers of More for saying that he refused the oath of "supremacy" when they should have said "succession". But I have shown that the oath was virtually one of supremacy, especially if the form was proposed which Lord Campbell has himself given.

§ 26 Henry VIII., c. L.

acknowledging the supremacy,* and it was declared to be high treason by words or writing to deny it."

"As More (and Fisher)† were now actually suffering imprisonment and forfeiture of their property for having refused to take the oath, it was impossible to make the enactment about oaths the foundation of a new prosecution, and the plan adopted was to inveigle them into a verbal denial of the supremacy, and so to proceed against them for high treason. With this view the Lord Chancellor, the Dukes of Norfolk and Suffolk, and others of the Privy Council, several times came to them in the Tower." ‡

It is remarkable that long before the making of the Act of Supremacy, Sir Thomas More, whose political foresight was almost prophetic, had written to his daugher, Margaret Roper, of his expectation of death by some new law to be made,§ and several months before the trial Cromwell had made an entry among his private memoranda: "*Item*, when Master Fisher shall to his execution?"‖ And here it may be asked, why, since Fisher and More both expected death and were prepared for it, they were so cautious, after the passing of the Act of Supremacy, in no way to violate it by denying the new title of the king. Was there in this no want of boldness in the profession of the Catholic faith? Would it not have been nobler to go forward spontaneously, as did the Carthusians, and like the bishop's special patron, St. John Baptist, say: It is not lawful? No, the cases were very different. Both Fisher and More had long ago, publicly and by writing, defended the supremacy of the

---

* 26 Henry VIII., c. 2. This is the formula I have given at p. 265. It is *virtually* an oath of supremacy.

† I have taken the liberty of applying to Fisher what was equally applicable though written only of More, who was the subject of the biography.

‡ *Life of More.*   § *English Works*, 1446.

‖ Mullinger's *University of Cambridge*, vol. ii., p. 1.

Holy See, and at this very moment were known to be suffering for their fidelity. They had, therefore, no need to profess their faith or to make protestation. The Carthusians on the contrary had at first accepted the supremacy, and now came forward to retract, and to die for their retractation. There was no reason why, being secluded from society (and their seclusion being in itself a public though silent protest), they should, by speaking, sacrifice life as well as liberty; while, on the other hand, by falling into the snare spread for them, they would have gratified the vengeful spirit of Henry, and involved judges and jury in the guilt of a legal murder. They therefore both resolved on silence.

The following details of the efforts to entrap the bishop into some verbal denial of the supremacy, when verbal acknowledgment could not be obtained, are taken principally from the depositions of the bishop's servant, Richard Wilson, George Gold the lieutenant's servant, and John à Wood the servant of Sir Thomas, who were subjected to interrogations on the 7th, 8th, 9th, and 11th June.[*] News first came to the bishop, with regard to the Act which made it high treason to deny any of the king's titles, about Candlemas,[†] 1535, from his brother Robert. Wilson says that on hearing it the bishop blessed himself, and said : "Is it so ?" A prophetic thrill of his martyrdom seems to have passed through his soul. Robert Fisher answered that the Commons had greatly hesitated at making mere words treason, and had inserted the word "maliciously"; adding, however, that "when it was put in it was not worth a . . . for they (the lawyers) would expound it at their pleasure". The event proved that Robert was right, but we shall see the bishop laying much stress on the word.

[*] *Letters and Papers*, viii. 856.
[†] The act of 26 Henry VIII., c. 13, was to come into operation on 1st February, 1535.

He was not destined to be the first sufferer under the new Act. He had had for some weeks companions in the Tower, whom the Holy See has placed in the same list of honour with himself. These were John Houghton, Prior of the Charterhouse, London ; Augustine Webster, Prior of the Charterhouse, Axholme, Lincolnshire ; Robert Lawrence, Prior of the Charterhouse, Bevall (or Beauvale), Notts ; Richard Reynolds, brother of the house of Syon, near London ; and John Hale, or Hall, Vicar of Isleworth, near London. It would be out of place to speak here of their heroic martyrdom. But it will help us to form a proper estimate of Fisher's " good confession before Pilate," if we listen to one of Pilate's friends in defence of his measures.

Soon after the death of the Carthusians, Dr. Thomas Starkey, who had been chaplain to Blessed Margaret Pole, Countess of Salisbury, and was now chaplain to Henry, wrote, by the desire of the king and of Secretary Cromwell, to Reginald Pole, then on the Continent, to induce him to return to England, and to defend the king's proceedings. The letter is useful, as showing the view the king wished to have spread through Europe, as regards the death of those martyrs, and that of Fisher and More, which was so soon to follow.

"At the last Parliament," he says, "an Act was made that all the king's subjects should, under pain of treason, renounce the Pope's authority,* to which the rest of the nation agreed, and so did these monks, three priors, and Reynolds of Syon, though they afterwards returned to their old obedience, affirming the same, by their blind superstitious knowledge, to be to the salvation of man of necessity,

---

* This expression of Starkey, sanctioned by the king, deserves notice. The Act made it treason maliciously to deny that Henry was "supreme head". Starkey and the Court considered this as equivalent to a positive obligation to renounce the pope, under pain of treason.

and that this superiority of the pope was a sure truth and manifest of the law of God, and instituted by Christ as necessary to the conservation of the spiritual unity of the mystical body of Christ. . . . Therefore they have suffered death according to the course of the law, as rebels to the same and disobedient to the princely authority, and as persons who, as much as in them lay, have rooted sedition in the community. . . . I was sorry to see a man of such virtue and learning [as Reynolds] die in such a blind and superstitious opinion. But nothing would avail. They themselves were the cause. It seemed that they sought their own deaths, of which no one [else] can be justly accused. *You may repeat this as you think expedient to those whom you perceive to be misinformed.*" *

The effect of this and similar letters, and of the cruelties of the king towards those who were faithful to the obedience of his own better days, was the very contrary of what had been hoped. Instead of being intimidated by the tortures, Pole was animated by the constancy, of the martyrs. We shall hear his own declaration on this subject by-and-by. For the present, having given Henry's view of himself, it may be well to contrast it with the words of an eye-witness and keen observer of all his actions, who had the privilege of expressing his thoughts freely—the imperial ambassador at the English Court. The letter was written on the 5th May, the day after the martyrdom of the Carthusians.

" The enormity of the case, and the confirmation it gives of the hopelessness of expecting the king to repent, compels me to write to your majesty that yesterday there were dragged through the length of this city three Carthusians and a Bridgettine monk, all men of good character and learning, and cruelly put to death at the place of execution, only for having maintained that the pope was the true head of

---

* Brit. Mus., *Cleopatra*, E. vi., 358. Abridged by Mr. Gairdner, in *Letters and Papers*, viii. 801.

the Universal Church, and that the king had no right in
reason or conscience to usurp the sovereign authority over
the clergy of this country. This they had declared to
Cromwell of their own free-will, about three weeks ago, in
discharge of their own consciences and that of the king,
and on Cromwell pointing out to them the danger, and
advising them to reconsider it before the matter went
further, they replied they would rather die a hundred times
than vary. Eight days ago the Duke of Norfolk sat in
judgment on them, as the king's representative, assisted by
the chancellor and Cromwell, and the ordinary judges of the
realm, and the knights of the Garter, who had been at the
solemnity of St. George. The monks maintained their
cause most virtuously. No one being able to conquer them
in argument, they were at last told that the statute being
passed they could not dispute it, and that if they would not
alter their language they were remanded till next day to
hear their sentence. Next day, in the same presence, they
were strongly exhorted to recant, and after a long discussion
they were sentenced by lay judges and declared guilty of
treason. Nothing was said about degrading them or changing their habits. And the same fate has overtaken a priest
for having spoken and written concerning the life and
government of this king.* It is altogether a new thing
that the Dukes of Richmond† and Norfolk, the Earl of
Wiltshire, his son (Lord Rochford), and other lords and
courtiers were present at the said execution—quite near the
sufferers. People say that the king himself would have
liked to see the butchery, which is very probable, seeing
that nearly all the Court, even those of the privy chamber,
were there, his principal chamberlain, Norris, bringing with
him forty horses, and it is thought that he (Norris) was
of the number of five who came thither accoutred and

---

* Blessed John Hale.
† The king's illegitimate son by Elizabeth Blount.

mounted like moss troopers,* who were armed secretly, with visors before their faces, of which that of the Duke of Norfolk's brother got detached, which caused a great stir, together with the fact that while the five thus habited were speaking,† all those of the Court dislodged.

"It is commonly reported that the king has summoned the Bishop of Rochester, Master More, a doctor who was lately his confessor,‡ a chaplain of the queen,§, and a schoolmaster of the princess,‖ to swear to the statutes made here against the pope, the queen, and princess, otherwise they would be treated no better than the said monks, six weeks being given to them to consider the matter. They have replied that they were ready to suffer what martyrdom pleased the king, and that they would not change their opinion in six weeks, or even in 600 years, if they lived so long; and many fear they will be despatched like the aforesaid.

"And it is to be feared that if the king is getting so inured to cruelty he will use it towards the queen and princess, at least in secret; to which the concubine will urge him with all her power, who has lately several times blamed the said king, saying it was a shame to him and all the realm that they were not punished as traitresses according to the statutes. The said concubine is more haughty than ever, and ventures to tell the king, as I hear, that he is as much bound to her as man can be to woman, for she extricated him from a state of sin; and, moreover, that he came out of it the richest prince that ever was in England, and that without her he would not have reformed the ecclesiastical affairs of the kingdom, to his own great profit and that of

---

* "Ceulx des frontieres d'ecosse."
† Mr. Gairdner seems to have read *parlant*. Mr. De Gayango\
in the *Spanish Calendar*, v. 156, reads *partant*, *i.e.*, departing.
‡ Dr. Wilson.   § Thomas Abell (*beatified*)
‖ Richard Featherstone (*beatified*).

all the people. Some time ago the queen suspected that
foul dealing had been used towards the princess, as appears
by a letter which she caused to be written to me, and which
I send to Granvelle. I forbear to write about the queen and
her affairs, as I presume she is doing it herself."[*]

In his letter to Granvelle of the same date, Chapuys adds :
"Even if the king wished to give up his abominable obstinacy, the lady and Cromwell, who are omnipotent with
him, would prevent it, knowing that it would be their
ruin".[†]

Such were the thoughts of those outside. We are all
familiar with the words of Sir Thomas More inside the
Tower. His daughter Margaret was still allowed to visit
him occasioually, and was standing by him in his prison cell
on the 4th May, when from his window he saw the noble
band being led out to execution : "Lo, dost thou not see,
Meg, that these blessed fathers be now as cheerfully going
to their deaths as bridegrooms to their marriage". We
now know also what were the sentiments of the holy Bishop
of Rochester. Richard Wilson, his servant, deposes that
the bishop said to him one day : "I pray God that no
vanity subvert them"—*i.e.*, no vain love of liberty or life.
After their death, George Gold, the lieutenant's servant,
brought to the bishop some scrolls of paper he had found
in their cells. They were scratches of writing with lead,
and letters pricked with a point. He had read for the
bishop from one of these the following words, spoken probably, or intended to be spoken, by one of them to the
chancellor : "My lord, ye should not judge me to death
this day, for if ye should, ye should first condemn yourself
and all your predecessors, which were no simple sheep in
the flock, but great bell-wethers. And, my lord, if ye
should 'n detestation of this opinion, dig up the bones of

---

* *Letters and Papers*, viii. 666 ; *Spanish Calendars*, v. 156.
† *Ibid.*, n. 863.

all our predecessors and burn them, yet should not that
turn me from this faith." The bishop, says George, looked
at the scroll and said: "They be gone; God have mercy
on their souls".* It was a little word, and all that he
cared to say to the gossiping servant of his jailor; but who
cannot surmise the deep, pathetic thoughts that scroll must
have aroused in his mind, and the strength it imparted to
his will? Yet he is said also to have remarked, two days
after the execution of the monks, that he marvelled at it,
since they had done nothing maliciously or obstinately, and
had not, therefore, violated the statute.

This was said on 6th May, which in 1535 was the feast
of Our Lord's Ascension, and we may imagine how the
fearless death of these monks, some of whom had been
personally known to him, and the certainty that his own
death would soon be brought about in a similar manner,
must have helped him to raise his heart from his dim prison
in the Bell Tower to the glory which his Divine Master was
preparing for him. "You are they who have continued
with me in my temptations, and I appoint to you, as My
Father hath appointed me, a kingdom, that you may eat
and drink at My table in My kingdom." †

He had not to wait in uncertainty. On the 7th May he
was visited by the Secretary of State, Thomas Cromwell,
and other members of the Privy Council. This visit, as
Mr. Bruce remarks, was quite "gratuitous, as nothing in
any Act of Parliament authorised the lords of the council to
inquire into the opinions of anyone on the subject of the
supremacy and king's title". But Sir Harris Nicolas writes
as follows on the subject of the Privy Council in the time
of Henry VIII.: "Combining much of the legal authority
with the civil and political, the council exerted a despotic
control over the freedom and property of every man in the
realm, without regard to rank or station. Its vigilance was

* *Letters and Papers*, viii. 856.   † *St. Luke* xxii. 28.

as unremitting as its resentment was fatal. . . . On charges of treason and sedition the conduct of the council was perfectly frightful. Its ears were always open to any accusation, however insignificant, which could possibly be construed into disaffection to the king or the laws, and many of the matters which were gravely investigated by Henry VIII.'s Privy Council would now only serve to raise a smile in the most sensitive of attorney-generals." *

In the present case the council did not listen to an accusation, but was sent by the king to create one, by forcing the bishop to speak, though he had no other wish than to remain silent. Cromwell and several other members of the council assembled in the Council Chamber in the lieutenant's house adjoining the Bell Tower, on Friday, 7th May, the day after the Ascension.† Of what passed we have but an imperfect knowledge. But we gather from the depositions of his man Richard, who loitered behind a screen, that the council asked the bishop two grave questions, and one of them regarded the new Act of Supremacy.‡ There was some discussion with a member named Thomas Bedyll; § and the bishop, when they were gone, asked Richard whether he had been too quick with Bedyll, to which he replied, No. The bishop also observed to his servant that he had given no [compromising] answer to their questions. The council read to him the two statutes, and afterwards the bishop procured a copy of them by means of his brother-in-law, Edward White, who paid him two visits. It was for what passed on this occasion, in all probability, that he was accused of high treason.

---

* *Proceedings and Ordinances of the Privy Council of England,* Preface, pp. xxiv., xxvi. Unfortunately, no records exist of the proceedings of the council till just after Fisher's death. There is a gap of a whole century between 1435 and 1540.

† This room is now the governor's dining-room.

‡ Fisher in his answer says he was asked one question only,

§ Clerk of the council.

A few days later the council paid a second visit and again subjected him to examination. The interview lasted long, but the bishop remarked to Richard that they were gone as they came. Having heard from the lieutenant's servant, George, that the council had also been with More, the bishop bade George ask him what answer he had given. Sir Thomas sent back a verbal message, that he had replied that he would not dispute about the king's title, but would give himself to his beads * and think of his passage hence. There then ensued some correspondence between the venerable confessors, carried to and fro principally by the lieutenant's servant. A letter having been intercepted, the servants and all other persons who had hitherto had any intercourse with the bishop were subjected to rigorous and repeated examinations as to letters and messages. The two principals also were plied with questions. Sir Thomas' answer was as follows :

" He had written divers scrolls or letters to Dr. Fisher, and received others from him, containing for the most part nothing but comfortable words and thanks for meat and drink sent by one to the other. But about a quarter a yeai after his coming to the Tower he wrote to Fisher, saying he had refused the oath of succession, and never intended to tell the council why; and Fisher made him answer, showing how he had not refused to swear to the succession. No other letters passed between them touching the king's affairs, till the council came to examine this deponent upon the Act of Supreme Head ; but after his examination he received a letter of Fisher desiring to know his answer. Replied by another letter, stating that he meant not to meddle, but to fix his mind on the Passion of Christ, or that his answer was to that effect. He afterwards received

---

* *I.e.*, prayers. The word was not yet restricted to rosary-prayers, much less to the material rosary.

another letter from Fisher, stating that he was informed the word *maliciously* was used in the statute, and suggesting that, therefore, a man who spoke nothing of malice did not offend the statute. He replied that he agreed with Fisher, but feared that it would not be so interpreted. After his last examination sent Fisher word by letter, that Mr. Solicitor had informed him that it was all one not to answer, and to say against the statute what a man would, as all the learned men of England would testify. He therefore said he could only reckon on the uttermost and desired Fisher to pray for him as he would for Fisher." *

From a paper signed by the bishop and still preserved we learn that about four letters in all were written by each party. † The first letter was written by More shortly after their incarceration to inquire what answer the bishop had given regarding the succession ; and the bishop had replied. No other letter of importance passed until after the first visit of the council regarding the supremacy. George had shown him a letter he was carrying from More to his daughter Margaret, regarding his answer to the council. As More's letter was obscure Fisher wrote to him to ask some further information. He does not remember More's answer. After a few days he wrote his opinion regarding the word "maliciously" in the statute, but asked no advice. He had burnt the letters and also the copy of the statutes lest, if they were found, the lieutenant might get into any trouble for his want of vigilance. ‡

The above details are gathered from authentic and un-questioned documents preserved to this day by the Government. Dr. Hall is the only authority for another "crafty and

---

* *Letters and Papers*, vii., n. 867.

† Sir Thomas however says eight pairs. Probably the bishop does not reckon the little notes of courtesy.

‡ The answers of the bishop are given in full in Lewis, vol. ii., Appendix 41.

subtle device," as he calls it, practised on the two prisoners at
this or a somewhat earlier period. As the whole matter has
been travestied by Baily, I will give the exact words of the
original biographer. "At solemn day appointed, when my
Lord of Rochester was called before them and there sore
urged to take the oath, they threatened earnestly upon him,
that he rested himself altogether upon Sir Thomas More,
and that by his persuasion he stood so stiffly in the matter
as he did; and therefore, to drive him from that hold, they
told him plainly and put him out of doubt, that Sir Thomas
More had received the oath, and should therefore find the
king his good lord, and be shortly restored to his full
liberty, with his grace's favour; which did at the first cast
this good father into some perplexity and sorrow for Sir
Thomas More's sake, whom for his manifold Divine gifts he
tendered and reverenced, thinking it had been true indeed,
because he mistrusted not the false trains of the counsellors.
But yet could not all this move him to take the oath.

"Likewise, when Sir Thomas More was called before them,
they would persuade with him, as they did before with my
Lord of Rochester, making him believe that he would never
have stood thus long but for my Lord of Rochester; and
then in the end told him that he (Fisher) was content to
accept the oath. Which Sir Thomas More suspected
greatly to have been true; and yet not altogether true,* for
that it was so given out by the lords (of whose sleights he
was not ignorant), but because it was a common talk among
divers others, as he understood by the report of Mistress
Margaret Roper, his daughter, who (upon special suit) had
free access to her father for the most time of his imprisonment. She had thus reported unto him upon occasion of
talk once with my lord chancellor, who on a time, as she
was suitor to him for her father's increase of liberty,

---

* He means: " And yet true, not precisely, for that it was given
out," &c.

answered her that her father was a great deal too obstinate and self-willed, saying that there were no more that sticked in this matter but he and a blind * bishop (meaning my Lord of Rochester), who is now content (said he) with much ado to accept the oath ; and so I wish your father to do, for otherwise I can do him no good.   And the like answer my lord chancellor made also to the Lady Alice Alington, the wife of Sir Giles Alington, and daughter of Sir Thomas More's last wife, when she at another time before was suitor for her father-in-law,† Sir Thomas More, in the same case."

Such is Dr. Hall's account of this plot.   The present writer is unable to reject it on *a priori* grounds, with Mr. Lewis, as being too foul an artifice to be employed by men who had any sense of honour, or because the king is represented as being privy to the lie.   Those who have studied the State papers of the period, who remember some of Henry's speeches about the divorce, or the way he tricked Rowland Lee into the secret marriage with Anne Boleyn, will find no difficulty in supposing the king a party to any mean plot ; nor were the members of his council men of too lofty principles to be his tools.   Audley, especially, the lord chancellor, was, as Lord Campbell calls him, " a sordid slave," capable of any dirty work.   Yet the story is unsupported by the biographers of More, and in the letter of Lady Alington, which I have already given, Audley does not say that Fisher has yielded, but simply reproaches him with his obstinacy.

Baily's account is given with details of all sorts, not found in Hall, or elsewhere, to my knowledge.   As it has been often quoted, it is necessary to note the points that he has added to the original narrative.   He supposes both More and Fisher conveyed to " court," *i.e.*, the king's palace.

* In the language of the period, blind means bigoted.
† Her stepfather.

Hall merely says "called before the council" apparently in the Tower. More is kept waiting "three hours"; when admitted, "the door was close shut," and he is urged for "about half-an-hour"; then he is "detained in custody within the court," and it is given out that he has yielded. The bishop is then also brought to the court. He has heard the rumours of More's compliance, and believes the assertion of the council, but charitably says : "I am not a fit man to blame him, in regard I was never assaulted with those strong temptations (meaning of wife and children), the which, it seems, have overcome him ". The bishop, however, is steadfast. "He was commanded to be withdrawn and kept close within a chamber of the court, which led towards the king's lodgings." Then the report is spread that he has succumbed. After this follows a long and minute account of a dialogue between Sir Thomas More and his daughter Margaret in the king's palace. If this is, as I take it to be, a sheer invention of Baily's, it is not only a very curious instance of literary forgery or romance, but it is important to stigmatise it, lest it should be copied by future writers as it has been too often already. According to Baily, neither Margaret's tale, told in good faith, nor the deliberate lies of the council, can induce More to believe that Fisher has yielded, and so he tells the council bluntly. In this he contradicts Dr. Hall, who says that More did give credence to the weakness or change of mind of the bishop, though he refused to imitate him. The language of Mrs. Roper, as described by Baily, is very different from what we know to have been hers, from her husband's *Life of More.**

* This passage of Baily, being taken for the original narrative of Hall, is the principal ground on which Mr. Friedmann, in his *Life of Anne Boleyn* (vol. ii., App. E), conjectures that Bishop Fisher after Christmas, 1534, really took the oath in some modified form, and was released for more than a month and frequented the king's Court at

Dr. Hall relates another attempt to entrap the bishop
more successful than the former; and as his condemnation
to death was the result of this stratagem (according to Hall),
it must also be given *verbatim*, for it has been again amplified and misrepresented by Baily. "About the beginning
of May, after this blessed father had been prisoner somewhat more than a year, the king sent unto him one Mr. Richard
Rich, being then his general solicitor, and a man in great
trust about him, with a secret message to be imparted unto
him on his majesty's behalf. Which message, though it
were, indeed, for a time very secret, yet fell it out at last to
be openly known to the world, both to the king's great displeasure, and perpetual infamy of the wicked and traitrous
messenger, as after shall appear. Nevertheless, this messenger, being come to the presence of this blessed father in
his prison, did there his errand, as it seemed, according to
the king's commandment; for it was not long after his
return to the king with an answer of his message, but an
indictment of high treason was framed against him, and he

Westminster, till he was sent back to prison in the middle of
February, 1535. The only grounds for this supposition are that a
Frenchman mentions an inquiry made at Court, "by Messieurs
Suffolk and Fischer". Mr. Friedmann suggests the natural explana-
tion that Fischer has been substituted by the editor for Wulchier or
Vulchier, as the French wrote Wiltshire (the Earl of Wiltshire, father
of Anne Boleyn); but he rejects this because of the general accuracy
of the editor. Yet in another passage, "Norfolk, Suffolk, Fischer,"
and others, are said to have "sat in council," where it is clear that
Wiltshire is meant, though even here Mr. Friedmann conjectures that
Fisher may have been *before* the council. He acknowledges that
such interpretations would be "hard to accept" were it not for two
things: 1. The fact that the lieutenant of the Tower's charges indicate
an absence of Fisher for forty days. But these charges I have
accounted for, not by absence, but illness and special attendance of
the king's physicians. 2. Mr. Friedmann refers to Baily (as above).
I think Mr. Friedmann has not shown here his usual acumen. The
idea of Fisher restored to liberty, and frequenting Henry's and Anne
Boleyn's Court in January, 1535, provokes a smile.

ırraigned and condemned at the bar, upon the talk that had passed between them so secretly in the prison, as after hall be declared unto you." *

* Baily does not imitate the reserve of Dr. Hall and content him-self with declaring the nature of this secret conversation from the evidence given at the trial; but, as if he had been present, gives a long discourse of Rich and a long answer of Fisher, and puts into both their mouths important matters of which Dr. Hall does not give a hint, and of which there is no confirmation from any source. He makes the solicitor-general say that (in spite of his rude treatment) the king holds the bishop's learning and judgment in the highest esteem, and will be guided by him. "And one thing more he wished me to acquaint you with, which is, that you may see how far his royal heart and pious inclination is from the exercise of any unjust or illegal jurisdiction, that if you will but acknowledge his supremacy, you yourself shall be his vicar-general over his whole dominions, to see that nothing shall be put in execution but what shall be agreeable both to the laws of God and good men's liking." In the answer of the bishop Baily puts a historical dissertation in justification of the English Catholics who withstood the pope in the time of Richard II., when he encroached on royal rights, and yet upheld him in his own. This may have been a common topic in 1655, when Baily wrote, but he had no right to put it in the mouth of Bishop Fisher, discoursing with Rich in the Tower.

CHAPTER XVI

WHILE the things just related were going on in the Tower, an event occurred in Rome which has been thought by some to have hastened the bishop's martyrdom. Pope Paul III. had succeeded to Clement VII. on 13th October, 1534. On 20th May he created seven cardinals, of whom "the Bishop of Rochester, kept in prison by the King of England," was one.* He was technically a cardinal-priest, of the title of St. Vitalis. If we could put any faith in the bragging letters of Sir Gregory Casale, one of Henry's Italian agents in Rome, the pope most humbly apologised to him when he heard how angry the king would be, and desired him to explain to the king what were his motives in selecting Fisher. His letter is dated 29th May, and is addressed to Cromwell:

"I wrote to you on the 22nd about the creation of cardinals, and amongst them of Rochester. As soon as I was well enough to go out, I visited all the cardinals who are our friends, and proved to them how rashly and foolishly they had acted in choosing Rochester for cardinal, thereby insulting and injuring a most powerful king and the whole English nation. I told them that Rochester is so boastful a man that, in his vainglory and the boastfulness which is

---

* Such is the entry in the *Diaria Pontificum*. The other cardinals were Nicolas Schomberg, Archhishop of Capua; James Simonetta and Jerome Ghinucci, auditors of the Chamber; John du Bellay, Bishop of Paris; Gaspar Contarino, a Venetian; Martin Carracciolo, protonotary.

natural to him, he will persist in his opinion against the
most serene king, for which reason he is in prison and condemned to death; besides that he is old and decrepit, and
utterly useless for the purposes for which they think him
fit. I made so much noise about the matter that it became
the talk of the whole city, and the pope consequently sent
for me. I said much more to him than I had done to the
others, and showed him that no greater blunder had ever
been committed. The pope appeared to be surprised at
the consequences I mentioned, and he tried to show by
many arguments that his intention had been good; for since
cardinals had to be created, he was led to choose one from
England for two reasons : first, because he had seen letters
of the most Christian king (Francis) in which he expressed
his wish that matters could be arranged with the King of
England, and that satisfaction could be given to him in the
affair of his marriage. Hence he thought that (in creating
Fisher a cardinal) he would obtain a proper agent to treat
of these affairs, and would do a thing pleasing to his
majesty. Secondly, that he was thinking much of a council ;
and since a certain constitution exacts that cardinals of all
nations should be present in a council, it had seemed to him
necessary to make some Englishman a cardinal. He had
not Rochester in his mind more than any other ; but when
it was said that the writings of Rochester were held in great
esteem, especially in Germany and Italy, and when Campeggio and others spoke so highly of him, it appeared to
him (the pope) that he should do a nice thing (*pulchrum
quiddam*), and give pleasure to the king in making him a
cardinal. I replied fully to all he said, and at the end
advised him, since such a blunder had been committed, and
most certainly a very great blunder, if only that it had been
done without consulting the king, that he should not proceed to send the red hat and cap till he had heard more
from England. The pope begged me most earnestly to do

everything I could to excuse this affair to the king; that he was extremely sorry for it, especially when I said that it was a matter too serious to admit of excuse." *

It is scarcely necessary to warn the reader to receive all this vainglorious boasting of Sir Gregory, and his account of the pope's abject apologies, with very large deductions.†

Sir Gregory was a man to whom lying came easily, and from a letter of his, written at the same time to Cardinal Bellay, we learn that Sir Gregory feared lest he himself should be suspected of having influenced the pope, and should incur the king's displeasure. A more truthful account is given by the Bishop of Maçon, the French ambassador in Rome, who writes to Francis I., on 29th May, that "the pope has asked him to beg Francis to use all his power with Henry in favour of the Bishop of Rochester. He had replied that he would write in that sense, but feared it would be of little use, for the Imperialists were saying that the creation of Fisher had been at the request of the King of France, hoping by such speeches to make Henry suspicious of Francis. If the latter should now intercede for Fisher the suspicions would be confirmed, and the request might be refused. The pope was greatly distressed and declared himself ready to pass a formal attestation, that he had not been requested by any prince to make Fisher a cardinal. If he had done so, it was merely on account of his fame for virtue and learning, and rather with the intention of pleasing the king than from any ill-feeling towards him." ‡

On 31st May, Dr. Ortiz, the imperial representative in Rome, writes to the Empress concerning the bishop's eleva-

---

* *State Papers*, vii. 425.

† In spite of the open schism in England, Henry kept his agents in Rome, negotiating in the hopes that Paul III. would rescind his predecessor's decision.

‡ *Letters and Papers*, viii. 779.

tion. He thinks, however, that before the bishop shall hear of it, Our Lord will have given him the true red hat, the crown of martyrdom.* By this time the story of the death of the Carthusians had reached Rome, and had excited great admiration for them and hatred of their murderer. It was generally felt that the pope had miscalculated—that, on the one hand, Henry was daring enough to vent his rage even on a cardinal; and that the jealousies and narrow views of the sovereigns of Europe would prevent any effectual interference on their part.

The Bishop of Faenza, papal nuncio in France, writes to Rome that he has spoken at length to the French king of the pope's concern about Fisher, and begged him to use his influence with the King of England for his liberation. Francis replied that there was no need to speak of his virtues, which were known to the whole world, and that no one had written better than he against the Lutherans. His holiness might be sure he would do all he could for his liberation ; but he doubted his success, for he feared this hat would cause him much injury, according to what he had heard from England, where they have been using strange measures against the Carthusians. He added that the King of England was the hardest friend to bear in the world ; at one time unstable, and at another obstinate and proud, so that it was almost impossible to bear with him. "Sometimes," said Francis, "he almost treats me like a subject. In effect he is the strangest man in the world, and I fear I can do no good with him ; but I must put up with him, as it is no time to lose friends."

The nuncio had offered to give the King of France the brief and hat for Fisher, and that all should be put in the Grand Master's hands, so that it might be done sooner according to the pope's will. Francis told the bishop to keep them, and he would be asked for them when it was time.

* *Letters and Papers*, 786.

"Cardinal Du Bellay has also promised to do what he can, but he fears this cardinalate will make Fisher a martyr. They will try to find some means to make the King of England take it as he ought. Will lose no time and do all he can for his liberation. Would rather see Fisher in Rome than be a cardinal himself, for he hears on every side that his virtue is not less than the world wants now." *

The news of the Bishop of Rochester's elevation reached England before the end of May. George Golde heard it from John Pennoll, the bishop's late falconer, and he from Bonvisi's servant, who had learnt the news at the French ambassador's. George also heard it at Mr. Thornton's house, and was told the news came from a servant of Lord Rochford. Richard Wilson told what he had heard to the bishop, and, according to his account, the bishop exclaimed: " A cardinal ! then I perceive it was not for nought that my lord chancellor did ask me when I heard from my master the pope, and said that there was never a man had exalted the pope as I had ". George Golde also told the news to the bishop, to which he answered, that " he set as much by that as by a rush under his feet ". The bishop's own testimony is, " that George brought him word since the last sitting of the council here, that he had heard say of Mistress Roper, that this respondent was made a cardinal. And then this respondent said, in the presence of the same George and Wilson, that if the cardinal's hat were laid at his feet, he would not stoop to pick it up, he did set so little by it."

Dr. Hall's account seems at first the very reverse of this. It is that the king sent Cromwell to the bishop, and that after talk on many matters : " My Lord of Rochester," said the secretary, " if the pope should now send you a cardinal's hat, what would you do? Would you take it?" "Sir," said he, " I know myself far unworthy of any such dignity, that I think nothing less than such matters; but if he so send it me, assure yourself I will work with it by all the means I can to benefit the Church of Christ; and in that respect I will receive it upon my knees." This reply, however, does not contradict the former. For the sake of the personal honour he would not stoop to pick up the hat; for the duties attached to it, and the honour of the Sovereign Pontiff, he would receive it on his knees.

Dr. Hall adds: " Mr. Cromwell making report afterwards of this answer to the king, the king said again with great indignation and spite: 'Yea, is he yet so lusty? Well, let the pope send him a hat when he will; but I will so provide that whensoever it cometh, he shall wear it on his shoulders, for head he shall have none to set it on.' "

That this right royal wit really came from the lips of Henry is both intrinsically probable, and is confirmed by the following letter of Chapuys.

He writes to the emperor on 16th June, 1535:

" As soon as the king heard that the Bishop of Rochester had been created a cardinal, he declared in anger several times that he would give him another hat, and send the head afterwards to Rome for the cardinal's hat. He sent immediately to the Tower those of his council to summon again the said bishop and Master More to swear to the king as head of the Church, otherwise before St. John's day they should be executed as traitors. But it has been impossible to gain them, either by promises or threats, and it is believed they will soon be executed. But as they are persons of unequalled reputation in this kingdom, the king, to appease the murmurs of the world, has already on Sunday last caused preachers to preach against them in most of the churches here, and this will be continued next Sunday. And although there is no lawful occasion to put them to death, the king is seeking if anything can be found against them, especially if the said bishop has made suit for the hat.

To find out which several persons have been arrested, both of his kinsmen and of those who live in the prison."*

"It is impossible to describe the distress of the queen and princess on account of these two persons; and they are not without fear that after them matters may be carried further than I have hitherto written. Since the said news of the bishop's creation as cardinal, the king, in hatred of the Holy See, has despatched mandates and letters patent to the bishops, curates, and others commissioned to preach, that they continually preach certain articles against the Church, and to schoolmasters to instruct their scholars to revile apostolic authority; and this under pain of rebellion; also that the pope's name should be rased out of all mass-books, breviaries, and hours, either in the calendar or elsewhere." †

---

* This refers to the examination of Edward White and the servants.

† *Letters and Papers*, viii. 876. Surely this deliberate perversion of the children was the last stroke of diabolical malice. Yet Gardiner was ready to co-operate. In a letter to Cromwell he mentions some verses he had written against the pope for the Winchester scholars. Henry's frenzy against the Vicar of Christ became so great that he had a picture painted for his palace at Hampton Court, which is thus mentioned in an inventory made in the first year of Edward VI.: "A table of the Busshopp of Rome and the four Evangelists casting stones upon him". (*Bib. Harl.*, 1419; quoted by Sir Henry Cole in his *Handbook to Hampton Court*, p. 53.)

THE news of the Bishop of Rochester's elevation to the purple reached England towards the end of May, 1535. Though his death was already determined on, and the council had early in May been engaged in the attempt to entrap him into words that could be construed into treason, it is probable, though not certain, that the papal honour accelerated his death.*

Until recently there hung much obscurity over the trial of the venerable cardinal. Some writers, partial to Henry, were unwilling to admit on Dr. Hall's, or rather on Baily's, testimony that he had been sentenced to death for no other crime than that of denying the king's supremacy; and as no official records of the trial were then accessible, they felt themselves at liberty to reject or question Baily's narrative, and to give reins to their own conjectures. All uncertainty, however, as to the nature of the accusation has been removed by the publication—it might almost be said the discovery—of the original arraignment and other official deeds regarding the trial. In 1836, the legal records of the

---

* Mr. Bruce, and after him Mr. T. A. Turner (in his Introduction to Lewis), have argued that Fisher's elevation could not have influenced the king, since the commission to try him was issued on 2nd June, before the news *could* have reached England. It is certain, however, from official depositions, that the news travelled fast, and reached England at the end of May. It seems, then, very probable that the commission was issued *because* of the news of the pope's action.

Court of King's Bench were transferred to the custody of
the Master of the Rolls.   Among these was what was called
the *Baga de Secretis* (or Bag of Secrets)—originally a real
bag, but long since transformed into a closet of which the
keys were kept by the Lord Chief-Justice, the Attorney-
General, and the Master of the Crown Office.   This *baga*
consisted of ninety - one pouches, containing principally
records of indictments and attainders for high treason and
other State offences, ranging from A.D. 1477 to 1813.
Pouch 7, bundle 2, contains the records of the trials of
Bishop Fisher, Sir Thomas More, and three of the Charterhouse monks.*

There is, unfortunately, no record of evidence tendered
and speeches made, and for these we have still to rely on
Dr. Hall.   But, so far as they go, the official papers not
merely prove the accuracy of Hall, but, by the coincidence
of their form with his history, show that he had access to
authentic sources.   I shall be careful, however, as I have
done hitherto, to distinguish between what rests on the unimpeachable evidence of original State papers, and what
depends on the veracity and accuracy of Fisher's biographer.

Before entering into details, it may be well to remind the
reader that he must not think of a State trial in the time of
Henry VIII. as of one in our own days.   Mr. Brewer, in
relating the proceedings against the Duke of Buckingham
(attainted in 1521), as related by Shakspere, observes that
the poet gives a true picture of justice as administered by
the Tudors.   "The presumption that men are innocent until
they are legally proved to be guilty, the facilities granted to
the accused for substantiating his innocence by retaining
the ablest advocate, the methods for sifting evidence now in
use, had no existence then.   In crimes against the sovereign,

---

* See *Third Report* of the Deputy Keeper of Public Records (1842),
pp. 16, 211.

real or supposed, men were presumed to be guilty until they had proved themselves to be innocent, and that proof was involved in endless difficulties. What advocate or what witness would have ventured to brave the displeasure of a Tudor king by appearing in defence of a criminal on whose guilt the king had pronounced already ? " *

The language of Justice O'Hagan is still more emphatic and precise. " It is singular," he says,† " that Mr. Emlyn " —the editor of *English State Trials*—"even while indicating the defects of the criminal law, claims for it a striking superiority over that of other nations. If it were so, God help the accused in other nations, for anything more iniquitous than the criminal procedure of England the imagination cannot conceive. . . .‡ In the first place, the prisoner was not allowed counsel to defend him in any case of treason or felony . . . he was left naked and helpless to contend with an array of learned, experienced, and too often unsparing and unscrupulous antagonists, bent on using all the resources of their powers and attainments for his destruction. It is true that if the ignorant prisoner could himself start any point of pure law, such as a defect in the indictment, he was allowed counsel to argue the point. In order to exercise this very poor prerogative, you will imagine that he was allowed to have a copy of the indictment. It would have raised the very hair upon the wig of one of the old judges to fancy the prisoner calling for a copy of the charge against him. He was entitled to have it read out to him, but that did not avail him much, for it was in Latin, and Latin of the most barbarous description. . . . Secondly, what will seem still more startling, no witnesses for the

* Introduction to vol. iii. of *Letters and Papers*, p. cxviii.

† Lecture in the Rotunda, Dublin, 1877.

‡ The lecturer remarks that he is speaking of past times, not of present, when the law "errs rather in affording loopholes for the guilty than in spreading snares for the innocent ".

prisoner were permitted to be sworn. They were allowed
to give testimony, indeed, but not upon oath, and the
Crown counsel, in their addresses to the jury, rarely failed
to descant on the superior credibility of the Crown witnesses
(though the most infamous of mankind) over the witnesses
for the defence, because the former were upon oath, the
latter were not. The force of injustice, you may fancy,
could not further go. And yet, such as it was, it was an
improvement on the practice of still earlier times. In the
reign of Queen Elizabeth and before that reign, incredible
as it may appear, no witness for the accused was heard at
all, either on oath or without oath. And, to complete the
picture, the witnesses for the prosecution were then, in
many cases, not put upon the table face to face with the
prisoner. The depositions of the witnesses were taken
behind his back, and upon the trial were simply read to
the jury, whose prearranged verdict of *Guilty* was delivered
as simply a thing of course. Thirdly, the most vital of all,
was the composition of the jury itself. The panel was
selected by the sheriff. The sheriff in counties at large was
the nominee and creature of the Crown.* In cities such
as London, and other great corporate towns, the appointment of sheriffs lay with the corporations. . . . In either
case the jury was, to use the familiar phrase, a packed jury.

"As to the State trials of former times, nothing that I can
say can go beyond the pithy expression of Lord Macaulay,
that an English State trial in those days was simply a murder
preceded by certain mummeries."

Lastly, Lord Chancellor Campbell, writing of these very
trials of More and Fisher, says: "There is a curious contrast between the history of France and England, that
assassination, so common in the one country, was hardly
ever practised in the other; but I know not whether our

* In Fisher's trial the sheriff for the county of Middlesex selected
the panel.

national character is much exalted by adherence to the system of perpetrating murder under the form of law ". *

We may now turn to the history of the legal murder of England's noblest and holiest son. On 1st June a special commission of Oyer and Terminer for Middlesex was directed to Sir Thomas Audley, chancellor ; Charles, Duke of Suffolk ; the Marquis of Exeter, the Earl of Rutland, the Earl of Cumberland, the Earl of Wiltshire, Thomas Cromwell, secretary ; Sir John Fitz-James, chief justice ; Sir John Baldwin, chief justice of the Common Pleas ; Sir William Paulet, Sir Richard Lyster, chief baron of the Exchequer ; and to Sir John Porte and Sir John Spelman, Sir W. Luke, Th. Inglefield, W. Shelley, and Sir Anthony Fitz-Herbert, justices.†

The cardinal, however, was not brought to trial until the 17th June. According to Hall the delay was caused by his great sickness. This I have before discussed. The interval was occupied in trying to collect evidence, and for this purpose all who had come into contact with him in the Tower were subjected to repeated interrogations, and the cardinal, as well as Sir Thomas, had to reply to a long list of questions, the answers to which were taken down in writing, and afterwards read to the prisoners, each page being signed by them in testimony of its accuracy. Of those submitted to the bishop on 12th June, I have already given the substance. They regarded principally his correspondence, and nothing was elicited by them that could be used for his prosecution. The most important answer is that to the fifth question regarding what he had written to More. He says that, " soon after the last being of the council in the Tower, More had communicated to him his wish to know his answer. And he had replied, that ' he

* *Life of Rich.* Lord Campbell is of course speaking of assassination by the Government.

† *Baga de Secretis,* and also Dr. Hall.

had made his answer according to the statute which con
demneth no man but him that speaketh maliciously against
the king's title; and that the statute did compel no man to
answer to the question that was proposed him; and that he
besought them that he should not be constrained to make
further or other answer than the said statute did bind
him, but would suffer him to enjoy the benefits of the same
statute'. *

"On 14th June he was asked:

"1. Whether he would obey the king as supreme head of
the Church of England? He stands by the answer he had
made at the last examination, but will write with his own
hand more at length.

"2. Whether he will acknowledge the king's marriage with
Queen Anne to be lawful, and that with the Lady Catharine
to be invalid? He would obey and swear to the succession, but desires to be pardoned answering this interrogatory
absolutely.

"3. For what cause he would not answer resolutely to the
said interrogations? He desires not to be driven to answer,
lest he fall in danger of the statutes."

The royal inquisitors having been baffled by these cautious
answers, and being unable to obtain any evidence against him
in his own confession, resolved to arraign and commit him
on a charge of words spoken on the 7th May. On Thursday,
therefore, the 17th June, he was brought to the King's
Bench at Westminster Hall, by Sir William Kingston,
constable of the Tower, says the official record; and (adds Dr.
Hall) "with a huge number of halberts, bills, and other
weapons about him, and the axe of the Tower borne before
him, with the edge from him, as the manner is. And because
he was not yet so well recovered that he was able to walk
by land all the way on foot, he rode part of the way on

* Lewis (ii., App. 41, p. 410), who gives the answers more fully than
they are given in *Letters and Papers*, viii. 858.

horseback, in a black cloth gown, and the rest he was carried by water, for that he was not well able to ride through for weakness." This is confirmed by Cardinal Pole, who writes that " when he was carried out to his trial, in the short journey, from utter exhaustion he was at the point of death ". *

Hall continues: " Being presented before the commissioners he was commanded by the name of John Fisher, late of Rochester, clerk, otherwise called John Fisher, Bishop of Rochester, † to hold up his hand, which he did with a most cheerful countenance and rare constancy. Then was his indictment read, which was very long and full of words, but the effect of it was this : ' That he maliciously, traitorously, and falsely had said these words *The king our sovereign lord is not supreme head in earth of the Church of England'.* ‡ Dr. Hall here forgets to mention that the words are said in the

---

* *Apology*, n. 20.

† In original it is thus: " Also called J. F., late of the city of R., bishop ". The title of Bp. of R. is not given.

‡ The words are: " Quidam tamen Johannes Fyssher nuper de civitate Roffen. in com. Kanc. clericus, alias Dominus Johannes Fyssher nuper de Roffen. Episcopus, Deum præ oculis non habens, sed instigatione diabolica seductus, false, maliciose, et proditorie obtans volens et desiderans ac arte imaginans, inventans practicans et attemptans serenissimum dominum nostrum Henricum octavum Dei gratia Angliæ et Franciæ Regem, Fidei Defensorem et Dominum Hiberniæ atque in terra supremum caput Ecclesiæ Anglicanæ, de dignitate titulo et nomine suis in terra supremi capitis Anglicanæ Ecclesiæ, dictæ imperialis coronæ suæ, ut præmittitur, annexis et unitis, deprivare, septimo die Maii anno regni ejusdem domini regis 27o apud Turrim London in com. Middlesex, contra legianciæ suæ debitum, hæc verba anglicana sequentia diversis dicti domini regis veris subditis, false maliciose et proditorie loquebatur et propalabat, videlicet, *The king our sovereign lord is not supreme head in earth of the Church of England*, in dicti domini regis injuriam, despectum, et vilipendium manifestum, ac in dictorum dignitatis tituli et nominis status sui regalis derogationem et prejudicium non modicum, et contra formam dicti alterius actus predicti anno 26° editi et provisi, ac contra pacem prefati domini regis," &c.

indictment to have been spoken (1) before several persons, (2) in the Tower, and (3) on the 7th May.

The judges had issued their precept to the sheriff of Middlesex for the return of a jury of inhabitants of the Tower,* *i.e.*, freeholders dwelling within "the liberties" of the Tower or the Tower district.

Before giving the result of the trial I must try to throw some more light on the exact nature of the indictment. Sir Francis Palgrave remarks that in former days, especially in cases of high treason, bills of indictment were virtually the depositions of witnesses or the confessions made by accessories. Hence we can often judge of the evidence offered by the perusal of the indictment. This is not the case with Cardinal Fisher's; but Sir Thomas More's indictment is more detailed and throws light not only on his own case but on the Cardinal's. It sets forth that on the 7th May, at the Tower, before Thomas Cromwell, Thomas Bedyll, and John Tregonell, and divers others the king's councillors, being examined on the king's supremacy, he replied: "I will not meddle with such matters". That afterwards, on 12th May, the said Sir Thomas, knowing that John Fisher, clerk, was then and had been detained in the Tower for divers great misprisions committed by him against the king, and *that the said Fisher being examined, had denied to accept the king* as before mentioned, wrote a letter to him, by which he agreed with Fisher in his treason, and intimated the silence which he (More) had observed, he also used the expression: "The Act of Parliament is like a two-edged sword, for if a man answer one way it will

---

* *Baga de Secretis.* Their names are given by Hall, which shows that he had access to documents. They are: Sir Hugh Vaughan, knight; Sir Walter Hungerford, knight; Thomas Burbage, John Newdigate, William Brown, John Hewes, Jasper Leake, John Palmer, Richard Henry Young, Henry Lodisman, John Carlington, and George Everingham, Esquires.

confound his soul, and if the other way it will confound his body ". Then afterwards More, fearing lest Fisher on his renewed examination should reveal what More had written, he (More) on 26th May sent other letters, requesting Fisher not to give the same answer, but to speak his own mind, lest the king's councillors should suspect confederacy. Nevertheless Fisher on 3rd June, when examined by Sir Thomas Audley, the Duke of Norfolk, the Earl of Wiltshire, and others, did refuse a direct answer, and said: "The statute is like a two-edged sword, &c., therefore I will make no answer in that matter ". That on the same 3rd June, More gave the same answer. Lastly, that on 12th June there was a dialogue between Richard Rich, the solicitor-general, and More which is there detailed, and is the same as in the evidence given by Rich on More's trial, and which More declared to be deliberate perjury. It does not, however, regard the bishop.

From all this it appears evident that "the divers true subjects of his majesty," to whom Cardinal Fisher was charged with having spoken the treasonable denial of the supremacy, on the 7th May, in the Tower of London, were Cromwell, Bedyll, Tregonell, and others of the king's council. The bishop, in his answer to the interrogations on 12th June, denies that he ever so committed himself. So did he to his servant Wilson, who thought the words had slipped from him. Wilson's answer made on 7th June to the inquisitions of the council in the Tower was that, standing behind the partition on the 7th May, the day after the Ascension, he overheard Mr. Secretary read the Act of Supremacy, and his master answered that he could not consent to take the king as supreme head; whereupon they read to him the Act making it treason to deny the king this title; that he (Wilson) cautioned the bishop to beware what answer he made to the supremacy.

On the 8th June, Wilson was again interrogated, and said

24 .

that after the second examination of the bishop, his master had said to him that the council had affirmed that on the 7th May he had declined to accept the supremacy, "and I," said the bishop, "remember no such thing". "Nor I neither," replied Wilson. "But a while after he came to his master as he was saying evensong, and said, 'Yes! that he had answered that he did not think the king might be supreme head'; *but his master denied having said so.*" *

I have given all this detail, because it has only recently been brought to light. It puts the indictment of Fisher in a somewhat different aspect from that in which it has hitherto been presented, though it is uncertain whether any of this evidence, such as it is, was used at the trial.

The legal papers in the *Baga* tell us how the bishop pleaded *Not guilty* to the indictment, how the *Venire* was awarded the same day, how a verdict of *Guilty* was returned, how judgment was given with the atrocious penalties usual in high treason, † and how Tyburn was fixed for the place of execution. (We shall see that several of these penalties were remitted, and the place of death changed to Tower Hill.) It may be remarked that the bishop, having been deprived by Act of Attainder of his bishopric, had not the trial of a peer, and that as little attention was paid to his clerical character as to his dignity of cardinal, so that there was not even an allusion to degradation previous to execution, which the law of the Church and of all Catholic countries required. Henry had fourteen years previously thus written of Luther: "We are daily listening for rumours

* *Letters and Papers*, viii. 856, n. 19, p. 328.

† The sentence was as follows (let those blush who enacted it, not those who transcribe it): "Your sentence is that you be led back to prison, laid on a hurdle, and so drawn to the place of execution, then to be hanged, cut down alive, your members to be cut off and cast into the fire, your bowels burnt before your eyes, your head smitten off, your body quartered and divided at the king's will. And God have mercy on your soul. Amen."

from Germany of men being raised from the tomb, and yet we not only hear of no one being cured, but of good and innocent priests cruelly slain by some of his satellites. This is no doubt for the purpose of teaching us that Order is no sacrament, that the priestly character is a figment, and that David was too timid when he was sorry for having touched the anointed of the Lord." * Since thus writing Henry had well succeeded in getting rid of all superstitious fears, and could slay God's prophets with as little remorse as an Achab or a Jezebel.

Official documents give us no further assistance regarding the nature of Cardinal Fisher's trial. They prove the important fact that the only charge made against him was denial of the new title of supreme head. He was found guilty of treason, but in his case what was called treason to his sovereign was in fact a higher loyalty and fidelity in refusing flattery and impiety, while it was also an act of allegiance to the Sovereign Pontiff, to his conscience, and to his God. Many Protestant writers have, with great candour and force of language, reprobated the absurd attempt of English law to affix the stigma of treason on acts like that for which Fisher and later martyrs suffered. "Treason," writes Hallam, " by the law of England, and according to the common use of language, is the crime of rebellion or conspiracy against the Government. If a statute is made, by which the celebration of certain religious rites is subjected to the same penalties as rebellion or conspiracy, would any man free from prejudice, and not designing to impose upon the uninformed, speak of persons convicted on such a statute as guilty of treason, without expressing in what sense he uses the words, or deny that they were as truly punished for their religion as if they had been convicted for heresy ? A man is punished for his religion when he incurs a penalty for his profession or exercise to which he was not liable on

* *Assertio Septem Sacram.* (De Extr. Unct.).

any other account.   This is applicable to the great majority
of capital convictions on this score under Elizabeth.   The
persons convicted could not be traitors in any fair sense of
the word, because they were not chargeable with anything
properly denominated treason." *

Mr. Bruce, who so patiently and successfully unravelled
the history of the Bishop of Rochester's sufferings and
death, expresses his opinion of his trial in the following
strong language : " The Act of Parliament upon which this
indictment was principally founded is certainly of a most
atrocious character, and evidences a state of society but
little removed from actual barbarism ; but the construction,
by which the mere expression of an opinion upon a disputed
point in theology was held to amount to a malicious and
treasonable attempt to deprive the king of his title of
supreme head, is, if possible, even more iniquitous than the
statute itself.   Every principle of legislation was violated by
the lawgivers, who created a treason out of men's wishes
and desires ; and not less violence was done to all rules of
construction, by stretching the latitude of this highly penal
statute, so that not merely wishes and desires, but even
opinions, were comprehended within its fatal enactments.

" Everything relating to the criminal proceedings of this
period was so irregular; humanity and even honesty were so
frequently absent from the judicial seats; the influence of
the monarch was so openly thrown into the scale by judges
who were the mere delegates of his vindictive spirit; there
was so much anxiety to obtain a conviction at whatever
cost and by whatever means—that those who infer that
Fisher *could not* have been convicted for the mere utterance
of an opinion, because such a conviction would have been
tyrannical and unjust, show, I fear, a disposition to judge of
the legal proceedings of the reign of Henry VIII. by the

---

* *Constitutional History*, ch. iii.

example of our own times rather than by that which they themselves exhibit." *

Mr. Gairdner also, besides remarking on the absence of malice in any words that may have been spoken, asks very pertinently: "How could Fisher, even if the word *maliciously* had not been in the statute, have been justly said to 'publish and pronounce' an opinion, for which he had been expressly asked in prison by members of the king's Privy Council?" †

We must now examine by what evidence was the supposed crime brought home to the prisoner. The place and the day are specified in the indictment, but not the occasion, nor the persons to whom the words were spoken, nor do we know from official sources the evidence that was offered. We know however, as has been said, that on the 7th of May the bishop had appeared before the council in the Tower, and had been questioned on the subject of the suprema y. Hence it is natural to conclude that the criminal words were charged as having been spoken on that occasion. Yet Dr. Hall gives a perfectly different account of the circumstances of the alleged offence and of the evidence offered. He does not mention the day, yet there is nothing in his version that could not have happened on the day and in the place alleged, though not before the council. If we are to suppose that the words charged as spoken in the Tower on May 7th were words addressed by the prisoner to the council, we must also suppose either that one or more of his majesty's Privy Council came forward as evidence, or that the mere written statem nt of the council, read to the jury, was considered

---

* Bruce. *Archæol.*, xxv., p. 83. He alludes especially to Mr. Turner's *Henry VIII.* This author had said that there *must have been* some other crime than "the mere theoretical refusal to acknowledge the ecclesiastical chieftainship," and that More and Fisher *must have been* convicted as abettors or participators in treasonable conspiracies !

† Introduction to vol. viii. of *Letters and Papers*, p. xxxiii.

sufficient and unimpeachable evidence for an immediate conviction.

This would, however, be to set aside the whole of Hall's account of the trial, which has hitherto been generally accepted as authentic, having been copied into the *State Trials*. Lord Campbell, accepting Hall's narrative without hesitation, writes as follows: "The only witness for the Crown was Rich, the solicitor-general, who, although he was supposed not to have exceeded the truth in stating what had passed between him and the prisoner, covered himself with almost equal infamy as when he was driven to commit perjury on the trial of More". He then goes on to abridge the evidence, the reply, and the judge's sentence as he found them in Baily.

I shall now therefore transcribe Dr. Hall's account of the trial in full, premising, however, that neither the certainty of the cause for which the Blessed John Fisher died a martyr, nor the certainty that he was put to death unjustly, even according to the law of England, in any way depends on the truth of the following narrative.

"These twelve men," writes Hall, "being sworn to try whether the prisoner were guilty of this treason or no, at last came forth to give evidence against him, Mr. Rich, the secret and close messenger that passed between the king and him, as ye have read before, who openly, in the presence of the judges and all the people there assembled (which were a huge number), deposed and sware that he heard the prisoner say in plain words, within the Tower of London: 'That he believed in his conscience, and by his learning assuredly knew, that the king neither was, nor by right could be, supreme head in earth of the Church of England'.

"When this blessed father heard the accusations of this most wretched and false person, contrary to his former oath and promise, he was not a little astonyed thereat; where-

fore he said to him in this manner: 'Mr. Rich, I cannot
but marvel to hear you come in and bear witness against
me of these words, knowing in what secret manner you
came to me. But suppose I so said unto you, yet in that
saying I committed no treason, for upon what occasion and
for what cause it might be said yourself doth know right
well, and, therefore, being now urged' (said he) 'by this
occasion to open somewhat of this matter, I shall desire my
lords and others here to take a little patience in hearing
what I shall say for myself. This man' (meaning Mr.
Rich) 'came to me from the king (as he said) on a secret
message, with commendations from his grace, declaring at
large what a good opinion his majesty had of me, and how
sorry he was of my trouble, with many more words than are
here needful to be recited, because they tended so much to
my praise, as I was not only ashamed to hear them, but
also knew right well that I could no way deserve them. At
last he brake with me of the matter of the king's supremacy
lately granted unto him by Act of Parliament, to the which
(he said), although all the bishops in the realm have consented except yourself alone, and also the whole court of
Parliament, both spiritual and temporal, except a very few,
yet he told me that the king, for better satisfaction of his
own conscience, had sent him unto me in this secret manner
to know my full opinion in the matter, for the great affiance
he had in me more than any other. He added further that
if I would frankly and freely herein advise his majesty of my
knowledge, that upon certificate of my misliking, he was
very like to retract much of his former doings, and make
satisfaction for the same, in case I should so advise him.
When I heard all his message and considered a little upon
his words, I put him in mind of the new Act of Parliament,
which (standing in force as it doth against all them that
should directly say or do anything against it) might thereby
endanger me very much, in case I should utter unto him

anything that were offensive against the law. To that he
told me that the king willed him to assure me on his
honour, and on the word of a king, that whatsoever I
should say unto him by this his secret messenger, I should
abide no danger nor peril for it ; neither that any advantage
should be taken against me for the same, no, although my
words were never so directly against the statute, seeing it
was but a declaration of my mind secretly to him, as to his
own person.   And for the messsenger himself, he gave me
his faithful promise that he would never utter my words in
this matter to any man living, but to the king alone.   Now,
therefore, my lords' (quoth he), 'seeing it pleased the king's
majesty to send me word thus secretly, under the pretence
of plain and true meaning, to know my poor advice and
opinion in these his weighty and great doings (which I most
gladly was and ever will be willing to send him), methink it
is very hard injustice to hear the messenger's accusation,
and to allow the same as a sufficient testimony against me
in case of treason.'

"To this the messenger would make no direct answer,
but with a most impudent and shameless face (neither denying his words for false nor confessing them for true), said,
that whatsoever he had said unto him on the king's behalf,
he said no more than his majesty commanded him.   'But'
(said he) 'if I had said to you in such sort as you have declared,
I would gladly know what discharge is this to you in law
against his majesty for so directly speaking against the
statute.'   Whereat some of the judges, taking quick hold
one after another, said that this message or promise of the
king to him neither could nor did by rigour of the law discharge him, but in so declaring his mind and conscience
against the supremacy, yea, though it were at the king's own
commandment or request, he committed treason by the
statute, and nothing can discharge him from death but the
king's pardon.

" This good father, perceiving the small account made of his words, and the favourable credit given to his accuser, might then easily smell which way the matter would go ; wherefore, directing his speeches to the lords his judges, he said : ' Yet I pray you, my lords, consider that, by all equity, justice, worldly honesty, and courteous dealing, I cannot (as the case standeth) be directly charged there-with as with treason, though I had spoken the words, indeed, the same being not spoken maliciously, but in the way of advice and counsel, when it was requested of me by the king himself. And that favour the very words of the statute do give me, being made only against such as shall maliciously gainsay the king's supremacy, and none other.' To that it was answered by some of the judges that the word maliciously in the statute is but a superfluous and void word ; for if a man speak against the king's supremacy by any manner of means, that speaking is to be understanded and taken in law as maliciously. ' My lords ' (said he), ' if the law be so understood, then it is a hard exposition, and (as I take it) contrary to the meaning of them that made the law. But then, let me demand this question, Whether a single testimony of one man may be admitted as sufficient to prove me guilty of treason for speaking these words or no, and whether my answer negatively may not be accepted against his affirmative to my avail and benefit or no ? ' To that the judges and lawyers answered that (being the king's case) it rested much in conscience and discretion of the jury, and as they upon the evidence given before them shall find it, you are either to be acquitted, or else by judgment to be condemned.

" The jury, having heard all this simple evidence, departed (according to the order) into a secret place, there to agree upon the verdict ; but before they went from the place, the case was so aggravated to them by the lord chancellor making it so heinous and dangerous a treason, that they easily perceived what verdict they must return, or else heap such danger upon their own heads, as was for none of their cases to bear.

"Some other of the commissioners charged this most reverend cardinal with obstinacy and singularity, alleging that he being but one man did presumptuously stand against that, which was in the great council of Parliament agreed, and finally consented unto by all the bishops of this realm, saving himself alone. But to that he answered, that indeed he might well be accounted singular if he alone should stand in this matter (as they said); but having on his part the rest of the bishops of Christendom, far surmounting the number of the bishops of England, he said they could not justly account him singular; and having on his part all the Catholic bishops of the world from Christ's Ascension till now, joined with the whole consent of Christ's universal Church, 'I must needs' (said he) 'account my own part far the surer. And as for obstinacy, which is likewise objected against me, I have no way to clear myself thereof, but by mine own solemn word and promise to the contrary, if ye please to believe it, or else, if that will not serve, I am here ready to confirm the same by mine oath.' Thus in effect he answered their objections, though with many more words, both wisely and profoundly uttered, and that with a marvellous, courageous, and rare constancy, in so much as many of his hearers, yea, some of his judges lamented so grievously, that their inward sorrow on all sides was expressed by the outward tears of their eyes, to perceive such a famous and reverend man in danger to be condemned to cruel death by such an impious law, upon so weak evidence given by such a wicked accuser, contrary to all faith and promise of the king himself.

"But all pity, mercy, and right being set aside, rigour, cruelty, and malice took place; for the twelve men being shortly returned from their consultation, verdict was given that he was guilty of the treason, which although they thus did upon the menacing and threatening words of the commissioners and the king's learned counsel, yet was it no doubt full sore against their conscience (as some of them would after report to their dying days), only for safety of their goods and lives, which they were well assured to lose in case they had acquitted him.

"After the verdict thus given by the twelve men, the lord chancellor, commanding silence to be kept, said unto the prisoner in this sort : 'My Lord of Rochester, you have been here arraigned of high treason, and putting yourself to the trial of twelve men, you have pleaded not guilty, and they notwithstanding have found you guilty in their consciences ; wherefore, if you have any more to say for yourself you are now to be heard, or else to receive judgment according to the order and course of the law'. Then said this blessed father again : 'Truly, my lord, if that which I have before spoken be not sufficient, I have no more to say, but only to desire Almighty God to forgive them that have thus condemned me ; for I think they know not what they have done'. Then my lord chancellor, framing himself to a solemnity in countenance, pronounced sentence of death upon him, in manner and form following : 'You shall be led to the place from whence you came, and from thence shall be drawn through the city to the place of execution at Tyborne, where your body shall be hanged by the neck, and half alive you shall be cut down and thrown to the ground, your bowels to be taken out of your body and burnt before you, being alive, your head to be smitten off, and your body to be divided into four quarters, and after your head and quarters to be set up where the king shall appoint, and God have mercy on your soul'.

"After the pronouncing of this horrible and cruel sentence of death, the lieutenant of the Tower * with his band of

* Probably it was the constable.

men stood ready to receive and carry him back again to his prison. But before his departure he desired audience of the commissioners for a few words, being which granted, he said thus in effect: 'My lords, 1 am here condemned before you of high treason, for denial of the king's supremacy over the Church of England, but by what order of justice I leave to God who is searcher both of the king's majesty's conscience and yours; nevertheless, being found guilty as it is termed, I am and must be contented with all that God shall send, to whose will I wholly refer and submit myself. And now to tell you more plainly my mind touching this matter of the king's supremacy: I think, indeed, and always have thought, and do now lastly affirm, that his grace cannot justly claim any such supremacy over the Church of God as he now taketh upon him, neither hath been seen or heard of, that any temporal prince before his days hath presumed to that dignity. Wherefore, if the king will now adventure himself in proceeding in this strange and unwonted case, no doubt but he shall deeply incur the displeasure of Almighty God, to the great danger of his own soul and of many others, and to the utter ruin of this realm committed to his charge, whereof will ensue some sharp punishment at His hand. Wherefore, I pray God his grace may remember himself in time, and hearken to good counsel for the preservation of himself and his realm, and the quietness of all Christendom.'

"Which words being ended, he was conveyed back again to the Tower of London, part on foot and part on horseback, with a like number of men bearing halberts and other weapons about him as was before at his coming to the arraignment. And when he was come to the Tower gate, he turned him back to all his train that had thus conducted him forward and backward and said unto them: 'My masters, I thank you all for the great labour and pains ye have taken with me this day; I am not able to give you anything in recompense, for I have nothing left, and, therefore, I pray accept in good part my hearty thanks'. And this he spake with so lusty a courage, so amiable a countenance, and with so fresh and lively a colour, as he seemed rather to have come from a great feast or a banquet than from his arraignment, showing by all his gesture and outward countenance such joy and gladness as it was easy to perceive how earnestly he desired in his heart to be in that blessed state for which he had so long laboured. Whereof he made the surer account for that he was thus innocently condemned for Christ's cause." *

In this account of Dr. Hall there is only one real difficulty. The indictment is for having "falsely, maliciously, and traitorously spoken and published" the words, "The king is not supreme head in earth of the Church of England," to divers true subjects of the our said lord the king (*diversis dicti domini regis veris subditis*). Now, if Rich was the only witness, and if he testified to words spoken secretly to himself, the indictment would not have been verified. To this it may be replied that such inexactness would have been easily condoned by the judges of those days. Perhaps this was the meaning of the cardinal's plea that one witness was not sufficient—a plea which was overruled by the lord chancellor. Strict legal justice was of little account in his eyes. Lord Campbell, writing of the very same commissioners and of the trial of Sir Thomas More, which was exactly parallel in all respects with that of Cardinal Fisher, says: " Trusting rather to *partial judges* and packed jury than the evidence which could be brought against him, a special commission was issued ".† And after relating the

* From Hall's MS.

† He says also: " We must regard" (Sir Thomas More's) "murder as the blackest crime that ever has been perpetrated in England under the form of law". I hesitate to assume that he would say *exactly* the same thing of Fisher's, since it is certain that Rich perjured himself against More; against Fisher he was merely treacherous and perfidious.

trial of Fisher and the ruling of Chancellor Audley, he says : " This *wicked judge* had not the apology of having any taste for blood himself, and he would probably have been much better pleased to have sustained the objection " (of the insufficiency of the evidence) " and directed an acquittal. He was merely the tool of a tyrant." This severe censure on the presiding judge is not founded on the single trial of Fisher, but on an accumulation of instances ; so that even if Hall's account were proved erroneous, Audley would not thereby have his character restored. Whereas the notorious injustice of Audley and the slavishness of his fellow judges in other cases, give a probability to Hall's account and remove the difficulty of reconciling the indictment and the verdict with the evidence.*

Similar reflections may be applied to the conduct of Rich. It is atrocious as represented by Hall; but from what is known of him, altogether apart from Hall's report of this trial, it is antecedently probable. He acted with even greater effrontery a fortnight later at the trial of Sir Thomas More ; and it is after a review of his whole career that Lord Campbell writes : " Rich was hardly free from any vice except hypocrisy ; he was one of the most sordid as well as unprincipled men who have ever held the office of lord chancellor in England ". Rich was then bidding for place; and to him conscience and honour were light things to bargain away for wealth and titles. Such men abounded in the 16th century. They cared neither for religion nor morality. They called themselves *politici*, and made their

---

* It was after a careful scrutiny of Audley's whole life that Lord Campbell pronounced him "a sordid slave"; and after weighing his conduct in the trial of Anne Boleyn, and of Archbishop Cranmer in her divorce, he sarcastically remarks: "It was well that Henry did not direct that Audley should officiate as executioner, with Cranmer as his assistant ; for they probably would have obeyed sooner than have given up the seals or the primacy ".

study in the arts of flattering the passions and prejudices of the great and powerful. The Court of Henry in his later days, as the Court of Queen Elizabeth afterwards, were their natural home. It is necessary to repeat things, with the authority of men trained in the law and well read as historians, like Justice O'Hagan, Lord Campbell, and Lord Macaulay, when attempts are being made to vindicate the tyranny of Henry, and to sneer at the obstinacy or want of moral courage and truthfulness of Bishop Fisher—one of the few fearless truth-tellers in that lying age.

There is, then, nothing antecedently improbable in Hall's account of the trial ; nothing is attributed to the witness or the judges or the jury but what we might expect from such men ; while it is extremely unlikely that Hall, being well informed as to the names of the judges and the jury, and the exact words of the indictment, should have been misinformed as to the nature of the evidence by which a conviction was gained. To suppose that he wilfully invented the whole episode of Rich's visit to Fisher in the Tower, and of his witness against him at the trial, would be to do him an outrage not justified by anything in his whole account of Fisher, or by anything we know of his personal character. If ever he gives a speech of Fisher, he is cautious to warn the reader that he is merely giving the *effect* or general bearing of his words ; and he contrasts most favourably with his injudicious plagiarist Baily, both in this and other respects. He gives no more of the interview between Rich and Fisher in the Tower than could be gathered from Fisher's own statement at the trial, whereas Baily, who in his account of the trial is cautious enough to follow Hall almost literally, has invented a long and improbable dialogue for the previous interview, which could never have been known to him even though it had been spoken.

It is to be regretted that from no other source can we clear up the obscurity, if it is judged to be such, regarding the evidence. The Bishop of Faenza, papal nuncio in France, writing from Paris on the 4th July, tells the rumour that reached him there as follows: "The cause of his death is rumoured in England to have been his writing evil of the king to Sir Thomas More, who was also in prison. And they have caused it to be said to his face by one of his chaplains, that he had written to More against the king on a bit of wood with a needle, having neither paper nor ink."* This remark is curious; for in the answers of George Golde, the lieutenant's servant, there is mention of some scrolls, found by him in the prison cell of the Carthusian monks, on which were "letters pricked with a point"; these scrolls, however, were not written by Fisher, but shown to him. Some gossip about this may have been the origin of the tale that reached the papal nuncio in Paris. Fisher had certainly no chaplains who could have appeared against him. As to his worthy servant, Richard Wilson, no one has thought that he was called to bear witness; and we shall see him still waiting on his master between the trial and the execution.

Writing on the 20th June, three days after the sentence and the second before the martyrdom, Chapuys, the cardinal's intimate friend, tells Dr. Ortiz, the emperor's ambassador in Rome: "On the 17th the Cardinal of Rochester was sentenced. He was told he did not appear to dispute, but to hear his sentence of death for transgressing maliciously the statutes of the kingdom, by which the king was head of the English Church. He replied that he had not contradicted those statutes maliciously, but with truth and holy intention, as they were opposed to Scriptures and to our faith. He was then sentenced to the same death as the Carthusians, on which he said that he was prepared to die, and hoped God would give him constancy. On his return to the Tower he was followed by a crowd of men and women in great grief,

* *Letters and Papers*, viii. 985.

who demanded his blessing when he crossed the water *
to enter the Tower." †

The procession with which Cardinal Wolsey's hat had
been brought to Westminster was magnificent, but how
much more glorious was this procession of the hatless
Cardinal Fisher to his place of martyrdom.

As a kind of appendix to this chapter I translate a
dissertation on the trials of Fisher and More, and the
contrast between their conduct, by Cardinal Pole. He
is writing to Francisco Navarre, Bishop of Badajoz. No
date is given, but by intrinsic evidence it was at the beginning of the reign of Edward VI. The bishop had
offered some friendly criticisms on certain passages in Pole's
book on the unity of the Church, and the cardinal accepts
some but refutes others : "You come now," he says, "to
the answer of Thomas More, in which you seem to find
fault that I, while eager to praise, have really cast a slur on
his virtue, if what I have related is true. Well, whether I
have narrated things as I should I cannot say, but I am
certain that I have told the truth. You do not approve the
studied silence of More, or rather that he kept silent so long
when asked his belief in a matter of faith, and you say that
I might have omitted that, since it does not tend to his
praise. But though I agree with you that there should be
no dissimulation when we are questioned on our faith, yet
it cannot be denied that everything has its proper time, and
there is a time to keep silence and a time to speak. The
time for speaking for More was, in my opinion, just when
he did speak, namely, after he **was** condemned by the

---

* Not the river Thames, for Westminster and the Tower are both
on the north side of the river ; but the Tower moat, over which was
a drawbridge leading to the entrance gate.

† The letter of Dr. Ortiz was written to the empress on 20th July,
but he says that he quotes from a letter written to him by Chapuys
on 20th June.—*Letters and Papers*, viii. 1075.

sentence of the judges. I do not think the same time was
the fit one for the Bishop of Rochester. For him the time
to speak out was immediately when he was questioned, for
this befitted his character of bishop. But More was a
layman, and since they were to condemn him by a civil, not
an ecclesiastical law, although the law was contrary to the
laws of God and the Church, it seemed to be more fitting
that, being asked about the law, he should answer according
to the law, snatching from them the arms of civil law which
they were using against him. This he did when he said
that, even if the law was just, he had done nothing against it
by word or deed, and therefore he could not be called to
account by them, and much less be condemned.

" Could anything be imagined more apt than this answer,
or more suitable to him who was most learned in the laws
of the kingdom, which as judge he had administered so
many years ; for by this one word he overthrew all their
efforts if they had only been willing to stand by their own
laws ? Hence I cannot think that More was wanting in his
duty to the Church because he did not immediately answer
that their decree was against the Divine law ; for about this
he was not asked, nor was he called to account for violating
Divine law, but human. When he understood that the
protection of human law was taken from him, and that he
was condemned contrary to the right of human law, then,
in the proper time, as it seems to me, he used ecclesiastical
arms, saying that, even if he had violated that decree, he
could not be condemned by Divine or human right, since
the decree was repugnant to Divine law.

" The more, then, I consider the result of those trials, the
cause and the persons who were tried, and the malice of
their enemies, the more I am convinced that those two men,
as in the matter itself they were taught and confirmed by
God, so also in their mode of defending themselves they
were guided by Divine rather than by human prudence, and

I have no doubt you will come to the same conclusion if you will consider the matter more attentively."*

From the unimpeachable testimony of Chapuys and Pole we must conclude that though both More and Fisher pleaded not guilty, yet, when the evidence was brought forward, More ably defended himself in the way described by Roper, and only confessed his faith after his sentence ; while Fisher before his sentence admitted his faith and his having already acknowledged it, but denied that malice could be imputed to him against the king or the law.

* Pole's *Letters*, vol. iv., p. 72

CHAPTER XVIII.

THE violent and cruel death of such men as Fisher and More, inflicted by sensual and heartless despots like Henry VIII., is one of the deepest and most awful mysteries of God's providence. Throughout the whole animal and insect world the small seem to be the prey of the great, the feeble of the strong. It is the same in human society, but with the additional perplexity that the best often succumb to the worst. Yet the Divine Master brings both these mysteries before our eyes, bidding faith and hope triumph over this spectacle of confusion and despair: "Fear not those that kill the body, but cannot kill the soul. . . . Are not two sparrows sold for a farthing? And not one of them shall fall on the ground without your Father. But the very hairs of your head are all numbered. Fear not therefore, you are of more value than many sparrows."*

The God who is the Author of life, and who with bounteous providence watches over life's preservation, clothing the indolent lilies with beauty, and feeding daintily the unthrifty songsters of the air, this God cannot be indifferent to death. Death is not the invading and conquering general of the armies of some other god, as Manicheans have dreamt, Death is the obedient servant of the one true God. Even among the lower orders of God's creation death comes only at the appointed time and in the appointed manner; however capricious his coming may seem to us, it is in reality "not

---

* *St. Matt.* x. 28-32.

without Our Father". The birds were created but for a few summers' mirth, the lilies but for a few days' splendour. How then should death come without their Father's providence to God's dearest and noblest children, for whom another and eternal life is reserved?

Yet death is terrible to man, however it may come. Though naturally mortal, he was not made for death. Death is to him the fruit of sin. The lilies and the birds know nothing of the death awaiting them, but man may die a thousand times by anticipation. To accept, therefore, even inevitable death, as from the hand of God, whether by sickness, by accident, in battle, or by the tyranny of a fellow-man, is an act of heroic virtue. But to go to meet death—to accept it when, by paltering with the truth or swerving from the right, we could still keep it aloof, is to be associated with the king of martyrs, and to gain a special aureole. How very few are willing thus to lose their lives that they may gain them! Men know they must die soon: they will squander life in war or duels, and imperil it for paltry gain. But few have faith enough in God to defy a tyrant for His sake. Look at the England of Henry VIII. "That the nation at large disliked the change [in religion] as it disliked the causes of the change, there can be very little doubt," writes Mr. Gairdner.* Yet when acquiescence in the change was required from the nation under penalty of loss of liberty or life, bishops, priests, and religious, nobles and plebeians, vied with each other in submission. "It is a curious fact," writes Lord Campbell—he might have said, "It is a shameful fact,"—"that against bills respecting religion, which must have been most highly distasteful to the great body of prelates, and to many lay peers, after the execution of Fisher there was not a dissentient voice, or the slightest audible murmur of opposition." †

* *Letters and Papers*, vol. viii., Introd., p. ĩ.
† In *Life of Audley*.

It is the contrast to all this in the life and death of the
Bishop of Rochester that gives them their intense and
abiding interest.   Yet the holy martyr did not rush upon
his death.   He took every precaution consistent with faith
and holiness to prolong his life.   He sighed for martyrdom ;
and when at length the hallowed morning came he exclaimed : " I most humbly thank the king's majesty that it
pleaseth him to rid me from all this worldly business ".
Yet he waited till God should deign to place the crown
upon his head, and dared not to snatch it from His hand.
Such deaths are precious in the sight of God and man.
" The hairs of your heads are all numbered," said Our Lord
when He sent His Apostles forth to martyrdom.   Therefore the Church has been wont not only to cherish the
relics of the martyrs, but to gather up and chronicle reverently their acts, to record all their words—those words that
" are given them " to speak in their last moments: We owe
a great debt of gratitude to Dr. Hall, that while those were
still alive who could speak as eye-witnesses, he wrote from
their report, and has preserved for us the acts of the martyrdom of Cardinal Fisher.   I transcribe his faithful and
pathetic narrative.   We have seen that the cardinal was
condemned to death and sent back to prison on Thursday
the 17th June, 1535.   The day of his death had not been
fixed.   It was, however, to be Tuesday the 22nd.   Hall
continues the history as follows :

"Thus being after his condemnation the space of four
days in his prison, he occupied himself in continual prayer
most fervently ; and although he looked daily for death, yet
could ye not have perceived him one whit dismayed or dis-
quieted thereat, neither in word nor countenance, but still
continued his former trade of constancy and patience, and
that rather with a more joyful cheer and free mind than
ever he had done before, which appeared well by this
chance that I will tell you.   There happened a false rumour

to rise suddenly among the people that he should be brought to his execution by a certain day, whereupon his cook that was wont to dress his dinner and carry it daily unto him, hearing among others of his execution, dressed him no dinner at all that day;* wherefore, at the cook's next return unto him, he demanded the cause why he brought him not his dinner as he was wont to do. 'Sir,' said the cook, 'it was commonly talked all the town over that you should have died that day, and therefore I thought it but in vain to dress anything for you.' 'Well,' said he merrily to him again, 'for all that report thou seest me yet alive, and therefore, whatsoever news thou shalt hear of me hereafter, let me no more lack my dinner, but make it ready as thou art wont to do, and if thou see me dead when thou comest, then eat it thyself; but I promise thee if I be alive, I mind by God's grace to eat never a bit the less.'

"'Thus while this blessed bishop and most reverend cardinal lay daily expecting the hour of his death, the king (who no less desired his death than himself looked for it) caused at last a writ of execution to be made and brought to Sir Edmund Walsingham, lieutenant of the Tower. But where by his judgment at Westminster he was condemned (as ye have heard before) to drawing, hanging, and quartering, as traitors always be, yet was he spared from that cruel execution, not for any pity or clemency meant on the king's part towards him, but the only cause thereof (as I have credibly heard) was for that, if he should have been laid upon a hurdle and drawn to Tyburn, being the ordinary place for that purpose, and distant above two miles from the

---

* This was probably on the 19th, on which day three Carthusians —Humphrey Middlemore, William Exmew, and Sebastian Newdegate—who had been indicted at the same time, but tried before him, were led out to execution at Tyburn. This was the second band of Carthusian martyrs.

Tower, it was not unlikely but he would have been dead
long ere he had come there, seeing he was a man of great
age, and beside that very sickly and weak of body through
his long imprisonment; wherefore, order was taken that he
should be led no further than the Tower Hill, and there to
have his head struck off.*

"After the lieutenant had received this bloody writ, he
called unto him certain persons whose service and presence
was to be used in that business, commanding them to be
ready against the next day in the morning. And because it
was then very late in the night, and the prisoner asleep, he
was loath to disease him from his rest for that time, and so
in the morning before five of the clock he came to him in
his chamber in the Bell Tower, finding him yet asleep in
his bed, and awaked him, showing him that he was come to
him on a message from the king, and after some circumstances used, with persuasion that he should remember
himself to be an old man, and that for age he could not by
course of nature live long, he told him at the last that he
was come to signify unto him that the king's pleasure was
he should suffer death that forenoon. 'Well' (quoth this
blessed father), 'if this be your errand, you bring me no
great news, for I have long time looked for this message.
And I most humbly thank the king's majesty that it pleaseth
him to rid me from all this worldly business, and I thank
you also for your tidings. But I pray you, Mr. Lieutenant'
(said he), 'when is mine hour that I must go hence?'
'Your hour' (said the lieutenant) 'must be nine of the
clock.' 'And what hour is it now?' (said he). 'It is
now about five,' said the lieutenant. 'Well, then,' said
he, 'let me by your patience sleep an hour or two, for I

---

* The above passage reflecting on the motives of the king is
omitted by Baily. He may have thought it improbable or uncharitable. It is, however, given as a matter of common opinion in a
letter of Erasmus that will be quoted presently.

have slept very little this night, and yet to tell you the truth, not for any fear of death, I thank God, but by reason of my great infirmity and weakness.' 'The king's further pleasure is,' said the lieutenant, 'that you should use as little speech as may be, specially of anything touching his majesty, whereby the people should have any cause to think of him or his proceedings otherwise than well.' 'For that' (said he) 'you shall see me order myself, as by God's grace, neither the king, nor any man else, shall have occasion to mislike of my words.' With which answer the lieutenant departed from him, and so the prisoner, falling again to rest, slept soundly two hours and more. And after he was waked he called to his man to help him up, but first of all he commanded him to take away the shirt of hair (which accustomably he wore on his back), and to convey it privily out of the house, and instead thereof to lay him forth a clean white shirt, and all the best apparel he had, as cleanly bright as may be. And as he was inraying himself, his man perceiving in him a more curiosity and care for the fine and cleanly wearing of his apparel that day than ever was wont to be before, demanded of him what this sudden change meant, saying that his lordship knew well enough he must put off all again within two hours and lose it. 'What of that?' (said he). 'Dost thou not mark that this is our wedding-day, and that it behoveth us, therefore, to use more cleanliness for solemnity of the marriage?'* About nine of the clock the lieutenant came again to his prison, and, finding him almost ready, said that he was now come for him. 'I will wait upon you straight' (said he) 'as fast as this thin body of mine will give me leave.' Then said he to his man, 'Reach me my furred tippet to put about my neck'. 'Oh, my lord' (quoth the lieutenant),

---

* This wedding-day of Blessed Fisher, 22nd June, is also the feast of St. Alban the protomartyr of Britain, as always celebrated by English Catholics.

'what need you be so careful for your health for this little, being, as your lordship knoweth, not much above an hour.' 'I think no otherwise' (said this blessed father), 'but yet in the meantime I will keep myself as well as I can, till the very time of my execution, for I tell you truth, though I have, I thank Our Lord, a very good desire and willing mind to die at this present, and so trust of His infinite mercy and goodness He will continue it, yet will I not willingly hinder my health in the meantime one minute of an hour, but still prolong the same as long as I can by such reasonable ways and means as Almighty God hath provided for me.' And with that taking a little book in his hand, which was a New Testament lying by him, he made a cross on his forehead and went out of his prison door, with the lieutenant, being so weak that he was scarce able to go down the stairs, wherefore at the stairs-foot he was taken up in a chair between two of the lieutenant's men and carried to the Tower gate, with a great number of weapons about him, to be delivered to the sheriffs of London for execution. And as they were come to the uttermost precinct or liberty of the Tower, they rested there with him a space, till such time as one was sent before to know in what readiness the sheriffs were to receive him ; during which space he rose out of his chair, and standing on his feet, leaned his shoulder to the wall, and lifting his eyes up towards heaven, he opened his little book in his hand, and said : 'O Lord, this is the last time that ever I shall open this book, let some comfortable place now chance unto me whereby I thy poor servant may glorify Thee in this my last hour'; and with that looking into the book, the first thing that came to his sight were these words : 'Hæc est autem vita æterna : ut cognoscant te, solum Deum verum, et quem misisti Jesum Christum. Ego te clarificavi super terram : opus consummavi, quod dedisti mihi ut faciam : Et nunc clarifica me tu Pater apud temetipsum, claritate quam habui prius, quam,'

&c.* And with that he shut the book together, and said : ' Here is even learning enough for me to my life's end '. And so (the sheriff being ready for him) he was taken up again among certain of the sheriff's men, with a new and much greater company of weapons than was before, and carried to the scaffold on the Tower Hill, otherwise called East Smithfield, himself praying all the way, and recording upon the words which he had read ; and when he was come to the foot of the scaffold, they that carried him offered to help him up the stairs, but then said he : ' Nay, masters, seeing I am come so far let me alone, and ye shall see me shift for myself well enough,' and so went up the stairs without any help, so lively that it was marvel to them that knew before of his debility and weakness ; but as he was mounting up the stairs, the south-east sun shined very bright in his face, whereupon he said to himself these words, lifting up his hands: ' Accedite ad eum, et illuminamini et facies vestræ non confundentur ".† By that time he was on the scaffold, it was about ten of the clock, where the executioner, being ready to do his office, kneeled down to him (as the fashion is) and asked him forgiveness. 'I forgive thee' (said he) 'with all my heart, and I trust thou shalt see me overcome this storm lustily.' Then was his gown and tippet taken from him, and he stood in his doublet and hose, in sight of all the people, whereof was no small number assembled to see this horrible execution. There was to be seen a long, lean, and slender body, having on it little other substance besides the skin and bones, in so much as most part of the beholders marvelled much to see a living man so far consumed, for he seemed a very image of death,

* *Joan.* xvii. 3, 4, 5. " This is life everlasting, that they may know Thee the only true God, and Jesus Christ whom Thou hast sent. I have glorified Thee upon the earth, I have finished the work that Thou gavest me to do."

† " Come ye to Him and be enlightened : and your faces shall not be confounded."—*Ps.* xxxiii. 5.

and as it were death in man's shape using a man's voice, and
therefore, monstrous was it thought that the king could be
so cruel as to put such a man to death as he was, yea, though
he had been an offender in deed. And surely it may be
thought that if he had been in the Turk's dominion, and
there found guilty of some great offence, yet would the Turk
never have put him to death being already so near death.
For it is an horrible and exceeding cruelty to kill that thing
which is presently dying, except it be for pity sake to rid it
from longer pain, which in this case appeared not, and,
therefore, it may be thought that the cruelty and hard heart
of King Henry in this point passed all the Turks and tyrants
that ever have been heard or read of.*

"When the innocent and holy cardinal was come upon the
scaffold, he spoke to the people in effect as followeth :
'Christian people, I am come hither to die for the faith of
Christ's holy Catholic Church, and I thank God hitherto
my stomach hath served me very well thereunto, so that yet
I have not feared death ; wherefore I do desire you all to
help and assist me with your prayers, that at the very point
and instant of death's stroke, I may in that very moment
stand steadfast without fainting in any one point of the
Catholic faith, free from any fear. And I beseech Almighty
God of His infinite goodness to save the king and this realm,
and that it may please Him to hold His holy hand over it,
and send the king good counsel.'"

I interrupt Hall's narrative for a moment. The last words
of a martyr are so precious that we must be sure we have
them as they were spoken. Hall's account is confirmed by
a letter written by the papal nuncio in France, on the 4th
July. He says the first report which reached him was that
the cardinal "spoke to the people boldly, telling them to
be loving and obedient to their king, who was good by

* Baily has omitted all this comparison with the Turk, yet it is certainly not exaggerated or unjust.

nature, but had been deceived in this matter ; that he was
led to death for wishing to preserve the honour of God and
the Holy See, at which he did not grieve, but was content,
for it was the will of God ". This was the first version, but
now he hears from the English ambassador that he only
said, that being of flesh which naturally feared death, and
knowing that Peter three times denied Christ through fear
of death, and having always had a mind to die, if necessary,
for the love of Christ and h.s holy Church, now that he was
come to it he begged all present to pray to God to grant
constancy and firmness to his fragile flesh to suffer cheerfully his approaching punishment. * This humble self-
distrust and earnest prayer for final perseverance is in perfect keeping with the saint's whole character, with what he
wrote in the Tower concerning the fall of great columns of the
Church who failed in humility,† and with his remark when
he heard of the constancy of the Carthusians at their trial :
" I pray God that no vanity subvert them ".

Dr. Hall continues his narrative : '" These or like words
he spake with such a cheerful countenance, such a stout
and constant courage, and such a reverend gravity, that he
appeared to all men, not only void of fear, but also glad of
death. Besides this he uttered his words so distinctly, and
with so loud and clear a voice, that the people were astonished
thereat, and noted it for a miraculous thing, to hear so
plain and audible voice come from so weak and sickly an
old body ; for the youngest man in that presence, being in
good and perfect health, could not have spoken to be better
heard and perceived than he was. Then after these few
words by him uttered, he kneeled down on his knees and
said certain prayers, among which (as some reported) one
was the hymn of *Te Deum laudamus,* to the end, and the

* *Letters and Papers,* viii. 985.
† In his treatise *De necessitate orana,*.

psalm *In Te Domine speravi*.   Then came the executioner
and bound a handkerchief about his eyes, and so this holy
father, lifting up his hands and heart to heaven, said a few
prayers, which were not long but fervent and devout, which
being ended, he laid his holy head down over the midst of
a little block, where the executioner, being ready with a sharp
and heavy axe, cut asunder his slender neck at one blow,
which bled so abundantly that many wondered to see so
much blood issue out of so lean and slender a body.   And
so head and body being severed, his immortal soul mounted
to the blissful joys of heaven." *

The king of martyrs has said : " Fear not them that kill
the body, and after that have no more that they can do ".
They can do no more to cause pain or fear, but they can
indulge in outrages on the mangled remains of their victims
to show their spite.   Several of such outrages were perpetrated on the lifeless body of Blessed Fisher.   Some of
these are too well attested to be called in question.   One,
however, is only given by Hall as a tale or report.   It is that
Anne Boleyn ordered the head to be brought to her, and,
looking at it for a time contemptuously, said these or the
like words : " Is this the head that so often exclaimed
against me ?   I trust it shall never do me more harm ; " and
striking the mouth with the back of her hand, received a
wound from a tooth that left a scar till her death.   Mr.
Lewis contends that this story is altogether improbable and
incredible, and, as it is not confirmed from any other source,
I have no desire to contest his view.   But the history of
Henry's brutality to the headless body is not so easily set
aside.   Dr. Hall says that the executioner "stripped the
body of his shirt and all his clothes, and left the corpse
naked on the scaffold, where it remained uncovered for the
most part of that day, saving that one for pity and humanity
cast upon it a little straw ; and about eight o'clock in the

* Hall's MS.

evening commandment came from the king's council to
such as watched about the dead body (for it was still
watched with many halberts and weapons) that they should
cause it to be buried. Whereupon two of the watchers took
it upon a halbert between them and so carried it to a churchyard there, called All Hallows, Barking,* where on the north

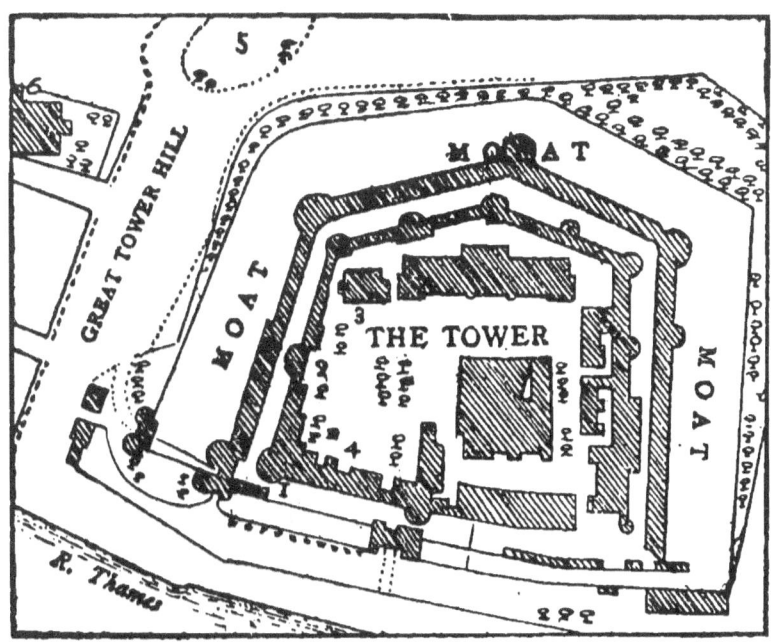

PLAN OF THE TOWER.

1. The Bell Tower.   4. The Lieutenant's Lodgings.
2. The Beauchamp Tower.   5. The Scaffold.
3. St. Peter's ad Vincula.   6. All Hallows Barking.

side of the churchyard, hard by the wall, they digged a grave
with their halberts, and therein without any reverence
tumbled the body of this holy prelate and blessed martyr
all naked and flat upon his belly, without either sheet cr
other accustomed thing belonging to a Christian man's
burial, and so covered it quickly with earth, following here-

* Called Barking, because in the patronage of the nuns of Barking.

in the king's commandment, who willed that it should be buried contemptuously."

I cannot be displeased with Mr. Lewis for arguing on the improbability of all these circumstances, since one would desire, for the sake of humanity, that they could be proved fabulous. He considers that no leave was necessary to bury a body that was not to be quartered and exposed, and that Fisher had many friends who would gladly have paid him the last rites. They certainly would had the king permitted it. But the Bishop of Faenza, writing from Paris on 4th July, says that he has just heard from the English ambassador—that is, I suppose, the French ambassador in London—that, instead of being hung, drawn, and quartered, "the bishop was merely beheaded, by the greatest grace obtained from the infinite fury of the king, *who finally was content that his body should be buried in the evening*".[*] That the body lay on the scaffold all day, and that the friends of the bishop were not free to dispose of it, is, then, no invention of Dr. Hall. And Cardinal Pole, who would certainly obtain authentic information on such a matter, writing at a later date, says: "Nor did Henry's unrelenting rage end with death. He was not satisfied unless the dead body was exposed to every kind of contumely. He ordered the body should remain quite naked on the place of execution as a spectacle to the people; and no one dared approach for fear of the tyrant, except those whose office it was to outrage or to strip it."[†]

---

[*] *Letters and Papers*, viii. 985. Baily has given occasion to objections by saying that leave came to bury the body from the "commissioners". Hall, however, says the council. Hall explains that the body was buried *contemptuously* by the king's orders; Baily omits this important fact.

[†] *Apologia*, § 20. "Nudum prorsus in loco supplicii ad spectaculum populo relinqui mandaverat, ad quod nemo accedere audebat tyranni metu præter eos qui contumeliæ causa accederent, vel qui mortuo indumenta detraxerant."

Fuller remarks: "The king vouchsafed him the Tower, a noble prison, and beheading, an honourable death; it is improbable he would deny him a necessary equipage for a plain and private burial". Unfortunately, many things happen that seem improbable, and history cannot be written *a priori*. Herod had a certain religious fear of John the Baptist, and when he was dead the king allowed John's disciples to bury his headless body. It seems improbable, then, that Herod could have given the head to a dancing girl for her and her mother to outrage. Yet this he did. As to the "noble prison"—not only adulterous queens and fallen statesmen were confined in the Tower, but many a common rogue also. Gangs of coiners were shut up within its walls at the very same time as Fisher and More.* If the bishop's dungeon was somewhat more honourable than theirs, it must be remembered that the king, throughout all the long months of the bishop's imprisonment, was eager to obtain his submission, and disappointment was converted into rage. If he remitted some of the sentence as too outrageous to be carried out on such a man, he did it reluctantly, and substituted other insults, a few degrees less villainous.

Dr. Hall continues: "The next day after his burial, the head being somewhat parboiled in hot water, was pricked upon a pole and set on high upon London Bridge among the rest of the holy Carthusians' heads that suffered death lately before him. And here I cannot omit to declare unto you the miraculous sight of this head, which, after it had stand [stood] up the space of fourteen days upon the bridge, could not be perceived to waste nor consume, neither for the weather, which then was very hot, neither for the parboiling in hot water, but grew daily fresher and fresher, so that in his lifetime he never looked so well. For his cheeks being beautified with a comely red, the face looked as if it had beholden the people passing by and would have spoke

* See returns of prisoners in *Letters and Papers*, viii. 1001.

26

to them, which many took for a miracle. . . . Wherefore
the people coming daily to see this strange sight, the
passage over the bridge was so stopped with their going and
coming that almost neither cart nor horse could pass; and
therefore at the end of fourteen days the executioner was
commanded to throw down the head in the night-time into the
river of the Thames,* and in place thereof was set the head
of the most blessed and constant martyr, Sir Thomas More,
his companion and fellow in all his troubles, who suffered
his passion the 6th day of July next following.''

In 1536, a long Latin letter was printed in Antwerp,
written professedly by Gulielmus Covrinus Nucerinus to
Philippus Montanus, on the 23rd July, 1535.† The letter
gives an account of the deaths of More and Fisher—of
More, principally from a narrative written in French by an
eye-witness, and circulated in Paris; of Fisher, from letters
of friends and general report. The writer of this letter is
commonly supposed to have been Erasmus, though he con-
ceals, or perhaps rather reveals, his identity by the words:
"What does our friend Erasmus feel, whose friendship with
More was so close that they had but one soul in two bodies?
Indeed, I fear lest the good old man die for very grief,‡ if,
indeed, he still survives." The writer accounts for his
knowledge of London and of English affairs by saying that
he was in the suite of Cardinal Campeggio. His account
of Fisher's martyrdom is as follows :

"On 17th June, John Fisher, Bishop of Rochester, a man
who proved himself a true bishop by the sanctity and austerity
of his life, by his administration of the sacraments, and his
assiduity in teaching both by word and writings, and by his

* Later on he says, "removed and hidden away". This is also
the expression of Erasmus.

† It was reprinted in 1563 with *Mori Lucubrationes*, and is also
given in *More's Life* by Roper (ed. 1729), p. 147.

‡ In Latin there is a pun—*Moro suo commoriatur.*

wonderful liberality to the poor and kindness to students, was taken from the Tower to Westminster Hall amidst a large number of armed guards, partly by boat and partly on horseback; for his body was very weak, not merely by old age, but by the sufferings of his prison, though, indeed, he had himself greatly undermined his health by fasting and watching, by study and toil and tears. Though he knew well what would be the issue of the trial, he was without fear, and with a placid and even joyful countenance obeyed the summons. There, according to the process followed in that country, which I have already described (in the case of More), he was condemned to death, and was to be executed when it should please the king. I suspect that this was added that, perchance, either by hope of pardon or fear of the torment, he might be led to change his mind. The kind of death was both foul and horrible, yet it was inflicted on some Carthusians—some say fifteen, but I can scarcely believe it. Along with these suffered a Brigittine monk named Reynolds, a man with the countenance and spirit of an angel, and of sound judgment, as I found by his conversation when I was in England in the suite of Cardinal Campeggio. I knew none of the Carthusians. Some of these are said to have been dragged along the road, then hanged, and their bowels were drawn out while they were still living, and some of them are said to have been burnt. But the constancy of all was incredible. Rumour generally exaggerates in such matters; but if this report is correct, it seems to be the intention of the king's advisers to frighten others by the cruelty of the torments.

"But to return to the Bishop of Rochester. On being conducted back to the Tower after that horrible sentence, he thanked the guards with a cheerful countenance for their attention to him, both in going and coming. You would have said that he was returning from a joyous feast; his colour was brighter, and his whole mien, as far as his gravity allowed, showed his gladness of heart, so that every one could see that the holy man, now near to port, was longing for that blessed rest. Nor was his death long delayed. On the 22nd June he was brought to Tower Hill, where, with a courageous and even cheerful face, he briefly addressed the people. He first prayed for the king and his kingdom, and then in a fervent but not lengthened prayer he commended himself to the mercy of God, and kneeling down, received the stroke of the axe upon his slender and feeble neck. . . . What grief this sight caused to all who had any piety, and who had seen how the spirit of Christ animated this holy pastor, anyone may judge from his own feelings.

"Some think the full severity of the sentence was not executed on him, lest if he had been dragged so far on cart or hurdle, old as he was and exhausted, he would have expired on the way. My own suspicion is that the more atrocious kind of death was threatened to strike terror and make him change his mind. It is also said that his death was hastened, because Pope Paul III., for his learning and holiness, had raised him to the cardinalate.

" Friends write to me that in Lower Germany it is reported that his head, when fixed on London Bridge, instead of shrivelling, grew more florid and life-like, so that many expected it would speak—a thing we read of in the acts of certain martyrs. When this fact or rumour got abroad, the head was taken away and hidden ; for the credulous people are easily moved by a slight occasion to make great tumults. Fearing lest the same thing should happen to the head of More, before it was exposed it was boiled in water, to inspire greater horror.* These and many other things are written from Flanders : I know not how truly. I wish we had here the acts of Fisher as we have those of More." †

---

* The same report reached Dr. Ortiz in Rome, and is mentioned by him in a letter of 22nd Nov. (*Letters and Papers*, ix. 873.)

† There is much more in the letter on the *policy* of the king, and

In this wish we cordially join. In the absence of more detailed records we gather up every scrap, and we are thankful that the recent publication of the letters of the imperial ambassador has added to our information three or four important facts—first, that an offer of pardon was made and rejected on the scaffold ; secondly, that Cranmer was given to the bishop as his confessor ; and thirdly, that the king's rejoicing over his death was even more abominable than those who think worst of him could have suspected. Chapuys writes to the emperor, on 30th June, a week after Fisher's death : " On the 17th the good Bishop of Rochester was sentenced to death, for refusing to swear to the statutes made to the prejudice of the pope and of the queen ; and on the 22nd his head was cut off in the place where the Duke of Buckingham suffered. The regret and compassion of the people is inconceivable. He was very earnestly solicited, after he mounted the scaffold, to comply with the king's wish on an offer of pardon; but he refused, and he died very virtuously.

" There was given him as confessor one of his great enemies, the greatest Lutheran in the world, and patron of all the *diableries* here ; yet he does not cease to say that one of the most holy men in the world has been put to death.*

" Cromwell told me that the pope was the cause of his death, who had done very ill and very foolishly in making him a cardinal, seeing he was the worst enemy the king his master had, and that his holiness had excused himself even more foolishly to Gregory da Casale, saying that he had

of the martyrs. It is enough to say that it is quite Erasmian—the policy of peace at any price. It does not harmonise with the death of martyrs.

* Can these words apply to anyone but Cranmer ? We know that he was appointed to be confessor of Anne Boleyn by the king. State prisoners had no choice of confessors ; and though Cranmer was excommunicated, schismatic, and heretic, he had jurisdiction *in articulo mortis*, and the martyr might accept his ministry.

done it because the pope intended to convoke the council, in which cardinals were to be present from all countries."*

On the same day Chapuys wrote to Granvelle. He sends him what he calls ironically a gallant and notable interpretation of a chapter of the Apocalypse, which was played on the eve of St. John. To see it "the king went thirty miles from here, walked ten miles at two o'clock at night with a two-handed sword, and got into a house where he could see everything.† He was so pleased at seeing himself cutting off the heads of the clergy, that in order to laugh at his ease and encourage the people, he discovered himself. He sent to tell his lady that she ought to see the representation of it repeated on the eve of St. Peter. Sends bills in accordance with this interpretation of prophecy, which will show what hope there is of putting affairs right again. If there be no remedy all will go to ruin. It is wonderful that the people are not Lutherans before this, considering what the king causes to be said."‡

At first this seems beyond belief, yet Chapuys had the play-bill, § and could scarcely be misinformed. The day he mentions, the eve of St. John, was the day immediately following that of Fisher's martyrdom, the "midsummer night" on which plays were wont to be acted. We know that he was guilty of abominable levity at the execution of Anne Boleyn, a fact which goes to confirm Chapuys' report.

* *Letters and Papers*, viii., n. 948. *Spanish Cal.*, v. 178.

† The original is: "Ce roy vint de trente milles loing diçy environ, les deux heures de nuyt, traverse dix mille a pied avec une espee de deux mains une bonne partie de la ville pour entrer en une maison ".
The Court was then at Greenwich. The king *came*, not went, and the representation must have been in London. I cannot understand the "ten miles," and suspect a fault of the copyist. Chapuys evidently says "he crossed a great part of the town (London) on foot ". Two o'clock at night may be two hours after sunset.

‡ *Letters and Papers*, viii., n. 949.

§ M. De Gayangos has translated this: " I send you *papal bulls* in conformity with the interpretation of the above mentioned prophecy ". (*Spanish Cal.*, v. 179.)

A few words more will complete all that can be said regarding the relics of the holy martyr. Dr. Hall writes: "Touching the place of his burial in Barking Churchyard, it was well observed at that time by divers worthy personages of the nations of Italy, Spain, and France, that were then abiding in the realm, and more diligently marked and wrote the courses of things, and with less fear and suspicion than any of the king's subjects might or durst do, that for the space of seven years after his burial there grew neither leaf nor grass upon his grave, but the earth still remained as bare as though it had been continually occupied and trodden".* Dr. Hall does not say that the holy body remained beneath this sterile earth, which seemed to protest against the outrage of which it had been the instrument; yet he says nothing regarding a removal of the cardinal's remains elsewhere. The *Gray Friars' Chronicle*—the jottings of a contemporary— after mentioning that the body was buried "in the church-yard of Barking by the north door," adds that after the death of Sir Thomas More, "then was taken up the bishop again, and both of them buried within the Tower".† Stow also records this reburial.

Whether this removal took place at the time of Sir Thomas' burial is uncertain, but it was effected by the care and influence of Sir Thomas's daughter Margaret. Weever says: "How long they lay together in this their house of rest, I certainly know not; yet this is certain that Margaret . . . removed her father's corpse not long after to Chelsea, and whether she honoured the bishop by another remove to the place of her father's burial or not, I know not; yet she might by all probability ".‡

* "Seven years." Perhaps the account Hall refers to was written seven years after the martyr's death.

† *Gray Friars' Chronicle* (Rolls Series).

‡ Weever's *Funeral Monuments*, p. 278. He is followed by Antony á Wood.

Weever does not give any authority for this translation, which he calls certain, of More's body to Chelsea, and other authors contest his accuracy. Of course, therefore, they do not admit a second removal of the remains of Fisher.*

It is not certain that those who visited the temporary resting-place of the martyr's body in All Hallows' Churchyard were unaware of the removal of the body, since the Chapel of St. Peter, being within the walls of the Tower, was inaccessible to them, and they might naturally pray where the relics had once rested. The first place of burial, then, was in the churchyard, "at the north side, hard by the wall," according to the biographer; "by the north door," according to the chronicle. A street now passes over this place, running by the north wall of the old church. The second burial-place is not far off.

In the north-west corner of the Tower is a small church very appropriately dedicated to St. Peter ad Vincula. An ancient feast of St. Peter's Chains has been kept on the 1st August to commemorate the Apostle's imprisonments in Jerusalem and Rome; and it was devoutly thought that those suffering captivity, whether justly or unjustly, might find consolation in the memory recalled by the Church's dedication. Criminals would say: "We indeed justly, but what evil had that man done?" and men wrongly accused would take courage from the Apostle's own words: "If you suffer anything for justice' sake, blessed are ye. And be not afraid of their terror, and be not troubled." † The church was ancient, but had been injured by fire and almost rebuilt (on a smaller scale) only two years before the Bishop of Rochester was committed to the Tower. In this building, which has lately been architecturally restored to the condition in which it then was, still lie (in all probability) the ashes of the Blessed John Fisher, mingled with those of the

---

* See Mr. Doyne Bell's *Chapel in the Tower.*   † 1 *Pet.* iii. 14.

Blessed Thomas More. The bodies were buried towards the west end of the church, near the entrance to the belfry. The state of this building, the burial - place of so many illustrious and unfortunate persons, had long been considered a disgrace to the nation, when in 1876 her majesty Queen Victoria gave permission for its repair and renewal. Burials had been so hastily made, and the bodies after death so disturbed by other burials, that it was found necessary to take up the floor and remove the human remains from the body of the church, and to rearrange those in the chancel. This was done with all care and reverence. "All the human remains which were found beneath the floor of the chapel were carefully collected and enclosed in boxes, with suitable inscriptions, and all the coffins which were found intact were at once removed to the crypt on the north side of the chapel."* It is probable, however that the remains of Blessed More and Fisher were not disturbed, since they are said to have been laid outside that main passage of the little church which it was necessary to relevel. Near the entrance-door at the west end has been recently placed a memorial tablet, of which the following is the inscription :

"List of remarkable persons buried in this chapel—
"1. Gerald Fitzgerald, Earl of Kildare, . 1534
"2. John Fisher, Bishop of Rochester, . 1535
"3. Sir Thomas More, ... 1535
"4. George Boleyn, Viscount Rochford, . 1536
"5. Queen Anne Boleyn, . . . 1536
"6. Thomas Cromwell, Earl of Essex, . 1540
"7. Margaret of Clarence, Countess of
"Salisbury, ... 1541,"
&c., in all 34, ending—
"34. Simon, Lord Fraser of Lovat, . . 1747".

* *The Chapel in the Tower*, by Mr. C. Doyne Bell, p. 15.

Just as the Blessed Margaret, Countess of Salisbury, whose ashes also lie in this chapel, had prepared for herself a burial-place that she was destined never to occupy, in the beautiful chantry at Christ Church, Hampshire, so had the Blessed John Fisher prepared his tomb within the chapel of St. John's College, Cambridge.   At the east end of the chapel were three arches in the north wall opening into a side chapel.   In this the bishop had prepared his tomb.   After the Reformation these arches seem to have been walled up and the chapel converted into a lumber-place.   The tomb had been taken to pieces, and the arms of the bishop, with his motto, over the chapel defaced, by order of Crom-well, "and monstrous and ugly antics put in their places ". In 1773, the tomb was found and carried outside, where it was soon destroyed by rain and frost.*

One who says he was a young scholar of St. John's Col-lege at the time of the bishop's martyrdom has recorded his recollections in a paper now in the British Museum : "He founded a chapel beside the high altar of the said college, and a tomb of white stone finely wrought, where he purposed to have been buried if God would so have dis-posed.   He founded a dirge to be sung yearly for him, at which the master of the college should have a noble, the president a crown, every fellow 3s. 4d., and every scholar 12d.   Also he founded thirty trentals to be said for him by the priests within that college, so that each should have said four trentals in one year." †

Besides these suffrages, the university had bound itself in 1528 to celebrate an annual obit, with dirge and requiem,

---

* See Mr. Turner's Introduction to Lewis' *Life of Fisher*, p. xxx., and Baker's *History of St. John's* (ed. Mayor), p. 567.   When the old chapel was taken down, the three arches, called the Fisher Arches, were re-erected in the new building on the left-hand side of the ante-chapel.

† MS. Harl. 7047, f. 16b.   See *Tablet Newspaper*, Jan. 29, 1887, p. 175.

as for founders of colleges and great benefactors.* His blessed soul had happily no need of these suffrages. It is, however, a pleasure to read that Catholic sympathy on the Continent supplied what tyranny forbade in England. One of Cromwell's correspondents writes to him on 1st September that he hears that "a great obsequy" has been made at Paris six days together, and at Rome for a month, for the late Bishop of Rochester and Sir Thomas More.† Nor is it likely that they were forgotten in Spain or Germany.

* The document is printed by Lewis, App. 21. The bishop's endowment, though made by royal licence, was confiscated in 1545 to the king's use by the Chantry Act.

† *Letters and Papers,* ix. 243 ; Letter of John Whalley.

CHAPTER XIX

THE public execution of a bishop and a cardinal, and of a bishop such as Fisher, whose reputation for sanctity and learning was European, could not fail to make a profound impression. We have seen something of it in the letter of Erasmus.

Chapuys has told us of the shock it gave to everyone in England who had any sense left of right and wrong. It is characteristic of Henry and of his sense of justice, that on the 25th June, three days after Fisher's death, and before the trial of Sir Thomas, the king, as if More was already found guilty and executed, sent round England a circular, in which, among other things, those addressed were commanded "to set forth the treasons of the late Bishop of Rochester and Sir Thomas More".* In England, however, there was a reign of terror, and few dared to express their thoughts. Let us see what was thought and felt and said in Rome and elsewhere.

A boastful letter of Casale, written from Rome immediately after Fisher's elevation to the cardinalate, has already been given. On the 1st June, he wrote again: "The French ambassador has received letters about certain monks executed in England for denying that the king could be supreme in the English Church.† A copy of the letters was read in consistory. They are full of pity for the monks;

---

* Burnet, vi. 106; *Letters and Papers*, viii. 921.
† These were the priors put to death on 4th May.

they make a great deal of the matter, and report that they gave most wise and holy answers to the king's council, and the kind of death is explained as most cruel. There was great talk in Rome on the subject, and some even of the cardinals said they envied such a death, and wished they belonged to the band. To those who related this to me, I replied that they might tell the cardinals, that if they really wished such a death, they might go to England and imitate the folly of the monks." But Casale adds immediately in cypher : " I really wondered that the French ambassador showed those letters, nor do I quite know what he means. . . . As regards the execution of the monks, it is Frenchmen especially who are surprised at it. . . . I have heard that directly after Rochester's elevation the imperial ambassador sent a courier to Flanders with orders to boast in the first letters written into England that he has been made a cardinal by Imperialist influence." *

The news of Fisher's death had not reached Rome except as a rumour on the 16th July, when Casale wrote again that the pope had sent for him and told him he had heard from the Imperialists that all England rejoiced at Rochester's promotion and praised the pope's goodness, and that the king of England had sent immediately to inquire of Fisher, if he had sought for the honour ; and when it was found that he knew nothing about it, the day of his death had been fixed, unless he should retract what he had maintained hitherto. " I laughed at all this," says Gregory, " saying that I would not answer such tales unless I saw letters from England or France. . . . The whole trick of Rochester's creation has now been found. It was an invention of the Archbishop of Capua,† who brought the pope to believe that he would gain eternal glory if he named Contarini and Rochester cardinals, without consulting

* *State Papers*, vii. 426.   † Nicholas Schomberg.

anyone.   And thus the archbishop did his own affair, for
he got the dignity he coveted with the rest."   He adds that
he thinks it better for himself to get away from Rome for a
time, so he will go and take the baths at Lucca.*

On the 27th July he writes from Ferrara that he does not
wish to return to Rome without instructions how to behave
and what to answer about all these matters.   The death of
the Bishop of Rochester was spoken of as certain in Rome
a month ago.   He had always said that both he and More
were condemned to death long before by Parliament, whose
statutes the king never opposed ; but he had mercifully
allowed delay that they might acknowledge their folly.   As
they would not recant he could not prevent justice taking
its course.   To those who have spoken of it since the news
came, he has denied that the king executed him because he
was created a cardinal, as he cared little what the pope did
in England in the way of making bishops or cardinals or anything else.   Still he asks for instructions.†   A correspondent
of Peter Vannes writes from Rome less boastfully : "The
pope has conceived incredible indignation.   A consistory
was held on the subject and I hear on good authority that
they will proceed to the utmost possible extremities towards
us.   The pope seems a resolute man, and would sooner have
seen his two grandsons slain."   Gregory de Casale has also
heard from Rome, and writes from Bologna, 20th July : "The
pope and Court are in the greatest indignation about the death
of Rochester ; they say the Court of Rome will make more
account of his death than of that of St. Thomas himself.
Cardinal Tournon's letter describing it moved everybody to
tears.   It was read in a consistory specially invoked."‡

* *State Papers*, vii. 429.   † *State Papers*, vii. 430.

‡ *State Papers*, vii. 621.   "Curiam pluris facturam hujus
hominis mortem quam illam S. Thomæ." Mr. Gairdner has translated this in *Cal.* (viii. 1144) : "His death will do more for the Court
of Rome than that of St. Thomas," which sounds selfish and is incorrect.   The true meaning will be seen in the pope's letters.

The result of this consistory may be seen in the following letter of Pope Paul III. to Ferdinand of Hungary, " King of the Romans":

"We doubt not that your majesty has heard of the cruel slaughter of John, Bishop of Rochester and Cardinal, and has been greatly shocked both on account of the dignity and sanctity of the man and of the cause of his death. . . . For Henry, King of England, had impiously and unjustly put away our dear daughter and your aunt, Catharine, Queen of England, with whom he had contracted marriage with the dispensation of the Apostolic See, and by whom he had children, and during her lifetime had by his own authority taken Anne to be his adulterous wife, and to veil his crime he denied the validity of his marriage with Catharine, and the power of the Apostolic See. He withdrew also his kingdom from obedience to the Apostolic See, to which it was tributary, and in many ways cast himself into the company of heretics, besides many other unworthy and impious deeds. And since these things displeased the good, if any found fault with his marriage with an adulteress, he caused them to be arrested, incarcerated, and put to death. For three whole years Christendom and this Apostolic See have patiently borne with his impiety, hoping for his amendment; but how fruitlessly his last deeds have shown. For when in our late creation of cardinals, to honour the virtue and sanctity of the Bishop of Rochester, we placed him among their number, hoping that that dignity, which is everywhere wont to be accounted venerable, would be effective in procuring his freedom, in this also Henry chose to be like himself in his former many cruelties, and like his forefather, Henry II., by whose hatred and persecution the Blessed Thomas, Bishop of Canterbury, became a martyr But this Henry has far exceeded the impiety of the former one. *He* slew one only, this man many. He slew the defender of the rights of one particular Church, this man the

defender of the rights of the Church universal. He an
archbishop, this man a cardinal of the Roman Church.
The former Henry, when obliged to clear himself before
Alexander III., cast the blame on others, and humbly
received the penance laid on him by the Roman Pontiff.
Whereas this Henry most obstinately defends his deed,
shows no repentance, but obstinacy and enmity. And he
has not the excuse that he has been injured by the Roman
Church, for by her he was adorned with the title of
Defender of the Faith, a title which he has ungratefully
wrested to the injury of the faith."

The pope then exhorts the King of the Romans, together
with his brother, the emperor, according to the piety of
their forefathers, to help the Holy See in the execution of
justice on a king who is heretic and schismatic, a notorious
adulterer, a public murderer, a sacrilegious rebel, guilty of
high treason against the Church, a despiser of the censures
of the Church, under which he has lain for two years, and
therefore rightly deprived of his kingdom. His messenger
will explain more.* This was written on 22nd July, 1535.
Four days later the pope addressed a similar letter to the
King of France.

"Expecting to hear from day to day of the liberation of
John, Cardinal of Rochester, having recommended him
most earnestly to Francis, has been astounded at the
announcement of his execution by King Henry. Doubts
not but that Francis is sorely grieved, seeing that his intercession would appear to have hastened the cardinal's death.
Deplores his loss to the Church, and especially the degrading mode of death inflicted on him. Regrets still more the
cause of his death—defending, not the rights of a particular
Church, as St. Thomas of Canterbury, but the truth of the
universal Church. Henry has thus exceeded his ancestor

* Printed by Chaco (Ciaconius) in his *Lives of the Popes and
Cardinals*, tom. iii., p. 574.

in wickedness. Not content with disregarding the censures of Clement VII., and remaining obstinate under them for two years, with the notorious adultery, which gives rise to scandal in the Church, with the sacrilegious slaughter of so many clerks and religious men, with heresy and schism, and the withdrawal of his kingdom from the universal Church and from obedience to the Roman Church, to which it is tributary, he commanded publicly to be executed a man who was elevated to the cardinalate because of his learning and holiness, after endeavouring to get him to recant and to deny the truth, which he would not do; and hastened his death on hearing of his creation as cardinal, thus committing the crime of lese-majesty, and incurring the usual penalties, especially that of privation.

" Is not ignorant of Henry's intrigues with Francis at the last meeting at Calais, tending to the universal destruction, nor of their repulse by Francis. Out of respect for Francis, and in hope of Henry's repenting, has for more than three years patiently borne many and great injuries, but has gained nothing. Is compelled therefore, at the unanimous solicitation of the cardinals, to declare Henry deprived of his kingdom and his royal dignity ; and the Roman Church has recourse to Francis, her most dear son,—having always been accustomed to have recourse to his predecessors in her oppressions,—and earnestly implores him to be ready to execute justice on Henry when required, remembering the great armies with which his forefathers avenged her injuries. Refers him to the Bishop of Faenza, papal nuncio, for further particulars.

" Rome, at St. Mark's, 26th July, 1535, pont. 1."

It is needless to say that the jealousies and dissensions of the kings of Europe did not allow them to heed these appeals of the Sovereign Pontiff, which were in harmony with tne public international law of Christendom as then accepteα. The bull of solemn and formal deposition was never published, though drawn up and printed, and to be found at the present day in the Bullarium of Paul III. It was about to be published when Catharine's death, 7th January, 1536, cooled whatever little warmth the emperor may have felt against his uncle-in-law; and the death of Anne Boleyn in May caused the pope to entertain hopes of Henry's repentance, the cause of his sin being removed. Meantime, whether it was that rumours of this action on the part of the pope had reached Henry's ears, or that he heard of the general indignation that he had stirred up on the Continent, and feared the effects, he thought it expedient to malign the men he had butchered, " with a meanness worthy of the ferocity which sent them to the scaffold," to use the words of a modern writer.*

The following is the letter written by Cromwell at Henry's dictation to Sir John Wallop, the king's representative at the Court of France : " Concerning the executions done within this realm, ye shall say to the French king, that the same were not so marvellous extreme as he allegeth. For, touching Mr. More and the Bishop of Rochester, with such others as were executed here, their treasons, conspiracies, and practices, secretly practised, as well within the realm as without, to move and stir dissension, and to sow sedition within the realm, intending thereby not only the destruction of the king, but also the whole subversion of the same, being explained and declared and openly detected, *and so manifestly proved before them, that they could not avoid nor deny it*, and they thereof lawfully convicted and condemned of high treason by the due order of the law of this realm, so that it shall and may well appear to all the world that they, having such malice rooted in their hearts against their prince and sovereign, and the total destruction of the common-weal of this realm, were well worthy, if they had had a thousand lives, to have suffered ten times a more terrible death and

* Turner, in his Introduction to Lewis, p. vi.

execution than any of them did suffer." As the indictments
of both Fisher and More are yet in existence, we know what
to think of the audacity of this lie. In another part of the
letter, which is too verbose to copy at length, the king, or
Cromwell in his name, says : " Touching such words as the
said French king spake unto you concerning how Mr. More
died, and what he said to his daughter going to his judgment,
and also what exhortations he should give unto the king's
subjects to be true and obedient unto his grace, I assure you
that there was no such thing, and the king's highness
cannot otherwise take it but very unkindly that the said
French king should so lightly give ear, faith, and credence
to any such vain bruits and fleeing tales, not having first
knowledge or advertisement from the king's highness here
of the verity and truths. . . .

" At Thornbery, the 23rd August." *

Meantime Cromwell's protegé Richard Moryson had
written home from Italy of the intensity of feeling prevailing
everywhere at the report of these executions : " Itali
Roffensis trudicatione gravissime commoventur, Mori autem
sic offenduntur ut nullis convitiis pæne temperent ".† To
counteract these reports, in September the calumny was
elaborated more fully in a Latin letter sent to Gregory da
Casale. The king is surprised that the pope and his Court
are so offended and indignant at the deaths of the Bishop
of Rochester and of More. The king owes no account of
his actions except to God, with whose will they are in perfect
harmony ; nevertheless, to put a stop to calumny, he will
relate the matter succinctly. When then the king by the
favour of God, and with the counsel of the most learned and
virtuous men of Christendom, whose minds and affections
were free from all bias, had brought his great cause to an
end, these good men, who were greatly disappointed, began

---

* MS. Harl. 288, fol. 39-46 ; Lewis, i., vii-xii.
† *Letters and Papers*, ix. 198 ; Letter of 27th August, 1535.

to turn their thoughts maliciously in another direction ; and when the king, as was his duty, was endeavouring to provide for the peace of his kingdom, and to reform the corrupt manners of his people, they tried, though fruitlessly, under specious pretexts to resist his efforts. The king had clear proofs of their wickedness, but he made light of them, hoping that his indulgence would lead them to a better mind ; for hitherto he had held them in some esteem, not really knowing their characters.

"They, on the contrary, led away by ambition, self-love, and their own private judgments, obstinately abused the kindness of their sovereign ; and when Parliament was summoned they began to inquire secretly with great care what matters would be treated and what measures taken ; and whatever they discovered by report, or from guess or usage, taking counsel together, they interpreted in a way adverse to the interests of the State, and opposed with such arguments and reasons as might easily have seduced the ignorant multitude.

"But as their evil consciences made them fear that the king was offended with them, and that they could not themselves easily carry out their secret projects, they made choice of some whom they knew to be bold, and fluent, and self-interested ; and, insinuating themselves into their friendship and familiarity, they poured out their venom into their minds, utterly forgetful of their faith and duty to the king and affection to their country. All this was not hidden from the vigilance of the king. The great iniquity of these men, who were thought so upright, was made manifest by witnesses, by letters in their own handwriting sent by the one to the other, and by their own oral confession. These and many other such matters at last compelled the most just prince to cast into prison these rebels, these enemies of their country, these disturbers of public peace, these impious and seditious men. Unless he wished the contagion to spread, to the neglect of his office, he could not act otherwise.

" In prison they were treated more gently and humanely than their crimes deserved. The king allowed them to converse with their relatives; their own favourite servants were permitted to wait on them ; such food was granted to them and such dress as their own relatives and friends judged most suited to their temperaments and the preservation of their health. But in spite of this mercy of the king, all good faith, all obedience, all love of what is right, utterly forsook these rebels and traitors; for when, after long and mature deliberation, with absolute unanimity certain laws and statutes were made in Parliament for the common good of the kingdom, and in perfect accordance with the true Christian religion, these men alone refused to acquiesce, always hoping that with time something might happen to favour their impiety, while they pretended that they had laid aside all thought of human affairs and were intent solely on the contemplation of divine things. In the meantime they gave all their thoughts and vigils, prisoners though they were, how they might elude and refute by their fallacies and juggling arguments these holy laws. Of their impious and perfidious minds there are most manifest proofs : their own handwriting in coal and chalk, when ink was wanting to them ; their secret messages sent backwards and forwards. They could not deny the letters that had passed between them and been burnt.*

" The most clement king might not longer tolerate such atrocious guilt, and committed them to open trial and judgment. They were found guilty of high treason and

* In the instructions given to Edward Foxe, Bishop of Hereford, when sent as ambassador into Germany, he is to say that More and Fisher " were of such traitorous hearts as even when in prison to plan an insurrection within the realm, as proved by a great number of honest men " ! (*Letters and Papers* ix. 215.

rebellion and condemned. Their punishment was far more lenient than the laws require or their fault deserved.

"From all this, anyone of unbiassed judgment can clearly perceive how rashly the Pontiff and Roman Court have taken offence. But when malicious men cease to make false suggestions, and the road of lies is closed against them, the Curia will lay aside its indignation. . . . Omit not, then, to make known everything that is here set down. His majesty will be delighted when pure and simple truth is no longer obscured by calumny. However, if lying reports so prevail that truth can find no place in their mind, his majesty with the aid of God will bear with their calumnies. He holds his kingdom in such peace and security, and is so sure of the fidelity and obedience of his subjects, that if any injury is offered to him from outside, he can with God's help easily repel and ward it off.

"From the king's palace at Brumham, Sept., 1535." *

It is perhaps needless to say that Henry's account of his proceedings found no more credence on the Continent than in England. There was one at least who told him openly what men thought and said of him. This was his relative, Reginald Pole, afterwards cardinal. The king had sent him a book, written by Sampson, in defence of the new supremacy, desiring to have his opinion on the subject. In the meantime occurred the martyrdom of Fisher and More. Pole sent the king a treatise, afterwards printed, on the Unity of the Church. He thus addressed the king:

"Is it possible? Could you slay men like these, who by your own judgment in former days, and by the judgment of all, were held in the highest esteem for innocence, virtue, and learning, and that for no other reason than that they would not violate their consciences by assenting to your impious. laws? Had you no care for your own judgment, no care for the judgment of other men, to say nothing of

* *State Papers,* vii. 436.

the judgment of God, though you knew that their memory
would be loved and venerated by all good men for ever?
Could you slay Fisher? Could you slay More? Could
you conceive such a crime, and bring on yourself such a
disgrace? I was not present, but when I think of it, it is
like a dreadful nightmare, and those who tell me of it seem
to be relating dreams. Why, Nero and Domitian, though
sworn enemies of the Christian name, had they known
these men as you knew them, could not have been so cruel
towards them. And I am bold to swear, that Luther himself, had he been king in England in your place, though
these two men were his direst adversaries, would not have
conceived the thought of avenging himself in such a way.
What great evil had they done you, these men who never
injured you in word or deed? They refused to subscribe
to your impious decree. But what if they refused; was
not perpetual imprisonment penalty enough, which already
you had inflicted on them, so that, when you dragged them
forth to death they had already for fifteen months endured
the squalor of their prison? O God, a torment like this
inflicted on such men, for no fault whatever but for their
splendid deeds, would have satisfied abundantly the cruelty
of the greatest barbarian; but yours it did not satisfy.
From their prison you dragged them out, like dead enemies
from their tombs, to feed your fierce and cruel will on the
butchery of their bodies. Condemned to perpetual prison,
they were as men dead and buried. What new thing had
they done that you should bring them forth to a second
death? Nothing whatever, but your impiety could not rest,
but pushed you on to add crime to crime. If you were not
driven on blindly by furies, you could give some kind of
reason (I do not say a just one, for such could not be
imagined, even though your law, instead of being unjust
and impious, had been most just), but at least some reason
with an appearance of legality. But how can such a reason

be found against men who even before the law was promulgated were condemned to perpetual bonds? They had no
longer the rights or name of citizens, and could not be
required to say whether they approved or disapproved of laws.
And More, who was so well learned in matters of justice,
objected this very thing on his trial. Never before was it
heard of that anyone who had violated the law neither in
word or deed should be condemned for mere silence.
But setting aside the injustice, what was your end and
purpose? What evil did you seek to avoid, what good
to attain? Tyrants have one or other of these ends in
view. I see what you wanted—to silence all; for who could
expect clemency when More and Rochester were condemned to death? But your counsel has been defeated.
The good, whom alone you feared, are by no means terrified.
They are encouraged by the example of More and Fisher.
If they were silent before, it was not from fear, but because
while those men lived they were not without hope of your
return to a sound mind. They did not wish to irritate you
by word or deed before the time. But now you have filled
all minds with indignation. Never was Christian king
spoken of in such words as are applied to you. I experience
a strange change in myself. Hitherto I ever kept silence,
and felt alarm; now I am bold to speak openly. I will tell
what has happened to me, and God is my witness that I
speak the truth. When first I heard of this slaughter, for a
month I was like one stupefied and without voice, being
stunned with the novelty of the thing and its unheard of
cruelty. But when I had recovered myself, as I had ever
been of the same mind as those men, I determined, not as
hitherto, to whisper what I thought into friendly ears, but,
in the words of Christ, to preach it from the roof-top." *

Pole was not ignorant of the probable consequences of
these burning words, not to himself, who was out of the

* *De Uniiate Eccl.,* lib. iii.

tyrant's reach, but to his mother and other relatives resident
in England. He was admonished by several to modify his
reproaches, but after long deliberation he could not find it
in his conscience to do so. It is well known that Henry,
not being able to revenge himself on the author of this
treatise, caused his aged mother, the Countess of Salisbury,
to be beheaded. Bishop Latimer reveals to us the instigator of this and the rest of the judicial murders.
It was Thomas Cromwell, Henry's evil genius. After the
Countess's attainder, Latimer congratulated Cromwell in these
words : "I heard you say once, after you had seen that
furious invective of Cardinal Pole, that you would make him
eat his own heart, which you have now brought to pass ; for
he must needs now eat his own heart, and become as heartless as he is graceless ".* What more striking evidence of
the havoc wrought in men's minds by the contagion of
Henry's blood-thirst than words so atrocious, gloating over
the expected death of a venerable lady and the broken
heart of her innocent and exiled son, because he had dared
to utter a protest against the cruelty that had robbed him
of his dearest friends and England of her noblest sons.

To these earthly judgments regarding the bishop's martyrdom I will add one which, if it is not directly a heavenly
communication, is at least the dream of one whose conversation was more in heaven than on earth :

"Memorandum, that I, John Darley, monk of the Charterhouse, beside London, had in my time licence to say service with a father of our religion named Father Raby, a
very old man, insomuch when he fell sick and lay upon his
deathbed, and after the time he was aneled and had received all the sacraments of the Church in the presence of
all the convent, and when all they were departed I said
unto him : 'Good Father Raby, if the dead may come to

* Wright's *Letters on the Suppression of Monasteries*, Letter 71
(Camden Soc.).

the quick, I beseech you to come to me,' and he said,
'Yea,' and immediately he died in the cleansing days last
past, anno 1534,* and since that I never did think upon
him to St. John Baptist day last past "—*i.e.*, two days after
the bishop's martyrdom.   He then relates an apparition,
when Father Raby told him of the glory of the martyred
prior, John Haughton, and the rest of his brethren, and
continues: "*Item*, upon Saturday next, at five o'clock in
the morning, he appeared to me again with a long white
beard and a white staff in his hand, lifting it up, whereupon
I was afraid.   And then leaning upon his staff said to me:
'I am sorry I lived not to I had been a martyr'.   And
I said: 'I think ye be as well as ye were a martyr'.   And
he said: 'Nay, for my Lord of Rochester and our father
was next unto angels in heaven'.   And then I said: 'What
else?'   And then he answered and said: 'The angels of
peace did lament and mourn without measure,' and so
vanished away.

"Written by me, John Darley, monk of the Charterhouse,
the 27th day of June, the year of Our Lord God aforesaid." †

The document just quoted must have got known and
been copied and spread abroad, since on 24th October,
1535, Dr. Ortiz, one of the emperor's envoys at Rome,
writes as follows: "Letters from England say that in the
Charter House of London various revelations have been
made by a deceased monk, who has appeared to many of
the brotherhood; which revelations had reference to the
glorious crown of martyrdom which the Cardinal of Rochester and the other saints lately executed have obtained, thus
opening for them the gate of paradise; and that Master

---

* *I.e.*, in Lent, 1535, New Style, since the year began on 25th
March. Lewis sneeringly says that Darley's vision occurred a year
before the bishop's death. If so, Darley would have been a prophet.

† *Cotton MS.* (Brit. Mus.), E. iv., fol. 129. Lewis, App. 37.

Cromwell—he that is bringing about all that Anne, the king's mistress, desires—has strictly forbidden the publication of the said revelations. Good Christians, however, have no need of such revelations ; martyrdom for faith they know opens the gates of heaven." *

The people of England were not slow in interpreting signs of God's displeasure against the king. On June 30th Chapuys urges certain measures to provoke a rising, "for many begin already to show discontent, saying that ever since these executions it has never ceased raining in England, and that is God's revenge" ;† and again on the 6th September : "The harvest has been very scanty indeed this year, and there is every appearance of a famine, owing to which your majesty cannot form an idea of the continuous importunities with which I am daily assailed on every side, soliciting the execution of the Apostolic censures, all people here believing that such a resolution on your majesty's part would be a sufficient remedy, considering the great discontent prevailing among all classes of society here at this king's disorderly life and government".‡

Lastly, not to forget the queen, to whom the death of her zealous champion must have been inexpressibly painful, Catharine wrote on 10th October, 1535, to her nephew the emperor, that "she finds a great consolation in the idea that she may, perhaps, have to follow so many blessed martyrs in the manner of their death. She is only sorry that she could not imitate them in life".§ On the 13th December the queen wrote again to her zealous friend in Rome, Dr. Ortiz, in answer to his exhortations to patience and hope : "You ought urgently to solicit from his holiness that the good work which the pope has commenced should be promptly executed. For, should there be the least hesitation or delay, it will be tantamount to letting the devil, who

* *Spanish Cal.*, v. 217. † *Ib.*, 179.
‡ *Ib.*, 201. § *Ib.*, 210.

hitherto has been only half bound, entirely loose and at liberty to do mischief. I cannot, indeed dare not, write to you in clearer terms. It will be sufficient if, as a prudent and wise man, you understand what I mean."*   In less than a month from writing this letter, this holy queen, whose last years had been one of the most cruel martyrdoms ever inflicted by tyrant, and one of the bravest ever endured by victim, went to join her friend and guide and comforter in paradise. She died 7th January, 1536.

* *Spanish Cal.*, v. 257.

CHAPTER XX.

T HE first apologists of the Reformation thought it necessary both to eulogise Henry and to depreciate his victims. William Thomas, who wrote in the time of Edward VI., and whose book has been reprinted by Mr. Froude, records Fisher's death in the following style : "The cardinal's hat was already upon the way coming to the Bishop of Rochester, not only as a worthy reward of his merit, but also as a buckler under the which the pope thought to handle his cruel sword. His highness, fearing the example of his predecessor, King John, or ever the hat arrived, shaved the bishop's crown by the shoulders, to see afterwards where the pope would bestow his cardinal's hat." * Bale, another contemporary, and a Protestant bishop, writes of Fisher, and Godwin, another Protestant bishop, copies him, with only a feeble apology that he is a little too severe (*paulo acerbius*) : "Fisher is described by Erasmus as a man stuffed full (*suffarcinatissimus*) of all episcopal virtues. . . . When the eternal truth of God began to shine upon the Germans from the Gospel, no one grew hotter, no one raged more mightily against it, than this Papistical driveller and impostor, with an eye only to his purse and his belly. . . . The mad old dotard suffered capital punishment." † These are but specimens which it would be easy, but nauseous, to multiply.

* *Il Pelerino Inglese*, or The Pilgrim, p. 31.
† Godwin, *De Præsulibus*.

At the present day very few followers of the Reformation would willingly speak ill of Fisher, or would care to defend Henry, yet they see no lesson for themselves in the contrast. Anthony à Wood greatly shocked Burnet when he wrote as follows about the Reformation : "Truth ought to take place and must not be concealed, especially when it is at a distance. And if our religion hath had its original or base on lust, blood, ruin, and desolation, as all religions or alterations in government have had from one or more of them, why should it be hidden, seeing it is too obvious to all curious searchers into records?" There was some candour in this language; but if Anthony à Wood meant that the Christian religion as well as the Protestant reform of it had its origin in the lust and cruelty of its founders, it is a reading of history that is new and paradoxical; nor is it easy to find any of these hateful *bases* of religion in its first introduction into England, as related by Venerable Bede. "Lust and cruelty" were its opponents then, as they were its "ruin and desolation" in the 16th century.

When it was found that the beginnings of Protestantism were such that no self-respecting historian could either defend or palliate them, recourse was had to the principle that God brings good out of evil, and even to the inspired words that He employs foolish things to confound the wise. Mr. Guthrie, in his *History of England*, writes : "As true history ought never to be a varnish of falsehood or softenings of prejudice, we are afraid of no censure in saying that the light of English reformation—as the Spirit of God did upon the earth when it was without form—moved upon a chaos of jarring, unconnected, repugnant, tyrannical principles. Order, indeed, arose out of this confusion, but the human agents are by no means to be justified." * Mr. Guthrie does not show how the light of the Reformation was distinct from the principles over which it moved; nor does

* *History of England*, vol. iv., p. 1036.

he explain wherein the order consists that was the result of this moving.

A writer of the present century, the Rev. Dr. Russell, is so delighted with this new genesis of Protestantism that he grows pious over the misdeeds of the reformers. "In reviewing," he says, "the great events of history, and more especially such as have had the most direct influence on the progress of religious truth, it must occur to every reader that there is a remarkable contrast between the instruments which have been employed by Divine Wisdom and the results which have flowed from their operation. Whether we look at the monastery of Wittemberg, or to the council chamber of Henry VIII., or to the castle of St. Andrews, nothing will be seen that can minister to human pride, or exalt our estimate of the purity and disinterestedness of human motives." * Let the reader pause for a moment at this astounding paradox, and imagine for himself an apologist for Christianity writing in this way of St. Peter and St. Paul, or of the assembly in the "upper room" at Jerusalem. Yet this principle, not of good out of evil, but of good by means of evil, appears now to have become an accepted commonplace among English Protestant writers. Quite lately Canon Jenkins wrote: "As the political divisions of the kingdom and the power of the collateral branches of the royal family had assisted in so great a degree the progress of the doctrine of Wycliff, so it was ordained that the excesses, and even sins, of the autocratic Henry should, by freeing the Church of England from the papal yoke, bring in the reign of a reformed Church and faith". †

The Rev. Dr. Knight, in his *Life of Erasmus*, writes: "It is an objection to the Reformation in England that Henry VIII. was a blustering prince, haughty and resolute, and affecting his own will and pleasure. It is enough to

---

* *History of the Church of Scotland*, ch. v.
† *Diocesan History of Canterbury*, p. 240.

say that a milder prince would not have done much in so
rugged a work.   When God has His providential works to
do, He knows how to raise up such instruments as are best
adapted to attempt, prosecute, and perform them in their
own time." *   This theory of God's wicked instruments is
not surprising in a writer of the 18th century; yet
Canon Perry, as lately as 1886, lays down the following
basis for his *History of the Reformation in England:* "It
would be impossible to find in all history a genuine record
of any great revolution, either in Church or State, wherein
all the agents had proceeded upon pure, disinterested
motives, and which was entirely uncontaminated by ambition, self-seeking, covetousness, or any of the baser motives
of human actions".   So far the proposition makes no great
demand on the candour of his reader; but as a sailor,
anxious to moor his vessel safe, throws to the shore a small
rope, and he who catches it soon finds that there is attached
to its end a great cable, the loop of which he is expected to
throw over a strong pillar, so acts the apologist of the
Reformation.   We have seen the small rope, now follows
the cable.   "Certainly," continues Canon Perry, "an exception to this cannot be claimed in favour of the English
Reformation of the 16th century, whether we look at the
usurping and tyrannical king, the timid and too subservient
clergy, or the grasping and unprincipled laity."   Another
pause, good reader.   The first proposition was that there
has been no great movement in which all agents were
absolutely perfect.   The second, introduced as a mere
exemplification of the first, is that in the Reformation all
the agents were thoroughly bad.   And now follows a third,
not that this is to be considered a blemish or a drawback,
but that it was a necessary condition of success.   The words
following immediately on the above are these: "Yet reflection shows that there were advantages in these evil

* *Life of Erasmus, Frei.. p. xli.*

features. Nothing less than the bold, overbearing temper of the king would have been adequate to head the movement which brought about the emancipation of England from the tyranny of Rome. A bolder struggle for ancient rights on the part of the clergy might have led to the utter apostasy of the State, and the covetous greed with which the laymen fell upon ecclesiastical property gave a stability to the work of change which it could not probably have acquired in any other way."[*] These are not the words of some bitter satirist, nor even of a Gibbon or a Macaulay. They are the calm reasoning of a dignitary of the Church of England. And to conclude this series of apologists for the Reformation in England with one who deserves to be found in better company than the above, Dr. Stubbs, the present Bishop of Chester, writes: "You will not suspect me of making Henry VIII. the founder of the Church of England; but I do not conceal from myself that, under the Divine Power which brings good out of evil and overrules the wrath of man to the praise of God, we have received good as well as evil through the means of this 'majestic lord who broke the bonds of Rome'."[†]

We are almost inclined to ask, Are these writers disciples of Christ or of Mahomet? Surely not of Him who sent out His disciples as sheep among wolves, and said: "Fear not, little flock, it hath pleased your Father to give you the kingdom". According to the above theories, victory is with the wolves, and a certain wolfishness is even a necessary condition of victory. Good out of evil, forsooth! Yes, for those who suffer the evil, not for those who do it; for the Fishers and the Mores, not for the Henrys and Elizabeths.

Let, then, the followers of the Reformation look back upon it from their own point of view; let them prove—and

* *History of Reformation in England*, p. 2.
† *Lectures on Mediæval and Modern History*, p. 262.

28

we will not contest their accuracy—that violence in the
king, servility in the clergy, avarice in the laity, were necessary conditions of its triumph; let them look with shame
on its heroes, and say with affected humility: "All glory be
to God, there is nothing here in which we can take com-
placency"; let them represent the Almighty, with Calvinistic blasphemy, as choosing evil tools, not to chastise His
loved ones for a time, but to build up His own work. The
Reformation has been a success; it has prevailed and it
prevails. Let its followers explain it as they will. As for
us, we know that there are successes which are failures.
There is no greater calamity or chastisement than when
God allows evil to prevail.

So also there are failures which are triumphs, and such
is generally martyrdom. But can this be said of Fisher, if
the cause which he opposed has been victorious? It may
be thought by some that the life of Fisher was lived in vain,
and his blood was shed to no purpose as far as this world is
concerned. And it might be said in explanation that England was reduced to such extremity by the sins of priests
and people that the few just men, as in the days of Ezechiel,
were ineffectual as intercessors. "If I send the pestilence
upon that land, and pour out my indignation upon it in
blood, and Noe and Daniel and Job be in the midst thereof;
as I live, saith the Lord God, they shall deliver neither son
nor daughter, but they shall only deliver their own soul by
their justice."* If we may be allowed reverently to conjecture the secrets of God's justice and of His mercy from
the page of history, such was not His wrath against England.
On the contrary, the influence of the holy lives, the fervent
prayers, and the heroic deaths of the first martyrs of Henry
has been wide and lasting, has gone on ever increasing, and
seems destined to be even more effectual in the future than

* Ezech. xv. 19, 20.

in the past. With a slight sketch of these consoling results I will close this study.

Before commencing the narrative of Fisher's life, I recalled the pathetic lamentation he made over the state of the world in the year 1505, when his prayer was that God would arise and have mercy upon Sion, for the time had come to have mercy upon her, the time had come. His prayer may have seemed to him to have been rejected. Things had gone from bad to worse, and were rapidly hastening to utter ruin. He could say with Elias : " With zeal have I been zealous for the Lord God of hosts : for the children of Israel have forsaken Thy covenant, they have thrown down Thy altars, they have slain Thy prophets with the sword, and I alone am left, and they seek my life to take it away ".* Indeed, there is something very gloomy in the words penned by him in the Tower, in the year 1534, when the shades of death were gathering round him. " Woe to us," he writes, "who have been born in this wretched age, an age—I say it weeping—in which anyone who has any zeal whatever for the glory of God, and casts his eyes on the men and women who now live, will be moved to tears to see everything turned upside down, the beautiful order of virtue overthrown, the bright light of life quenched, and scarce anything left in the Church but open iniquity and feigned sanctity. The light of good example is extinguished in those who ought to shine as luminaries to the whole world, like watch-towers and beacons on the mountains. No light, alas ! comes from them, but horrid darkness, and pestilent mischief, by which innumerable souls are falling into destruction." †

These words, however, were not a cry of despair, they were not a lamentation over hopeful prayers poured out to

* 3 *Kings* xix. 10.

† *De necessitate orandi. Ratio tertia.* This passage is omitted in the old translation, recently reprinted.

deaf ears. On the contrary, they occur in a treatise on prayer, and are part of an exhortation to go with confidence to the throne of grace to find help when most in need of it. It was not granted to this great servant of God, to this perpetual intercessor for God's people, to see all the fruit of his prayers. Of course he never doubted that in England, as well as throughout the whole breadth of the Church, there were many holy souls. It was a favourite saying of his that the Holy Ghost, who ever inhabits the Church, cannot remain idle.* But he was not to learn till after death by what magnificent creations of sanctity the Holy Ghost was already in those last days of his on earth beginning to renew the face of the Church. He lamented especially the state of the clergy. Yet what holy popes, bishops, priests, founders and reformers of religious orders, legislators, and missionaries were even then at work, or preparing for their work by a most holy life. The prospect before his eyes was that of a people betrayed by their pastors, of pulpits long silent and now vocal only with insults to God's vicar, and of the glorious Church of St. Gregory and St. Augustine foundering in heresy and schism. Yet on the feast of Our Lady's Assumption, the 15th August, 1534, while he, a bishop, banished from his people, deposed from his see, shut in a dark prison, without mass, without communion, was calling on the Queen of Mercy to stay the arm of God's vengeance, in Our Lady's Church at Montmartre in Paris the Blessed Peter Faber was offering that eventful mass at which St. Ignatius, St. Francis Xavier, with four companions, whose names are hardly less illustrious, pronounced their first vows and laid the foundations of the Society of Jesus. Could Fisher in spirit have seen

---

* "Sancti Spiritus non otiosa in Ecclesia residentia" (*De Sacerd.*, col. 1241). "Non otiosus esse potest, qui ad tantum negotium, tam inciytus, a tam eximiis personis, Patre videlicet et Filio missus esse non ambigitur" (*Assert. Lut. Conf.*, col. 287).

that act and known its consequences, he would have known that his prayer was answered beyond his hope or imagination.

This was but little. When the beacons seemed to him extinguished, they were being kindled on every mountain. Michael Ghisleri, afterwards better known as Pope St. Pius V., was sanctifying the order of St. Dominick ; St. Thomas of Villanova, afterwards Archbishop of Valencia, as provincial of the Augustinians in Spain, was making reparation for the apostasy of Luther in Germany ; St. Peter of Alcantara, in his poor Franciscan habit, was in ecstasy before the Blessed Sacrament ; Blessed John of Avila was exercising his wonderful apostolate in Andalusia ; St. Cajetan was, by his example and his preaching, kindling the fires of divine love in Naples ; St. Jerome Emilian was drawing near to the close of his holy life in Rome ; St. Lewis Bertrand, a holy child of nine, was beginning those austerities which gave supernatural vigour to his missionary labours in America ; St. Andrew Avellino, a young cleric of fifteen, was growing into that perfect spirit of the priesthood, of which he was to be so great a promoter among the clerks regular ; th spirit of God had already drawn St. Philip Neri to Rome, where, at the age of twenty, he was mature in sanctity ; and St. Francis Borgia, then known as the young Marquis of Gandia, was leading, in the married state, a life so pure and lofty that he was as perfect a model for noble laymen as he afterwards became for priests and religious. I have mentioned only such as were already or were one day to be priests, and have chosen only names that are familiar. Who that knows the meaning of the article of his creed, " I believe in the communion of saints," can doubt that Blessed John Fisher's life and prayers were among the efficient causes of the graces poured out so abundantly on the Church, and that on the other hand the prayers and merits of saints unknown to him were strengthening him in his heroic confessorsi..p and martyrdom ?

We have seen that the fame of his martyrdom soon
spread through Europe; and during the last three centuries,
though the Church, from prudence probably, and not to
stir up fierce fanaticism in England, had delayed to enrol
him in her catalogue of canonised saints, or to give him a
place in her martyrology, the name of John Fisher, the
champion to death of the rights of the Holy See against the
tyrant Henry, has been a household word with every educated
Catholic in Christendom.   Nor was it altogether forgotten
even in his own ungrateful country.   It was certainly the
memory of his constancy that touched the hearts of Tunstal
and Gardiner with sorrow for their weakness and made them
bold to endure years of imprisonment, even before their
reconciliation with the Church.   It was the example shown
by him that upheld the English hierarchy at the accession
of Elizabeth, and prevented them from imitating the recreancy of the courtier bishops of Henry.   I have alluded to
the saints who sprang up so numerously in Europe after the
great apostasy of the 16th century.   But there is one
country especially rich in saints, and of saints who rank in
the first order, that of martyrs.   That country is the land of
Fisher.   Other Churches were the joyful mothers of confessors; the English Church, in her humiliation and agony,
was to bring forth martyrs.   Before the close of the century
which witnessed Fisher's death, hundreds would like him
endure spoliation and imprisonment, and hundreds like him
would be faithful unto death.   And it must be observed
that all, or nearly all, died for the same cause—for resisting
the usurpation by the civil power of supremacy over the
Church.

It is this that has made a thoughtful German writer
remark, that if Anglicanism has kept more of the externals of
the Catholic Church, and seems like Henry himself to have
retained more of the Catholic faith and worship than the
Churches of Luther and of Calvin, yet in reality it is more

deeply opposed to the Divine constitution of the Church and more deeply branded with injustice and cruelty. Not much Catholic blood was deliberately and legally shed in Calvinistic Scotland and Switzerland, or in the Lutheran parts of Germany. It was in England, Wales, and Ireland, where the royal supremacy was forced on unwilling populations, that martyrs were made. "Germany," writes Dr. Kerker, " would not submit to a despotism so gross as that which weighed on England. Her revolutionary movement was the work of theologians, not of princes; not princes but theologians formulated her doctrines and her discipline; and the civil and ecclesiastical powers have ever been kept distinct. In England, on the contrary, though episcopacy has been retained, it derives its jurisdiction from one who makes no pretence to be a bishop. By virtue of civil power alone the State decides for the Church her doctrines and regulates her discipline. It is the most odious form of the Protestant revolt."*

These words of a modern German remind me, by way of a very curious contrast, of a letter written by an Englishman in the 12th century. When Frederick Barbarossa was troubling the face of Christendom, John of Salisbury asked indignantly : "Who has made the Germans judges over the nations? Who has given to these rude and impetuous men authority to set, at their pleasure, a prince over the heads of men? I know well what this German emperor is plotting, for I was at Rome when Eugenius was pope, at the time when the first embassy was sent, at the beginning of this emperor's reign; and their intolerable pride and unguarded tongues laid bare the impudence of their designs. He promised that he would reform the government of the whole world, and bring it all into subjection to Rome, if only the Roman Pontiff would favour his plans. His plan was that against whomsoever the emperor should draw the sword, the

* *Life of Fisher,* part iii., ch. xv.

Roman Pontiff should also draw the spiritual sword. But he has not found yet anyone who will consent to such iniquity."[*]

This ancient plan of tyranny, by making the spiritual power the tool of the civil, and thus degrading both, was one of the favourite schemes of the 16th century. A suggestion was made to the Emperor Charles V. during the siege of Rome in 1527, that either the papacy should be kept low, and made to do the bidding of the empire, or that it should be abolished, and each king should set up a patriarch as the creature and puppet of his own will in his kingdom.[†] By God's providence the emperor consented to neither project. Yet it was in that moment that Henry thought to make the pope the aider and abettor of his own lawless passions; and failing in that, he adopted the scheme of the puppet-patriarch or primate. It is very notable that, in that very crisis of the papacy, the two men who after-wards died for it were upholding it with their prayers. More, we are told, in his parish church of Chelsea, with his family, made earnest supplication for the deliverance of the Holy Father. And Fisher was so zealous in the same holy cause that Wolsey knew no better way to insinuate himself into his confidence, than by speaking to him of public prayer and penance to be done for the wants of the Holy See.[‡] Such men were already martyrs in heart. It was by a special providence of God that Fisher was not called on

---

* Ep. 59 (*Bib. Max. Patr.*, t. xxiii., p. 423).

† See Mr. Brewer's Introduction to vol. iv. of *Letters and Papers*, p. 170.

‡ See p. 153. When Wolsey left Rochester he proceeded to Canterbury, and there presided at the litanies and solemn supplications that were being made for the pope. During these he wept bitterly. Mr. Brewer thinks it was at the foresight of his own ruin. Cavendish, who wit-nessed it, thought it was from compassion for the Holy Father. Though his conduct was not loyal to the Sovereign Pontiff, yet there is no need to reject the view of Cavendish, as if noble thoughts and compunction never visited him.

to shed his blood for any of the sacraments he had maintained against Luther and Œcolampadius, nor More for his
defence of Catholic traditions against Fish and Frith and
Tyndal. They died for something more fundamental still
—for the Divine constitution of the Church, the pillar and
foundation of all truth. Their example thereby became
more practical for all times and persons. It has been often
said, by way of removing from Protestantism the odium of
these cruel deaths, that the Reformation was not begun in
England when More and Fisher died, and that they died by
the hands of a fierce persecutor of Protestants. But if
Henry was neither Lutheran nor Zuinglian, he was the
founder of that which is the essence of Anglicanism, the
supremacy of the civil power in the things of God. He laid
down the doctrine of the Supreme Head, which God's providence, I would almost say His Divine irony,* reduced to
its most ludricous forms in the headship of his child-son
and his bastard and shameless daughter, and showed in its
absurd consequences in the three systems of religion produced by the same authority in those three reigns. It was
against this public tampering and trifling with all truth,
with the very existence of objective and permanent truth
upon the earth, that these noble martyrs protested by their
death. No one can say with any plausibility that they were
victims to their prejudices, or to the superstitions in which
they had been educated, or that they died from obstinate
resistance to progress and blind conservatism. It was, on
the contrary, from a narrow conservatism that the rest of
the bishops yielded to Henry. He was the enemy of
heretics, they thought, the protector of the Church in her
honours and riches in their day. More and Fisher cared
little for this, when they saw him introducing a principle
which might be the source of every error.

   Their crime was said to be treason, not heresy, for fidelity
* " Dominus subsannabit eos " (*Ps.* ii. 4).

to the Church under this new impiety had become treason to the sovereign. They were thus the fitting leaders of a series of martyrs, all of whom were branded as traitors. Even when the charge was that of offering Holy Mass, it was only as treason to the sovereign that it became a deadly crime. The State had long punished heresy with death, considering it a treason against God, and an attack on the fundamental unity of the nation and of Christendom ; but it had neither taken on itself to decide what was heresy, nor to make the malice of heresy consist in resistance to the dictation of the civil power in things Divine. A new crime, that of treason for adhering to the unity of Christendom, was invented by the odious tyranny of Henry, and by him handed down to his successors. Fisher and More died, not merely for fidelity to conscience, a glory not denied to them even by those who think their conscience erroneous and unenlightened. They died for the rights of the human conscience to receive religious Truth from God only, through His own appointed channels ; and not from human power, to which Truth is nothing else than State Expediency.

Yet the death of More and Fisher has also an important bearing even on those works of controversy which were un-connected with the charge of treason, since it proves beyond gainsay their authors' conscientiousness and love of truth,* and explains the only point requiring explanation or apology —a certain asperity that is common to them both. There is no unfairness in their controversy. Fisher quotes his opponents in full, and gives their own words and context, and then meets them openly. Sir Thomas neither under-states the arguments of his antagonists, nor imputes to them

* Dr. Knight, in his *Life of Colet*, has dared to say : "Sir Thomas More was a leading reformer, but human fears and worldly policy stopped him short and turned him out of the way he saw to be right" (p. 147).

what they would repudiate. But they both handle their opponents severely and defend the severity of their language. Why was this? I have already remarked that they were arguing with apostate Catholics, and had a right to use a tone which would ill befit us in controversy with modern Protestants. But there were special reasons for such severity. The controversy of the first Protestants adopted two forms—that of indignant invective or that of unctuous piety. According to their bias, they sought to copy the denunciations of the Prophets or the exhortations of the Apostles. And this language imposed upon the people. When they read the impetuous declamation of Luther against the pope, they were hurried away into the belief that nothing less than some dread mystery of iniquity could have aroused such passion. When they read the "sweet reasonableness" with which Œcolampadius argues against the Real Presence, it seemed the very tone of adoration in spirit and in truth. So it was with our English heresiarchs, with whom More had his encounters. They took both styles as it suited them. Now that which gives freshness and human interest to the writings of More and Fisher, even at the present day, is to see how the mask was stripped off these hypocrites or self-deceivers by both the Churchman and the Statesman. Neither Fisher nor More was naturally disputatious; they had not grown up amidst polemics. The candour of both had long been shown in bewailing or denouncing and correcting the evils that disfigured the Church they loved. But the keen sight of a saintly and contemplative mind made Fisher see through the pretences and shudder at the blasphemies with which the revelations and institutions of God Himself were now attacked; and a similar spiritual sensitiveness, together with a practised wit and shrewdness, made these even more apparent to Sir Thomas. If they had both died full of honours, we might still have appreciated the sincerity and singleness of their hearts in their warmest controversy; but their patient endurance for truth, their death rather than swerve even a hair's-breadth from what they knew to be right, from the path of honour and conscience and allegiance to God, oblige us to admit that zeal for truth, and not for party, had alone sharpened their pens in controversy.

It will, of course, be said that some of the opponents of More, at least, died for their convictions, and that such deaths on either side proved only ardour or sincerity, and not truth. Even were there no difference in the cases, I would reply that my argument at the present moment is for sincerity and simplicity of character rather than objective truth. But the calm dignity with which More and Fisher went to their deaths from amidst dignity and honours may well challenge comparison with the hot enthusiasm or evasions and retractations and relapses of the greater number of Foxe's martyrs. The former died for the one Catholic and Apostolic faith, the latter for private fancies and enthusiasms. To lay down one's life in duty to one's country and to perish in a duel are two different things.

This connection between the writings and the deaths of More and Fisher has been admirably stated by Cardinal Pole. "The disputes," he says, "that the conduct of Henry has aroused in England have brought everything into doubt; men do not know what to believe, which side to take. How can we know, they ask, when clever men, learned men, and, as far as we can see, good men, take opposite sides? Would you not, then, if you could, send ambassadors to Jesus Christ to ask Him to decide? But, you say, this is not serious. Cities of Greece could send ambassadors to consult the oracle, but Christ is in heaven. Nay, but listen : Supposing that you could send an embassy, whom would you send? Not priests only, but priests and laymen—at least one of each class. Now, had you to choose among all the priests and bishops in England, would

there have been any hesitation? Would not all by acclama
tion have selected the Bishop of Rochester? What other
have you, or have you had for centuries, to compare with
Rochester in holiness, in learning, in prudence, and in
episcopal zeal? You may be, indeed, proud of him;
for, were you to search through all the nations of Christendom in our days, you would not easily find one who was
such a model of episcopal virtues. If you doubt of this,
consult your merchants who have travelled in many lands ;
consult your ambassadors; and let them tell you whether
they have anywhere heard of any bishop who has such a
love of his own flock as never to leave the care of it, ever
feeding it by word and example ; against whose life not even
a rash word could be spoken ; one who was conspicuous not
only for holiness and learning, but for love of country?"
After further commendation of Fisher, he proceeds :

" Do you seek a colleague worthy of such a man—a layman of great learning and sanctity, but without superstition
or weakness ; a man acquainted with public affairs and with
men? Again there will be no hesitation. More is that
man. Brought up amongst clever men, learned, incorrupt,
holy, familiar with matters of State, loving his country,
there is no one else in whom all such qualities are united,
at least in such a degree.

" Well, would you not send these on your embassy? But,
see, of their own accord, before you thought of it, they have
undertaken the task and have brought back the answer from
Christ. Both of them by their learned writings have told
you what to think of the disputes of our days; and now,
lest you should doubt whether they really speak in Christ's
name, He has set the same seal on them that He gave to
Himself and His Apostles. He allowed Satan to open the
gates of hell against them and to try them to the utmost,
and He gave them strength in the sight of the whole Church,
of men and of angels, to undergo a contest and win a crown,

than which none more glorious has been won since the days of the Apostles. What! my country, were you not a spectator of this, when every deceit was practised, every snare was spread—on one side the favour of the prince, power, honour, and whatever is delightful to men, and on the other side prison, torment, infamy, and death, or rather deaths? From these two gates all the armies of Satan issued forth and assaulted these two soldiers of Christ to drive them from the citadel of truth. You saw this, my country; you saw not only that they did not faint for fear, nor were driven from the battlements, but, on the contrary, the enemy was repulsed, his war-machines were broken, and they remained more constant than ever in the possession of the truth. You beheld this, and did you not admire? Did you not gather from your admiration how true was their doctrine, how agreeable to the will of Christ? It was not mere death that they encountered with constancy, as even criminals may sometimes do, but they chose it in preference to the favour of the king, to riches and power and honour. This they could not have done without the assistance of Him who gave victory to the martyrs and Apostles." *

Can I better conclude than by again putting before the reader the martyr's own words, already quoted in the first chapter: "Set, O Lord, in Thy Church strong and mighty pillars, that may suffer and endure great labours, watching, poverty, thirst, hunger, cold, and heat, which also shall not fear the threatenings of princes, persecution, neither death. Oh! if it would please Our Lord God to show this goodness in our days, the memorial of this His so doing ought of very right to be left in perpetual writing, never to be forgotten of all our posterity, that every generation might love and wor-ship Him time without end."

The feast of the English martyrs, John Fisher, Thomas More, and others, is kept on the 4th May.

* *De Unitate Eccl.*, lib. iii.

ORATIO.

Deus, qui beatos martyres tuos, Joannem Pontificem, Thomam eorumque socios, veræ fidei summique sacerdotii propugnatores, inter Anglos omni ex ordine suscitasti: eorum meritis ac precibus concede: ut ejusdem fidei professione unum omnes, sicut tuus rogavit Filius, efficiamur et simus: Qui tecum vivit ac regnat in unitate Spiritus Sancti, Deus, per omnia sæcula sæculorum. Amen

CHRONOLOGY AND INDEX OF FISHER'S LIFE.

			PAGE
1469.		Birth at Beverley, ...	6
1483.		Enters Cambridge, ...	11
1487.		B.A., ...	13
1491.		M.A. and Fellow of Michael House, ...	13
1494.		Senior Proctor — Makes acquaintance of Lady Margaret, ...	19
1497.		Master of Michael House, ...	19
1501. July 5.		S.T.P., ...	19
,, ,, 15.		Vice-Chancellor of University, ...	19
1502.		Confessor to Lady Margaret — Resigns Mastership of Michael House, ...	19
1503.		Lady Margaret Professor of Divinity, ...	21
1504.		Chancellor, ...	26
,, Nov. 24.		Consecrated Bishop of Rochester (age 35),	56
1505. April.		Foundation of Christ's College begun, ...	21
,,		Master of Queen's, ...	27
,,		Visit of Henry VII. to Cambridge—Feast of St. George, ...	27
1506.		Second Visit of Henry VII., ...	28
1509. ,, 21.		Henry VII. dies—The Bishop preaches his Funeral Sermon, May 10, ...	106
,, June 29.		Lady Margaret dies—The Bishop preaches at her "Month's Mind,"	106
,,		Foundation of St. John's College begun, ...	28
1512. Feb. 4.		Colet's Sermon before Convocation, ...	84
,, ,,		Appointed to be King's Orator in Council of Lateran (does not go), ...	71
1511-1513.		Erasmus at Cambridge, ...	93
1514.		Chancellor for Life, ...	35
1515. Sept. 5.		Wolsey made Cardinal, ...	80
1516.		Fisher learns Greek—Visit of Erasmus, ...	94
1518. Lent.		Speech before Legatine Council, ...	75

29

			PAGE
1519.	Book against Jaques Le Fevre (*De Unica Magdelena*), ...		108
,,	Learns Hebrew, ...		95
1520. June 7.	Field of Cloth of Gold, ...		81
1521. May 12.	Sermon at Burning of Luther's Books, ...		50
1523. '	Opposes Subsidy in Convocation, ...		89
,, ,,	Publishes *Lutheranæ Assertionis Confutatio*,		112
1524.	Publishes work on St. Peter in Rome against Ulrich Willen, ...		112
1525.	Publishes Defence of the King's Book against Luther, ...		111
,, ,,	Publishes Defence of Sacred Priesthood, ...		111
,, August.	Eck of Ingoldstadt visits Fisher, ...		114
1526.	Writes in Defence of Blessed Sacrament against Œcolampadius, ...		122
1527. Quin. Sun.	Preaches at Retractation of Dr. Barnes, ...		51
,, May 6.	Rome Sacked by the Imperial Army, ...		122
,, ,, 17.	Collusive Suit before Wolsey and Warham against Marriage of Henry and Catharine,		150
,, June 2.	Fisher writes Letter in Defence of the Marriage, ...		150
,, July 4.	Attempt of Wolsey to circumvent Fisher, ...		153
,, Dec. 7.	The Pope escapes from Rome, ...		153
1528. June.	The Sweating Sickness, ...		157
,, Oct. 8.	Campeggio arrives in London as Legate regarding the Divorce, ...		159
,, ,, 25.	Campeggio confers with Fisher, ...		160
,, Nov. 8.	The King's Speech at Blackfriars' regarding the Legates, ...		147
1529. May 31.	Legatine Court opened, ...		165
,, June 28.	Speech of Fisher against the Divorce, ...		170
,, Oct. 25.	Sir T. More, Lord Chancellor, ...		170
,, Nov. 3.	Opening of the "Long Parliament" of Henry, ...		181
,, ,,	Provincial Council of Canterbury, ...		79
,, Dec.	Fisher accused of Disparaging the Commons in Parliament, ...		185
1530. Sept. 12.	Proclamation against obtaining Bulls from Rome, ...		190
,, Oct.	Fisher Arrested for Appealing to the Holy See against Parliament, ...		189
,, May 24.	Proclamation against Heretical Books, ...		191
,, Nov. 26.	Death of Wolsey, ...		193

PAGE

1531. Feb. 11.   The Clergy acknowledge Henry Supreme
                 Head "as far as God's Law permits,"   202
  „   Feb. 20.   Attempt to Poison Fisher, ...   213
1532. May 10.   Fisher consulted by Convocation, ...   220
  „   „ 16.   Sir Thomas More resigns the Great Seal—
  „   Parliament refuses the Pope Annates,...   222
  „   June 8.   Fisher preaches against the Divorce,   ...   224
  „   Aug. 23.   Archbishop Warham dies, ...   206
1533. Jan. 25.   Anne Boleyn secretly married to Henry,   ...   225
  „   March 30. Cranmer consecrated, ...   225
  „   April 6.   Fisher's Second Arrest (Palm Sunday),   ...   226
  „   May 23.   Cranmer gives Sentence against Henry's
                 Marriage with Catharine, ...   227
  „   June 1.   Coronation of Anne Boleyn (Whitsunday),   228
  „   „ 13.   Fisher released, ...   228
  „   July 11.   The Pope annuls Cranmer's Proceedings, ...   228
  „   Aug. 8.   Brief of Censure against Henry, Anne, and
                 Cranmer, ...   228
  „   Sept. 7.   Elizabeth born, ...   225
  „   Dec.   Great Illness of Fisher, ...   247
1534. Jan 15.   Opening of Session, ...   251
  „   Feb. 21.   Act of Attainder against Fisher on account
                 of Holy Maid of Kent introduced,   ...   259
  „   March 23. Clement VII. gives Final Sentence on
                 Henry's Marriage Case, ...   261
  „   „   30. Fisher's Attainder passed by King, ...   260
  „   April 13. Fisher refuses the Oath of Succession—Sent
                 to Tower, ...   274
  „   May 1.   Oath again proposed, and refused by Fisher,   280
  „   Sept. 26. Death of Clement VII., ...   274
  „   Oct. 12.   Cardinal Farnese becomes Pope Paul III.,
  „   Nov.   Fisher attainted of Misprision of Treason a
                 second time, ...   283
  „   „   18. Henry declared by Parliament Supreme
                 Head—Treason to refuse the Title,   ...   317
  „   Dec. 22.   Fisher writes to Cromwell from Tower,   ...   290
1535. May 4.   Martyrdom of Three Carthusian Priors, of
                 Reynolds, and Thomas Hale, ...   340
  „   „   6.   Feast of the Ascension, ...   345
  „   „   7.   Fisher, called before the Council, refuses to
                 admit the King's Supremacy, ...   345
  „   „ 20.   Fisher created Cardinal, ...   354
  „   June 1.   Special Commission for Trial of Fisher,   ...   365

				PAGE
1535. June 3.	Bishop interrogated in Prison,	...	...	345
„ „ 12,14.	Do.	...	...	347
„ „ 17.	Trial at Westminster,	... ...	...	365
„ „ 19.	Three Carthusians (the second band) martyred,	... ...	... ...	391
„ „ 22.	(Monday, Feast of St. Alban.) Martyrdom of Blessed John Fisher (age, about 66),			393

www.ingramcontent.com/pod-product-compliance
Lightning Source LLC
Chambersburg PA
CBHW052345110726
47901CB00005B/1367